EXIT THROUGH TORTUGA BAY

ESCAPE IN PARADISE (BOOK 2)

ALICIA CROFTON

3DIMPLES

Copyright © 2021 by Alicia Crofton

Book design by Erik Ebeling

Editing by Sarah Pesce

Proofreading by Anne Victory

ISBN 978-1-7352353-7-0 (paperback)

ISBN 978-1-7352353-5-6 (ebook)

To my sister and mother; my tribe.

Only when we are no longer afraid do we begin to live.

— DOROTHY THOMPSON

CHAPTER ONE

Noah rolled over in his bed, his muscles aching in protest. Tangled strands of brunette hair draped across the pillow reminded him he wasn't alone. The taste of the brunette's cigarette mouth lingered on his tongue.

Was it Bridgette? Brianna? He couldn't remember. Either way, it was a mistake. The last time he would let a cougar in his bed for a one-night stand, or so he told himself for the hundredth time.

It was as if Noah had a bull's-eye on his forehead for tourists looking for a good time, and the bar had been swarming with them last night. Brittney—or Blanca?—had been very handsy. He had cabbed home in a drunken stupor with her paws in his pants and a whispered list of all the things she planned to do to him. Fuzzy memories confirmed she had gotten to them all, only this time he shuddered at the thought.

He was done with these casual flings.

All he had wanted was a night out with friends, drinking away his problems as if they didn't exist. That had been his plan anyway. But like all the plans he had tried to make, it failed the moment Bianca or Brenda showed her vulnerable side.

Brenda. That had to be her name. Recently divorced with two kids in high school. It was all coming back to him now. His drunken heart had been swallowed whole the moment her eyes had shimmered in unshed tears as she talked about the fifteen years she had given that *bastard*. Her words.

He shouldn't have taken her home, but that eighth shot of chiliguaro had taken charge at some point, abusing its responsibilities of helping him forget about his bigger problem. More specifically, the problem waiting for him at the warehouse.

It was no ordinary problem either. No broken faucet or running toilet. It was far more serious.

Two hundred kilos of cocaine had been stashed in their family's business. For weeks.

Two. Hundred. Kilos. The weight of a male tiger. Or a moose. And Noah wasn't even a drug dealer. Or a drug user. The blow had shown up one day out of the blue, compliments of his oldest brother, Raffi, who had accidentally involved himself with a cartel.

Who accidentally gets involved with a cartel? An idiot, that's who. That summed up his older brother in a nutshell.

Now a mountain of drugs worth at least thirty million dollars was currently stashed in their coffee delivery van, waiting for Noah and his more reasonable brother, Kai, to anonymously drop it off at the Limón police station.

Stress levels were high, to say the least.

Brenda moaned into the pillow, blinking a few times, and then pulled the hair off her face. Charcoal smudges blended in with dark circles under her eyes. Fine lines emerged across her forehead and around her mouth. Under the soft glow of the Costa Rican sun, Noah estimated she was at least fifteen years older than he was.

Noah didn't understand how this kept happening. It was a curse really. He couldn't go anywhere without being approached by an older woman. He was a good-looking guy but not any better-looking than his brothers, and they never had the same problem.

He had been told before it was his charm that wooed the ladies. And if he were being honest, he always liked the attention from older women. They made him feel mature and respected—unlike how he was at home with the constant belittling he got from his two older brothers and the babying he got from his mother. Older women treated him like the adult he was.

He had been happy to go along with the cougar phenomenon for a while, but lately the one-night stands had left him feeling empty and alone. He would've probably been better off if he had just stayed home.

"Good morning," Brenda said, her voice scratchy.

"Morning."

"I had a really good time last night," she said, tracing Noah's shoulder with her finger. Her fingernail snaked up his neck and behind his ear. The gesture felt forced, her eyes not quite reaching his. He could almost see the escape plan forming in her mind.

She didn't need to pretend this was anything more than what it was. He had thought he'd made that clear last night, but then again, he had thought he'd taken off his shoes too, but he felt them tug against his cotton sheets.

Had he had sex with nothing on but his Air Maxes? He peeked under the covers to confirm. His dumb ass had been too drunk to take them off. At least he hadn't tracked too much sand into bed from the beach bar.

"I had fun too," Noah said, stopping her hand from caressing him any further. He gently gave it back to her before pulling his fully laced shoes out from under the covers. "I've gotta head to work." He slipped his shoes through his boxers—not an easy task on the first try. Was he still drunk? "I can show you out before my mother wakes up."

"Your *mother*?" She shot up, covering herself with the bedsheet. "You still live with your mother?"

"Well, yeah. Did I not mention that?" Noah said, scratching the back of his head. "I've been helping with the family business and—"

The woman cocked her head to the side, narrowing her eyes. She zeroed in on his face. "How old are you?"

"Twenty-two."

She gasped. *"Twenty-two?"*

"Did I forget to mention that too?" Noah winced. "Sorry. I was so drunk and—"

"Oh my god, oh my god," she repeated, over and over again.

His charm had apparently worn off. The woman frantically gathered her clothes while holding the white sheet to her chest. Her hands shook as she reached for her bra, which was hanging over the edge of the bed. Noah grabbed the lacy fabric and handed it to her.

She snatched it, avoiding eye contact while she dressed. "This was a terrible mistake," she said, slipping on her tank top and grabbing her heels.

Yep. He couldn't have agreed more, but it was too late for that now. Regardless, he hated to see a woman in distress, and he stalked over to her, placing his hands on her shoulders to calm her down. "We had a good time. Don't sweat it." He smiled, coaxing a grin from her.

Brenda pulled her blouse over her head. "I should go," she said, storming toward the door in a frenzy, reaching for the knob.

"Wait, hold on," Noah said, stopping her from heading out

first. He nudged her aside and opened the bedroom door, sticking his head out into the hallway toward his mother's room.

Clanking plates and water running in the sink drew his attention toward the kitchen instead.

"Ma is up. We can either go through the window, or I can sneak you through the front door."

The woman's mouth dropped in horror. "I'm not climbing through *that*."

"All right, then you'll have to follow me. Don't get caught."

"Are you serious?" Brenda huffed.

"Just tiptoe behind me and you'll be fine."

"This is ridiculous."

"Shh," he whispered. He tiptoed down the hall and poked his head into the kitchen.

Ma's back was turned, her round hips jostling while she whisked a bowl of eggs. Bacon crackled on the stove.

"Now," he mouthed, ignoring Brenda's scowl.

Grabbing hold of her hand, they crept past the kitchen and dashed through the living room, out the front door. Noah pulled Brenda onto the front step, lightly closing the door behind him. He let out a breath of relief. "We did it," he said, beaming.

"I can't believe I just had to sneak out of your mother's house," she said, strapping on her heels.

"Yeah, but it was fun, right? Sneaking around like a teenager?"

Brenda's mouth tilted into a smile.

"There's that smile," Noah said, nudging her with his elbow.

"You are quite the charmer, aren't you, Noah?"

"And you are quite the woman, Brenda."

Brenda's face fell, and she turned to leave.

"Was it something I said?"

"I knew this was a mistake," Brenda huffed before turning back around to face him. "My name is *Belinda*."

"Shit." Noah cringed. "Sorry."

"Whatever." With a flick of her long, uncombed hair, she turned on her heel and thundered down the sidewalk.

"Can I at least call you a cab?" Noah shouted.

"I've got it," Belinda said, not bothering to turn around. She pulled out her cell phone while she marched down the sidewalk.

Noah crossed his arms at his chest, watching her take her post at the street corner. He waited to make sure she got into her ride safely. Of course she didn't look back to wave goodbye.

The emptiness was back, only this time it was worse. He had never, ever made a woman feel as insignificant as he felt after a one-night stand.

Never again, he told himself.

Noah lumbered toward the rolled-up newspaper at the end of the driveway. It was his best excuse for having gone outside in his underwear and his damn *shoes*. And he needed to prepare for the interrogation he was about to get from Ma.

Creeping back through the front door, he jumped at the sight of her in the kitchen, standing with a hand on her hip and a spoon raised in the air. Long strands of white hair had fallen out of her bun. "What did I tell you about bringing women over to my house?" Ma said in English with her thick German accent, waving her spoon at him.

"What are you talking about? I was just getting the newspaper."

"Don't you dare feed me those charming lies of yours, boy. I can see right through you."

Noah cowered. "Sorry, Ma," he said, plopping the newspaper in the basket by the door. He averted her icy glare as he slumped his shoulders.

"When are you going to stop fooling around and find yourself a nice college girl? Someone your own age?"

Noah leaned down to give her a kiss on the cheek. Although she fought it, her lips curled into a smile.

"I've already kissed my chances at college goodbye, remember? I've got responsibilities here." Noah had dropped out of his first semester of college when his father had become ill and his company was on the brink of bankruptcy.

"You're not tied to the business anymore. Kai is going to sell it."

"Yeah, but we still have that damn van of cocaine to deal with. If Kai hadn't run out of the house for some chick last night, this whole ordeal would be over by now."

Ma harrumphed. "Just let Kai handle the business stuff. You're my baby. I can't have anything happen to you."

There she goes again. Always putting his older brothers in charge. And now that Raffi, the oldest of the three, had royally messed up by getting involved with the cartel, it was up to Kai and Noah to clean up the mess.

"It's a lot of cocaine, Ma," Noah said. "It's too risky for Kai to handle it on his own."

Noah still hadn't gotten used to talking to his mother about the drugs. He and his brothers had tried keeping it a secret from her, but she had eventually found out. Now she was an accomplice, whether she wanted to be or not.

"Also, Ma, you gotta stop treating me like a kid. I'm an adult now."

Ma squeezed Noah's cheeks, giving them a tough yank. His pounding head felt like it would split in two. "You'll always be my baby," she said, returning to the stove. "Now get some clothes on and eat some food. I cooked this American breakfast for you, just how you like it."

After a quick rinse in the shower, he slipped on a pair of shorts and a shirt with the Greene Coffee Roastery logo printed on the front.

The surfboard in the corner of his bedroom called to him. He needed to clear his head.

Tomorrow. He would surf tomorrow after the cocaine was out of his life forever. He'd baptize himself in the holy ocean and pray to the surfing gods for forgiveness for missing a day.

Noah had just finished pulling on his sneakers again when a knock came from the front door. He looked out his window to find a police car parked in the middle of their driveway.

Noah's heart leaped in his chest. Muffled voices echoed from the living room. He opened his bedroom door a crack, pressing his ear against the edge of the doorframe.

"We have a warrant to check the warehouse," a male voice said in Spanish.

"The warehouse? For what?" Ma shrilled.

Fuck.

Fuck fuck fuck fuck. How did they know? Who could have tipped them off?

A voice came over the policeman's radio, and the air in his room stood thick and heavy. He had to do something. He had to get rid of the cocaine before the police got the wrong idea. They had never wanted the drugs in the first place, but the police wouldn't understand.

If Noah didn't do something now, his mother and his brothers would pay the price.

"I'm sorry, ma'am," the officer said. "I can't say."

"Officer, I...," Ma stammered. "I mean, I am shocked."

"We'd appreciate it if you'd come with us to the warehouse."

Noah's stomach sank. He had to go right now. Grabbing

his keys and his cell phone, he opened his window and leaped out into the bushes. Tiny branches scratched his ankles.

He hunched down low, scurrying to his car parked on the street.

Luckily, the cops were still in the house while he slipped into the driver's seat.

Ma would eventually notice he was gone. Hopefully she could stall them while Noah got rid of the van with the cocaine.

Noah's blood pumped furiously through his veins as his shaky key scraped against the ignition.

Maybe this was his chance to prove to Ma and Kai that he could handle things himself. He was a man after all. Tired of being treated like a kid.

Okay, so he was scared shitless, but he'd be damned if he didn't save his family from going to jail for a crime they didn't commit.

CHAPTER TWO

Noah tore through his father's office, or what used to be his father's office. Kai had taken over and reorganized everything. The keys to the van were normally on the hook by the garage door, but they weren't there this time. He checked all the drawers and cabinets before he had the idea to check the van itself.

Sprinting back to the garage, he climbed into the van's driver seat, frantically searching the glove compartment and console. He stuffed his fingers in the seat cushions and under the floor mats.

Nothing.

Noah didn't know how much time he had, but it couldn't be long until Ma and the policemen arrived at the warehouse. The cocaine had already been stuffed in cardboard boxes in the back of the van. All he needed to do was drive away before he was seen.

Noah pulled down the visor, and the small ring of keys fell into his lap. "Finally," he muttered as he turned on the engine and hit the garage door opener. He looked back at the cardboard boxes and cursed under his breath. What the hell was he going to do with two hundred kilos of cocaine? Where would he go?

Pulling out of the warehouse, he noticed a car parked across the street. A baby-blue Mercury Sable with two men sitting in the front seats.

That was unusual. Nobody ever parked there this early.

Noah's muscles tensed.

Paranoia settled into his bones as he pulled onto a main road, keeping an eye on the Sable in his rearview mirror.

It was probably nothing, Noah assured himself. If the cartel knew how to find the cocaine, they would have come for it days ago. Weeks ago, actually. It was impossible to think they would just show up today, of all days, while the police were on their way.

The Mercury Sable slipped out of view. Noah sighed, running a nervous hand through his damp hair. He wasn't sure where he was going, but he knew he needed to get out of Limón.

Noah pressed the gas and drove forward, nervously tapping on the steering wheel.

This was all his brother's fault. Raffi was a certified idiot.

Noah used to look up to Raffi as a kid, but that was a long time ago. It was hard to forgive him for dumping all his problems on the family. Granted, Raffi had tried handling things himself, but he only made matters worse, finding himself in jail for a completely unrelated crime.

Moron.

Noah pulled up to a stoplight as a prickle crawled up his neck. When he checked his rearview mirror again, his body seized.

It was the damn baby-blue Mercury Sable, pulling up right behind him.

Fuck.

This was just a coincidence, right? Maybe they were

hanging out in front of the coffee warehouse to figure out their directions. Or maybe the driver got lost on their way to brunch. That's it. They were going out to brunch. Definitely. Probably meeting their mother at the diner down the street. The one with the really good churrasco and eggs.

When the stoplight turned green, Noah inched forward, expecting the Sable to make a left turn, but it drove straight through instead.

"The diner is that way," Noah said aloud, hoping that somehow they'd realize their error and make a sudden turn.

Nope. They tailgated him instead and followed his next turn, despite Noah's attempt at pulling the wheel last minute.

Okay, new plan. Noah reached for his cell phone and dialed his brother.

Kai's voice came on the other line. "Hey, Noah. I was just on my way over to—"

"Kai," Noah cut him off. "I may have done something really stupid."

"What is it? What's wrong?"

Noah proceeded to tell him about the cops showing up at Ma's house and the blue Mercury Sable on his tail. "You need to go check on Ma," Noah said. "She's with the police now, but if these guys knew where to track down the cocaine, they might show at the house. You need to get there, now."

"Fine," Kai growled. "I will take care of Ma, but then I'm coming to help you. Give me a time and place."

A time and a place? Seriously? When could he have possibly come up with a plan? He was surviving by instinct. "I can't. I don't know where I'm going."

"Pick a town. Any town."

Noah looked in each mirror. The Sable was unrelenting in its pursuit. To keep his family safe and out of jail, he only had one option.

"I can't pick a town because I'm going to try to outrun them," Noah said.

"That is a terrible plan!" Kai shouted. "You'll get yourself killed."

"I've got this. You deal with Ma."

"Noah, please," Kai said urgently. "Don't go—"

Beep. The phone shut off. The battery icon appeared on the screen, mocking him for forgetting to charge his phone last night during his drunken escapade.

Noah threw the cell phone in the seat and pulled up to another light. He made a right turn, and sure enough the blue Mercury Sable tailed close behind.

The signs for the highway came into view, and he did the only thing he could think to do: he pressed on the gas.

He might not have had a plan, but he knew he had to get the hell out of Limón and get rid of this cocaine once and for all.

The van rattled down the highway. Noah wiped his forehead with the back of his hand, his eyes frantically shifting between the road ahead and the rearview mirror.

The men in the Sable had been driving for almost three hours, and Noah's pounding hangover headache had lingered the whole way. He had hoped that the men would eventually give up the chase or run out of gas, but they hadn't backed down.

The exit sign for San José zoomed overhead. The city might be his only chance of escape—that is, if he was able to lose them in the intense traffic clogging the streets.

Giant towers sprang into view, surrounded by a jungle of buildings atop rolling hills. The San José Mountains anchored the skyline with clouds settled around the peaks.

The fresh, salty air was replaced by wafts of exhaust fumes and wet cement after the rain. The clouds had begun to part, and the sun shone down through the windshield, directly into Noah's eyes.

Noah yanked the steering wheel to the right, cutting off a truck full of chickens. A series of bawks and high-pitched clucks filled the air as he skidded over a median onto an exit ramp. Fixating on the rearview mirror, he prayed the Sable didn't see his exit off the highway.

He held his breath, pumping the brakes as he pulled up to a stoplight.

Just as a victorious smile reached his lips, the Sable snaked around a city bus and onto the exit ramp, picking up speed.

Shit.

Noah's heart pounded in his chest, and he gunned the van forward, driving over the sidewalk to pass the car ahead. He made a turn, cutting off a cab that slammed on its brakes with a loud screech. An angry horn quickly followed.

"Sorry!" Noah yelled out the van window.

He tore through the streets, dodging between cars and cutting corners.

It was beginning to look like he had lost the Sable between Avenue 16 and 18. He felt a wave of relief, and his breath began to normalize.

There was a brief opening in oncoming traffic, and Noah jerked the wheel to the left, nearly swiping a moped. More horns blared as Noah swerved around a businessman. He looked back in his rearview mirror as squealing tires were followed by crunching metal, the Sable colliding with a black SUV. All the cars in the intersection came to a halt. The Sable's headlight hung from its socket.

"Yes!" Noah yelled, adrenaline ringing in his ears. He pumped his fist in the air, tearing up the street before he made a hard-right turn. The wreck slipped out of view. This was his chance to make his big escape. But where would he go?

At the next stoplight, he could finally relax. Music from the shops and restaurants seeped into the van. A swarm of people crossed the sidewalk, ambling around with coffee cups and cell phones in their grips.

A billboard over the freeway featured a setting sun over the ocean. A silhouetted surfer held his board under neon-pink letters that read THIS WAY TO TORTUGA BAY.

That seemed as good of a place as any.

He checked to see if he had enough gas to get to the west coast and took the exit onto Highway 27.

Tortuga Bay, here I come.

CHAPTER THREE

Grace took a big, gulping sip of her spiked cider while she worked up the courage to talk to Todd Meyers, the sexiest man in Traverse City, Michigan.

He had asked for her number once—for work, of course —but he had never used it. And it was driving Grace wild.

"Just go ask him out," Tessa whispered. "There's no better time than now."

"Easy for you to say, Tony Robbins. I've never done anything like this before." Grace had talked to boys, but she'd never asked them out. And they were never *men*. The guys in college were nothing compared to this strong, manly man with sexy stubble and a chest for days.

Grace didn't have time to have a normal life, and she especially didn't have time to date. But Tessa had given Grace the bright idea to try squeezing in her dates during lunch breaks. At first Grace hated the idea, but the more she thought about it, the more she liked it. It was practical and pretty much the only way she would ever get to kiss Todd Meyers.

"But what if he's not interested in dating over lunch breaks?" Grace said.

"If he's not interested in a lunch date, then he's not worth your time."

Grace pulled her orange soda lip balm from her pocket and swiped it across her lips. The citrus scent soothed her nerves. "I guess you're right. And it's not like I have any other options." Grace looked around at Maritime's employees scattered across the grassy field, Solo cups in hand. The grumpy tech nerds hovered around picnic tables and lawn games in little clusters divided between their fandom of *Star Wars* and *Star Trek*.

But not Todd.

Todd was in sales, just like Grace. It was fate. It had to be. The problem was he wasn't making the first move.

Grace was no longer satisfied with the stolen glances in staff meetings or the casual smiles they exchanged down the halls. Grace was ready for more. And this was her chance.

Todd tossed a bean bag with poetic precision, landing in the three-point hole. The little fan club surrounding the cornhole game burst into cheers.

Grace sighed behind her Solo cup, watching the man of her dreams give high fives all around.

"What would I even say to him? 'Hey Todd, nice cornhole. Want to have lunch sometime?'"

"You should totally lead with that." Tessa snickered, taking a bite of her cider donut. She groaned, rolling her eyes to the back of her head. "Oh my god, this is so good." She moaned so loud people turned their heads.

"I give that a level six on the foodgasm scale," Grace whispered. "Not quite as lively as your level-eight cheese pizza earlier today."

A dusting of cinnamon and sugar flew out of Tessa's mouth as they both keeled over in a fit of giggles.

"Hello, girls," a woman's voice announced. Tessa's spine stiffened. "Having fun?"

Jane Lambert appeared in their periphery. Future CEO and official pain in the ass.

"I see you're enjoying the *donuts*."

Grace wasn't sure how Jane made that sound like an insult, but she had.

Tessa licked the sugar off her lips. "Hi, Jane," she said flatly.

Tessa had been tasked to help Jane with her accounts. Jane insisted she was too busy to cover them all. Maritime Marketing Services was a company that sold experience packages to hotels and resorts. From wine tasting to ice cave hiking, Maritime offered it all. And it was the sales team's job to constantly find new experiences and new clients while also acting as the liaison between the *Star Wars*-loving tech team and their customers.

Tessa and Grace were lowly sales associates compared to Jane, who was a *senior* sales associate only because she was the CEO's daughter. Jane spent all her time bossing around employees as if they reported to her when they actually all reported to the same director. She was clueless when it came to the technical part of their job and didn't care to learn, so she would pretend to "mentor" the other sales associates, but in reality, she was only using them to do all her grunt work.

"Great turnout, isn't it?" Jane surveyed the company picnic as if it were her very own kingdom.

Both Grace and Tessa muttered some version of *mm-hmm* in their cider cups.

Despite her better judgment, Grace turned toward the menacing blonde, mostly to be polite but also because Tessa was blatantly ignoring Jane and making their small talk uncomfortable.

Jane was in her late forties, tall and slender with perfect

breasts stuffed in a cream turtleneck sweater. Her black leather leggings were painted on runway-model legs. Her sleek blond hair was cut in an angled bob that looked great on her but would add ten pounds of cheeks to anyone else.

Grace looked down at her own mustard cable-knit sweater ladened with pills and snags from overuse. The maroon corduroys she had bought in high school still fit but were frayed at the hem.

As much as Grace wanted to look as beautiful as Jane, she couldn't afford it, and she didn't have the time. She let her chocolate-brown hair grow long and the spattering of freckles across her cheeks go without a touch of makeup.

Jane's mouth twisted into a mischievous smirk. "I couldn't help but notice you were staring at Todd Meyers, Grace."

Grace exchanged a look with Tessa.

"Not really. We were just watching the cornhole game," Grace said.

"He is cute though, isn't he?" Jane said, nudging Grace with her elbow. "Maybe a little old for you though."

Grace held back her retort. How young did Jane think Grace was? Todd couldn't have been more than five years older than her own twenty-four years. He wasn't too old. He was perfect.

Either way, it didn't matter. Jane didn't need to know about her crush on Todd, so she bit her tongue. "Like I said, I was just watching the game."

From across the grass, Todd's honey-brown irises flicked up, and a slow smile emerged on his scruffy face.

A frenzy of butterflies emerged as he waved at her. Grace's heart rattled in her ribs like a caged animal.

He *waved*. To her.

Grace's heart was in her throat.

But something felt off. A prickling sensation at the back

of her neck. She turned to find Jane glaring down the hill, her eyes darkening. A shudder ran down Grace's spine.

"I've got to go mingle," Jane said, blinking away the darkness in her eyes. "Enjoy the rest of the picnic."

"You too," Grace said.

"Oh, and Tessa?" Jane said pointedly.

Tessa looked up over her cup, her brown eyes like giant rounds of chocolate cake. "Yeah?"

"Send me all the files you have on the Tortuga account before you head out," Jane said. "Please," she added a beat too late. "I want to make sure I don't have any *flaws* in this pitch."

Tessa gulped, nodding her head. "Sure. I'll send them out tonight."

"Perfect," she purred, although the look in her hooded eyes indicated otherwise. She sashayed down the grassy hill, her high-heeled boots aerating the grass along the way.

"What the hell was up her butt?" Grace said, looking over Tessa's paled face.

"Jane's on a rampage," Tessa said. "Ever since her husband left her for a younger woman, she has it out for us younger girls. Like we're competition or something."

Grace shook off the creepy-crawlies in her spine.

"I didn't help things by calling her out on an error in front of a client today. She's pissed."

Grace winced. "Oh no."

"And now she wants me to send all those files. That can only mean one thing."

"What?"

"She's going to take me off the Tortuga account, that's what. I'm not going to get my chance to go to Costa Rica."

"Don't say that," Grace said, rubbing Tessa's shoulder. "She can't be that catty, can she?"

"You don't know Jane like I do," Tessa said. "She *is* that

catty. And mean. And I swear to God, if she takes me off this account, I'm going to quit. I hate this job."

Grace scrunched her nose. "I know you wanted to go to Costa Rica, but Jane has been making you miserable. Maybe getting off the project isn't the worst thing in the world."

"But... *Costa Rica.*"

Grace sighed. "There will be other chances to go. I promise. Maybe you and I could go sometime."

Tessa rolled her eyes, calling her bluff.

"Okay, maybe not in the *near* future. But one day. Just don't quit on me, okay? I don't know what I'd do without you. You helped get me this job; you can't strand me here."

"Yeah, you're right," Tessa huffed. "I promise I won't quit."

Grace smiled, putting her arm around her friend. "Good."

"And who knows, maybe Jane will cool off and everything will go back to normal tomorrow."

"There's the spirit," Grace said, happily turning back toward the cornhole game.

"Enough about me," Tessa said, giving her a nudge. "You know what you have to do now."

Grace took a deep breath, her heart fluttering. "You're right. It's now or never."

"Thatta girl."

Grace had every intention of bounding down the hill and saying hello, but her Doc Martens were rooted to the ground, her limbs frozen in place.

"Oh, for heaven's sake, go!" Tessa said, giving Grace a big shove, putting her in motion. Slowly she made her way down the hill. Her pulse quickened with each stride toward Todd and his posse.

Was she really doing this? Would he really go for dating... at work? Her palms were sweating, sticking to her cup.

Todd scored another three-pointer, and the crowd

roared. He proceeded with his high fives. One by one, he eventually made his way to Grace.

She held her hand up and got a solid thwack from his palm. She might never wash her hand again.

"Nice job," Grace croaked. She cleared her throat.

"Thanks," Todd said, brimming with pride.

"You've got great cornhole— I mean, your cornhole game is great." *Oh God, this is a disaster.*

Todd's mouth tilted into an easy smile as he looked her up and down. His gaze left a tingling trail over her body.

"Thanks," Todd said. "I could actually use a break. You want a turn?"

Grace's eyes widened. "Oh gosh, no. I'm not a cornhole kind of girl. I was actually going to ask—"

"Come on. Try it," he said, handing her a bean bag. He gestured to the other players to pause the game. "Let's give Grace a try, guys."

"No, really. I don't throw things. I have zero hand-eye coordination."

"It's easy," Todd said, his eyes glittering like a Christmas tree. "You just give it an underhand toss. Like this." He stood behind her, the heat of him giving her heart palpitations. Then he took her arm and motioned it back and forth, mimicking a throw in slow motion. His fingers pressed into the skin near her elbow, and her insides turned into spiked rum-flavored jelly.

"Like this?" Grace said, swinging her arm back. Her fist connected with something behind her.

"Ergh!"

Todd hunched over, holding his crotch, and Grace realized what she had done.

"I'm so sorry!" Grace said, dropping the bean bag to the ground in horror.

Todd's face twisted in agony. "It's fine. I'm fine," he grunted. He waved off the crowd, regaining his composure.

"I'm seriously so sorry—"

"Don't sweat it," he said through labored breaths. "My nuts are made of steel."

Grace was just about to run away in shame when Todd interrupted her exit plan.

"Hey, wait. Don't go. I wanted to talk to you about something."

"You did?"

"Do you mind if we go somewhere a little more quiet?"

Oh my god. Oh my god. Oh my god.

Her stomach did a somersault. Was he really asking if they could be alone? She almost squealed with glee.

"Sure," Grace said, hampering the extra octave in her voice.

He smiled before biting his lower lip. Promises of languid kisses and sweet caresses were written all over his face.

This was it. The moment she had been waiting for. Ever since she first laid eyes on the man, she'd dreamed of their first kiss. If it was even a fraction of what she imagined, she'd be floating in the clouds.

"Look over there." He pointed across the park. "There's a playhouse behind the trees, next to that swing set."

Grace's heart sputtered. She looked up the hill to find Tessa's bright smile and two encouraging thumbs-up.

There's no time like now. "That sounds great."

"Excellent," he said, holding out an elbow to escort her.

Holy moly. This was really happening. She was finally going to be alone with Todd Meyers.

As they strolled through the park, Grace felt her hands tremble. She squeezed his bicep as she stepped onto the playground box. The taut arm muscle flexed under her fingertips. She tightened her grip to steady herself.

Todd pointed up toward the top deck of the playhouse. "Here it is." The wooden structure was just big enough for two adults to fit in. A plastic fishbowl window overlooked the scenic park, and a steering wheel was mounted on the opposite wall.

"After you," he said, grinning from ear to ear.

Grace stepped up the wooden slabs and entered the club house, sitting in the far corner.

"Ahoy," Todd said, ducking to get inside. He looked out the fishbowl window. "I don't think anyone noticed us go up here, do you?"

"I don't think so." Except for Tessa, who had been silently dancing at the top of the hill.

Todd took a seat next to her, his knee lightly grazing hers. The touch brought an earthquake of sensations. She hadn't been touched by a boy since college. It had been too long.

Silence filled the space.

"So," Grace said.

"So," Todd replied.

Grace's heartbeat went into hyperdrive as his eyes trailed down her sweater.

"I like your outfit," Todd said. "You've got a Velma Dinkley vibe goin' on. It's cute."

Grace blushed. He thought she was cute. That was a good thing, right? "Why does that name sound familiar?"

"She's from *Scooby-Doo*. You know, the smart one in the van."

"Oh right," Grace murmured, remembering the nerdy character from the show. Her heart sank. The word *cute* no longer felt like a compliment.

"I'm sorry," Todd said, running his hands over his stubbly cheeks. "You don't actually look like Velma. I mean, she had short hair and glasses, and you obviously don't. Crap. I don't know why I'm rambling. I think I'm nervous."

"You are?"

Todd cleared his throat, shifting his weight back until he leaned against the wall. He peered out the fishbowl window, deep in thought.

The brightness in his eyes was gone, and Grace sensed the shift in his mood. She waited for him to say what was on his mind. She'd talk more about cartoons if he wanted, anything to get his mouth moving and eventually on hers.

"So," Grace said, "you wanted to talk?"

Todd glanced at Grace nervously. "Right. Yes." He pressed his lips together, gazing into Grace's eyes. He leaned forward.

This was it. The moment she had been waiting for. Well, a little out of order of how she had imagined things, but that was okay. Kissing first. Lunch dates later.

She sucked in a breath and held it the moment he stopped leaning forward. He placed his elbows on his knees and cradled his chin in his hands.

"I was going to ask about Jane."

"Jane?"

"I saw you talking with her up the hill. Are you two friends?"

Grace's mouth dropped open. "Friends? With Jane?" She couldn't think of the word she would describe her relationship with Jane. What do you call someone you avoid entirely?

"Did she say anything about me?"

Grace choked on the saliva that slipped down the wrong tube. "What?" She felt her face grow hot as she coughed and gagged on her own spit. She grabbed her cup of cider and slugged the last of it to calm her throat. "She didn't mention you. Why?"

"Well," he started, scratching the back of his head. His face scrunched up, turning a deep shade of pink. "I…"

Oh.

The words he couldn't get out, the agony in his face. Grace should have known.

He liked Jane. Of course he liked Jane. Sure, she was twenty years older than him, but she acted young. She was beautiful and confident and impeccably dressed. How could Grace have been so foolish to think Todd might actually be interested in her instead?

Hopes and dreams burst like bubbles blowing into a barbed wire fence.

"I didn't realize you liked her like that," Grace said quietly.

"Actually, there's something else. I—"

"Aha!" Jane trilled, appearing at the foot of the playhouse with her cell phone in hand. "Smile for the camera!" A burst of light blinded Grace.

"Jesus. You scared the crap out of me," Todd said.

"Oh, I'm sorry. Was I interrupting something?" Jane said, batting her eyelashes.

It all made sense now, why Todd had waved in the first place. She had been standing next to *Jane*.

"I was just leaving, actually," Grace said.

"Oh, come on, Grace," Jane crooned. "I didn't mean to break up your little party."

Grace stepped down from the playhouse, catching a glance at Todd. At least he had the courtesy to appear sad that she was leaving. The crease in his forehead was a nice touch.

"I'll leave you two alone."

"Grace, wait," Todd called out.

She looked over her shoulder to find Todd pleading with his eyes. "Don't go."

It almost seemed like he truly didn't want her to leave. But that couldn't be. He was only being polite. Grace squashed the kernel of doubt and turned to go.

She stepped off the play structure and onto the bark

chips. Before she took another step, she heard Jane's muffled words behind the plastic fishbowl window. "She's a bit of a party pooper, isn't she?"

Grace didn't linger to hear Todd's response. She marched over the bark chips, gritting her teeth. With a heavy heart she slogged back to the company picnic, fighting the tears that threatened to spill on her Velma Dinkley sweater.

Marching past the cornhole game, she found Tessa standing by the round of ladder golf.

"I'm heading home," Grace said.

Tessa's eyes widened in surprise. "You are? What happened? Did he hurt you? I'll cut him."

Grace shook her head. The lump in her throat was too heavy to overcome.

"It's okay. There'll be other guys."

Grace sniffed. "You've seen the guys here. There's literally no other man here who wears deodorant."

Tessa brought her in for a hug, letting Grace rest her head on her shoulder. She smelled like pineapple rum and cinnamon.

"Want to talk about it over coffee tomorrow?"

"Sure," Grace said, releasing her friend. "See you in the morning."

Grace took a few steps up the grassy patch when she heard, "Watch out!" A pink golf ball tied to the end of a rope was flying through the air. The golf ball collided with her cheekbone with a hefty thud, and she found herself lying on the cool, damp grass.

"Grace! Are you okay?" Tessa's voice warbled around in her head.

She lay there with a shattered heart and a splitting headache. Two solid reminders why it was better to just stay home.

CHAPTER FOUR

"Good grief! What happened to you?" Aunt Judy trilled from under a mountain of blankets. The television lights flickered, illuminating her worried, wrinkled expression as Grace hung her purse by the front door.

"I got hit in the face with a golf ball." Grace slipped out of her muddy boots and plopped on the couch.

"You look like hell," Aunt Judy said.

"Gee, thanks." Grace put up her feet, crossing her ankles on the coffee table. She took a big whiff. "Why does the house smell like pee?"

Aunt Judy frowned. "Bobblehead over there made brussels sprouts." She groaned, motioning toward the kitchen. "You might as well put me out of my misery and shoot me now."

"I heard that!" Tamara's voice sprang from behind the kitchen wall. Tamara poked her head around the corner and gave Grace a friendly wave. She had teased her hair out particularly big that day.

Grace bit back a laugh. "I'm sorry," she mouthed.

Tamara shook her head, a hand perched on her hip. She

and Aunt Judy were always bickering, but deep down, Grace suspected they were friends in secret. Tamara was the best worker at Sunrise Homecare, if only because she showed up to work on time and helped cook dinners, even though the latter wasn't in her job description.

In the past year, Judy had cycled through many Sunrise workers who consistently showed up late, if at all. Not to mention that they constantly messed up her medication schedule as well. Sunrise was not the best-ranked institution in the state, but it was all Grace could afford on her sales associate salary.

It was better than a nursing home. At least that's what Grace kept telling herself.

Grace's aunt had been diagnosed with multiple sclerosis right around the time Grace's parents died. Aunt Judy had saved Grace from the foster care system then, and now Grace was returning the favor, saving her aunt from the nursing home. Even if it meant foregoing the preschool teaching career Grace had wanted for herself. A teaching salary wouldn't pay for the expenses Grace needed to keep Aunt Judy out of a home. Luckily, Tessa had helped her land a job at Maritime, which covered the cost of Sunrise and kept Aunt Judy safe and sound at home.

"Can I grab you a bag of frozen peas for that eye?" Tamara said.

"I got it," Grace said, pulling herself up off the pillowy cushions.

"Sit down," Tamara said, emerging with a bag of peas. "You need to take it easy."

Grace thanked her, accepting the bag. The icy plastic crunched on her cheekbone, and she winced. The initial bite of cold settled against her skin, and she sat back down.

"I was just about to head out. Brussels sprouts and baked chicken on the stove," Tamara said.

"Thanks, Tamara," Grace told her.

Aunt Judy stuck her tongue out. "Bleh."

"Can I do anything else before I leave?"

"Yeah, you can put that garbage you just cooked in the trash and order us a pizza."

Grace glowered at her aunt.

"Ignore her. Have a great night." Grace didn't bother to ask if she was able to get Aunt Judy outside today. She already knew the answer. Aunt Judy refused to go outside in the cold, blaming it on the damn wheelchair, cursed by the devil himself. Grace had stopped asking a while ago.

Tamara shrugged on her coat. "I'll see you bright and early tomorrow."

"Don't let your hair blow you away on your way out," Aunt Judy said.

"Always a pleasure, Judy," she deadpanned.

Aunt Judy lifted her middle finger in response. Grace caught Tamara's smile before she walked out the front door.

"Be nice," Grace scolded her aunt.

"I am nice," Aunt Judy retorted, snuggling up with her favorite cream afghan with tassels worn into tangled clumps of yarn.

Grace rolled her eyes and turned toward the television. "Which movie will we be watching tonight?"

"*Magic Mike* is on cable."

Grace stuck her tongue out. "How about something a little more romantic and less thrusty?" Her aunt had a slightly more scandalous taste in movies than Grace. "What about *The Sweetest Thing*?" Grace said. "Or any Meg Ryan movie."

"All right," Aunt Judy said, pointing to the remote control. "You can pick since it looks like you had a rough day."

"You have no idea," Grace said, grabbing the remote control. She was sure *Sleepless in Seattle* was still in the DVD player from the last time they'd watched it, and she hit Play. The tension left Grace's forehead as the familiar jazzy notes came over the speakers.

This was her happy place. Chick flicks and comfy blankets. Sheltered from the cruel, dangerous world. Protected from menacing golf balls and real-life rejection.

"Do you want to use the dinner trays tonight?" Grace said.

"Sure, but I may never be able to watch Tom Hanks again without the lingering taste of piss in my mouth."

Grace chuckled. "They're just tiny cabbages. Get over it." Grace stood up from the couch and nudged Aunt Judy's shoulder on her way to the kitchen. She cut up Aunt Judy's dinner into tiny pieces to make it easier for her to eat. Her MS brought on a fierce trembling in her hands, making it impossible for her to eat with a knife and fork.

Grace placed the food in a bowl, grabbed a spoon, and set up a dinner tray in front of Aunt Judy's recliner chair. She tucked a napkin in Aunt Judy's shirt and brought over her water.

"You all set?"

"Mm-hmm. Thanks, sweetheart," Aunt Judy said, an appreciative sparkle in her eye. "You're too good to me. Before you put the movie back on, tell me about that picnic. Did you finally get the nerve to ask that boy out?"

Grace sighed, picturing Todd and Jane together in that playhouse. "He likes someone else."

Aunt Judy frowned. "Then he can eat a bag of d—"

"Don't you dare finish that sentence!" Grace gasped.

"What?" Aunt Judy shrugged.

"You're a bad influence."

"Well, someone ought to be."

Grace rolled her eyes. "Not this again." She felt a lecture coming on.

"You know, you should really get out more."

"I get out plenty," Grace said, setting up her dinner tray in front of the couch. "I have a job."

Aunt Judy snorted. "I'm talking about going out. Living a little."

Grace groaned.

Aunt Judy was always giving her a hard time about being a homebody. What she didn't realize was Grace was doing it for her. Somebody had to rake the leaves and do the dusting. Water the plants. Pay the bills. It was her duty as Aunt Judy's only living relative. And it was the least she could do after Aunt Judy took her in and raised her as her own.

"I've been giving it a lot of thought, and I've been a burden on you long enough. I think it's time we consider putting my old withering ass in a nursing home."

"No! Aunt Judy! That's crazy. I'm not sending you to a nursing home."

"No offense, Grace, but look at ya." Aunt Judy pointed. "You're wearing a sweater I bought in the seventies. You haven't had a haircut in over a year. You haven't been out on a date since… ever. You're not living your life, Grace. And it's all because of me."

Grace's heart clenched. "But I like being here with you. I like watching Meg Ryan and Tom Hanks movies. I like my life just the way it is."

The few white hairs left on Aunt Judy's eyebrows slid up her forehead. "That's just the thing, Gracie. You're too comfortable. And if I don't get out of your hair now, you'll never have a life of your own."

"But—"

"Stop right there. Let's say you asked out that dreamboat and he said yes. What was your game plan? How were you planning on going out on a date if you've gotta be home before Dolly Parton needs to clock out?"

Grace frowned. "I figured we'd have lunch."

"Lunch?" Aunt Judy gasped, clutching her chest. "You're not going to snag a husband having *lunch*. You'd be better off going to the senior citizens' happy hour at Applebee's."

Grace stuck her lip out. "Actually, that's not a bad idea."

"You're hopeless! This is no way to live at your age. Your parents—"

"My parents were reckless and irresponsible," Grace snapped. "They got out. Lived their lives to the fullest. And look who paid the price."

Aunt Judy's face softened. "Now, Grace, I didn't mean to upset you."

Grace's cheeks burned. She turned away, hating the fact that after so many years she could still be upset with them. It's not like it was their fault the helicopter pilot lost control of the damn thing, but they were foolish enough to get on it.

"I like my life here with you," Grace said. Safe and controlled. The way life ought to be.

The silence was heavy, like a thick cloud hovering between them.

"Grace, I'm afraid this just isn't up to you," Aunt Judy said.

"Please don't leave me," Grace said, unable to escape the quiver in her voice.

Aunt Judy's shoulders slumped as she released a deep breath. Her hazy gray eyes seemed to droop even more. "All right, fine. I won't leave you until you're ready. But we have a problem."

"What problem?"

Grace recalled her aunt's doctor's appointment earlier in the week. Had they found something serious? She had been feeling a little light-headed lately. The last time they checked her blood, her platelets were low.

Grace wouldn't be able to take the bad news. Her Aunt Judy was her everything. Her only family. Grace noticed her head trembling in a way it did when she was nervous. Stress had a tendency to flare up her symptoms.

Grace braced herself for the news.

"I received a letter the other day from Sunrise. Turns out they're raising their rates. Probably trying to get an old grump like me out of their registry."

Grace let out a breath of relief. "I thought you were going to say something way worse." Grace sank into the cushions. "How much is the increase?"

"I don't want to say."

"Aunt Judy. Cough it up."

Aunt Judy shook her head like a petulant child.

"Tell me right now, or I'm going to have to tickle it out of you."

"You wouldn't dare," Aunt Judy snapped.

Grace stood up, her fingers curled, twitching in the air, threatening to tickle Aunt Judy's toes until she fessed up. It was a little cruel, but it worked.

Grace's fingertips just barely grazed her aunt's stockings when Aunt Judy kicked wildly in response. "Fine! You win, you evil child!"

Grace giggled, smiling triumphantly before resuming her seat on the couch.

"Twenty percent."

"Twenty percent?"

"And on top of that they've added an additional annual registration fee. Fifteen hundred dollars."

Grace's eyes grew wide. Her mouth fell open. "Are you serious?"

"They're crooks."

Grace set her jaw. A twenty percent raise and an annual fee was more than they could manage. She had barely been able to cover the costs as they were. "There's got to be another option."

"Yeah. It's called a nursing home," Aunt Judy said, pointing toward the remote in her nonverbal way of telling Grace their conversation was over.

"I can make more money."

Aunt Judy scowled. "No, Grace—"

"I'm going to ask for a raise."

"Nonsense. The nursing home around the corner is half the cost we're paying now," Aunt Judy said. "Sweetheart, I know you're not ready for me to leave, but you've got to find a way to let go."

"No. I can take care of this on my own."

"What you should be doing is taking care of yourself. Now put Tom Hanks back on the screen before I really get upset."

Grace hated when she did that, using the TV to end their discussion. She had always found a way to get the last word. And Grace had let her.

But not this time. Not when it involved breaking up her family of two.

Grace reached for the remote and pressed the power button. The television went black.

"Wh-what are you doing?" Aunt Judy stammered.

"I'm asking for a raise whether you like it or not. I will not move you into a nursing home if I'm perfectly capable of taking care of you myself."

"But—"

"No buts. I can handle this. And I don't want to hear another word about that damn nursing home or the fact that I don't have a life!" Grace's voice echoed off the paisley wall-papered walls. "I've had enough!"

Grace had never shouted at her aunt before. Regret instantly consumed her, but she held her ground. She would not back down. Not this time.

Aunt Judy sat in stunned silence. Her mouth opened and shut like a fish out of water.

"Okay," Aunt Judy said finally, her hands floating up in surrender. "But you'll have to do one thing for me first."

"What is it?" Grace said more softly this time. "I'll do anything for you."

"Good, 'cause I just crapped my pants."

The sun peeked behind the trees, reflecting off the large panel windows of Maritime Marketing Services. An icy breeze from Lake Michigan blasted her in the face. Grace shuffled toward the front door, a steaming to-go cup of coffee warming each hand. The weather was just beginning to turn into one of Michigan's never-ending winters. Frost had already coated the grassy lawn out front, and it was only October.

Grace's teeth chattered but not from the cold. Her nerves were getting the best of her. Asking for a raise was not something she had ever done, nor was it something she looked forward to. To help get her mind off the impending task, she stopped by her favorite coffee shop on the way to work.

Grace loved surprising Tessa with coffee. Her excitement for the little things in life was infectious, and Grace could use all the enthusiasm she could get today.

Plus Tessa certainly needed a little pep too, given everything going on with Jane Lambert, evil manipulator and stealer of men.

Grace hoped that Tessa would still get to go to Costa Rica. She had been talking about it for weeks. But also, selfishly, Grace was excited to live vicariously through her. She couldn't wait to hear about Tessa's trip.

Grace yanked the front door open and waltzed inside,

grateful to be out of the cold. She took her first step up the stairs when the elevator pinged in the back of the lobby, catching her attention. Most people didn't use the elevator. The building had only two floors.

Out of curiosity, she peeked around the corner to see who was stepping through the sliding doors.

Tessa's reddened face emerged. She was holding a cardboard box in her arms.

"Tessa?"

Tessa let out a snort that was a half sob, half laugh.

"What happened?" Grace said.

"She fired me. She freaking fired me."

"Who fired you?" Grace said, switching to a whisper. "Jane?"

Tessa sniffed, gesturing for her to follow her out the lobby, back into the cold. As soon as they gave the building enough clearance, Tessa went on a warpath, setting her box on the trunk of her Toyota Corolla.

"I knew that wench had it out for me," Tessa said. "I just knew it."

"But how can she fire you if you don't report directly to her?"

Tessa rubbed her face, wiping away the smeared mascara underneath her eyes. "Jane can get anyone fired. All she has to do is call Daddy, and they'll find some excuse. HR called me in this morning and said I was getting laid off due to 'budgetary reasons.' It's all crap. I know Jane was behind it."

Grace rested the coffees on the car hood and brought Tessa into a hug. "I'm so sorry. That's awful. She's awful."

Tessa wiped away a tear. Her eyes drifted toward the coffee cups. "Are one of those for me?"

Grace nodded her head. "I was going to surprise you."

Tessa smiled, her skin blotchy. "You're the best."

"This probably isn't going to help you feel any better, but

here you go." Grace grabbed one of the cups and handed it to her. "Is there anything I can do?"

"You know what you can do?" Tessa said, straightening her spine. "You can stay away from that shrew. She'll make your life a living hell." Tessa took a sip of her coffee, and her face brightened a touch. "Thanks for this. It does help." She closed her eyes for a moment. "Honestly, I think this was the best thing for me. I've been unhappy here for so long. It's time I find a new gig."

Grace put a hand on Tessa's shoulder. "I'm just sorry it had to end on Jane's terms, not yours."

"Meh," Tessa said. "Screw her. She's dead to me now. I don't have to put up with her crap anymore, so there's a silver lining for ya."

"That's true. I'm sure she'll be on to harassing her next victim in no time."

Tessa handed her coffee to Grace while she opened her trunk, setting her box of personal belongings inside. She pulled Grace into another hug and squeezed. "Better get inside. You're shaking."

Grace nodded.

Tessa grabbed her coffee and sat down in the driver's seat. She closed the door, rolling down her window. "You know, you never told me what happened with you and Todd yesterday."

"Oh right," Grace said. "Come by the house tomorrow, and I'll fill you in. I've gotta be with my aunt all day."

"That sounds good."

"I'm going to really miss having you here at work."

"I'm going to miss you too." Grace grabbed her coffee from the hood and stepped away for Tessa to back out of her spot. She watched as her best friend drove out of the parking lot and onto the road of a fresh start.

Grace stood in front of her boss's office, her heart pounding. Her fingernails biting into her palms. She raised her hand to knock, but it hovered in front of the door, unmoving.

Raises were not something that were handed out like Halloween candy. Grace would likely have to work for it. She'd beg if she had to. She'd do anything to keep her aunt at home.

What if her boss said no? What then?

Would Grace have to find a second job?

Maybe she could work on the weekends. The housework would suffer, but Grace could learn to live a little less tidy.

Who was she kidding? She couldn't work weekends. She was already putting in hours of work on Saturdays and Sundays as it was. Grace didn't have time for a second job.

This raise was her only hope.

Her hand remained frozen, suspended in the air, unable to knock.

Knock, gosh darn it! You can do this.

Just as her knuckles grazed the door, it swung open. Miranda squealed, clutching her chest. "You scared me," Miranda said. Her face paled, nearly matching her white hair. "Good heavens, what happened to your eye?"

Grace reached for her cheek. "I accidentally got in the middle of a ladder golf game at yesterday's picnic."

Miranda winced. "Ouch."

"Do you have a minute? I wanted to talk to you about something."

"Sure, come on in," Miranda said. "What's on your mind?"

Grace sat in the chair across from Miranda's desk. The metal frame felt cool against the heated skin of her forearms. She looked up to find Miranda comfortably leaning back in her chair. Waiting.

Miranda's brows were plucked so thin they were just faint lines across her face. She wore a power-red lipstick and a white collared shirt. Miranda was usually easygoing, but today she looked like Meryl Streep in *The Devil Wears Prada*.

"Yes?" Miranda said, her chin in her hand.

"I was wondering if it would be possible to ask for a raise?"

Miranda jerked her head back. "Oh, I see."

"As you know, I've been working really hard. I acquired my own account earlier this year. I'm full of ideas. Lots of ideas. Brimming, even. Anyway, my family is in a bit of trouble and—"

"Say no more," Miranda said.

Grace opened her mouth, then promptly shut it.

"You have been doing a great job as an associate, I will give you that. But I can't just go around handing out raises."

Grace looked down at her hands.

"I've got a better idea," Miranda said, prompting Grace to look back up into Miranda's eyes.

"Tell me what to do. I'll do anything. I'll take extra work if I have to. Please. I can't tell you enough how much I need this."

An image of Aunt Judy sitting in a four-walled cell floated across Grace's mind.

"As you may know, Maritime is about to land our first-ever international account."

Grace sucked in a breath. "The one in Costa Rica?"

"Exactly." Miranda formed a tight-lipped smile.

The room blurred. Grace attempted to focus on Miranda's head, but for a moment there, she had three.

"You mean… the account Tessa was on?"

Miranda frowned. "Yes. Unfortunately, Tessa was impacted by a recent layoff. For budgetary reasons, of course."

Grace clenched her jaw.

"Jane needs to acquire that account. And I need a strong sales associate like you to help her do it."

"Me? But—"

"As you know, rumor has it that Jane is next up as CEO. When that happens, her role opens up." *Senior* sales associate. Grace hadn't even dreamed of getting a fancy title, but if it would help keep her aunt from moving into a nursing home, she was on board. The promotion should be enough to cover the home care expenses.

"Go with Jane to Costa Rica. Help her land that account. If you can impress her and get her to recommend you for the job, it's yours."

Slight problem. Grace had never flown before, and Costa Rica was a long way away.

She felt the blood drain from her face and the back of her neck begin to itch. How could she get in a plane after what had happened to her parents? It was risky and unsafe to fly. Could she really get on an airplane and travel across the world? Could she leave her aunt behind with full-time home care?

"Are you all right?" Miranda said. "You look gray."

"I'm fine." Grace swallowed. A cold sweat emerged above her brow. "I just need to figure out how I'm going to pay for my aunt's home care while I'm gone."

"Expense it. Expense anything you need to land Tortuga Bay."

Grace stared, wide-eyed. She was out of excuses not to go, other than fear itself.

"Is it a deal?" Miranda said, her eyes fixated on Grace's hairline, probably watching her sweat beads form into giant droplets.

Grace couldn't say no to an opportunity like this. This

was more than she could have ever asked for, despite having to work with Jane.

Tessa had warned her about Jane, but what other choice did Grace have? She could get along with Jane. She had to. For Aunt Judy.

Grace nodded her head yes, the word stuck in her throat.

"Great. Well, I suggest you pack your bags then. You're headed to Costa Rica in a couple of weeks."

CHAPTER FIVE

The traffic had cleared up once Noah left the city. A plan had begun to take shape. He could dump the cocaine near a police station, make an anonymous call to let them know, then find a place to lie low for a while, preferably on a beach somewhere where he could stay out of sight.

Noah rolled down the window, letting the wind whip through the van while he zoomed through the smaller towns on the outskirts of San José. After an hour had passed, the sun was shining directly in Noah's eyes. He squinted under the glare, cursing himself for not remembering his sunglasses.

The highway eventually cut through a vast mountain range covered in the greenest grass he had ever seen. Emerald-green palm trees covered the rolling hills, and fresh air barreled in, replacing the lingering fumes of the city.

When a gas station came into view, he was tempted to stop. He needed water and shades. His mouth was parched, and his eyes were strained from darting between the road ahead and the rearview mirror. If he could just make it to Jaco, he'd stop for gas and supplies.

He hadn't seen the Sable since he left the city, but those men could have gotten Noah's license plate. They could have eyes all over the country. Noah could only guess how connected they were.

He had heard of the horror his older brother had seen when the last delivery went awry; the dead bodies everywhere, the gore. Noah had never seen Raffi so shaken up before.

Noah would have gladly handed over the drugs to those men if he hadn't been afraid of getting gunned down. The cartel were dangerous, obviously. He would have to be careful wherever he went.

Noah cursed out his older brother again for tangling him up with the cartel. He had been a good kid growing up. He had played by the rules—well, mostly, when he wasn't cutting classes to surf. But he was a straight-A student and had been accepted into the best universities in Costa Rica.

He had the perfect life planned out. He'd graduate with a degree in hospitality and work his way up the ranks until he managed his own hotel. And he would have pursued all that if his father had been in better health and hadn't needed Noah's help.

How could Noah leave for college while Pop was in the hospital and his business was failing? He couldn't do that to him, or Ma. They'd needed him, so he'd stayed. But working at the roastery had opened Noah's eyes to how bad things had gotten.

His father had made several bad investments with little return. He bought a fancy technology system that would open up their distribution across the country but then didn't have anyone to sell their coffee to.

Pop had big dreams but no follow-through.

When Pop had put Raffi in charge of sales, it only got worse. Raffi was a wild card, disorganized and unreliable. In the last year of Pop's life, they had lost more accounts than they gained.

Noah witnessed the downfall of his father's health and business firsthand, watching failure after failure. It was heartbreaking and disorienting to see his idol fail at the thing he desperately wanted to get right.

Noah had insisted that he could jump in and help with sales, but Pop and Raffi said no, demanding that Noah work the roaster or make deliveries instead. *You're too young*, they had said.

And Noah had let it go. His first big mistake.

Maybe he should have been more persistent. Maybe he should have demanded that he step up and take charge. But he had kept quiet, afraid that if he had stepped up, he would have failed just as they had.

No fancy college degree could fix the fuck-up gene that ran in his blood. Noah was just like them.

If Noah could have it his way, he'd escape it all. He'd build himself a yurt off the coast somewhere and surf all day.

It wasn't that Noah didn't want to work; he just didn't want the big responsibility anymore, especially when it came at the expense of others. Noah's dream to manage his own hotel one day was out of the question now. If it turned out he was as big of a failure as Pop, it would impact hundreds of people. Noah couldn't have that weight on his shoulders.

He'd rather find a job helping people where the stakes weren't so high. A job he knew he'd be good at and not disappoint himself along the way. Maybe he could teach kids how to surf or learn to be a tour guide in a rainforest. Whatever it was, it had to be simple and only involve himself.

He wanted a stress-free life without the drama of the cartel on his ass, without the women that left him feeling empty inside. He wanted *pura vida*, the simple life. The reason he fell in love with Costa Rica in the first place.

Noah sighed, resting his elbow out the window, letting the wind cool his skin.

A street sign zoomed past him, reminding him of his destination. He was just outside of Jaco, off the Pacific coast. It was only a matter of time before he would be free from the cocaine, free from the burden that plagued his family the moment Raffi decided to make the cartel his get-rich-quick scheme.

He couldn't wait for a fresh start even if he had to stay in hiding the rest of his life.

CHAPTER SIX

"You're going to Costa Rica?" Tessa exclaimed, grabbing a soda from the fridge.

"Costa Rica?" Aunt Judy shrieked from the living room. She strained her neck toward the kitchen where Tessa and Grace stood in front of the microwave. "What do you mean you're going to Costa Rica?"

Grace finished explaining what had happened with Miranda just as the microwave dinged. A waft of buttery, hot popcorn spilled out of the paper bag.

"I was going to tell you last night," Grace said, "but I'm not even sure I can go through with it."

"Of course you can." Tessa bopped Grace's shoulder. "You have to."

"Are you upset that I took your place?" Grace said, pouring the popcorn into one giant bowl for Grace and Tessa and into a smaller bowl for Aunt Judy.

"I'm not upset, but I'm a little worried for your sake," Tessa said. "Jane is going to make your life miserable if you don't kiss her ass."

Grace whimpered, carrying the bowls into the living

room. She set one on Aunt Judy's lap and the other on the coffee table before taking a seat at the far end of the couch. Tessa followed suit, draping a blanket over their laps.

"But you'll be fine," Tessa amended. "You're far more patient than I am. You can deal with Jane better than I ever could."

"I'm not stressed about Jane, really. It's the trip to Costa Rica that has my guts all twisted up. I've never been on an airplane before."

"Are you flying first class?"

"Business class," Grace said. "I don't even know what that means."

"It's basically first class. Spacious. You're going to love it," Tessa said.

"Great. I'll be nice and comfy while I plummet to my death."

Tessa and Aunt Judy exchanged a glance, like a silent negotiation to figure who would address Grace's irrational fear this time. They'd been a tag-teaming duo ever since Grace brought Tessa over to her house for the first time when the girls were twelve.

Tessa leaned back and proceeded to stuff her mouth with popcorn while Aunt Judy straightened in her chair. "What happened to your parents was a fluke. You hear me? Airplanes are completely safe."

"Let's say I get there safe," Grace said, her heart pounding in her chest. "I'd be in a foreign country. I don't know the language. I don't know my way around there. What if I get lost on my way to the resort? What if—"

"Relax," Aunt Judy said. "Breathe. You'll be fine."

"What about *you*?" Grace said. "I'm going to be leaving you for three nights. I'll have to hire the night shift. Are you even comfortable with that?"

Aunt Judy placed a kernel of popcorn in her mouth and

leaned back in her chair. "If you set me up in a nursing home, then you wouldn't have to deal with that, would you?" she said with a smug tilt of her head.

"We're not talking about this right now," Grace said stubbornly.

"I'm just sayin'," Aunt Judy said, pressing Play on the remote. The beginning credits of *You've Got Mail* danced across the screen.

Conversation over.

"She'll be fine, right, Tessa?"

Tessa turned off her phone and grabbed another handful of popcorn. "You're going to have so much fun. I mean, this is an experience of a lifetime."

Of all the words for Tessa to say, she chose the ones her parents used before they hopped in that Alaskan helicopter, never to return home again.

Grace shoved down the niggling fear and replaced it with a handful of popcorn and a swig of diet cola. Then she looked over at the collection of snow globes on the mantel, each a memory of her parents' adventures. The globes reminded her of her parents and the happiness she always felt when they came home. But they also reminded her of the Alaskan globe she never got and the price they all paid for an *experience of a lifetime*.

"This will be good for you," Aunt Judy said, following Grace's line of sight. "Maybe you could bring back a snow globe to add to your collection."

There was empathy in her aunt's voice. Empathy and love. She knew how hard this was going to be for Grace.

Grace guzzled the rest of her soda until she felt the fizz in her nose. Settling under her blankets, she took a shaky breath. The fear of flying and the guilt of leaving her aunt behind would all have to take a back seat. She was going to Costa Rica in two weeks, and that was that.

Nothing would stop her from keeping her aunt out of a nursing home.

Nothing.

❀

Grace fumbled with her buckle, eventually getting her shaky hands to cooperate and click it into place. She struggled to focus on the flight attendant's directions on how to put on her mask. Shouldn't they practice this before takeoff?

Outside the airplane window, the sky was an inky blue. Grace watched airport workers in bright orange vests transport a cart of luggage. Each bag tossed into the belly of the plane made a large thump, jostling the aircraft and her nerves.

"Champagne?" the flight attendant asked sweetly, holding a tray of flutes.

"No, thanks," Grace said. She was sure her trembling hands wouldn't be able to hold the stem without spilling it all over herself.

"Champagne?" the flight attendant asked Jane across the aisle.

"Do you have anything stronger?" Jane said.

"Yes, but you'll have to wait until our flight service."

Jane pursed her lips and grabbed a flute anyway. "I don't usually drink," she told Grace, taking a sip of her bubbles. "But it's been a long day and I hate airplanes."

Grace shifted in her seat. "I'm not a fan either."

Jane smiled, holding her champagne flute out as if she were toasting Grace.

The engine—or whatever was making all that racket— was getting louder. Grace squeezed her eyes tight.

"Want one of these?" Jane said, breaking Grace's focus on each sound the plane made. Grace couldn't tell what was normal and what was a mechanical failure the technicians had missed. She opened her eyes to find Jane holding a white oval pill in her hands. "It'll help with your nerves."

"No, thanks."

"Suit yourself," Jane said, popping the pill in her mouth.

The plane pulled forward, picking up speed.

This was it. There was no turning back.

All of a sudden, she was hot. Really hot. Sweating. Her thermal shirt was sticking to her back. Grace reached for the nozzle above her head, pointing the air toward her damp face.

Her stomach lurched with the plane as the ground drifted away.

"Are you okay over there?" Jane asked.

"Fine. Just fine." A lie. She needed something to distract herself from the impending doom. Her thoughts drifted to Todd and Jane, an upsetting distraction. She pictured them in the playhouse during that company picnic, and a jolt of turbulence shook the question right out of her mouth. "So what's going on with you and Todd?" she blurted out, hating herself for it. But then again, it was helping her forget about being hundreds, possibly thousands, of feet in the air.

"Nothing," Jane snapped. "Why do you ask? Do you think he's too young for me or something?"

"No, not at all. I asked because I got the impression that he liked you."

Jane arched an eyebrow. "Is that so?"

"He was asking about you when you showed up at the playhouse that one day. I figured you two might be dating or something."

Jane tossed her head back with a laugh. "You are so precious, Grace. I'm not dating Todd. I can't be in a relationship with anyone at work if I'm going to take over the business one of these days." She looked down at her flute, studying the bubbles before drinking it down in two gulps. Her eyes glittered under the overhead light. "Between us girls though, I will admit I do like toying with him."

Grace wondered if Todd knew he was being used as a toy. Or if he cared at all. Either way, he had made it clear he preferred Jane over her, so it shouldn't matter anymore, despite the lingering ache that came with an unrequited crush.

"Young guys give me a little boost, you know?" Jane continued. "After what Bobbie did, it's nice to be reminded that I've still got it."

"Who's Bobbie?"

"Bobbie is my piece-of-shit ex-husband."

"Oh right. I'm sorry."

The overhead speaker crackled on, and the captain announced they'd hit thirty-five thousand feet.

Grace took a deep breath. As painful as this conversation with Jane was, at least she'd made it through takeoff.

"Don't be sorry for me. I'm *fine*," Jane scoffed, leaning back in her chair. She crossed her legs with her empty flute dangling in the aisle. "Can someone please take this before I break it?"

A flight attendant rushed over and whisked away the empty flute.

"Anyway, if Bobbie thinks he's better off with a perky college student, that's *fine* with me." Jane reached for her purse below the seat and pulled out a tube of bright pink lipstick, applying it in the compact mirror while she spoke. "I'm having the time of my life being single again." She blotted her lips with a pop.

She was silent for a moment, staring at herself in the mirror, inspecting the skin under her eyes and around her mouth. "It's a good thing we couldn't have kids after all," she said quietly. Grace almost didn't hear her under the hum of the airplane.

Jane snapped her compact mirror shut and shifted in her seat. There was pain in her eyes, despite what appeared to be an attempt to hide it with her smile.

Grace didn't know what to say or how to console her.

"Wipe that pity off your face," Jane said. "I told you I was fine. Never been happier. Truly."

All of a sudden the air blasting overhead had become too much. Grace shivered under the icy whoosh. She quickly turned the nozzle off.

The flight attendant appeared, setting a small cup of ice on Jane's tray. A tiny bottle of vodka and a can of tonic water followed. "Compliments from the gentleman in 6C."

Jane's eyes widened in surprise, exchanging a look with Grace as if to say she couldn't believe it either. Together, they turned their heads to check out the man three rows behind them.

The man in 6C was wearing a business suit. His hair was slicked back with speckles of white on the sides, contrasting with his deep brown skin. He held his drink up, saluting Jane from across the seats.

"Oh em gee," Jane mouthed to Grace. "He's a hunk."

Grace nodded in agreement. He looked like one of those beautiful Latino men in a telenovela.

"What do you think; should I go over there?" Jane said, not even looking up for Grace's response as she poured the contents of her little mini bar into her cup and unbuckled her seat belt.

Jane slapped on her dazzling smile and sauntered over to 6C. She took the empty seat next to him and began chatting.

Grace turned back around, wondering what it would be like to meet a man like that. To be desired instantly. She looked down at her oversized I [HEART] NY sweatshirt her father used to own. She wore plain black leggings and her favorite Christmas socks she wore all year long. Dirty sneakers on her feet. She was like a walking man repellent.

Grace hated to admit it, but something needed to change. If she really wanted a boyfriend, she might actually have to put more effort into it and not just her looks.

She shut her eyes, deciding she would worry about it another day. She needed to focus on getting some rest during this red-eye flight so she could be fresh for the presentation tomorrow.

CHAPTER SEVEN

The captain's voice shook Grace out of her dream, informing the cabin and crew they were ready for their descent. Grace rubbed the sleep out of her eyes and looked over to Jane's seat.

Jane wasn't there.

Grace peered behind her chair toward 6C, but the hunky businessman wasn't there either.

Grace rubbed her forehead. Panic settled in. *Did she oversleep?* Had she missed her stop entirely? Did that even happen on flights? Her pulse quickened. Was she missing the presentation this very moment?

The bathroom door opened, and the hunky businessman stepped out, running a hand down his shirt, adjusting his belt buckle as he strolled down the aisle.

Grace let out a relieved sigh. She shook off the rest of her brain fog and relaxed in her chair.

A moment later, the same bathroom door opened, and Jane emerged and walked back to her seat. She sat down gingerly, snapping her buckle in place.

Did she just...

Did they...
Oh.

Grace had heard of the mile-high club before, but she didn't think people did it for real.

Jane looked out her window. The back of her hair was a wild mess with chunks of hair going in every direction. And as Jane leaned even farther, looking out the window, her heel turned up. A long sheet of toilet paper was speared at the tip.

Twenty minutes later, they landed in the San José airport before the sun had a chance to rise. Jane carried the streamer of toilet paper all the way to baggage claim.

The airport was surprisingly busy at five in the morning. A crowd of people, including Jane, stood around the baggage carousel, but Grace gawked out the sliding doors instead. The sky had turned a deep purple, the hint of early-morning light. Palm trees lined the median between a two-way street, and a rush of warm air washed over her every time someone walked through the sliding doors.

The clicking sound of Jane's heels drew near, and Grace turned to see Jane's frantic face.

"What's wrong?" Grace said.

"I forgot the portfolio," Jane said, her face turned white. "I think I left it on the plane. Why didn't you remind me to get it?"

Grace gaped at her. *Me? Remind you?*

Technically, they didn't even need the boards. And technically, they could have done their presentation on a video call and saved the company thousands of dollars, but Jane had insisted on taking the old-fashioned approach. She had said it gave them an edge to sell their concepts in person, and the boards were meant to show her *human side*.

"Don't worry. I have everything saved on a PowerPoint. We can project from my computer."

"No!" Jane's eyes were wild. "I'm not good with all that technology stuff. We need to reprint."

Grace bit her tongue. Their whole company was based on technology and web development. The fact that Jane couldn't handle a simple PowerPoint presentation was a little unnerving if she was going to be the CEO.

"We only have four hours until our presentation. It's going to take at least an hour and a half to get to the resort. We don't have time."

"Yes, we do. We can check in at the hotel and find a print shop nearby. I'm not giving a presentation without my boards!"

Grace blinked at her.

There was no sense in arguing. Not if Grace needed to stay on her good side. She nodded her head and followed Jane out the doors toward the line of cabs.

This was going to be a very long two-day trip.

Grace opened her hotel room and gasped. Giant sliding glass doors showcased the garden just beyond her patio. Palm trees swayed in the breeze, welcoming her to the gorgeous resort. The ocean glittered in the horizon.

She had never seen anything so beautiful in her entire life.

She opened her patio door, and the salty air rushed in.

A white king-size bed with two magenta roses sitting on top of a folded swan towel held a handwritten note from Fernando, the hotel owner.

I HOPE YOUR STAY HERE IS VERY PLEASURABLE. WE ARE ALL LOOKING FORWARD TO MEETING YOU SOON.

SINCERELY,
FERNANDO RODRIGUEZ

Grace glanced at the alarm clock on the nightstand. They were running out of time. She threw down her carry-on and tore through her clothes, letting them fly wildly in her perfectly clean space. If she didn't help Jane get this account and her promotion to CEO, she'd have to get that second job and learn how to live like this all the time. Why not start now?

She picked a navy pencil skirt and a cream floral blouse that she'd found at a thrift store. It seemed like a good idea at home, but it looked out of place in this tropical resort. *Ah well.* It's not like she had better options anyway. She got dressed and dabbed a little orange soda lip balm on her lips.

Grace knocked on the hotel suite door that connected her room with Jane's. "Are you ready?"

The door opened, and Jane was holding an earring to her ear. "Come in."

Jane's charcoal eyeliner and long false lashes brought out her hazel eyes. She wore a white sheath dress that hugged her in the middle and around her slender hips.

Grace looked like a spinster next to Jane.

"Are you sure we have enough time?" Grace asked, clutching her computer bag as if it were keeping her afloat.

"Of course we do."

They didn't.

It was a quick trip to the print shop, but the language barrier had slowed down their process of printing seventy images. Jane must have spent a fortune on reprints of the same pictures, over and over again. And she completely underestimated the amount of time it would take to cut everything out and paste them on the boards the way she wanted them.

By the time they were done, they only had fifteen minutes to get to their meeting.

Grace's stomach began to ache. She didn't want to make a bad first impression, especially when the account was so important to Maritime.

"Pulling up an Uber now," Grace said, stepping out onto the sunny parking lot.

Jane was shielding her eyes, overseeing the strip mall when she paused.

"Check out that hottie," Jane said.

Grace waited for the Uber app to pull up before following Jane's gaze toward the gas station next door.

A young guy, probably around Grace's age, was standing near a white van with a Greene Coffee Roastery logo plastered against the side.

"A hottie who delivers coffee," Jane purred. "Two of my favorite things."

"Mm-hmm," Grace said, typing in the resort address into her phone.

"I wouldn't mind letting him roast my beans," Jane said, giggling to herself.

Grace pinched the bridge of her nose. Scanning the app, her mouth flew open. "There are no Uber drivers out here."

"What? Let me see that," Jane said, tugging Grace's phone from her hands.

Grace ran her fingers through her hair. What were they going to do? "I'll have to call a cab."

"A cab will take too long. I have another idea." Jane handed Grace's phone back and marched across the parking lot toward the gas station.

Grace's stomach dropped when she realized she was approaching the van guy.

Oh no. No. No. No.

She wasn't about to ask a stranger for a ride, was she?

Grace trotted behind her. "Jane. Whatever you're think-ing, it's probably best—"

"I know what's best," Jane snapped, continuing with her long strides.

"You can't ask a stranger for a ride. Especially one with a windowless van! Jane, please. This isn't safe. This is how girls' faces get put on milk cartons."

"Let me handle it. If he gives off a creepy vibe, we'll call the damn cab."

Grace stopped in her tracks. "Can't we just call and tell them we're going to be late?"

Jane ignored her, merely yards from the guy now. He was putting the gas nozzle away when Jane approached. "Hey! You there!"

The guy looked up and smiled. As Grace got closer, she could see that he had freckles across his sun-kissed nose and cheeks.

"Hi," he said. "Can I help you?" He had an accent of some kind. It sounded American but with a hint of something. British, maybe? German? Grace couldn't quite put her finger on it.

"I'm sorry to bother you," Jane said, fixing her hair. "But my assistant and I are in a bit of trouble."

Assistant? Grace bit her tongue.

"We have a presentation to be at in ten minutes, but there are no drivers to take us in time."

Van Guy got an eyeful of Jane, then turned to Grace. His eyes flared. They were a stormy sea green. His mouth twitched into a smile, sending Grace's pulse humming in her veins.

"Would it be too much to ask for a quick ride? The resort is only one mile away," Jane said.

"You need a *ride?*" The guy looked at his van and rubbed his neck. "I don't know if that's a good idea."

"Surely you have room for the both of us. I'll pay you. Twenty bucks."

"I'm sorry," Grace cut in. "Jane, we can't just interrupt this guy's day like this. He's probably super busy with important things or whatever one does with a windowless van."

Van Guy tilted his head, his eyes twinkling in amusement.

"Don't be a prude. He's our only chance."

"But he's a *stranger.*" Grace felt Van Guy's eyes on the side of her face, but she refused to look up at him.

"Easily fixable," Jane said, holding out her hand. "I'm Jane. This is Grace. See? Now we're not strangers."

Grace found the strength to look up and saw the flicker of concern on his face.

"Fifty bucks," Jane burst out. "If we leave right now."

Van Guy glanced at Jane and then back at Grace, his hands on his hips. He finally said, "I'm Noah. Noah Greene."

Greene. Just like the logo on the van. Somehow that made Grace feel better. A serial killer wouldn't plaster his name all over his own moving vehicle, would he?

"It's nice to meet you," Jane said.

"The pleasure is all mine." The sparkle in his eye had Grace forgetting how to use her tongue. She gaped at him, unable to process a consistent string of thoughts.

This is not a good idea.

Why is he so good-looking?

Hitchhiking in a foreign country is not safe.

But his dimple is so mesmerizing.

Get yourself together, Grace.

"Let's get you to that meeting," Noah said.

Jane squealed. "Thank you! Thank you!" She pulled him into a hug and jumped into the passenger seat.

Grace stood frozen in place, assessing his extraordinarily

white teeth. Homicidal psychopaths didn't have white teeth like that, right? Or were they more likely to have white teeth? A shudder went down her spine.

"You'll have to sit in the back," Noah said. "Is that okay with you?"

Grace nodded, watching the muscles in his arms flex as he opened the back doors. He smiled, holding the doors open for her. His boyish grin was disarming, and Grace lost all sense of reason.

"I will admit, you don't give off a creepy vibe," Grace said.

"Thanks?" Noah said, furrowing his brow. "You don't either."

Grace peered in the van. "What's in the boxes?"

"Body parts. Kidneys. The usual black-market stuff." Noah grinned, holding out his hand.

"Funny," Grace said, eyeing him cautiously.

Noah continued holding out his hand. "It's just coffee," he said, a slight tic in his jaw.

There weren't any knives or hooks or body bags from what Grace could see. And it did smell like coffee, which was reassuring.

"You better not be lying to us, Noah Greene."

Noah smiled, shaking his hand for her to grab it. "You asked *me* for a ride, remember?" he said.

Grace slid her hand onto his palm. His fingers clasped around hers, helping her into the van. An odd sense of calm coursed through her. The tensed muscles in her neck and shoulders relaxed.

Noah held her hand a millisecond longer than necessary, probably to make sure she was steady on her heels. "You can grab onto the handle over there," he said, pointing to the bar above her head. "But I'll drive nice and slow for you," he said with a playful shimmer in his eyes.

Boxes covered the floor bed, unmarked with strips of red

duct tape sealing the seams. It seemed odd to have duct tape, not packing tape, on the boxes, but what did she know?

Grace found a place to sit while Noah waited patiently.

"Are you going to be okay back here?" Noah asked.

Grace nodded, and he shut the doors and ran to the driver's side.

"I don't know how I got so lucky to have two beautiful ladies riding in my van today, but I'll take it. Maybe this is the universe making up for some of my bad luck."

"What kind of bad luck?" Jane said. Her hand rested on the back of Noah's chair.

"I'm just having a hard time with this coffee delivery. That's all." He put the van in drive, and as he promised, he drove slowly over the bumps in the road.

His gaze caught Grace's in the rearview mirror, and she couldn't look away.

Her stomach did a cartwheel, and tingles rushed down her spine.

"You doing okay back there, Blue Eyes?"

Blue Eyes? She had never been given a nickname before.

Grace flushed, not sure if she was okay or not.

CHAPTER EIGHT

Chauffeuring two women in a van full of cocaine was probably not his best move. But what else could he do? They needed him. *Grace* needed him.

Grace. Noah loved that name.

She thought he was busy and important. Ha. Nobody ever thought that about Noah. He had to admit it felt nice for someone to assume he had more pressing things to do than help a couple of ladies out of a jam.

She was gravely mistaken, though. He wasn't anything special.

Noah rubbed his jawline, looking in the rearview mirror again, catching her intoxicating aquamarine eyes staring back at him. They were staggeringly blue, like two tropical lagoons.

Every glance felt like magic, the kind that could make him fly from thinking happy thoughts.

He almost forgot she was sitting on thirty million dollars' worth of drugs.

Almost.

Guilt festered in his gut, mingling with the anxiety from

the day. He felt bad about lying, but it wasn't like he could have told them what was actually in the boxes.

"So where are you ladies from?" Noah asked, turning his left blinker on.

"Traverse City, Michigan," Jane said. "Have you heard of it?"

Noah tapped on the steering wheel. "The mitten state, right?"

"You're correct," Jane said, holding up her hand. Her fingernails were pristinely manicured like the rest of her. She looked like a fembot. Like she wasn't even real. She was nothing like the natural beauty sitting in the back. "We're right here," she said pointing to where the top of her pinky touched her ring finger.

"I knew it," Noah said proudly. Geography had always been his favorite subject in school. Probably because their family had moved around the world so much when he was young. They had lived everywhere, from Barcelona to San Francisco. He loved studying maps.

"How about you?" Jane said. "Where are you from? You're obviously not Costa Rican."

"Did you pick up on that?" Noah said teasingly. "I was born in Germany, but we used to country hop with my father's company. We settled down in Costa Rica about twelve years ago when Pop decided to start his own coffee business."

Noah saw Grace nod her head in the rearview mirror. A flicker of understanding crossed her face as if she had just fit two puzzle pieces together.

"I went to English-speaking schools my whole life," Noah said. "A lot of them were American."

"Ahh. That explains your accent," Jane said, touching his shoulder with her fingertip.

Noah followed Jane's arm with his eyes and was met with two smoldering hazel irises.

Uh-oh. Not again. She had that look he knew all too well.

"How old are you?" Jane said.

Noah checked his mirror, looking for Grace's reaction to Jane's direct question, but Grace remained expressionless.

"Twenty-two," Noah said finally.

"You're young," Jane purred. Her finger trailed up his arm, circling the top of his shoulder. The sensation made his neck itch.

"Can you guess how old I am?"

Noah sent an SOS through the rearview mirror, but Grace was shaking her head. She shrugged as if to say *You're on your own, pal.*

Noah laughed off his nervous energy. "I don't particularly care about a woman's age, as long as she feels comfortable in her own skin."

"Is that so?" Jane purred, removing her fingers from his collarbone much to Noah's relief.

Noah shuddered, shifting in his seat.

Jane was beautiful, sure, but he was done with her type: desperate and seeking attention from a young guy to prove she wasn't old. She had that pseudoconfidence that women had after being freshly Botoxed and waxed. It was a facade though. It wasn't real.

Noah was done being cougar bait. Plus he had big problems to deal with, and pleasing a needy out-of-towner was not one of them.

He checked for Grace's reaction in the mirror and was met with a solid grimace.

"Have you ever—"

"Hey look, we're here," Noah said, interrupting Jane, pressing firmly on the gas as he pulled up toward the resort entrance. He'd never been so glad to pull into a porte cochere in his life.

The Tortuga Bay Resort was a sprawling two-story building nestled against the coast with white stucco walls and a terra-cotta roof. Two large potted palms in cobalt-blue vases stood on either end of the main lobby doors.

Jane looked in her purse. "Shoot, I don't have cash on me right now, and we only have a minute to get to our meeting. Can you wait here until we're done?"

"Don't worry about it. I've got to get back to my delivery."

"No! I insist. Please. I won't take no for an answer."

"Can you let me out?" Grace said from the back.

Noah jumped out of the van, jogging to the back door. He pulled the door open and offered his hand, but Grace waved him off.

"I've got it, thanks," Grace said, gripping the side of the van to steady herself in her skirt that wouldn't budge. She bent sideways, awkwardly teetering on one foot, then attempted to jump. Unsuccessfully. She tumbled into Noah's arms.

"Whoa there," Noah said. "Are you okay?"

She was delicate and soft, and Noah instantly felt the urge to protect her. Like getting smacked in the face with his new life's purpose. It stunned and disoriented him while she pressed herself off his chest.

Noah caught a whiff of oranges, only sweeter, and found himself wanting more of her scent. More of her delicate softness.

"I'm fine," Grace said, grabbing her giant folder. "Thanks for the ride."

"Come on, Grace," Jane said. "Noah, I'll meet you in the lobby when we're done with our presentation, okay? It'll be about an hour."

"Yeah, but—"

"Bye!" Jane yelled, slipping through the lobby doors.

Grace gave him an apologetic look before mouthing a silent thank-you as she trailed behind Jane.

Hot damn, she was cute. He couldn't leave now, not with Blue Eyes giving him all the feels. Who was this girl? And why did he have this intense urge to stay and get to know her?

A parking attendant jogged out of the hotel and looked as though he were about to take Noah's keys.

"Sorry. I was just leaving." He hopped in his van and started the engine.

He should go, he told himself. The cartel might still be on his tail.

He didn't care about the fifty dollars Jane promised him, and he might as well try to forget about the blue-eyed beauty. She was likely only in town for a few days anyway, just like the rest of the tourists who came and went out of his life.

But she was different somehow. He couldn't quite put his finger on it.

She hadn't flirted with him like women usually did. Hell, she might not have been interested in him at all. But he felt a tug on his chest the moment he touched her hand. An instinct that told him to stay.

It wasn't safe to hang around there. And he really needed to dump the cocaine.

But he really, really wanted to get to know Grace.

Noah stepped on the gas and pulled through the porte cochere. His brain directed him to drive toward the main road, but his heart had him pulling the steering wheel down a street a block from the resort. He parked along a palm tree-lined road, just far enough away from the condominium complex across the street and the public beach ahead.

He needed to think.

Noah peered down the road toward the sliver of ocean.

Surfers bobbed in the waves like happy little blueberries. They called to him.

Stay, the ocean waves said.

He killed the engine and looked around the quiet street. It didn't seem like anyone would bother him there, at least for a little while. And come to think of it, he *did* need a place to lie low where the cartel might not be able to track him down. Perhaps this was as good a place as any. His van blended in with the other vehicles parked along the street and didn't look too out of place.

Noah tapped on the steering wheel as he thought some more. Raffi would have asked the pretty blue-eyed girl if he could stay in her hotel room for the night. Kai would have left, keeping a safe distance between himself and the girl. It was the better option, and Noah knew it.

And yet he found himself slipping out of the van and walking up the street anyway. He headed back toward the resort like a moth being drawn to the blue light in Grace's eyes.

If the cartel had a tracking device in the van, they'd find it. And if they did drive across the country to get their stuff, they could take it. All of it. It'd make his job a lot easier than dumping it near a police station after the sun went down.

Noah kicked the gravel on the street before turning down the entrance to the resort hotel. This was the safest option, he told himself. The cartel wouldn't be able to find him at the resort. Putting distance between himself and the van was the right choice for now.

He just needed to decide if he would book his own room or charm Grace into staying in hers for the night.

Wait, no. That was the old him. Noah was done with one-night stands. He'd book his own room. He had money saved for college, and it wasn't like he'd be going anyway. He could afford at least one night at a nice hotel.

Noah stepped into the main lobby. Decorative surfboards were bolted to the back wall of a seated area. Giant wicker fans swirled the air around the room, making the large potted palms in each corner sway to the ambient music in the background.

A concierge with a name tag that read CYNTHIA stood behind a long rectangular desk, her hair pulled back tight. She offered him a bright smile with crater-sized dimples on each cheek.

"Welcome to Tortuga Bay Resort," she said in English.

"Thank you. Cynthia, is it?" Noah said in Spanish.

She nodded.

"You have a lovely smile, Cynthia."

A slight blush swept across Cynthia's face. "Gracias. How can I help you?"

"Do you have an extra room for one night?"

"We have a two-night minimum here, but I can check our availability." Cynthia's fingernails clicked on the keyboard until she pulled up a large king room with a view by the pool. "That'll be four-hundred and twenty-three dollars."

It was more affordable than he was expecting, but it didn't stop him from wincing at the price tag. He handed Cynthia his card. "Do you have a phone charger I could borrow?"

Cynthia said she would check after she finished booking his reservation.

Noah tapped his hotel key on the counter, reading a brochure about baby sea turtle hatchlings, when Noah heard footsteps echoing from down the hall. Jane and Grace emerged, a little less frazzled than when he had last seen them.

"Done so soon?" Noah said.

"We were stood up," Jane said, crossing her arms. "We rescheduled for tomorrow."

Noah caught Grace's blue eyes staring at him just before she looked away. The tips of her ears turned a deep fuchsia.

"The good news is they're comping another night, which means we just earned us an extra day at the hotel." Jane looked up at him with sultry promise in her eyes. He had seen that look on a woman's face before. Only this time he wanted nothing to do with it.

"I'm sorry, Noah," Cynthia chimed in. "We had lent out all our iPhone chargers. Maybe you could check back with us later?"

"You need a charger?" Jane said.

Noah looked down at his phone. "My phone is dead. I'm supposed to be giving my brother a call."

"You can use mine," Jane said. "Come on"—she snaked her hand around his arm—"I'll let you charge your phone in my room."

"Your room is just on the left," Cynthia said to Noah, handing him a key. She pointed toward the pool. "There's a stairwell by the exit there. It will take you to 208."

"Thanks," Noah said, waving his key in the air.

"You're staying at the hotel too?" Grace said, her face scrunched in confusion.

"Uh, yeah." Noah stalled, trying to think of an explanation that wasn't too suspicious. "I'm a long way from home. Figured I'd camp here for the night."

Grace wrinkled her brow, her head tilted to the side.

"I... uh," Noah stammered. "I decided to take a last-minute vacation. It's been a rough couple of weeks."

Jane squealed, but Grace narrowed her eyes before turning away.

"I'm so happy you're staying here too." Jane squeezed his arm, letting her fingers linger over his skin a little too long.

"I'm heading back to my room," Grace grumbled, turning on her heel. She was gone before Noah could utter a weak "wait." Great. Now he was stuck with the cougar alone.

"What's with her?" Noah said, pointing his thumb.

"Oh, Grace? Who knows? I think she's a hermit."

Noah angled his head.

"She's very dull," Jane drawled, leading him out toward the pool.

Noah cringed. Jane was staking her claim, scaring poor Grace away.

Jane led him around the pool, walking behind the lounge chairs full of couples relaxing under the warm sun. The turquoise pool was in the shape of a sea turtle, he noticed, with blue and green decorated tiles along its edge. A bar was perched under a cabana with room for four stools, one taken by a burned man in a straw hat.

"Do you want to grab a drink first?" Jane said, gesturing toward the bar.

"No, thanks," Noah said.

"Lunch then? I can order room service."

"Nah," Noah said. "I really need to call my brother."

They strolled slowly, as if Jane hadn't heard he had things to take care of. Perhaps he needed to give her a stronger hint to back off. "Does Grace have a boyfriend?"

Jane scoffed. "No." She paused. "Why do you ask?"

Noah shrugged. "I don't know," he said, feeling a smile come along. "I think she's cute."

"She likes a guy in our office. Todd."

"Oh," Noah said, looking down at his shoes. *Todd. Screw Todd.* "But she's single…" He let the words hang heavy between them, and he could feel the heat of Jane's frustration.

"Enough about Grace, okay?" Jane said, stopping him in front of a hotel room. She placed a hand on his chest, lightly caressing his sternum with her long, manicured fingernails. "I want to learn more about *you*."

Jane looked up through her eyelashes and licked her upper lip.

"I just really need a charger," Noah said, clearing his throat.

She eyed him up and down. "Sure," she said with a devious smile. "Come in."

She opened her door, leading to a large room with a king-size bed and a sofa perched in front of two french doors. Beyond the doors were a garden patio, palm trees, and the sprawling ocean behind it.

"Nice room."

"Thanks," Jane said. "Definitely a perk being in the biz."

"What is it that you do?"

"I'm in sales for my father's company. We build experiences for clients like this resort."

"Experiences?"

"Yeah, things that their customers would like to do during their stay. Kayaking, wine tasting, adventure hikes. That sort of thing. Our company does all the partner setup and the web development to get them up and running."

"That's pretty cool."

"It is, isn't it?" Jane smiled brightly. She slipped out of her heels. "Do you mind if I change? This dress is terribly uncomfortable."

Noah stood frozen, not sure if he should stay or go, but the answer was right in front of him as she turned her back to him, looking over her shoulder. "Can you please help me unzip?"

Noah had seen this porno before. He needed to be careful. He inched toward her anyway, unzipping her dress from the top to the lowest curve of her spine. She had a nude, lace bra on top of silky, tanned skin. Four or five tiny birthmarks spanned her back.

Jane's dress dropped to the floor, and Noah promptly turned around. He heard the telltale sound of a bra unclipping before he saw it flung across the room in the corner of his eye.

"Is that phone charger around here somewhere?" Noah asked, his voice cracking.

"It's over by the nightstand."

Her naked silhouette reflected off the framed poster above the bed. She was shimmying herself into a dress when he forced himself to focus on the cord plugged into the wall. As he picked up the end of it, he noticed the flat nub.

It was the wrong fit.

"Any chance you have an adapter?"

"Oh shoot. I thought you had the same model. I don't have that adapter thingy with me." She sat on her bed in a red sundress, letting the strap slip over her shoulder. Jane wet her lower lip before taking it between her teeth.

"I should go," Noah said, turning to leave.

"Hold on," Jane said. "Don't forget about your money." Jane sauntered across the room, bending down to open the safe in her closet, a little triangle of nude underwear on display.

"Here you go," she said, emerging with cash.

She held it out for him, just far enough that Noah had to step forward to grab it. Jane flicked her wrist away before he could snag the fifty-dollar bill.

"You sure you don't want to stay and play?" she said, teasingly.

Noah grinded his teeth. "Yeah, I'm sure." He reached for the bill before she swiped it away again, taunting him with that playful grin of hers.

"Ah, ah, ah," Jane said. "You have to be faster than that."

Noah felt his blood pressure rise. He clenched his jaw, about to walk out of there without the money when she stuffed the fifty-dollar bill in her cleavage, a little corner of it poked out. "You'll have to come a little closer to get it," she said.

This lady was out of her goddamn mind.

"You know what?" Noah said. "You can keep it."

He turned on his heel, ignoring the scoff behind him as he reached for the door.

"Come on, Noah. I'm just having a little fun. Here," Jane said, holding out the money. "Take it, for real. I'm not playing anymore."

Noah blew out through his nose, closing his eyes. He gripped the door handle firmly, teetering on the decision to take the money or run.

He slowly turned and lumbered back to Jane's outstretched arm and took the money out of her hands, shoving it into his pocket.

"You see? I can play nice," Jane said, sitting back down on the bed, crossing her legs. "I'm sorry." She looked away. The edges of her ears turned pink. Her hand rose up to her nose, and she sniffed.

Fuck. Were those real tears?

A squeak escaped her throat, followed by a snort.

Dammit, that was a cry. Noah gripped his fists and stalked toward her. His mother didn't raise him to leave a crying woman alone. It was his Achilles' heel.

"Are you okay?" he asked gently.

Jane snorted again. "I'm sorry. I'm fine. I just feel really foolish."

Noah felt his face soften. "It's okay," he said gently. "Don't cry." He found himself sitting next to her, hating himself for falling into what was probably a trap.

She turned toward him, the skin around her eyes blotchy and swollen.

Noah's heart sank.

"I'm too old for guys like you. Aren't I?"

He pictured the very upset woman storming out of his house that morning. "Actually, you're not too old at all."

"Really?"

"You're beautiful," he said. It was a reflex. He always defaulted to telling a woman she was beautiful even if other descriptors came to mind: desperate, manipulative, pushy.

Jane smiled, resting a hand on his shoulder. She blinked, and a tiny little black streak of mascara smudged under her eyes. "You think I'm beautiful?"

He really needed to get out of there now.

Her eyes drifted to his mouth, and she leaned forward.

Shit. He leaped off the bed. "I'm sorry. But I really need to make that phone call. Do you think Grace might have a charger I could borrow?"

Jane blinked at him, stunned, as if she had never been turned down from a kiss before.

"It's urgent. Really. I have this delivery and—"

"She's in there," Jane snapped, nodding toward the wall. "Next door."

"Right here?" Noah said, pointing at the connecting door. He took a few steps toward it. "You sure you're going to be okay?"

Jane wiped her eyes and forced a smile. "I'm fine." She didn't look fine though. He fought the urge to stay and console her, as he had done for women so many times before. But it was easier to leave this time, knowing Grace was just beyond the door.

"Why don't we hang out later?" Jane sniffed, putting on a brave smile. "Platonically, of course." The curve in her lips gave away her true intentions.

He blinked at her, then nodded politely, although he had no desire to see her again.

Noah knocked on the door, and a moment later, Grace appeared, her eyes wide. "Noah?"

"Get me out of here," Noah mouthed.

CHAPTER NINE

"It's just one more night," Grace said. "I'll be there before you know it."

"No problem, but I'll have you know, Tamara's cooking is going to kill me before you get here," Aunt Judy said on the phone.

"I'll make your favorite chicken enchiladas when I get home. I promise."

"I don't like the night lady that came last night either. She smells like rotten cabbage dipped in cheap perfume. The fruity kind. You know how much I hate fruity perfume. It flares up my symptoms."

Grace rolled her eyes. "Okay. I'll remind Sunrise to tone down the perfume."

"You can also tell 'em to cut down on the hair products. Dolly Parton over here went a little overboard on the hairspray. I'm afraid she's going to catch fire any minute."

"No hair products. Check."

"Thanks, sweetheart. Good luck at the presentation tomorrow. Tamara, do you have anything to add?"

"Aunt Judy! Was Tamara standing there this whole time?"

"She's holding up the phone. You're on speaker."

Grace smacked her head with her palm. "Hi, Tamara," she said apologetically.

"Hi, Grace," Tamara said flatly. "For the record, I use dry shampoo to fluff up my hair. Not hairspray."

"It's fine. Ignore my aunt. She's just being crankier than normal."

"Oh really? Here I was thinking she was having one of her better days."

"Witch," Aunt Judy muttered under her breath.

"She's been such a pleasure today." Tamara's words dripped with sarcasm.

Grace winced. "I'm sorry."

"It's fine. Nothing I can't handle."

"Okay. Gotta go. I'll call you tomorrow."

She shut off her phone and relaxed, trying not to let Aunt Judy's mood bring her down any further. Seeing Jane sink her claws into the cute guy with the van had put Grace in a funk. She had been crazy to think they might have had a connection on their ride to the resort. She could have sworn there was a spark the moment he helped her up in the van.

It didn't matter now.

Jane had called dibs. Noah didn't seem like he was all that interested in her, but it didn't matter. Grace already knew Jane always found a way to get what she wanted. Which meant Noah was completely off-limits.

Grace's ears perked up at the sound of a shutting door. That must be Jane and Noah now. Getting his "phone charged." The thought made her queasy.

Their muted voices seeped through the wall.

Grace either needed to get out of her room or put her noise-canceling headphones on. She reached in her bag and remembered she had left them at the office. She'd have to pop in her regular earbuds instead.

Getting comfortable in her desk chair, she turned on her favorite playlist and worked on her email to Sunrise.

Just as she hit Send, someone knocked at her door. Grace jumped, startled by the intrusion. She pulled out her earbuds and stumbled over her suitcase and the pile of clothes that had been draped across the floor. The experiment of living in a messy room was not working.

She yanked open the door to the hallway and found no one there. The knocking continued, and she realized it was coming from the connecting door between her and Jane's rooms. She opened it and gaped at the broad male chest in front of her. Noah's body took up nearly every inch of space of the doorframe. Her eyes leveled with the Greene Coffee Roastery logo on his shirt.

She had to extend her neck to look up and see the panicked look on his face.

"Get me out of here," he mouthed, his eyes a desperate plea for help.

Grace stepped back in surprise.

"Can I borrow your phone charger?" he said, his hand gripping the doorframe so tightly Grace was concerned the wood was about to bow.

"What's wrong with Jane's?" Grace said, crossing her arms.

"My connector didn't fit," Jane said, a bite in her voice.

Grace poked her head in. Jane was sitting on the bed, scrolling through her phone. She looked up for a moment to dismiss them as if she was done with the conversation for now.

Grace blinked at Noah, assessing his hair. It didn't look like they had had sex, but then again, Jane was in a different dress than before. Maybe they had a quickie and she was already done with him.

"Please?" Noah said.

Grace shrugged and stepped out of the way for him to come in. He closed the door behind him. She picked up a few things from the chair and tossed them into the corner of the room.

Noah looked around the room, his hands on his hips. "It looks like a bomb went off in here."

"It's an organized chaos," Grace said. "The cord is plugged into my computer over there."

"It's impressive is what it is." He scratched the back of his neck, his T-shirt lifting up just enough for Grace to catch a glimpse of his abs.

She felt her cheeks turn red.

"Are you okay?" he asked, a slight tease in his voice.

"Of course I'm okay," Grace said, flustered. "Are *you* okay? What happened back there?"

"Jane's pissed I didn't play her little seduction game."

"I see." Grace threw a pair of shorts into her luggage. It would have bothered Grace if he had become another one of Jane's playboys. She was relieved he hadn't.

Noah perched his hands on his hips and looked around the room. "I'm just so amazed that such a tiny person can make such a big mess."

Grace chuckled. "What can I say? It's a gift."

"One of many, I'm sure," Noah said. The flare in his eyes left a little flutter in Grace's belly. He really was a flirt.

Grace brushed off the remark and pointed to the cord connected to her computer. "You can make your call in here if you want," Grace said. "I'm going to sit outside for a bit."

"Thanks," Noah said, stepping over a pair of heels. He lifted the end of the cord and held it out for her to see. "Hey, look. It's the perfect fit." He beamed, slotting the end of the rounded connector into his phone.

Grace found herself lost in his smile and those perfectly

white teeth. *How does someone in the coffee industry have such white teeth like that?* It defied all reason.

His smile was infectious. She felt her own smile coming on just before her bossy brain reminded her to lock it down.

Shake it off, Grace. He's off-limits. If Jane found out Grace was attracted to Noah, the talons would come out. Jane was too competitive to let Grace win Noah's affections. And heaven forbid, if Grace was caught flirting with him, Jane would never make the recommendation Grace needed to get her promotion.

"I'll be outside."

Sliding the glass window open, the heat wrapped around her like a warm blanket. She sat in the plastic patio chair and released a shaky breath.

Noah's presence had all her nerve endings on alert. Her heart was working overtime to keep herself calm. She needed a distraction from the buzz in her head.

She needed Tessa.

Grace: Tessa, help. There's an extremely hot guy in my hotel room right now, and I have no idea what to do.

Tessa: Hell yeah! [double high-five emoji] It's about time you got a little action.

Grace: It's not like that. Although he's been flirting with me. What do I do?

Tessa: Hit that! If he's interested, you should go for it.

. . .

Grace: There's something about him…

Tessa: YASSSSSSSS, GIRL. Get it.

Grace: I just met him!

Tessa: K, then get to know him first before you schlob his [eggplant emoji].

Grace: You are ridiculous. Why are we friends again?

Tessa: Cause I'm the only one who puts up with your neurotic tendencies.

Grace: Oh right. [eye roll emoji]. Remind me to get better friends.

Tessa: You love me tho. Now go tap that ass [finger pointing emoji] [peach emoji].

Grace: …

"Hey," Noah said, interrupting Grace's emoji search. He had stuck his head out the door with a big silly grin.

"Hey." Grace fumbled her phone in her hands. It dropped

to the stone patio floor. She reached down to pick it up. Luckily there were no scratches.

"Do you mind if I join you?" he said, stepping outside. "I need to give my phone a minute to charge before I can make my call. It's superdead."

"Sure." Grace smiled, tucking her phone between her legs. That felt awkward, so she pulled it out and placed it face-down on her lap. The phone buzzed with more text messages. Probably Tessa sending her more inappropriate emojis. Grace silenced her phone.

Noah sat in the chair next to her, his leg bouncing up and down as he crossed his arms over his chest, looking out onto the garden.

"You look stressed," Grace said. "Is everything okay?"

Noah leaned forward, resting his elbows on his knees. His fingers ran through his dusty brown hair. "Is it that obvious?"

"That must be some coffee delivery," Grace said, tilting her head to the side. When she did, her breath caught in her throat. Even with that troubled look on his face, he was truly beautiful. She'd never seen such a handsome face in person before. Not even Todd could compare.

"It's really, really complicated."

Grace cleared her throat. "Try me," Grace said.

Noah let out a big sigh, staring out into the bright blue sky. He leaned back in his chair, attempting to release his arms to his sides, but he looked stiff and agitated. "I feel like I'm on a wild-goose chase. I have to get rid of—I mean drop off—this special delivery, but I don't have a place to put it."

"You don't have an address?"

Noah shook his head and laughed ruefully. "I was supposed to figure that out on the way here, but then my phone died. I thought I could handle this on my own, but I guess I was wrong." He paused, looking out toward the ocean.

"You seem like a smart enough guy. I'm sure you can figure it out."

Noah's eyes went vacant for a moment, like he had gone to some other place in his head. When he came back, his eyes had darkened like the sea before a thunderous storm. "I did what my oldest brother would have done. I acted without thinking. Without a plan." Noah shuddered. "I'm in over my head."

"You have a brother?" The poor guy needed a distraction, and it was all she could think of to say.

"I have two, actually. Raffi is the oldest. He's a dumbass." Grace snorted. The way he said dumbass sounded polite somehow. His peculiar accent popped up in the most unexpected ways. "Then there's Kai, the middle child. The responsible one."

"So that makes you the—"

"Baby. I know. I hear it *all* the time."

A sore spot, Grace presumed.

"I think you're lucky. I didn't have any siblings, growing up. I was very lonely."

Noah's mouth lifted into a wicked grin. "So, are you lonely now?" he drawled. "I can keep you company."

Grace's eyes bugged out at his flirting. Her eyes drifted beyond Noah's head toward Jane's patio, confirming that her door was still closed. She couldn't have been listening.

Grace let out a breath of relief. "You can't say things like that."

"Why?"

"Because of her." Grace gestured toward Jane's room.

"What about her? What's up with you and Jane anyway?"

"To be honest," Grace said, looking down at her hands, "she scares me."

"You and me both."

They exchanged wary smiles.

"She was coming on really strong," Noah said.

Grace snickered. "Was it that bad? I thought guys liked that kind of thing."

Noah shook his head. "No way. Not like that. She was too aggressive. But it was nothing I couldn't handle until she started crying."

Grace covered her open mouth. "What did you do?"

"I got the hell out of there. But she might think there's a chance we're going to hang out." Noah settled his elbows on his knees. "I don't want to hang out with her. At all." His eyes darkened again. "I'm going to need your help with keeping her away from me."

"How am I going to do that?"

"I don't know. Maybe you can tell me where she's going to be so I can avoid her. I need some sort of heads-up if we're all staying here together."

"You want me to help you hide from Jane? You know, most men fawn over her."

"Why, because she's hot?"

Grace shrugged. "I guess."

"Then most men didn't meet you at the same time," he said with a lazy grin.

A rush of blood pricked her cheeks. Grace opened her mouth, then promptly shut it.

Flirtypants was good. Flirtypants was really good.

Grace cleared her throat. "Don't you have a call to make?" she said, her voice an octave higher than normal.

Noah smiled, tilting his head to the side. "Trying to get rid of me already?"

"It's not that. It's just…"

"You're not used to compliments?" The sparkle in Noah's eyes turned her bones into goo.

She couldn't think straight, despite her brain attempting to shut everything down.

"I'm sorry if I made you nervous."

"You didn't," Grace said, swallowing an alarming amount of saliva.

"My phone is probably charged enough to make that call now," he said, ambling toward the door.

"Okay."

He winked, pulling the sliding door open. The moment he was gone, Grace felt his absence like a dark thundercloud blocking the sun. She felt the urge to turn around and watch him through the glass, but she held steady.

She was in uncharted waters. Never had she felt so easy around a guy in her life. Of course it had to be with someone Jane had sunk her fangs into.

He is off-limits, she repeated to herself. But her mantra didn't stop the wide smile from spreading across her face.

❀

Noah's phone came alive. Three voice mails from Kai. He took a seat in the chair and played the messages.

"Noah, listen. The police already know about the van. Raffi fessed up. I have a plan, but you need to call me, okay? Everything will be fine."

Beep.

"I'm really worried about you, man. Please call me."

Beep.

"Noah. Dammit. I can't take this anymore. If someone hurt you, I'll kill 'em."

Strong words from his mild-mannered brother.

So... Raffi fessed up? Holy shit.

The dumbass finally did the right thing by confessing. And if the police already know, that must mean they were almost out of this mess, right?

Kai picked up the phone after one ring. "Noah, are you okay?" Kai's voice was frantic.

"I'm safe, man. I lost the Sable back in San José. At least I'm pretty sure I did. They got in a wreck in the middle of the city."

"Where are you?"

"I made it to Tortuga Bay."

"That's clear across the country!"

A car horn blared into the phone, followed by a whistle in three loud bursts.

"I'm moving. Jeez," Kai muttered under his breath.

"Where are *you*?" Noah asked.

"I just dropped Ma off at the airport. She's on her way to Berlin."

"Good," Noah said, sinking into the chair. He felt his lungs expand, as if it was his first full breath of the day. "I assume she'll stay with Aunt Ida?"

"Yes. I booked a one-way trip. I told her she's not allowed to come back until things calm down. I'm working with the police now, but it's gonna take some time before it's safe at home."

"I wish I would have known you were working with the police before I drove all the way out here." *And spent a small fortune on a hotel room.*

"No, it's okay. At least you're safe. But we have to hand over that cocaine before we get in any more trouble."

"Any *more* trouble? Are we going to jail too?" Noah's pulse quickened.

"No, we're in the clear. Raffi is taking responsibility for everything."

"Still. I messed up," Noah said, running his hands through his hair. "I should have never left."

"Go easy on yourself, man. It's good that you got out of town. We still don't know if there are other people looking for the drugs. The police said they were going to set up surveillance at the house, but it isn't here yet and it might take a while. You're safer out there."

Noah looked out the window. Grace was propped up in her chair, scrolling through her phone, her face scrunched in the most adorable way.

Fuck me, she's cute. He should probably stay away from her though. With all the drug dealer drama going on, it probably wasn't wise to get close to anyone. But he might actually die if he didn't get a taste of those orange-scented lips before he left.

Focus, Noah. Focus.

"What do I do?" Noah said.

"I have a number for you to call. A detective. Her name is Clara Ramirez." After a moment of heavy breathing in the phone, apparently searching his pockets, he recited Clara's number, and Noah jotted it down. "She'll be able to tell you what to do next."

"Thanks, man."

"You know"—Kai paused for a moment—"I'm really proud of you."

"Oh stop."

"No, really. I'm really proud of how you took charge. I'm sorry I wasn't there this morning."

"What are you talking about? I totally fucked this whole thing up. I should have never taken the van. I just wish I had known the police weren't going to throw us all in jail."

"Never mind that. I just wanted you to know that I appreciate what you did. You were trying to save us all from getting in trouble for Raffi's mistake."

"It was reckless and impulsive. Something Raffi would have done."

"No. It was selfless and brave. And you're nothing like Raffi."

"Yeah, yeah, yeah."

"Listen. Even though Pop isn't here to tell you this, I think he'd say he was proud of you too."

Noah felt a flush of warmth in his chest. "I hate when you get all sentimental and shit," Noah said. "Stop being nice. It's making me uncomfortable."

Kai sighed. "We've been through a lot these past weeks. I'm allowed to be a little emotional."

"You're getting soft," Noah said. "Or is it the girl? Jolie, right? Is she the reason you've turned into a squishy teddy bear?"

"I'm not a squishy teddy bear," Kai said, but Noah could swear he heard him smiling. "I'm just glad this whole nightmare is almost over. Before you know it, you'll be in school and getting on with your life."

Noah's body tensed. "About that," he said, running his hand through his hair. "I don't think I'm going to go to college anymore." Not to mention, he'd already begun spending the money he'd saved up.

"What the hell are you talking about?"

Noah winced. "I just don't think I'm cut out for it."

"Why? You've always been at the top of your class."

"It's not the school that I'm concerned with; it's the after-school part. I just don't see the point of trying to be successful at anything if I don't have it in my blood."

"What the hell kind of thought process is that?"

"Look at Pop. Look at Raffi. They were both screwups. Just like me."

Kai growled. "Don't make me drive all the way over there and knock some sense into you."

Noah clenched his fist. He had just proved to Kai that he could handle the van of cocaine on his own, and it still wasn't enough to convince him Noah wasn't a child anymore.

"I don't want to talk about it right now, okay?"

"Easy, easy," Kai said. "We don't have to discuss this now, but I do want to continue the conversation later."

"There's nothing to say. Plus I'm having to spend the college money I had saved to be out here."

"Noah!"

"Gotta go."

He pushed the End button.

Kai wasn't his father, and yet he had insisted on acting like it even when Pop was alive. Noah didn't want to be told what to do anymore. He could make his own decisions. And his decision was to enjoy life—not waste it on silly dreams that would get him nowhere.

He dialed the detective's number.

"This is Detective Ramirez," a voice answered.

"Hola," Noah said, flipping to Spanish. "This is Noah Greene. I understand you're helping with my case?"

"Noah Greene," she repeated. "The one we've been trying to track down?"

"That's me."

"Sounds like you and your brother got in quite some trouble."

"You're telling me," Noah said, running his hand through his hair.

"Tell me what happened and where you are."

Noah relayed what he could in a loud whisper, keeping his eyes anchored to Grace through the window. He wasn't quite ready to tell her the truth, for fear of scaring her off.

He told Clara he had never gotten a good look at the men's faces, but he could tell they were men by their broad shoulders and the outline of their hair.

"I need to get rid of this van," Noah said. "I'm afraid they're tracking me still."

"Don't worry, I'm going to send the local police there to

come pick up the contraband. They'll scan the van for a tracking device at the station."

Noah let out a sigh of relief. It was going to feel so good to be rid of this burden that had been plaguing him for weeks.

Noah sank into the hotel chair, his hand in his hair. He supposed he should be grateful that he wasn't in trouble for playing keep-away with the cocaine for so long. They should have called the police all along, if it hadn't been for their fruitless attempts at protecting their brother.

"What's going to happen with Raffi?"

"I can't say, honestly. He's doing the right thing, complying with the police and helping us with the investigation. His trial won't be for another few months or so. We'll have to wait and see."

"What about the drug dealers that were following me? Do you think they'll come looking for me?"

"I can't say for certain, but we're on the hunt for them. In the meantime, I suggest you lie low for a while."

"That's the plan," Noah said, looking around the room. He still needed to check into his own hotel room and make a plan for his life that didn't involve colliding with the cartel. "Should I be in witness protection or something?"

Clara paused. "I'm not sure you'll qualify. But if we catch these guys and have to bring you in as a witness, then we can file a request."

"Okay."

"Hang tight. I'll make the call and will let you know when the police will be dispatched."

Noah glanced through the window to find Grace's aquamarine eyes fixed on him. She quickly looked away, focusing her attention on the palm planted on the patio.

If she found out he had been hiding cocaine, she'd probably tell him to take a hike.

You better not be lying to us, Noah Greene rang in his ears.

Noah thanked Clara for her help and clicked off the phone. The proverbial two-hundred-kilogram weight had been lifted off his shoulders. One problem down. Another cartel-size problem left to go.

Noah got up and poked his head out the back door.

Grace was resting both her feet on the wicker coffee table, scrolling through her phone, pretending as though she hadn't been caught staring at him moments ago.

"Hey," Noah said with a smile.

"Did you get everything worked out?" Grace asked, looking up from the screen.

"Sort of, yeah. I figured out who I'm working with now. Her name's Clara. I'm waiting on instructions, but things are in motion."

Grace crossed her arms, leaning back in her chair with a pinched expression on her face. "Clara's going to help you with your complicated coffee delivery?"

"Yeah," Noah said, studying the way Grace's face had slacked. "Are you all right?"

"I'm good."

Noah smiled, not wanting to leave her room, but he needed to be ready to meet the police by the van soon. "I better get going."

"Okay." Grace stood up from her chair. "It was nice meet—"

"What are you doing later?" Noah interrupted her, the words tumbling out of his mouth without thinking. He should stay away from her and hide out in his room… but those eyes. And those lips. And the funny way she scrunched her nose. All beckoned him to learn more.

"Me?" Grace looked up, her eyes widening into giant swimming pools. "I'm having dinner with Jane."

Noah and Grace cringed at the same time. Grace put her hand over her mouth, holding back a giggle.

"Can't you get out of it?"

Grace shook her head. "Not really."

Her eyes locked onto his and held tight. Something in that exchange gave him hope that this would not be their last time together. He would just need to find a way to see her again without Jane nearby.

"What about tomorrow?" he said. "You wanna grab a coffee or something?"

Grace's freckles darkened in a flush, and a soft smile emerged before vanishing. "That's probably not a good idea."

Ouch. He wasn't expecting that. "Why not?"

She shrugged. "If Jane saw us hanging out, she might get a little jealous."

"Who cares?"

"I do," Grace said. "I care."

Noah felt his face contort with confusion. "Why? I don't understand. I thought you didn't like her."

Grace ushered him inside, sliding the door behind her. "I need to stay on Jane's good side to keep my job. She's the CEO's daughter and basically controls everything and everyone."

"That sounds miserable."

Grace shook her head, staring off into the distance. "It *is* miserable."

"Then why work there?"

Grace pressed her lips together, staring at Noah for a long while as if she were deciding how much she wanted to tell him. Her finger twirled around a lock of hair as she appeared to be mulling it over in her head.

"Come on, you can tell me. I won't say anything to her. Obviously."

"You promise?"

"Cross my heart and hope to die." Noah even made the sign with his hand.

Grace's eyes turned to slits, jutting her hip out. "How old are you?"

She was cute when she was sassy.

"Forever young," he said, beaming from ear to ear. "So, what's the deal? Why work for her when you could work for anyone else?"

"The deal is, Maritime pays really well. Above market average. Especially for someone like me who had zero experience in sales to begin with. And I need the money for my aunt's home care expenses. In fact, I need a promotion to keep up. And if I don't kiss Jane's ass, I'm going to lose my aunt forever to some four-wall asylum for old people with bad tempers."

Grace's hair had wrapped so tightly around her finger the pink skin bulged between the strands.

"Oh man, that's... a lot of responsibility," Noah said. He stared at her finger and watched her unravel her hair. It was hypnotizing in a way that made him forget what they were even talking about.

Grace took a deep breath. "So...," she said.

"So...?"

"Jane likes you. I need to stay on her good side. That's that. You should probably stay away from me."

"What if I can't?"

"Can't what?"

"Stay away."

Grace hitched a breath. "You hardly know me."

"That may be true, but something tells me if I walk out that door, I won't be able to stop thinking about you."

A flush rushed to Grace's freckled cheeks again. "You are a flirt." She playfully shoved his chest. Her small hand lingered a tad longer than was necessary to make her point, and Noah felt his nether regions twitch. He wanted her to touch him again. If it took more cheesy come-ons, then so be it.

"Ditch Jane and have dinner with me," Noah said, stepping closer.

"I told you. I can't," Grace said, putting a strand of hair behind her ear. She looked up at him through her thick lashes. "I mean, I really shouldn't."

Noah's phone buzzed in his hand. It was Clara, letting him know the police were on their way.

"Hold that thought. I gotta run. I'll come find you later."

"No, you won't."

Noah headed toward her door and opened it, a big smile on his face. "Yes, I will."

"No, you won't," Grace said, obviously holding back a smile. Her blue eyes twinkled.

"Yes. I. Will," Noah said in the hallway.

"No. You. Will. Not," Grace said, charging toward the door.

He was pretty sure he saw a hint of a smile before she closed the door in his face.

CHAPTER TEN

A tall black Sprinter van pulled down the street and parked behind the van, and two strong Costa Rican men from the Jaco police department with two very serious faces exited the vehicle. Noah was hiding in the bushes, relieved to see their police uniforms the moment they stepped out onto the sidewalk. He couldn't take any risks in case the cartel got to him first.

Noah exhaled. The tension in his spine released as he welcomed the two men with a wide grin, plucking leaves off his shirt. "You have no idea how glad I am to see you." He shook the officers' hands as Officer Rico and Officer Gareth introduced themselves.

"Where is the contraband?" Officer Rico said in Spanish.

"In here," Noah said, opening the back doors.

Officer Gareth took out a pocketknife and sliced through the duct tape, opening up a box. He held one of the plastic wrapped bricks in his hand and exchanged a look with Officer Rico.

"This is a hell of a lot of cocaine," Officer Gareth said.

Officer Rico muttered something into his radio and slid it

back in its holster before crouching down next to another box. He took out a blade and opened it, peeking into its contents.

"Let's take it away," Officer Rico said.

Noah helped them load the boxes into their van. By the time the last box was set, his shirt was sticking to his chest and back. Beads of sweat dripped down his hairline. Noah wiped his forehead with the back of his forearm and watched with a heaving breath as the policemen locked up the van.

Officer Rico muttered another code into his radio while Officer Gareth took out a pad of paper.

"So," Noah said, stuffing his hands in his pockets. "What happens next?"

"We'll need a brief statement from you," Officer Gareth said, licking his thumb and flipping to a new page in his notebook. "And a driver's license."

"Sure," Noah said, pulling out his wallet. "What do you need to know?"

"How you came into possession of the cocaine would be a good start."

Noah gulped. His brother had already confessed everything, so hopefully what he was about to say wasn't new information. He proceeded cautiously. "My brother, Raffi, took up a side gig. He did deliveries for the wrong people. They never told him what was in the boxes, and he never asked, supposedly. I believe him because he's a big dumbass."

Officer Gareth chuckled.

"One day he showed up to one of the drop-off locations, and everyone had been shot dead. He panicked and came straight to our family's warehouse with the boxes in his van. He was in shock."

"When you realized there was cocaine in the van, did you call the police?"

Did he need a lawyer for this? "Um…" Noah's eyes darted

between the two officers who were staring at him intently. "We didn't know what to do. We didn't..."

"It's okay," Officer Rico said. "Ramirez has a protective hold on you. You're not in trouble. Just tell us what happened."

"It's kind of a wild story."

"We're listening," Officer Gareth said.

Noah nodded, licking his dry lips. The sun beat down on him like an investigation lamp light. "Raffi showed up at our warehouse with the van," he started. He relayed the events leading up to that morning. How their neighbor had found out about the drugs. How he tried to blackmail them. How Raffi's attempts at fixing the problem himself made everything so much worse.

It wasn't until Raffi found himself in jail that Kai and Noah could do the right thing and get rid of the cocaine. And they would have, if the cartel hadn't shown up that morning and chased him all the way across the country.

The two officers gaped at Noah with their mouths open.

"I told you it was a wild story," Noah said.

Officer Gareth held out the notebook he had written on. "I could write a book with this content."

Noah laughed. "Yeah, you could. But that's been my life for the past couple of weeks. I'm worried the cartel is still tracking me."

"Follow us to the station. We can have a team search the van for a tracking device."

"Thank you," Noah said. "I tried looking for one myself but didn't see anything."

"Honestly, they probably don't have one. It sounds like it took them a couple of weeks to figure out where the cocaine was. If they had a tracking device on you, they would have shown up earlier."

Noah blew out a shaky breath. "That's what I was hoping."

"You should be fine," Officer Rico said. "But to be safe, I'd suggest you stay away from home for a while."

Noah nodded.

"Let's head out," Officer Rico said, hopping in the driver's side of the Sprinter.

Noah got in the van and stuck the keys in the ignition, smiling to himself. The nightmare was almost over.

Cranking his wrist, the engine roared to life. He slid the gear into drive and drove forward an inch when the van puttered to a stop.

What the hell? The check engine light appeared, mocking his optimism. He pressed on the gas pedal again, but the van wouldn't budge.

Noah flagged down the policemen to pull up beside him. Officer Gareth rolled down his window. "What happened?"

"My van just died," Noah said. "My dashboard looks like a New Year's fireworks show."

Officer Gareth frowned. "I'll call you a tow. We need to head to the station. Are you going to be okay here?"

"Sure."

"See you at the station," he said, giving Noah a salute. They drove off and out of sight.

Noah was left to wait in his hot van. He texted Clara the update and then stared out toward the horizon where the ocean met the sky. He let the varying shades of blue, his favorite color, calm his nerves, a practice he would do in the mornings while he warmed up to surf.

As he focused on the blue of the ocean, he realized he had a new favorite blue, the color of Grace's eyes. Vibrant. Electric. A shade of blue that not only calmed him but excited him at the same time. Looking into Grace's eyes was like drinking a vodka Red Bull, intoxicating and invigorating, a dangerous combination.

It was too bad she was American and lived so far away. She would have been someone he'd ask out on a real date. Someone he would have been proud to take home to meet Ma and not have to sneak out the front door.

But she'd be gone in a matter of days. He'd have to settle with being friends—that is, if she'd even let him.

A tow truck pulled up beside the van. The driver smiled and waved, a cluster of bracelets jingling around his wrist. Then he backed up his truck and maneuvered behind the van. It took a few tries to line it up just right. Noah waited for him on the sidewalk.

A good-looking guy with light blue eyes and shaggy blond hair stepped out of the truck. He looked to be in his midthirties. He was Australian, from what Noah could tell by his accent. "Hola, mate," he said, assessing the back bumper of Noah's van. "I hear I'm taking you to the police station."

"That's right," Noah said, introducing himself. He shook the man's hand.

"The name is Ivan. Let's get you rollin'."

Ivan hooked up his truck to the back of the van with a series of hooks and levers. It was a whole process that took longer than Noah was expecting. His stomach growled, reminding him he hadn't eaten all day. He could have grabbed food at the market across the street, but before he could suggest it, Ivan told him he was ready to go.

Noah took the seat in the passenger side of his truck. Ivan had a flower lei wrapped around his stick shift and rose quartz crystals dangling from his rearview mirror.

Ivan got into his seat and followed Noah's gaze. "The crystals bring good energy," he said. "This is a good energy zone only. No bad energies allowed in here."

"I'll have to shake off the bad day I'm having then."

"That's right. Gotta leave all that stuff behind ya." Ivan put his seat belt on and inched forward, checking his rearview mirrors while he slowly merged onto the right side of the street.

"I take it you're from Australia?"

"Yeah. Came here 'bout five years ago or so now. Had a nasty divorce in Brisbane and needed to get away. I came here for a holiday, then never went back."

"No kidding."

"This place is paradise. I couldn't get myself to leave. Found a quiet apartment right off the beach. Taught myself how to surf. Got a job. And yeah, here I am."

Noah's jaw dropped. "What you just described is exactly what I want. Just a simple life. No hassles. Just the basics, and a beach to surf, of course."

Ivan rubbed the stubble on his tan chin. "It definitely has its perks." His brow creased as he looked out onto the road. There was something he wasn't saying. Ivan's hand reached up for one of the crystals, and he rubbed it between his forefinger and his thumb.

He must have seen the curious look on Noah's face because Ivan began to explain. "I have to remind myself sometimes how lucky I am to be here. That I'm okay without all the things I used to have back in Brisbane." He laughed to himself, his eyes glittering with a memory. "Can't afford fancy cars and steak dinners anymore."

"What did you do there?"

"I was a salesman. Made good money selling computer chips for a living. But I gave all that up for my life here." Ivan flicked on the turn signal as he pulled up to a stoplight.

"Are you happy?" Noah said.

Ivan grew quiet for a while. He rubbed the quartz crystals again. After an awkward silence, he brought his hand back to his steering wheel. "Yeah. I'm happy. For the most part."

The green light flashed, and Ivan made a turn left onto a busy road in town. "But there are days when I think about the work I was doing. The people I was around. I had lots of friends and coworkers to grab a beer with. Here… it's just me. The women I meet don't stick around longer than a night or two. I had always thought I'd be a father one day, but it turns out nobody's willing to have a baby with a guy who just wants to surf."

Noah hadn't thought of that. He had been so focused on cutting out all the drama from his life that it didn't occur to him he could be cutting out the chance at having a family too. He was too young for all that now, but who knew what he would want when he was older.

"It's all a trade-off, you know. Life's about making choices. And then dealing with the ones you make." The police station came into view, and Ivan pulled into the parking lot. "I've been instructed to take your van around the back."

"Sounds good," Noah said, still thinking about what Ivan said about choices. That dream of living on a yurt near the beach didn't seem as glamorous as it had before.

"You want to rub the crystals before you head out? It'll bring you good vibes."

Noah's eyes grew wide. "Oh no, thanks, man. That's your thing."

"Come on. I insist. Something tells me you need this more than I do."

Noah stared at the crystals while Ivan parked the truck in front of a warehouse behind the main station.

The cartel was still out there, and they might or might not be looking for him.

What the hell. It wouldn't hurt.

Noah rubbed one of the quartz rocks with his fingers, much to Ivan's delight.

"There you go, mate. Here's my card," Ivan said, handing Noah a business card.

IVAN LANSER
PURA VIDA TOWING
REIKI MASSAGE
ENERGY CONSULTANT

"Call me if you need a tow. Or a reiki massage," he said.

"Thanks," Noah said, staring at the card. "I might take you up on that tow if I have to bring the van to the shop."

"Good to meet you."

"You too," Noah said, shaking Ivan's hand. *It was definitely enlightening*, Noah thought as he got out of the truck.

The strangest feeling washed over him as he stood on the pavement and watched Ivan release his van from the tow. Like his life had just flashed before his eyes, but he didn't love what he saw.

Perhaps he might need a new plan for his life. One that didn't involve relying on rubbing crystals to remind himself that his loneliness was worth the choices he made.

CHAPTER ELEVEN

Grace followed Jane onto the outdoor patio. The host greeted them with a smile and brought them to a table near the stone edge overlooking the beach. The sky was a bouquet of pinks and oranges, and the warm breeze tickled Grace's cheeks. Votive candles on white tablecloths twinkled brightly as the sun ticked behind the horizon.

The band that had been setting up on the terrace started playing an Afro-Caribbean tune. The drums worked their way into Grace's veins, lifting her spirit. Even though she had been dreading this dinner with Jane, she could at least enjoy an evening in paradise.

Jane was rambling on about the time she went to Cabo with her ex while Grace scanned the restaurant. There were mostly young couples, probably on their honeymoon. A family with the cutest set of twins, about four, Grace guessed, sat in the middle of the restaurant. The children bounced and swayed in their chairs, warming Grace's heart.

Everyone seemed so joyous and carefree. Even the staff looked happy to be there. The servers waiting in the back swayed their hips to the music.

A flash of white caught Grace's attention. At the restaurant entrance, Noah stood tall in a fresh white collared shirt with the resort logo over the breast pocket. He must have picked it up from the hotel gift shop. A flutter in her stomach had her shifting in her chair at the sight of him. The host greeted him and grabbed a menu.

Wait. He had asked her to warn him so he could keep away from Jane, but Grace hadn't gotten his number. Now it was too late. The host sat him at the table behind Jane, who was too busy yapping to notice.

Just as Noah took a seat, he locked eyes with Grace, then noticed Jane sitting in right in front of him. He almost jumped out of his chair.

"Oh shit," he mouthed. He yanked the menu off the table and pulled it over his face. He peered over it, doing a double take at Jane.

Grace stifled her laugh.

"I wonder where that cutie went off to," Jane said, sipping her water.

"Cutie?" Grace cleared her throat. "Who knows? He's probably taking care of that coffee delivery."

The votive candle flickered in Jane's eyes. "I think he was playing hard to get," Jane said dreamily.

Noah cowered in his chair, shielding himself with his menu. He held out a shaky fork as if it were a sword.

Such a goof. If he really wanted to avoid Jane that badly, he could just leave.

The theatrics were kind of entertaining though. Grace appreciated the distraction.

The server showed up to take their drink orders.

"I'll have your house wine, please," Grace said.

"Vodka tonic," Jane said. "And we're ready to order."

The server smiled, pulling out his notepad.

"I'll have a salad with a grilled chicken breast on the side."

Jane continued her order with precise directions on how to cook the chicken and a list of other specific requests that were not on the menu.

The server was writing down Jane's custom order feverishly on his notepad.

When it seemed like Jane was done, the server looked to Grace for hers, exasperation set deep behind his eyes.

"Arroz con pollo, please," Grace said, handing him her menu before he scurried off toward the kitchen.

"What do you think? Am I too old for a guy like him?" Jane said.

"Uh." Grace felt trapped. "The server?"

"I'm talking about the coffee delivery boy."

"Oh. I don't think you're too old for a guy like him," Grace said, ignoring Noah, who was waving his hands wildly in the air to halt the conversation. Perhaps Grace could help him out a bit and throw Jane off his scent. "But…"

"But what?" Jane pushed. "*You're* not into him, are you?"

Grace's mouth went dry. "Well, um. I—" Grace caught Noah's intense glare over Jane's shoulder. He leaned forward in his chair, listening intently. "I—" Grace looked down at her water glass and remembered something Noah had said earlier. "He has a girlfriend," Grace lied, catching the confused tilt of Noah's head in the corner of her eye.

"A girlfriend?"

"He said something about her when he was charging his phone." It wasn't a complete lie. He had mentioned someone named Clara after all.

"Ahh, that explains why he was so skittish in the hotel room," Jane said, her eyes flared with excitement. "But that hasn't stopped men before. They just need a little persuasion."

Noah ducked under his menu again, exaggerating the tremble to his hands.

"Men are like puppies. They do what you want when you have the right treat."

Grace felt instantly ill.

"How do you think I got my husband in the first place?" Jane laughed. The server placed her drink on the table, and Jane appeared too deep in thought to acknowledge his presence.

Grace thanked the server for her wine and took a large gulp.

"He was dating a pretty thing too," Jane said, staring off into the distance. "I love a good challenge." Her eyes darkened. "All I had to do was dangle a treat in front of him for a while, and eventually he came."

Grace's eyes grew wide at the innuendo, then she exchanged a terrified glance with Noah.

Grace had made matters worse. Now Noah was an even bigger challenge, and there was no sign Jane would back down.

Perhaps she should change the subject. "I was thinking about something," she said, her eyes darting around the restaurant for inspiration. She had to start talking about something else, anything to divert the conversation back to safe ground. She eyed dishes being placed on a table across the restaurant.

An idea struck.

"What do you think about adding local restaurants to our experiences?"

Jane jutted her chin forward, appearing a little perturbed. But she seemed to be thinking it over anyway. Grace praised herself for steering the conversation back to work.

"The resort would lose revenue if their guests ate somewhere else," Jane said. "You know that. The point of Maritime is to bring them experiences that they can't get on location."

"What if the hotel got a percentage of the sale, just like all our packages?" Grace said. The idea was forming in her mind as she spoke.

Jane sneered. "We're talking about a trickle of revenue. Pennies. It's not worth our time."

Grace glanced over Jane's shoulder. Noah's eyes were fixed on Grace, a slight curve to his lips.

For reasons Grace couldn't explain, she decided to continue despite Jane's initial rejection of the idea. It was a good diversion from Jane's obsession with Noah, at the very least.

"Let's say we found the top three or five restaurants around here and developed a prix fixe sample-size menu. The portions could be small so that the guests can stop by multiple places on the same day. Like a dinner crawl." Grace paused a moment, picturing how it would work.

"Imagine," Grace said. "They would get to try the town's best food in one night. Cocktails at so-and-so bar. Mini crab cakes at yada yada restaurant. Prize-winning chocolate soufflé at the best dessert place in town." Not that Grace had ever tried anything so extravagant, but she had seen the menus on fancy restaurants before.

"And we could create a VIP experience where the guests don't have to wait in any lines. They just sign up for the local food-tasting experience at the resort a day in advance." The more she talked, the more she fell in love with this idea. "All the restaurants involved could be prepared. Have a table ready for them. The food or drinks, whatever their specialty is, prepped and ready for them to arrive at their slotted time. The guests get to experience the best of the local cuisine in one town and won't feel the need to go out again."

Grace felt her pulse quicken, her fingers clammy around the wine stem. It was exhilarating and terrifying to spill out an idea without days or weeks of preparation. It was so unlike her she hardly recognized her own voice. Despite Jane's frown, Grace pushed forward with her pitch.

"The resort wouldn't lose any money. If anything, they might make more money because the guests would have satisfied their need to try the local food in one night instead of multiple nights, so more dinners at the resort overall."

She chanced a look over Jane's shoulder and was rewarded by a soft, proud smile on Noah's face.

Grace felt her chest fill with something warm and light, the way a balloon must feel with helium. She nearly floated over her seat, waiting for Jane to say something about this great idea that had spontaneously gushed out of her.

"It won't work," Jane said, crossing her arms.

The proverbial balloon in her chest deflated like a worn whoopee cushion. "It won't? Why not?"

"For one, it's too many businesses to coordinate for one experience. Think of the paperwork," Jane scoffed.

"But we have tons of paperwork for all our experiences," Grace said. "I can handle—"

"No restaurant would agree to something like this. What's in it for them?"

"They'd get the traffic. The social media attention. The—"

"Listen. It's a cute idea. Really. You're adorable. Ideas like these are great in theory, but they don't work. They're impossible to execute. Think of the technology involved in coordinating with just one company. Imagine doing that with multiple restaurants who might not even have a website at all. What you're proposing is a logistical nightmare. It just won't work."

Grace fought the disappointment bubble in the back of her throat. "But we have the tech—"

"Grace. No. I'm sorry. If you want to be senior sales associate, and I know you do, then you have to learn how to think bigger."

"You knew I was going to apply for the job?"

"Of course. Miranda filled me in on your little arrangement. And I understand you need me to put in the recommendation."

Grace shrank in her chair.

"Don't worry. I can help you." Jane leaned forward. "I can teach you about the laws of costs and benefits. How to properly pitch a business idea. If you're going to replace me, you need to come off less amateur."

Grace avoided Noah's eyes on her but felt them like a rake pushing on hot coals.

"You're lucky to have me," Jane continued. "I can save you from embarrassment. Just listen and learn. Don't ever pitch an idea before vetting it first."

Grace fumed. Sure, her idea hadn't been vetted, but it was just an *idea*. Jane wasn't even CEO yet, but she sure as hell acted like it anyway. Not to mention that she didn't have the technical know-how to see the possibilities.

"Don't worry. We'll let this little mishap slide for now. You still have ample opportunity to impress me at tomorrow's presentation."

Grace swallowed the lump in her throat, embarrassed that she let her imagination run wild in front of Jane, of all people. Too ashamed to look up at Noah's face from behind Jane, she hadn't seen that he had gotten up from his chair. He was stalking toward them. His jaw set as if he were about to give Jane a piece of his mind.

No.

Grace burst out, "I have to pee!"

Noah towered behind Jane, his chest heaving, waiting for Grace's next move. He was too close, merely inches from Jane's chair.

"Okay," Jane said, knitting her brows together. "Be my guest."

Grace stood up from her chair on wobbly legs, setting her napkin down. She backed away slowly, away from Jane, away from Noah, who had taken a step back to not be seen.

Grace zoomed through the outdoor restaurant and into the lobby. She ducked behind the wall that led toward the restrooms and clung to it as if it were holding her upright.

A moment later, Noah appeared, his eyes round and worried. "Hey. Are you all right?"

"What are you *doing*?" Grace whispered. "I thought you were trying to avoid her."

"What am *I* doing? What are *you* doing? How can you let her talk to you like that?"

Grace sucked in her cheeks, folding her arms. "You heard her. I need her recommendation so I can get that promotion. And I need that promotion to pay for my aunt's home care. There's no sense in arguing over a stupid idea," she said, tugging at her dress. "I shouldn't have said anything."

"Hey," Noah said, putting his hand on hers. "That was a great idea. I'd go on one of your restaurant crawls in a heartbeat." He paused for a moment, his eyes darkening. "She's probably just jealous she didn't think of it herself."

Grace harrumphed. Tessa would have said the same thing.

Noah's hands cupped her shoulders, giving them a little shake. "Don't doubt yourself. Just because the idea seemed impossible to her doesn't mean it is impossible."

"I should have known better than to just blurt out ideas like that. That was so unlike me."

"I could tell you were trying to distract her. For me." Noah smiled. "I appreciate it. But if it's going to cost your promotion, then don't sweat it. If she sees me, then I'll handle her. I'm sorry that I stuck around. I shouldn't have stayed."

"It's okay," Grace said. She drew in a shaky breath as her focus shifted to the strong hands that had remained on her shoulders. The strength and weight of them was probably meant to calm her down, but they were doing precisely the opposite. Her pulse quickened under the gentle stroke of his thumbs.

She stared into his eyes, getting lost in the soothing sea green while her heart thumped in her ears. Her eyes dropped to his mouth the moment he wet his lips, igniting a fire in Grace's belly. She suppressed the urge to reach up and kiss him and cleared her throat instead.

"Thanks for the pep talk, but we shouldn't be seen together. I should go."

Noah pressed his hand against the wall, boxing her in. He leaned in close. Grace could smell the hotel soap he used, a mix of ylang-ylang and green tea. The nearness of him made her body tingle; her fingers itched to touch him.

"Why don't you ditch her?" he said, whispering in her ear. "Come have dinner with me instead."

The soft tickle of his breath on her neck made her body arch toward him. It was dangerous to be so close to him when her body seemed to have a mind of its own. She didn't trust herself around him, not when she was supposed to stay away. Jane would be wondering where she was if she didn't get back.

"I can't. I'm sorry."

His eyes locked onto hers, a touch of sadness in their depths. "Come meet up with me later then," he whispered, his finger cupping her chin. His eyes dropped to her mouth, and a jolt of energy zipped through her spine. A blossom of warmth spread from her chest and traveled down to her fingers and toes.

She wanted to kiss him with an urge that scared her. What had gotten into her? She was never this impulsive.

"I can't."

"You can," Noah pressed. His smile was full of promises,

leaving her light-headed. She could only imagine what he had in mind with that sinful glint in his eyes and the cocky twitch of his mouth.

Maybe if they just kissed and got it out of the way— No. She wasn't thinking clearly. One kiss with him would be her undoing. It would be her luck that Jane would walk in on them and see, and then… She couldn't stomach the rest.

"I'm sorry," Grace said, turning to leave.

"Wait." Noah's hand grabbed her arm.

Grace looked up to find Noah's face had fallen into concern.

"I meant what I said. It was a really good idea."

Grace's chest tightened. "Thanks."

Noah released her arm, letting her go.

She offered him a soft smile. A silent goodbye. She had no business lurking in the shadows with Jane's latest target.

It was the right decision, she told herself, stalking back toward the patio. She willed herself to not look back.

Grace slumped in her chair across from Jane and stared at the food placed in front of her, no longer hungry. Jane rattled on with business advice, but Grace wasn't really listening. The only thing she noticed was Noah's empty table, and she wondered how it was possible to miss someone she just met.

Noah got a call from the police station the moment Grace left. His van was ready to be picked up, and they confirmed there were no tracking devices. Noah's shoulders slumped with relief.

Without tracking, the cartel would have a hard time finding him on this side of the country. He was pretty sure he had a decent head start after that wreck in San José. He might just be in the clear after all.

Noah pulled out Ivan's business card and gave him a call, asking if he could tow his van to the nearest auto shop. He agreed, then asked Noah if he wanted to go surfing together, and they arranged to meet up the next morning. Noah could borrow an extra board and wetsuit if he needed.

By the time Noah got off the phone, he was exhausted. The thought of sitting at a restaurant with Jane in the vicinity no longer appealed to him. Especially when Jane was the reason Grace wouldn't submit to the fiery spark between her and Noah.

He saw the way Grace responded to his touch. The way she primed her lips to be thoroughly kissed. She wanted him even though she was too stubborn to give in. He'd have to find another way to see her. Even if they could only be friends.

CHAPTER TWELVE

Grace kicked off her sandals and put on her flannel pajamas. The ones with the penguins in Santa hats. They were her favorite, warm and soft and cozy and familiar. Yes, she was in Costa Rica, but her air-conditioning was on full blast, and she was ready to dive into bed, watch a movie, and forget all about the fact that she'd turned down Noah tonight.

Regret had seeped into her bones even though it was the right choice to walk away.

She sighed, climbing onto her bed. She flipped through the channels, landing on Lifetime, when a soft tap on her sliding door made her jump.

Noah stood behind the glass, holding a bottle of champagne and grinning slyly. Her heart fluttered in her chest. She couldn't deny how happy she was to see him.

Grace padded to the door, not bothering to open it.

"You shouldn't be here."

"Can you let me in?" he whispered, barely audible through the door. His breath was blowing steam onto the glass. "Don't let her see me." He smashed his face and hands against the door like one of those cartoon characters getting smushed by a giant wrecking ball.

Okay, that was adorable. She opened the door a crack.

"What are you doing here?"

"I thought we could celebrate," he said, holding up a bottle of champagne.

"Celebrate?"

"My coffee delivery. It's all taken care of."

Grace narrowed her eyes at him. "I find that a very odd thing to celebrate."

The sound of a sliding door caught both their attention, and they looked toward Jane's room. Her light had flicked on.

"Get in." Grace opened her door all the way and pulled Noah inside, her heart racing. She softly closed the door and slid the blinds closed.

"I told you we can't do this," she said, her breath regulating.

"Do what? Be friends?"

Grace crossed her arms, jutting a hip to the side. "Is that what we are? Friends?"

"Sure. I was going to ask if you wanted to go see the—" Noah paused, his eyes raking over her body. "Nice pj's."

Grace's cheeks grew warm as she remembered the penguins in Santa hats. "They're comfortable."

"Are you going to bed?"

"Well, no. I was just about to watch a movie." Grace looked at the TV. *A Prince for Christmas* flashed on the flat-screen, sleigh bells and a wintery wonderland in the backdrop.

"You're watching a Christmas movie in your Christmas jammies?"

Grace scoffed. "Yeah, so?" She folded her arms. "What's wrong with that?"

"First of all, it's October."

"Your point?"

"You're one of those crazy Christmas people, aren't you? The ones who keep their holiday decorations up all year long."

Grace stilled.

"You *do*, don't you? I bet you have Christmas lights on your house right now."

Grace crossed her arms. "Actually, I haven't been able to get Christmas lights up. The ladder terrifies me."

"But you would if you could, right?" Noah said.

She loved Christmas. And she might have set up a tiny tree in her bedroom a few years ago and never put it away. She had told herself she was too busy, but in truth, she just loved seeing it every day.

Christmas brought back her favorite memories from her childhood. Her father used to make a big show of his Christmas light displays, competing with the neighbors to see who had the biggest, brightest house on the street.

It *was* her favorite time of year, but she refused to give Noah the satisfaction of being right.

"No," she said.

Noah angled his head, appearing as though he was deciding if he wanted to press any further. He must have decided against it as he walked over to the counter and set the champagne bottle down. "Do you like champagne?" he said, unwrapping the foil.

"I—"

A knock at the connecting door had them both jolt, exchanging a look of terror.

"Grace?" Jane's voice called from behind the door.

"Hide," Grace whispered. "One second!" she called to the door.

Noah leaped over the bed, ducking down on the other

side, but he was too tall. The top of his head peeked up like a Whack-a-Mole.

"I can see you. Go in the bathroom."

Noah darted up and raced across the room, tripping on a shoe before tucking himself behind the wall. As soon as he was out of view, Grace opened the door.

Jane had put on a tight white dress and fire-red lipstick.

"Hey Jane, what's up?"

Jane glanced at Grace's pajamas, not bothering to hold back her laughter. "Cute pajamas."

"Thanks," Grace bit out.

"I was going to go to the bar, hoping I might run into that coffee delivery boy."

Grace's spine stiffened.

"I wanted to see if you wanted to come." Jane trailed off, eyeing Grace up and down. "But I see you've already made plans." Her eyes landed on the nearly opened champagne bottle. "Celebrating something?"

Grace glanced toward the bathroom to make sure Noah couldn't be seen. "Yeah," Grace's voice cracked. "Just celebrating my first airplane ride with some champagne and a movie."

"How precious," Jane said, sticking her bottom lip out in that patronizing way of hers. "Well, enjoy. Don't get too drunk. We have a big presentation tomorrow, and I need you to be clearheaded for all that technical crap our customers always ask about."

"I'll be fine. Have fun," Grace said, closing the door. She rested her forehead on it for a moment, letting her heartbeat slow.

"Is it safe to come out now?" Noah whispered, his head poking out from behind the bathroom wall.

"Jane's looking for you."

"I heard." Noah shuddered.

"You have to go."

"Hell no. Come on, Grace. This is the perfect hiding place for me. She already knows my hotel room number. The concierge said it right in front of her. I can hide here with you, and she'll never find me."

"Noah! You're not staying here tonight."

"That's not what I—" Noah cursed under his breath. "I just want to hang out for a little while. As friends. Please?"

Grace narrowed her eyes, cocking her head to the side. "I'm not sure we can be friends."

"Sure we can." Noah slipped off his shoes and climbed into bed.

Grace gasped. "What the heck are you doing? I haven't agreed to this yet."

"Yes, but you were going to." Noah winked. "We're watching a movie, right?" he said, tucking himself under the covers.

"I said *I* was watching a movie. You were on your way out."

"Come on, Blue Eyes." Noah patted the bedspread next to him. "I promise to behave. Scout's honor."

Grace let out an exasperated sigh. "You are incorrigible." She bit down the smile that threatened to reach her face and lost. He looked so cute, cozied up in her bed. It was like all her Hallmark fairy godmother dreams had come true.

"Get in," Noah said, smiling. "I want to see what this *Prince of Christmas* is all about."

Grace slipped under the covers next to him, the heat under the sheets radiating up her legs. She was careful not to touch him for fear of bursting into flames.

They settled in bed together, watching the movie quietly a few moments before Noah leaned in to whisper, "This is really good." His eyes widened as a herd of elves bombarded the screen, their faces painted like orange Oompa-Loompas.

"I speak fluent sarcasm, you know." Grace nudged him with her elbow.

He nudged back, and the contact had her lady parts undulating with need.

The temptation of touching him was getting harder and harder to fight. Every nerve ending pointed to Noah, tempting her to scoot closer. To press herself against him.

They sat in silence for a while, at least pretending like they were watching the cupcake baker run into the prince for the first time. Grace couldn't concentrate on anything but the intoxicating heat under the covers.

When she glanced up to see if he was paying attention to the movie, his stormy jade eyes were on her.

Liquid hot magma. She had become a pool of lava.

"You're not paying attention," Grace rasped.

"I'm not?" he said with a lazy smile, his eyes drifting to her lips.

"You're not even looking at the TV."

"Because I've got something better to look at."

"Ugh! Noah. Your lines," Grace said, making a gagging sound. "I thought we were just friends."

"I don't want to be just friends," he muttered out of the corner of his mouth.

"But you said—"

"Forget what I said," Noah said softly. "Unless it's what you want."

Grace chewed on her lip. She didn't know what she wanted anymore. Before Noah, she had thought she wanted a relationship with someone like Todd. But now... she was confused. And turned on by the cocky stranger in her bed.

If she gave in to this newfound desire, it'd be short-lived. A fling. Something Tessa would encourage her to do but wouldn't solve her need to find her own Meg Ryan, Tom Hanks-style happily-ever-after.

"I don't know what I want," Grace said. "But we're not going to be more than friends if you keep feeding me cheesy lines."

"Those don't work for you?" Noah said playfully. "Would you rather I act like the prince in this movie? All proper and stuffy?"

"Something tells me you couldn't if you tried."

"Sure I could."

Grace jerked her head. "A prince would never climb in bed with a woman without asking."

"I'm pretty sure that's historically false."

Grace giggled. "I mean in the movies."

"So, you *do* want a prince from a movie."

"Not exactly. I don't need to be showered with gifts or taken on magical carpet rides. I just want a normal relationship."

"With Todd?" Noah said, arching a brow.

Grace gasped. "How did you know about Todd?"

"Jane told me you have a crush," he said, his eyelids lowered. "What does this Todd have that I don't?"

Grace snorted. "Literally nothing. I moved on the moment I found out he likes Jane."

"Then he's an idiot."

"I can't blame him for liking someone more beautiful than me."

"Don't you dare say that," Noah said. His eyes darkened. "No one is more beautiful than the girl I'm looking at right now."

"Psh." Grace chuckled uncomfortably. "You are brimming with lines, aren't you?"

"I speak the truth," Noah said, leaning back on the pillows. "Now quiet down. I'm trying to watch the movie." He focused on the screen, pretending to watch with exaggerated concentration.

"What are you doing?" Grace said. "You obviously don't like it."

"I'm taking notes on how to be a prince for you," he said, a sly grin on his face.

Grace couldn't help but smile at the sparkle in his eye and the dimple in his cheek.

She was in trouble.

Grace turned to him. "I'm not going to sleep with you. In case you were wondering."

"Oh, thank God," Noah said. "I was worried you were trying to seduce me."

Grace gasped. "Me? Seducing you?"

Noah laughed. "Yeah, with those penguin pj's. They're a real turn-on, you know."

"Can you ever not be a flirt?"

Noah pressed his palm against his chest. "You wound me."

"I'm sure," Grace said with a roll of her eyes.

"And of course I can. Not be a flirt, that is."

"Let's see," Grace said, folding her arms, challenging him. "Tell me one nonflirtatious thing."

Noah looked at her while he was deep in thought. He tapped his lips with his finger, a flicker of mischief in his eyes. "I can tell what size shoe you wear, just by looking at your feet."

"What?" Grace said. "Impossible."

"No, it's true. Let me see your flippers."

Grace jutted her chin. "I don't believe you, but you've certainly piqued my interest." She pulled the covers down her legs and then paused. "Wait a minute. You don't have some sort of foot fetish or something, do you? Because I'm not into—"

"No, not at all." Noah laughed. "I swear. It's just this weird gift that I have."

"Well then, let's see what you got." Grace pulled out her feet from under the covers and flexed them for him to assess.

Noah took a foot in his hands, cupping her heel, and turned it side to side. Shivers ran up her leg. Then he closed one eye and yanked her foot up to his face as if he were looking into a microscope.

"What's the verdict, Dr. Scholl?" Grace said, jerking her foot back, confident that he would never guess it right. She had long, slender feet, making them look smaller than they actually were, when in fact they were well above average for her petite five-foot frame.

"Nine," he said smugly, sitting back on the pillows and focusing on the TV.

Grace's mouth flew open. "How the hell—?"

Noah grinned so hard it looked like his cheeks were going to bust. "I'm just that good," he said. "And damn, girl. That is an impressive size for a little thing like you."

Grace blinked, unable to comprehend how someone could possibly know the size of shoe someone wore by looking at their foot.

"My aunt always says I'm well-grounded," Grace said, smiling.

Noah chuckled. "You must be pretty sturdy on those things."

"I am," Grace said, unashamed. "I'm still stuck on the fact that you figured it out. How?"

Noah placed his hands behind his head and cradled his neck. He waited a tick before he said, "Your shoe."

"What?"

"Your shoe, over there," he said, pointing. "When I tripped on it, I saw the size of your shoe in the sole."

"Oh my god," Grace said, laughing. "You tricked me." Her hand swatted his arm. "I believed you."

"I'm. Sorry. But," Noah said in between swats, "it was just too easy."

They giggled until Grace's belly hurt, and she slumped back down on her pillows, shoving her feet under the covers.

"It's your turn," Noah said.

"My turn for what?"

"Tell me something nonflirtatious."

Grace rolled her eyes. "I'm not the flirty one. You are."

"Then this should be pretty easy for you."

Grace huffed, pulling her covers up to her chin. She hated talking about herself, especially when the person's eyes glazed over and they just waited for her to be done. It happened every time.

Noah studied her for a moment. "Jane told me what you do for a living. You must have tons of stories from all those experiences you create. What's the most fun thing you've ever done?"

Grace's mouth opened to speak, but the truth held her back. She hadn't gone on any of the experiences they created for their clients. Except for that one cheese-making company she and Tessa had visited over their lunch break last year. That hardly fit what Noah was talking about. "I actually haven't done any," she said solemnly.

"Really?"

Grace sank farther in her bed. "Really."

"Why not?"

"Because I'm not interested in white-water rafting. Or snowshoeing. Or parasailing. It's not safe."

Noah shifted his weight, facing her now. His head was propped up on his hand as if he were waiting for her to continue.

"Are you scared?"

Grace thought about that for a moment. "Yes and no."

"How can you be both scared and not scared?"

"You don't need to hear the whole story," Grace said, waving him off.

"I want to," Noah said sincerely.

His willingness caught her by surprise. All the cheesy lines and cockiness was set aside as he draped over her bed, waiting to listen, eagerly.

Grace took a deep inhale. "My parents were big adventurers. They were constantly doing things, going places, exploring. That sort of thing." She paused. "A part of me wanted to be just like them when I grew up."

"But…"

"They died in a helicopter crash when I was nine."

"Oh shit," Noah said. "I'm so sorry. I can't even imagine going through something like that at such a young age. That must have been really hard for you."

Grace nodded. "I'm still a little mad at them for it. No matter how unreasonable that may be."

"It's not unreasonable," Noah said. "You're allowed to feel however you feel."

Grace jutted her chin forward. She had never been told that before. The novelty of it felt like a snuggly blanket around her heart. For years, she was told to let go. To forgive and move on. To not let her parents' deaths prevent her from experiencing life. Aunt Judy was not exactly an inspirational life coach, and she didn't believe in therapy.

You're allowed to feel however you feel. Grace loved that. It was refreshing. Liberating.

She looked into Noah's eyes. They had softened, watching her intently. He didn't look bored or uninterested at all.

So Grace continued. "I loved my parents. I still do. I just wished they hadn't had this need to constantly be out of the house. They did everything. Went everywhere. Without me."

"Did that upset you?" Noah said. "Did you feel left out?"

Grace chewed the inside of her cheek. "It wasn't that I felt left out. It's more that they chose to leave, you know? They made a choice to do all these risky, adventurous things. They chose that life over me."

Noah nodded in understanding.

"The last thing I want is to do the same thing to my aunt. To leave her behind. She can't do much because of her MS. I need to be there for her, and it's not fair for me to be having fun while she's cooped up at home."

Noah looked thoughtful for a minute, his eyes drifting across the ceiling, fixating on the fan that swooshed the air around. After a while, he said, "But you're here now. In one of the most beautiful countries on the planet. It would make no difference to your aunt if you stayed in your hotel room or if you went out and did something fun, right?"

"Yes, but if something were to happen to me or if I died in a freak accident, she'd be left alone forever."

"So you need something safe. An adventure, but nothing dangerous."

"Exactly."

His eyes brightened. "I've got the perfect idea."

Grace turned her head, eyeing him cautiously. "I don't like the sound of that."

"I promise you, it's completely harmless. You need to get out, and there's something I want to show you."

Grace stared back at him. He had that excited sheen in his eyes that had Grace's stomach doing flips, but the thought of leaving the comfort of her own bed was almost too much to bear. "It's nine o'clock!"

"So?"

"Nothing good happens after nine o'clock."

"Everything good happens after nine o'clock," he said, smiling.

"But how will I know if the girl gets her prince at the

end?" Grace said, pointing to the television, knowing full well that the girl always got her prince.

"Come on, Blue Eyes. It seems to me like somewhere, deep down in your genetic makeup, you have a desire to explore. To see the world."

"I—"

"It's buried. But it's there. I can see it. You even said so yourself—you thought you'd end up being adventurous just like your parents one day."

"Yeah, but that was until they died."

"Listen. There's something outside I want you to see. It's not dangerous at all, I promise. It's just an experience that you won't regret."

"I don't know," Grace said, trying to tamp down the excitement that was beginning to surface. She thought back to her text conversation with Tessa. Tessa would have definitely encouraged her to go.

"Come with me," Noah said, sliding off the bed. He reached out his hand to help her up.

Grace stared at it, a shot of adrenaline coursing through her veins. "But what about Jane?"

"What about the life you're not living because you're too scared to live it?"

Grace zipped her lips. He had her there. "I'm wearing my pajamas," she said, looking down at her buttoned-up flannel.

"Keep 'em on. Your seduction technique will eventually wear off on me," he said teasingly.

Grace snorted, shaking her head. The dimple on his cheek made an appearance as his smile brightened.

"You can trust me," he said, more seriously this time, an unsaid plea in his voice.

Grace found herself placing her hand in his, allowing his fingers to wrap around hers.

"Well," Grace said, pulling herself up off the bed, "I've

already gotten into a stranger's van today. Why not top it off by going out into the night with no clue of where I'm going?"

Noah chuckled. "It would be a shame to stop while you're on a hot streak."

❦

Noah pulled Grace behind a tree, checking if the path through the garden was clear. Being on the lookout for Jane was exhausting and annoying, but something told him Grace was worth the extra effort.

Grace's shiny blue eyes glistened in the moonlight as she continued to prod. "Seriously, Noah, where are you taking me? I can't stand surprises."

"We're headed to the beach," Noah said, squeezing her hand.

"Oh," Grace said with a faint smile. "Okay."

The ocean breeze cooled his skin, a soothing respite from the heat generating from Grace's hand. Touching her was like sitting too close to a bonfire, with the occasional spark shooting up his arm, but in a very good way.

The roaring crash of waves grew louder as they found the sandy path. Grace stopped to take off her flip-flops, and Noah noted that she still held his hand while she balanced on one foot. His chest tightened at that small act of trust.

A few people were standing on the beach with flashlights several yards away, crouched down on their haunches.

"What are they looking at?" Grace said in wonder.

"You'll see in a second," Noah said.

A woman with a flashlight on her head and a chart in her hands approached and introduced herself as a nature guide. "Are you here to see the baby sea turtles?"

Noah watched Grace's eyes grow wide. "Sea turtles?" she gasped.

"Yep," Noah confirmed.

"All right then," the lady said. "A couple of things you should know. There are only about seven nests on this beach. You can see each one is marked with caution tape. The hatchlings range from there"—she pointed to a few people clustered around a patch of sand—"to that point way out there. We just ask that you stand behind the lines, and don't touch the hatchlings. Let them do their thing."

"You got it," Noah said. He thanked the lady and led Grace to a patch of eggs a few yards up the coast where there weren't any people hovering over them.

The moon was so bright it illuminated the hole in the ground with round sand-covered eggs piled together. Some eggs had already been broken, while others were still intact.

A lone baby sea turtle and its sibling were making the trek toward the ocean, and another baby was struggling to get out of its shell.

"They're so cute!" she said, covering her mouth.

They both plopped down, their feet in the cool sand. Noah pulled out his phone and flashed a light on the pile of eggs. "Look," he whispered.

A tiny crack had formed on one of the eggs, and a small piece chipped off as the turtle started breaking through.

"Wow," Grace breathed in almost a whisper.

They watched in silence as the little guy made his way out of the egg. Noah resisted the urge to help him out as it wriggled within its shell. Its little face appeared, and Noah felt his heart clench.

"Okay, that is really cute," he said.

He looked next to him to find Grace's eyes fixed on the new hatchling. Her eyes were glossy.

Noah put his arm around her shoulders, pulling her into a hug, a move he hoped she wouldn't think was too forward. When Grace melted into his side, he sighed in relief.

Goddamn, she felt good under his arm. This petite little thing. She fit perfectly.

"I can't believe I'm watching this right now," Grace said. "How did you know?"

"I saw it on a brochure when I was checking in," Noah said. "They usually hatch during this time of year. I guess we got lucky."

Another big piece of an eggshell broke off, and the baby's little flipper was free.

"This is the most amazing thing I've ever seen in my life," Grace said. Her fingers covered her mouth. "Thank you for bringing me here."

Noah gave her a little squeeze. She nestled in closer in response.

"Where's their mother?" Grace said, searching around.

"I think she's back in the ocean."

Grace stilled. "These little guys are on their own? They have to find their way to the ocean all by themselves?"

"Yeah, but look," he said, pointing at the three babies that had almost reached the ocean's edge. "They don't need their mother. They have a natural instinct to head straight toward the water."

Grace sat up, alert, scanning all the eggs as if she had become personally responsible for each and every one of them.

"It's hard to just sit back and watch, isn't it?" Noah said.

"I want to help them so bad," Grace said, her eyes glittering.

Noah chuckled. "Me too. Check out that one," he said, pointing to the baby that had reached the water.

"Oh my god."

They sat quietly, watching the sea turtle take to the waves, be carried in, and then pushed out. The struggle was both heartbreaking and magical. Eventually the sea turtle was out of sight, into the great ocean.

"A part of me feels silly now," Grace said softly.

"Silly? Why?" Noah sat up, leaning toward her.

"For feeling sorry for myself, having to grow up without my parents, when these guys do it from the very beginning. They're not even remotely scared."

Noah smiled, resisting the urge to touch her again. "Who said they weren't scared?"

"They don't look scared."

"It doesn't mean they aren't," Noah said. "Their little baby sea turtle brains are probably thinking, *Holy crap, what the hell am I doing?*" Noah used his best Kermit the Frog voice for effect, generating a bubble of laughter from Grace, encouraging him to go on. *"Why do I have this sudden urge to plunge into that big moving thing? Do you know, sis? Bro? No? Me neither. Let's do it anyway."*

Grace giggled so hard she had to wipe the tears from her eyes. It was probably the best sound he had ever heard, second to the ocean waves roaring in front of them.

"Kermit the Frog?"

"Yep."

"That's pretty good."

"Thanks. I practiced my entire life for this very moment."

Grace locked her gaze on his, smiling shyly before returning her attention to the baby sea turtles.

"I'm inspired," Grace said with a smile.

"Oh yeah? I can teach you to do the voice."

Grace chuckled. "Not by you," she said, playfully shoving him with her hand. "I'm inspired by the baby sea turtles."

"Ah."

"This whole time I've been the baby turtle that just wants to stay in its shell," she said thoughtfully. "I mean, I have my reasons to not go out. I have to take care of my aunt."

"That sounds like an excuse to me."

Grace bit her lip, looking out onto the ocean. "I guess you're right. I'm full of them." She paused thoughtfully. "Better to be full of excuses than full of shit though, right?"

Noah cocked his head to the side. "You said shit."

"Yeah? So?"

"Your little potty mouth is cute on you."

"Potty mouth?" She shrugged. "I do swear, you know. I'm not that much of a prude."

"Oh really now?" Noah said, watching the twitch in her mouth as she took her lip between her teeth. He'd love to test out how *not that much of a prude* she really was.

"My father used to tell me that we are defined by our excuses," Noah said. "And I guess that always kind of stuck with me."

Grace seemed to be taking in that advice. Her eyes darted between the eggs and the ocean for a while until she straightened her back and said, "I don't want to be defined by my excuses anymore."

"Good. So what does that mean for you?" he said softly.

Grace sat quietly for a moment before looking up. "Maybe I'll finally get the courage to put up my own Christmas lights this year."

"Oh yeah?"

"Ever since you mentioned it, I can't stop thinking about them. When my parents died, there was no one left to put them up. The ladder freaks me out, so I just don't bother. But every year at Christmas time, my bare house is just another reminder that they're gone. Maybe this year I'll ask my friend to hold the ladder for me."

"There you go; that's a start."

Grace looked up with her sparkly blues. "I can't thank you enough for bringing me out here."

Noah pulled her into a hug. "I'd be happy to get you out

any time." He breathed in the sweet orange scent of her, and she swung her arms around him.

"Did you say you're leaving tomorrow?" Noah asked.

"Tomorrow night, yes. We changed our flight to a red-eye."

"When's your presentation?"

"In the morning. Why?"

Noah tapped his finger to his lip, thinking of what they could do before she left.

"What's that face?" Grace said. "What are you brain-storming over there?"

Noah squared his shoulders, facing her. "Let's go on an adventure tomorrow afternoon. You and me."

Grace's eyes went wide. "An adventure? Noah, I don't know. I said I'd get out of my shell, but—"

"But what? I thought you were done with excuses."

Grace gave him an admonishing look.

"I can teach you how to surf."

"Oh no," Grace said. "No way. Not doing that."

"Come on. It'd be perfect. With big ol' flippers like yours, you'd be a natural."

Grace chuckled, playfully swatting him across the shoulder.

"I'll think of something," Noah said. "What's your number? I'll text you in the morning." He pulled out his phone and opened a new contact.

"What's your last name?" he asked.

"McKinsey."

"Grace Blue Eyes McKinsey." Noah typed it into his phone. "I like that. All right. What are your digits?"

Grace recited her number, and Noah sent her a quick text. "Thanks."

"Jane and I need to leave the resort by six o'clock to get to San José."

Noah frowned. It wasn't enough time. He only had just met her, but he wasn't ready for her to go.

"Any chance you could extend your stay?"

Grace shook her head. "I have to get back to my aunt. My company is helping pay for the extra night care expenses, and I can't afford that on my own.

"You don't have anyone else in your family to help?"

Noah saw a flash of pain in her eyes, but she had quickly blinked it away.

"It's just the two of us," she said. Her voice had grown quiet.

Noah studied her facial expression. She looked like she wanted to say more, but she dragged her finger in the sand instead, leaving a swirling pattern near his feet.

"Tell me about your aunt," Noah said.

Grace released a long, hard breath. "You sure? I don't want to bore you."

"You could never bore me."

Grace pressed her lips together, smiling shyly. "She's... a handful." He waited patiently until she spoke again. "She took me in after the accident even though she had just gone on disability. She could hardly support herself, but she couldn't let me go into foster care."

"You were going to go to foster care?"

An image of a small blue-eyed girl, alone, her bags packed on a doorstep, emerged in his mind. His heart ached for her.

"The paperwork had been filled out and everything, but then my aunt showed up, raising hell. She would have burned down the building if they hadn't let her take me home."

"She sounds like a good lady."

Grace laughed. "That's not usually how she's described. But she is good underneath all her snark."

"That's sweet, in its own way."

"It's impossible to find good care for her. But I can't let her be alone in a nursing home. Not when she has me."

Noah noticed a flyaway strand of her hair dancing in the breeze. His fingers itched to touch it. To put it back in place, to smooth her hair, and rub her back. God, he desperately needed another excuse to touch her.

"You're truly amazing, you know that?" Noah said.

"Nah," Grace said, poking her finger into the sand. Her eyes fixed on the nest of eggs. "I'm just trying to do for her what she did for me."

Noah sat quietly, computing how much time he could get with her before she had to go back. As much as he wanted to convince her to stay longer, he understood the additional night care expenses would put her in a jam.

Unless...

An idea brewed in his head.

Unless he could delay their presentation so that her company would pay for an extra night. Just as a plan began forming in his mind, he saw two men strolling down the beach.

His body tensed.

The men had large, squared-off shoulders and big puffed-out chests. They were marching with purpose.

It couldn't be...

Could it?

Noah felt his body go rigid.

"Do you mind if we head back?" Noah said, his voice cracking, eyeing the two figures coming their way.

"Really? Now?" Grace said, following his line of sight toward the men barreling at them like a freight train.

"Yeah," Noah said. "It's getting late. You've got your presentation tomorrow."

Grace blinked a few times. "Okay."

Noah shuffled to his feet, holding out his hand to help her up.

Grace stared at it. "Why are you being so weird all of a sudden?"

"I'm not weird. You're weird." Noah's voice was high-pitched. His heart was pounding in his chest. His brain screaming at him to get the hell out of there.

Take my hand. Take my hand. Please now!

By the time Grace placed her hand into his and got to her feet, Noah was full-on sweating.

"Why is your hand so clammy?" Grace said.

"I'm just nervous for you and your presentation," he said, guiding her into the brush.

"Noah, the path is over there."

"We're going on an adventure path. I'm warming you up for tomorrow." Noah stepped in between the bushes, but the plants scratched at his ankles and shins.

"Ouch," Grace said, holding her foot up. "These bushes are sharp."

Noah scooped her in his arms, hoisting her up.

"Noah!" she squealed.

"Shh," Noah said nervously. "You don't want people to think I'm kidnapping you."

Just as he scampered up the hill, his ankles feeling like a kitty scratching pole, he glanced down to see the two men advancing down the beach.

He could see now under the glow of the moonlight they were both wearing track suits. A waft of cigar smoke blew up the hill. Then Noah heard the faint echo of one of the men talking in Spanish in a low, gruff voice, complaining about his lower back pain.

Noah let out a breath of relief.

They were just two men on a power walk, smoking cigars.

Not the cartel guys.

"Noah, put me down!"

Noah stepped over the last bush and set Grace on her feet on the manicured lawn near the garden sidewalk.

Grace playfully smacked his chest. "Are you crazy?"

Noah smiled, looking down at his feet riddled with red lines. They stung like hell, but he didn't care. "Maybe a little bit," he said, smiling, gesturing with his hands.

Grace shook her head, a sweet smile on her face. She bit her lip again, sending a rush of heat through his body. He watched her mouth, imagining what it tasted like. What it would feel like around his—

"So what kind of adventure are we going on tomorrow?" Grace said, breaking his train of thought. "I told you that I hate surprises."

"The surprise is part of the adventure."

"Keep in mind I'm a virgin adventurer," she said. "You'll need to go easy on me."

Noah's dick sprang to life. "I'll go easy," he said, his voice strained. "I promise."

The small part in Grace's lips didn't go unnoticed. It was taking every ounce of self-restraint to not scoop her up in his arms and take her to bed. But if she wanted Prince Charming, she was going to get Prince Fucking Charming.

"Come on, I'll walk you to your room," he said, holding out his elbow. He maneuvered his hips just enough to shield her from seeing the pitched tent between his legs. "You're going to need a good night's sleep for an action-packed day tomorrow."

Grace's eyes twinkled.

"I promise you, it'll be fun. And safe."

He just needed more time. It was a good thing he had all night to come up with a plan.

Grace followed Noah through the garden path back toward her room. It didn't go unnoticed that he kept looking over his shoulder, afraid of running into Jane.

Grace held back the urge to hold his hand, although she desperately wanted to feel the warmth of it again. She walked faster, falling into step beside him. When he draped his arm around her shoulders, she molded herself into his side.

When she spotted her patio, she frowned. Their night was over so soon. It was sweet he cared about her presentation, but coming home early was not what she was secretly hoping would happen that night. Especially after he had been such a good listener on the beach.

They approached her patio door, but Grace didn't open it. She stared at the handle, hoping Noah would ask to come in.

"Thanks for coming out with me," Noah said, running a hand through his hair. He had a tortured look on his face as if he wanted to say more.

"It was fun," she said, locking eyes with his. It became a standoff. She wanted to feel the press of his kiss, his hands around her waist, pulling her close. She wanted to feel the weight of him on top of her and his mouth on her breasts—

"I should get going," he whispered.

Grace took a step back. "Are you sure? You did leave that half-opened bottle of champagne in there. Do you want to come in for a bit?" She couldn't believe the words had escaped her mouth. This guy was turning her into an impulsive, wanting bundle of nerves.

And yet, somehow, she didn't mind.

Noah looked through the door, his face contorting in pain. "I want to so bad," he said. "You have no idea."

Grace looked up into his troubled eyes, waiting for him to explain, but nothing came out.

How could he be such a flirt one minute and not accept an invitation to come in the next?

Grace looked down at her penguin pajamas and her dirty, sandy feet.

Right. Her outfit wasn't exactly screaming *come ravage me.*

Grace felt his finger tilt her chin up, and she looked into his eyes.

"Whatever you're thinking, it's not the reason I'm not coming in your room."

"It's okay. I understand."

"You don't," Noah said, leaning forward. His eyes were ablaze, drifting to her lips.

Grace fluttered her eyes closed, awaiting the impact of a kiss, but felt his cheek against hers instead, his breath on her ear as he whispered, "The old me would enjoy peeling off those pajamas and licking every inch of your body until you scream my name."

Grace sucked in a breath.

Noah straightened, giving her more space than she desired. "The new me would also enjoy those things very much, but I want to do this right." He swallowed hard. "And if I go in there tonight…"

He didn't finish his thought. *Why didn't he finish his thought?*

Grace wet her lips, caught between wanting to show him what he's missing and wanting to show him how much she appreciated his self-control. Because the truth was, she didn't trust herself around him. She wouldn't have taken it slow. He had enraptured her so quickly it was rendering her senseless and spontaneous, completely unlike herself. Before she built up the courage to do what she would later regret, he gave her a peck on the forehead.

"See you tomorrow," he whispered.

Grace blinked, stunned by the swirling emotions storming her head and heart. Noah was gone. But he left behind a burning heat deep in her core. And that tingling warmth in the pit of her stomach stuck around the rest of her sleepless night.

CHAPTER THIRTEEN

Grace wrapped her hands around her large cup of steaming coffee, pressing the rim to her lips. She closed her eyes, savoring its warmth while the morning ocean breeze kissed the back of her hands.

The sun broke through the clouds, and she tilted her head to the side, letting the sunrays caress her neck. She imagined Noah's mouth on her shoulder, placing warm kisses toward the spot just behind her ear.

A shiver ran down her spine, remembering his smoldering eyes and the way they drifted to her mouth last night. She could no longer think of anything else. She had spent an unholy amount of time imagining his mouth on hers, wondering what he tasted like.

She took another sip of her coffee to bring her back to that dreamlike state. She imagined his hands cupping her face, his lips pressed firmly to hers. She felt her breath catch as she pictured his hands making a slow crawl to her aching breasts. Kneading and massaging and—

A plate of fruit dropped on the table, shaking Grace out of her trance. Jane had arrived for breakfast, and the tables scattered across the patio were suddenly full of people. The patio had been empty when she had first sat down. How long had she been daydreaming?

Jane wore a formfitting, knee-length black dress. A hint of puffiness settled under her eyes. For once, she didn't look perfect.

"Did you have fun last night?" Grace said.

"Ugh. I never did find Noah. But I did drink my weight in vodka tonics. How was your movie?"

Grace's eyes grew wide. "Good." She couldn't remember a single thing that had happened in it with Noah sitting so close to her. Grace hoped Jane didn't press for more details. She was terrible at lying under pressure.

"Glad to hear it," Jane said, looking out onto the ocean.

Grace poked at her toast. It was cold and hard. "Are you ready for the pitch?"

Jane sipped her coffee. "I was born ready. And I remembered to bring the portfolio this time too," she said, tapping the binder propped up on the table leg.

Grace reached for her coffee, pressing the cup against her lip, when she looked up. Time stood still as Noah strolled up from the beach, his wetsuit unzipped to the waist, revealing his bare chest, more muscular than Grace had imagined. His hair had curled, dripping water onto his bare shoulders. He was walking with a blond guy with a deep tan, and they stopped, chatting at the edge of the stone patio.

Jane might have been saying something, but Grace only heard the thumping of her own heart as she took in his wet, naked torso glistening in the morning sun.

He was like an angel. A surfing angel.

His eyes locked onto Grace, and her stomach hollowed. Noah smiled, lifting a finger to his friend as if to tell him to wait a minute. Then he started to approach the table.

Shit. He hadn't seen Jane. Grace panicked. She signaled

with her eyes that Jane was sitting at the table with her, but he wasn't getting her cues.

Grace made a tiny shake of her head. *Look! Look!*

Noah finally stopped, his eyes landing on the back of Jane's head. He froze, then quickly turned on his heel, but the surfboard he was carrying hit a woman in the face.

The lady screeched.

Oh no.

Orange juice was everywhere, dripping down the woman's nose. Noah muttered soft apologies, taking a napkin from the table to wipe her face, but his surfboard swung around, hitting another man across the aisle.

"Watch it!" the man scowled.

Grace could feel everyone on the patio turn to watch the spectacle. A soft hum of whispers followed.

Jane appeared to notice too and turned in her chair.

"Noah?"

Noah froze, plastering a smile on his face. "Oh hey," he said, setting down the napkin. He turned back to the disgruntled patrons and apologized again.

"Causing trouble over there?"

Noah laughed nervously.

"Come on over," Jane said, waving her hand.

Grace winced, exchanging a glance with Noah as he tiptoed across the patio with the surfboard tucked tightly against his body.

"Where'd you get the surfboard?" Jane said.

"My friend's letting me borrow it," Noah said, pointing behind him with his thumb. The handsome tanned guy waved from across the patio. "How are you ladies doing this morning?"

"Better now that you're here," Jane said. "I was looking all over for you last night."

Grace took a jittery sip of her coffee before setting it

down. It clanked loudly against the saucer, bringing Jane's attention along with it. "Grace, you remember Noah, right?"

Grace gulped. Her face flushed with heat. "Right. Yeah. Phone charger. Noah. Yep."

Blubbering fool.

Jane scrunched her nose at Grace before turning back to Noah. "Have breakfast with us."

Noah's eyes darted around. "I'm sorry. I've got to get back to my friend."

"That's perfect. He can join too so Grace doesn't feel like a third wheel."

Grace's eyes grew wide, pulling her coffee cup to her mouth. It sloshed around, splashing on her nose and lip. She quickly grabbed her napkin to blot her face. She thought she might have gotten away with it, but when she looked up, Noah's eyes were on her with a wicked grin.

"We should get going." Grace's voice squeaked. "For the boards. The poster boards. You know? We have to set up."

Smooth, Grace. Real smooth.

Jane whipped her head around, reprimanding Grace with her icy glare. Then she turned back to Noah and plastered her sticky-sweet smile on her face.

"What are you doing later?" Jane said. "Wanna grab lunch? It'll be my treat."

Noah scratched the back of his neck. "I'm sorry. I've made plans for the rest of the day."

Jane stuck her bottom lip out. "Okay then. How about tonight before I leave? We can grab a drink."

Noah shook his head. "I'm sorry. I'll be in the middle of a... project." His eyes drifted to Grace. Only Noah could make the word *project* sound sexy.

Grace's cheeks and ears were on fire. She turned away, pretending to be very interested in the surfers out in the ocean.

"Your loss," Jane said, shrugging her shoulders. "See you around, coffee boy."

"Enjoy the rest of your trip." He turned to leave, his surfboard grazing a man's toupee. The man looked up, eyeing Noah guardedly.

Grace's spine stiffened as she waited for the man to notice his hair was askew, but he immediately returned to his food instead. She exchanged a relieved glance with Noah before he scampered back to his friend, looking over his shoulder one last time before they took off.

"Good Lord, what's wrong with your face? You look like a tomato," Jane said.

"Oh. I've probably been sitting out here too long."

"Let's go then. Can't have you looking like a ripe cherry while we're presenting." She stopped and leaned in to whisper, "I know this is going to sound weird, but did you see Noah's nipples? I wish I could bite 'em," she said, placing a cube of cantaloupe between her teeth.

"I can't say I did," Grace said. She had been too busy staring at his abs and the sun-kissed freckles across his beautiful face.

"I like a man with a strong pair of nipples," Jane whispered. She heaved a deep breath before standing up from the table and waltzing away.

Grace grimaced, feeling the blood drain from her face. She and Noah had planned to meet by the pool after her presentation, but it all felt wrong with Jane pining for his nipples like that.

If Jane saw them together, she would be furious, and only God knew what she would do to retaliate. A shudder ran down her spine.

Was it worth the risk? It wasn't like Grace was entirely comfortable with going on an adventure in the first place. She didn't even know what he had in mind. He wouldn't tell her. The anticipation of it all had been eating away at her all morning.

The only reason she hadn't found an excuse to bail was because she had been fantasizing about his kiss.

Grace followed Jane between the tables and chairs and through the open courtyard full of big ferns and giant green plants. Colorful flowers were sprinkled throughout the resort, including birds of paradise, her favorite, unlike any flower she had seen back home.

A gurgling water fountain calmed her nerves, but it wasn't enough. The question remained: Should she meet up with Noah or stay in?

After a moment's thought, she determined that not seeing Noah again would be far worse than the anxiety of going out.

She pushed all that aside for now as she trotted behind Jane into the conference room.

This was what she should have been focusing on, winning their first-ever international account, not dreaming about his tongue between her—

No. She had to stop. She couldn't mess this up.

Jane had just finished critiquing Grace's poster board placement when a tall and slender man, wearing a cream-colored dress shirt, walked in. He introduced himself as Fernando, the hotel owner. His eyelashes and eyebrows were so thick it was hard to look at anything else.

He firmly shook Grace's and Jane's hands, then introduced them to Diego, his hotel manager.

"Thank you again for being so flexible," Fernando said. "My sincerest apologies for having to reschedule. I trust you are finding enjoyment at this resort?"

"Very much," Grace said.

"Top-notch," Jane said. "You're running a wonderful operation here."

"Shall we get started?" Fernando said, gesturing toward

the table. His eyes were noticeably secured to Jane's ass when she turned toward her first poster board.

Grace took a deep breath, waiting for the rest of Fernando's team to file in and sit down.

Jane smiled. "Good morning. Welcome. Thank you for having us. I'd like to start by—"

NURT. NURT. NURT.

A blaring fire alarm startled everyone in the room. Fernando's brows pinched together like two kissing caterpillars.

"I'm so sorry. That seems to be our fire alarm. Please. Come," Fernando said, ushering everyone out of the room.

Grace's pulse quickened. Could there really be a fire? Was she going to die in a hotel fire, thousands of miles from home?

Just as she set foot into the hallway, the sprinklers blasted on, raining down on her head, soaking her navy floral dress. The wet fabric clung to her body like plastic wrap.

She looked back to find Fernando's cream-colored shirt had become translucent with two brown eyes peering back at her.

If Jane's got a thing for nipples, she's going to get a kick out of Fernando's shirt.

Jane shouted, "I'm drenched!"

"Please exit to the parking lot," Fernando said. His hair had come undone from his perfectly coiffed style, flattened against his head.

Everyone shuffled out the door when Jane stopped and turned. "My boards!"

Jane started toward the lobby, but Fernando held his hand out to stop her. "It is not safe to go back there right now."

Jane looked at Grace, her eyes were desperate. Pleading.

"I'm sorry," Grace said softly, clutching her purse to her

chest. "We can use my computer. I have everything saved in PowerPoint."

Jane huffed, pouting her lip.

"Don't worry about the boards," Fernando said. "You've already sold us on the concept over the phone. We're more interested in the technical stuff anyway. Diego wants to see an example of how it works."

"Oh," Jane said, wiping the mascara under her eyes. "Well then. We can do that."

"Perfect. We'll reschedule for tomorrow, and we'll comp you another night. I'll be in touch. But in the meantime, if you can excuse me, I must tend to this emergency," he said, pointing to his phone. "Hola." Fernando stalked off, speaking loudly in Spanish over the fire alarm.

When the alarm stopped, people waited around for instructions on what to do. It turned out the only part of the building affected was the main office where their presentation was, so Jane and Grace walked back to their hotel rooms to change clothes.

"I'll text you when I hear from Fernando about the time for the meeting tomorrow," Jane said.

"Sounds good."

Grace opened her room and gasped at the sight. Noah was stretched across her bed, a smug smile on his face, leaning his head back on his hands.

"How did you—?"

"Shh!" Noah whispered, pressing his finger to his lips. He spun his legs off the bed and stalked toward her. "You left your patio door open," he said quietly.

He took a few strands of her damp hair between his fingers, his eyes glittering with amusement. "You're wet."

"There was a fire. A fire alarm. Water came from the ceiling." She was a mumbling mess.

Noah shook his head with a growing smile. "There's no fire."

Grace gasped. "Did *you* do this?" She pointed at his chest.

"I might have." Noah's shoulders inched toward the ceiling.

"You could be put in jail! Do you know how serious this is?"

"Yes, but does it mean I get an extra day with you? Because if it does, it was worth the risk."

Grace's mouth dropped open. "You've got to be kidding me."

"I figured if your presentation got delayed again, you might get to stay another night. And your company could help pay for your aunt's night care."

"Noah!" Grace whisper-shouted. "How could you do something like this? You're absolutely crazy."

"I'm sorry, but I needed more time."

"More time?" Grace said. "More time for what?"

Noah grew quiet for a moment, looking beyond Grace's shoulder. "More time with you." The sparkle in his eye made her weak in the knees.

She was in real trouble now.

"I don't know when we're rescheduling our presentation," Grace said lamely. "They could change it to this afternoon, for all I know. Then I won't get to spend any time with you at all." The thought made her ache.

"I'm sure it'll work out," Noah said, looking out the patio door. A menacing smile appeared.

"Don't tell me you have a backup plan."

Noah shrugged. "I really don't want to use it, but I do have one."

"You're out of your mind," Grace said, pushing his chest.

She stormed toward the bathroom and grabbed a towel. Noah followed close behind.

"Plan B is a little crazy." Noah said. "Plan C, however, is cuckoo for Cocoa Puffs. Let's just hope we don't get to plan C."

Grace rolled her eyes, although his master plan to spend more time with her was kind of sweet in its own way.

"There will be no plan B. And for God's sake, there will be no Cocoa Puffs."

Noah looked away, heartbroken. Grace couldn't bear it. She was about to reach for him when a ding from her purse caught her attention. She pulled out her phone and gaped at the text message from Jane. *Meeting got moved to tomorrow morning.*

"What is it?" Noah said.

A smile warmed Grace's lips as she looked up. "Do you always get what you want, Noah Greene?"

Noah caught his lower lip between his teeth, his face brightening. "Get dressed. I've got somewhere I'd like to take you."

CHAPTER FOURTEEN

The wind whipped through Grace's hair as the cab drove out of the resort and onto the palm tree-lined highway. Noah sat beside her, his elbow hanging out the window and a smug smile on his face. He shifted in his seat, spreading his legs out. His knees were dangerously close to touching hers.

"How did you get out of hanging out with Jane all day?" Noah said.

"She wanted to lay out by the pool. I told her I didn't bring a bathing suit, which is true."

"You didn't?" Noah said, cocking his head to the side.

"I didn't think I'd have any time to go swimming. Plus my skin doesn't do well in the sun. I told her I wanted to check out the cultural museums in town, knowing she wouldn't want to come with me."

"Naughty girl," Noah said, his pearly whites beaming in the sunlight.

"I guess you're rubbing off on me," Grace said, knocking his knee with hers. She ignored the playful hint of a smile in his eyes. "I don't know how Fernando's schedule suddenly became jam-packed this afternoon, and I don't want to know. But I do know that you are sneaky and a bad influence."

Noah snickered devilishly, his sea-green eyes sparkling with trouble.

"So, where are we going? The suspense is killing me."

"We're on our way to Jaco," Noah said. "From there, we'll take a shuttle for a little sightseeing."

Sightseeing? Grace let out a shaky laugh. Okay, she could handle sightseeing. A small bubble of nervousness formed deep in her belly. She had heard about the aerial trams offered just outside of Jaco. They were famous for them. In fact, it was one of the experiences she and Jane had included in their pitch. That must be what he meant when he said *sightseeing*.

They'd be high up, but it couldn't be as scary as flying in a plane. She could do this.

Grace stuck her hand out of the cab, feeling the wind between her fingers and up her arms, smiling at the palm trees.

"What are you so smiley about?" Noah said. He leaned in close, looking out her window, and placed his hand on the seat as he leaned forward. His fingertips lightly brushed her leg.

All she could think about was the soft brush of his fingers against her skin and the lingering smell of ylang-ylang and green tea. Her body sizzled in her seat.

When Grace could gather her wits, she said, "I was just admiring the palm trees. We don't have them in Michigan, but I wish we did."

Noah's eyes dropped to her lips before he leaned back in his seat. Grace tried concealing her disappointment he hadn't made a move. She was ready to kiss him, especially with Jane nowhere in sight.

"They're my favorite," Noah said, his eyes sparkling.

"Mine too." Grace smiled. "You mentioned that you've lived all over. Is Costa Rica your favorite?"

"Hands down," Noah said. "There's no other place like it. Everyone is so laid-back and happy here. I can surf every day. Watch the sunrise over the ocean—well, at home at least. It's paradise."

Grace looked down at her hands, imagining what life would be like to live in Costa Rica, without the changing leaves in the fall or the brightly colored blooms coming back to life in the spring.

"You don't miss the seasons?"

Noah shrugged. "I don't know. It's been a long time. I remember the one winter we spent in Chicago. It was super-cold. I was six. My mother bundled me up with a blanket tucked inside my jacket, with two pairs of gloves and earmuffs. It was definitely one of the most fun times I remember as a small kid."

Grace giggled. "I can picture that. I bet you were cute when you were young."

"Hell yeah, I was," Noah said. "In fact, we had a neighbor in Chicago who would come out and watch me play in the snow. She used to tell Ma I was the cutest of her boys, which ticked my brothers off, and they would pummel me with snowballs."

Grace stuck her lip out. "Poor thing."

"Nah, I was all right. They toughened me up."

"I didn't have siblings to play with, but I would still spend hours outside, building snow forts and snowmen with my dad. Then we'd come inside and sit by the fireplace, with big mugs of hot chocolate warming our fingers," Grace said. "I should really fix our fireplace at home. The gas valve has been broken for years. One of many things I haven't had time to take care of."

Noah looked at her for a while, thinking deeply. His eyes twinkled for a moment until he visibly shrugged off the thought.

"I'm sorry," Grace said. "We were talking about seasons. Not my to-do list when I get home."

"It's okay. It was on your mind. I like knowing what's on your mind."

Grace blushed, feeling warm everywhere.

"I like the seasons all right," Noah continued. "But Costa Rica has something that no other place does. They have this saying here: *pura vida*. It means simple life. It's a way of living here that is different than anywhere else. People take it slow. No one is in a hurry for anything. We don't require much to be happy."

"*Pura vida!*" the cab driver shouted. The sweet man didn't speak a lick of English, but he must have picked up on the phrase.

"*Pura vida*," Noah said with a smile, patting the man on the shoulder. He said something else in Spanish that made the cab driver nod his head a few times, and then Noah turned back to Grace. "I just told him that I was explaining the concept of *pura vida* to you."

"So, you like the simple life. This is what you want?" Grace said.

Noah looked out his window. The passing palm trees zoomed by. "Yeah," Noah said. "At least I thought I did. I don't really know what I want right now."

"That's okay," Grace said. "You're still young. You've got your whole life to figure out what you want."

"I know, but part of me feels like I'm at a fork in the road. You know? Like the next choice I make is going to affect my future somehow, and that kinda scares the shit out of me."

Grace noticed how Noah's knee bobbed up and down.

The closer they drove into the city, the more violently it moved.

"I used to think that I wanted to get a college degree and start my own business. Own a hotel or a chain restaurant. Something like that. But then I saw how much my pop worked on his own business and how he failed. And what it did to his health."

Grace frowned. "Is he okay?"

"He died a few months ago. He literally worked himself to death."

Grace cupped her mouth in shock. "I'm so sorry."

"Thanks," Noah said, looking straight ahead. "The late nights, the booze, the cigar smoke, the lopsided balance sheets. It just all caught up to him."

His jaw tensed and he made a fist, tapping on his knee.

"That must have been hard for you to watch," she said softly.

"It was brutal. And the bitch of it all was that even though he gave his life for that business, he was just barely making a profit. It was all for nothing."

"Is that why you changed your mind about going to college?"

Noah nodded. "It doesn't seem worth my time and money to pursue a big, fancy career if it's not going to give me anything in return, you know?"

Grace frowned. "Are you not passionate about anything?"

"Sure. I love to surf. I like helping people, making them smile. But I'm not exactly in love with the idea of getting my hopes and dreams up only to fail in the end."

"Everyone's afraid of failure, Noah. But you have to try something."

"That's the beauty of living here," Noah said. "I don't. I can get a job doing anything and spend most of my time surfing and just hanging out. It's all the same but without the looming disappointment that comes with a failed career."

"Is that really what you want?" Grace said. "To surf all day and just hang out?"

Noah let out a sigh, his eyes meeting hers. "Would you be less attracted to me if that were the case?"

Grace scrunched her nose. "I don't know. Ambition can be both attractive and unattractive on people. But if you have a gift, like making people smile, then you should use that gift. If you don't, I would find that wasteful."

Noah fidgeted with the pocket on his shorts and chortled at a thought that seemed to emerge. "You know, if you had asked me two days ago what I wanted, I would have told you I just wanted a yurt on the beach. Nothing else. I figured it would be all the same if I got some job, serving ladies drinks with tiny umbrellas."

"Like a cabana boy?"

Noah shrugged. "I'd be putting a smile on a woman's face."

Grace pursed her lips.

"But that was before I met you. And Ivan."

"Who's Ivan?"

"Oh, my new friend. The guy I went surfing with. He's basically living my dream, only the guy doesn't realize he's not happy."

"Why is he not happy?"

"Because he doesn't have a woman willing to stick around." His eyes softened. "Someone as beautiful and smart and sexy as you."

Grace bit her lip before she realized it was just another one of his lines. She really needed to get ahold of herself. "Your lines are so—"

"Charming? Working for you?"

Grace slapped his shoulder playfully before looking away,

not giving Noah the satisfaction of her smile. He was breaking her resolve to not become a blubbering bowl of woman jelly.

"Not that my opinion matters, but you could be so much more than just a man who can make a woman smile."

"More? I don't know about that. More is the opposite of less. And living with less is the essence of *pura vida*."

"*Pura vida!*" the cab driver chimed in again, pumping his fist.

Grace giggled at the intrusion.

"Anyway," Noah said, "I don't know what I want. And I didn't realize when I got into this cab that I'd be driving with a career counselor."

"I'm sorry, we can talk about something else."

"No, it's good. I need to make a decision soon. I can either use the money I saved up for college or use it to buy a place to live."

"I'm not really sure that's something I can help you with."

It was hard to comprehend the concept of living simply. That was never an option for her. If she really thought about it, living in Michigan was kind of a pain in the butt. The leaf raking, the snow shoveling, the rain. The layers of clothes to manage through the blistering cold. And of course, there was the general way of life up there, the American dream. The work-hard mentality that Grace had adopted not because she wanted to but because she had to, to make ends meet for her and Aunt Judy.

Grace looked at Noah's carefree smile and pocketed the thought that they were truly from two different worlds. Whatever was going on between them had an expiration date.

She needed to remember that the next time her lady parts yearned to be touched by him.

Noah said something to the cab driver, who immediately

pulled over to the side on a busy street. They had entered Jaco. People strolled down the sidewalk, music thumped from outdoor-seated restaurants, and the buzz of cars zoomed all around.

"We're here," Noah said, pulling out his wallet. He handed the cab driver a few bills, patting him on the shoulder. They exchanged a few words in Spanish before Noah darted out of the cab, holding out his hand to help her out. "My lady."

"I see you paid more attention to that movie than you let on."

Noah winked. "You deserve the very best, princess. Welcome to Jaco," Noah said, spreading his arms out wide.

The small city radiated with energy on that bright, sunny day. Grace took a whiff from the restaurant nearby. It smelled like warm spices.

"Are you ready for our big adventure?" Noah said.

Grace took a breath, envisioning a leisurely aerial tram ride through the jungle. She could handle that, she convinced herself, ignoring the butterflies in her stomach.

"I'm ready," Grace said, taking his arm.

They wandered down the sidewalk, past several souvenir shops. "I'd like to get a souvenir before we head back to the resort."

"Oh yeah? What were you thinking?"

Grace looked up thoughtfully, tapping her finger to her lips. "I think I want a baby sea turtle souvenir. In a snow globe."

"Snow globe?" Noah laughed. "You do know that sea turtles would die in the snow, right?"

Grace's eyes bugged out. "Well, obviously it's not real. But my parents used to bring home a snow globe from their travels."

"I see. Well, it might be hard to come by, but if you want a baby sea turtle snow globe, we will get you a damn baby sea turtle snow globe."

Grace squeezed his arm, plastering a smile on her face. She pushed the truth deep down: Noah would never leave Costa Rica, Grace would never leave her aunt in Michigan, and a souvenir would be the only thing she could take back with her to remember him helping her get out of her shell.

"I don't know why you insisted on covering my eyes," Grace said. "I already have a pretty good idea about what we're about to do.

"You do? Really? Am I that predictable?" Noah said as they bumped along on the shuttle taking them through the winding jungle path. The canopy overhead blocked the sun, and the temperature had dropped about ten degrees.

The shuttle bus was full of chatting families and couples, trying to talk over the party music blaring over the bus's speaker system.

"I've never done this before," Noah said. "The concierge said this one had the best views on the west side of the country."

Grace had a flutter in her stomach. She had never been so high up before—well, apart from the airplane ride, of course. But if she could handle that, she could handle an aerial tram. Right?

"Are you nervous?" Noah said.

Grace pressed her lips together. "A little," she admitted.

Noah threaded his fingers through hers. Holding his hand felt like liquid sunshine. It warmed her body and her chest. She squeezed back in response.

As much as it felt good to hold his hand, she couldn't ignore the tug at her heart. Whatever this was, whatever they were together, it was only temporary. Grace gathered her wits, telling herself to just enjoy the time now and not worry about the future.

Pura vida, she thought to herself.

"No offense," Noah said, "but I'm surprised at how cool you're being about this. I thought you were going to put up a fight."

Grace raised her shoulders to her ears. "I did come up with a million excuses to not come with you today."

"What made you decide to do it?"

Your dimple.

Your smile.

The way you make me feel inside.

"There was something you said last night. How the baby sea turtles were probably afraid, but they went to the ocean anyway. I guess I never realized it was okay to be afraid."

Noah smiled. "Good. In that case, in the spirit of conquering your fears, I want to ask you something."

"What is it?"

"On this trip, there are two stops," Noah said. "There's the family stop. It's not as high up, and it's easier. Then there's the main stop. It's at the highest point and requires some effort to get up there. I was planning on taking you to the family stop, you know, to ease you into this whole adventure thing." He paused, looking deep in her eyes. "Would you rather do the main one? At the top? Or would you rather do the family-friendly one?"

Grace gulped. She hadn't realized there would be two options for aerial trams. But it made sense for kids who wanted to go with their parents and needed more seats.

The main stop probably had a better view but would be scarier than the other one. And a longer drop if they were to fall.

Grace swallowed hard. "Which one do you want to do?"

Noah shook his head. "Whichever one you want." He looked up through the windshield. "It looks like we're almost at the family stop, so you'll have to decide now."

Grace's heart raced. Would she really be testing herself if she chose the safer option? Her hands felt clammy. She released Noah's grasp and looked out the window.

The shuttle came to a stop, and the music shut off. The guide stood up and explained they had made it to the bunny-hop stop, and a family got up from their seats to file out.

A bunny-hop stop sounded safe. It was predictable. It was the old Grace.

"Let's do the main stop," Grace said.

"Are you sure?"

"No, but I know I'll regret it if we don't."

"Okay then," Noah said, smiling slowly before sitting back in his seat. "I'm proud of you."

He tried to hold her hand, but she dodged it, pulling her hand into her chest. "I'm kind of sweaty, sorry. I'm getting nervous."

"Your sweaty hands don't bother me. Gimme." He held his hand out.

The bus roared to life, and Grace's heartbeat quickened. She stared at his hand, instantly craving the soothing calm of his touch. She wiped her hand on her shorts and placed it into his. He clasped around her hand, firm and yet soft at the same time. A wave of peace rushed through her.

She could handle this.

When they got to the top of the hill, everyone filed out of the shuttle bus and stood around the guide who explained the safety protocols. For a minute there, it sounded like this aerial tram required people to wear harnesses, but he must have been talking about the tram itself.

Then one of the guides opened the back door of the shuttle and started handing out helmets.

"Helmets?" Grace heard herself say. She hadn't pictured herself needing a helmet, but she took her hair out of her ponytail and put it on anyway.

Next came the handlebars and the harnesses.

"Make sure the clip goes in the middle, just like this," the guide said, demonstrating how to put the harness on.

"I'm all about safety," Grace said. "But this seems a little excessive for an aerial tram ride, no?"

Noah stopped adjusting his harness and looked up at her. "What?"

"I said that all this gear was more than I was expecting for a tram ride."

Noah's eyes grew wide. "Grace. This isn't a tram ride."

"What is it?"

"We're zip-lining."

"Zip-lining?" Grace croaked. She had lost her voice. The ground dropped from her feet.

"I thought you knew," Noah said, unhooking his helmet. "This whole time you thought…"

Grace covered her mouth. "What were you thinking?"

"I was thinking we were going to go on the bunny-hop zip line. But then you were talking about facing your fears and all that, so I thought I'd give you the option to go on the main one."

They both looked up at the winding staircase. It led to a platform where someone had just launched off at the top. Their squeal echoed through the trees as they zoomed down the line overhead.

"Oh my god. Oh my god. Oh my god," she said, dropping her helmet to the ground.

"Is everything okay?" the guide said.

"We're fine," Noah said. "Just give us a minute."

Noah led Grace to the opposite side of the bus, away from the crowd. "We do not have to do this. Okay?"

Grace was taking deep, ragged breaths, her chest pumping wildly for air. "This is too much."

Noah wrapped her in his arms. "It's okay. We don't have to do anything you don't want to."

Grace sank into his chest, wrapping her arms around his waist. That sense of calm washed over her again. She let him hold her for a while until her breath normalized.

"I'm so sorry. I had only meant for you to take baby steps. It was a bad idea."

There was something in the sound of his voice that made her look up into his eyes. He truly didn't mean to push her this far. He was only trying to help her live a little.

Zip-lining was something her parents would have done. She recalled how they had bungee-jumped in New Zealand once. All their adventures had sounded so cool to Grace at the time—that is, until they didn't come home.

What was it about her parents that made them thrill-seekers? And why didn't she have that gene? Or did she, and it was being masked by her own fear?

If those little sea turtles could be brave, then so could she.

"Excuse me. We're about to go over the instructions," the guide said, popping his head around the bus.

"I'm sorry, but we decided to—" Noah started.

"We're doing it," Grace blurted out.

"We are?"

"Yeah," Grace said, taking a deep breath. "I need to do this. I need to get over this silly fear of everything. I need to live my life."

"Ayeeeee!" Another zip-liner screamed overhead.

"It does sound like they're having fun," Grace said. "That's gleeful screaming, right? Not screaming toward imminent death?"

Noah chuckled, looking down at her with the biggest, caring eyes. "You sure?"

"I'm sure."

"That's my girl," he said, giving her a kiss on her forehead. A flood of endorphins rushed from the top of her head to her lady parts.

My girl.

If only that could be true.

Her body shimmered from the impact of his kiss. Even if she were to die today, she would at least die next to a man who could make her feel like she was the center of the universe.

"Let's do this," she said, putting her helmet back on.

CHAPTER FIFTEEN

The wooden platform towered over the trees, sitting on top of a jungle that led to miles and miles of coastline. Grace's stomach sank at the sight.

"Wow. We're really high up," Grace said, her voice strained. Her heart pumped wildly in her chest. There was a difference between now and how she felt on that airplane ride to Costa Rica, a buzz in her veins.

Grace felt like she had somehow summoned her parents' adventurous spirit. A spirit that had been dormant inside her for years, never allowed to come out and play. This side of her had been cloaked and hidden, tucked away until now.

This must be what they had felt like, she mused. The bungee jumping, the rock climbing, the cliff jumping. A small part of herself began to heal with the new understanding of why her parents sought adventures all the time. Her parents were chasing this... this *feeling*.

"Grace? Are you okay?" Noah asked, snapping Grace back to the moment.

"I'm okay," she rasped, studying the wrinkle in his forehead.

A loud clink, metal on metal, caught both their attention as they watched the zip line guide clip a teenager to the line. The zip line guide was a beautiful woman with light brown skin and light brown eyes, staring in Noah's direction.

"Seems like you caught someone's attention," Grace whispered.

"The only attention I want is yours," Noah said. He rubbed his hands down her arms, drawing a shaky breath from her.

The guide went about the safety checks and tugged on all the buckles and snaps, then positioned him at the edge of the platform, instructing him to keep his feet up.

"Ready?" the guide said.

The teenage boy replied, nodding his head. His eyes locked on the giant cable and gripped his handlebars with a leather-on-leather squeeze.

"*Pura vida!*" the guide yelled, pushing the kid forward.

The boy hadn't made a peep until he got about a hundred yards into the vast open air over the jungle and yelled, "¡*Mierda*!"

Grace felt herself pale.

Noah slipped his hand in hers, curling his fingers against her skin. "It's okay to be scared," he said.

She looked down at their hands, and her face softened. "You have this amazing ability to calm all my nerves."

"Is that all I'm good for? Calming your nerves?"

Grace looked into his eyes and felt the color come back to her cheeks. "You might do something else to my nerves as well."

"Like, get on them?" Noah quipped, his eyes glittering.

Grace snorted. "Not yet, at least."

Noah leaned closer. "I'm sure I'll get there soon enough," he said teasingly. His fingers grazed her jawline, and Grace felt a shiver down her neck.

"You certainly are good at distracting me," Grace said huskily. She had all but forgotten she was about to launch off this wooden platform into the jungle below.

"Who's up?" the female guide said. They both whipped their heads to her.

"Do you want to go first? To get it out of the way?" Noah said.

She shook her head violently. "No. No way," she said, peering over the platform. The hot thrill she felt earlier had turned to icicles down her spine. "You go first. This was your idea."

Noah set his jaw. "You're right. This was my idea. I'll go. Just don't leave me hanging down there alone, okay? You gotta jump."

Grace squeezed his hand before letting him go. "I'll do it. I promise."

"Remember the baby sea turtles," he said.

Noah approached the guide, letting her snap his harness into place. He positioned his handlebar on the line and looked back at Grace.

The zip line guide performed all her checks. Grace noticed how the girl's fingers lingered around his buckles longer than what seemed necessary. She stopped to ask him if he spoke Spanish, and when he nodded, she launched into an entire monologue in the language. Grace narrowed her eyes on the girl, not knowing if she was giving him information on the zip line or if she was telling him her life story.

Noah responded with something in Spanish that made her laugh, her hand draping over her chest.

The guide tossed her long ponytail over her shoulder and continued talking in Spanish as she batted her eyes and smiled in a way that made Grace's blood boil, reminding her that there would be other women ready and willing to fight for Noah's attention. And they'd be here when Grace went back home.

As if Noah could sense Grace's jealousy, he cranked his neck to look back and mouthed the words, "I'm sorry."

Grace's heart grew twice its size in that moment, looking into Noah's eyes. She felt her legs moving before she realized what she was doing. Marching toward the launch platform, she took a giant step and grabbed his face with her hands.

"Grace, what are you doing?"

Grace cupped his chin, feeling the soft prickle of facial stubble that she hadn't seen with her eyes. A flicker of surprise crossed his face as Grace pressed her lips against his. The world faded into a swirling blur.

She swept her tongue over his, awakening every cell in her body. He tasted like coffee. And chocolate. Sweet. Just as she had imagined.

Noah released a low groan into her mouth before Grace pulled away and admired her handiwork. His eyes were half-mast in a sleepy haze.

"What was that for?" he said in a low whisper.

"I wanted to give you a proper send-off," Grace said, her cheeks flushed. She stepped down from the launch platform, pressing her fingers to her lips. She couldn't believe she had done that.

"Oranges," Noah said.

"What?"

"You taste like oranges. Just as I dreamed last night."

"Ready?" the guide said, clearly not amused with Grace's interruption.

After a kiss like that, he was ready for anything. He was

proud of Grace for stepping in, like she was claiming him. He wanted more of it. More of Grace.

He gripped his handlebars firmly and nodded his head. "Ready."

The guide pushed him off the plank, yelling, "*Pura vida!*"

Noah soared through the sky, his boner like a mast on a pirate ship gliding through the ocean. The whir of the zip line buzzed in his ears. His stomach dropped somewhere between the launch and the clearing as the zip line took him above the jungle canopy.

He gasped at the sight. Miles of coastline and white-peaked ocean waves. He saw tiny buildings and ant-sized people walking around town. The colors were so rich and vibrant; he strained his eyes to take it all in. The vivid turquoise ocean, the rich green palm trees, the bright blue sky.

Before he knew it, he was hurling through a jungle tunnel, darkened by the thick forest. His feet nearly touched the leaves below. His handlebars caught on something that slowed his descent as he zipped down, reaching the platform with another guide waiting to catch him.

When he came to a stop, the adrenaline from both Grace's kiss and the zip line had him reeling. He couldn't wait to see her face. To touch her. To kiss her again.

He took off his harness and his helmet and waited.

And waited some more.

The guide shifted his weight back and forth on each foot, his eyes glued to the zip line the entire time.

God, Noah hoped she wasn't chickening out.

He waited some more, staring at the zip line. Willing her with his mind to take the leap.

The guide's radio transmitter went off, but Noah couldn't understand what was said.

"Is everything okay?" Noah said to the guide.

The guide shrugged. "Sometimes it takes a little extra time."

Noah blew out an aggravated breath. It felt like it was taking longer than it should have. Had she given up? Had she bailed on him?

A moment later, he heard the faint sound of Grace's squeal echoing through the trees. Grace appeared, gliding down the zip line, her feet in the air. The whites of her teeth gleamed under the pockets of sunlight. She was glowing with glee.

The guide caught her harness and brought her to a full stop.

"You did it!" Noah shouted, waiting for the guide to untangle her from the straps and the clips.

"That was amazing!" Grace shrieked. She leaped off the platform and into Noah's arms. He lifted her up, and she wrapped her legs around his waist in a full body hug.

Noah twirled her around once before setting her down. Staring deep into her eyes, he cupped the back of her neck and crashed onto her mouth. Her body leaned into him, returning his kiss with reckless abandon. They pulled and tugged and writhed. Her velvety mouth lingered with one last devastating kiss, leaving nothing but their beating hearts and jagged breaths and—

"Ahem."

A very uncomfortable guide, waiting for them to get off the platform for the next zip-liner.

The shuttle dropped them off at a busy corner in front of a string of tourist shops. He was intoxicated from their zip line high and the sense of normalcy in their stroll down the sidewalk hand in hand.

If they headed back to the resort now, they'd have to worry about running into Jane, which would surely put a damper on the fun they were having. Plus Grace wanted a souvenir. He couldn't deny her the opportunity when souvenir shops were right in front of them.

Noah pushed down his sense of unease to being in the sea of people and squeezed her hand, leading her to a store with colorful scarves and trinkets spilling onto the sidewalk.

Wafts of patchouli and jasmine greeted them as they stepped inside. A popular Latin-American pop song played overhead, and the store clerk acknowledged them with a kind smile.

"I still can't believe I did that," Grace said starry-eyed as she scanned the turnstile of magnets and key chains, Pura Vida written across them in a rainbow of colors.

"I'm really proud of you," Noah said. "That was a scary thing."

Grace picked up a sea turtle figurine and stuck her lip out. "Look how cute this is."

"Can I get that for you?"

She shook her head. "No, thanks. I'm still on the hunt for a snow globe."

Noah laughed, shaking his head. "I think it's funny you're dead set on that."

"My parents used to bring me snow globes from all their adventures. Now that I've been on my own, it's only fitting."

"I see," Noah said, scanning the wall of shot glasses and picture frames.

"I'm hungry, you?" Grace said.

"Oh yeah, I guess we never ate lunch, did we? I could eat."

"I saw a ceviche place up the street. I've never tried that, but I've heard it's good."

Noah raised his eyebrows. "You want ceviche?" Noah would've preferred sneaking back into the resort, ordering room service, and staying in bed all day, but that would have defeated the purpose of her experiencing new things.

They left the shop, and he took her hand again like it was made for his. Her touch was addictive. Every slight movement, the swing of her arm or the tug on his fingers, left him wanting more.

She smiled, looking up with her stark blue eyes.

"Whatcha smiling at?" Noah said.

"You," Grace said dreamily. "This trip. I don't think I've ever been this happy."

Noah squeezed her hand in response. Her glow radiated up to his heart. "Me either."

"I don't want this feeling to end," Grace said, her eyes dimming just enough to crush him.

He had been ignoring the fact that they had a deadline. She would be heading back to Michigan tomorrow, and that would be it. The end of whatever this thing was between them, so unlike any other relationship he had had in the past.

He'd never had a problem with short flings before, so why did this one feel so different? Why did the thought of her leaving make him feel like he had a rotting hole in his gut?

A small toddler ran out of a store, stopping right in front of Grace. His cheeks were blotchy red, and he tugged on her leg as if he thought she was his mother.

Grace crouched down, letting go of Noah's hand to comfort the little one. "There, there. It's okay. Where's your mommy, darling?"

The boy held his arms up, as if he wanted to be picked up. Without hesitation, she bundled him in her arms and looked around. "We'll find your mommy. Don't worry." She soothed the crying toddler with soft sways, rocking him side to side as she stepped into the shop he had come from.

A woman had been shouting at the back of the store, but neither Noah nor Grace could see her. A moment later, the woman came flying out of the dressing room. Her eyes were wild. Her shirt was halfway pulled over her head, and her jean shorts were unbuttoned and sagging down her hips.

When her eyes settled on her son, her body slumped. "Thank you so much," she said in Spanish. "He's always running off on me at the worst times."

Grace yanked on Noah's arm. "What did she say?"

Noah, staring at the wall, away from the half-dressed woman, translated in English for her as Grace gave the woman's son back.

"I'm glad I was there to catch him," Grace said kindly. "He is the most adorable thing," she said, staring at the little boy with his curly locks draped over his puffy eyes.

"He can be adorable sometimes," the woman said in English. "When he's not being so sneaky." She gave the boy's cheeks a little pinch. "Say gracias to the kind lady, Miguel."

Little Miguel held out his hand, opening and shutting his fingers in a gesture that looked like a goodbye.

Grace clasped her hand over her heart. "Goodbye, Miguel." She turned to leave, catching Noah's gaze. Her big, round eyes were shimmering.

Noah's chest filled with what felt like soft, warm sand, sputtering down an hourglass hole.

"You have a way with children," Noah said, leading her out the store and onto the busy sidewalk.

"I guess," Grace said. She placed a loose strand of hair behind her ear and nestled into his side so people could walk around them.

"You have that same look in your eyes that you had last night with the baby sea turtles. A motherly instinct."

Grace looked straight ahead. "I wanted to be a preschool teacher."

"Why didn't you?" Noah said gently.

She shrugged. "It didn't pay well enough to cover the

medical bills and home care. Gosh, I haven't thought about it in forever. I was offered a teaching job the same day Aunt Judy had this awful seizure. It was clear she needed help at home while I was at work. So my friend, Tessa, helped me get a job at Maritime instead."

Noah grew quiet for a moment. "Do you still have your teaching license?"

Grace nodded. "My certificate was good for five years. I have one year left." She shook her head. "But it doesn't matter. My aunt needs me."

The CEVICHE sign came into view on the other side of the street, when Noah's eyes caught on a light blue car parked a few yards up. His spine stiffened at the familiar lines of what looked like a beat-up Mercury Sable.

His throat constricted, and his feet came to a stop.

"What's wrong?" Grace said.

"I… uh…," Noah stammered, feeling the heat rise up his neck. His eyes darted to the shop they were standing next to. A clothing store. "Do you mind if I pop in here for a quick second? I need another clean shirt." He didn't wait for her response as he yanked her inside.

He grabbed the first shirt on a hanging rack inside the store. It was black and had a collar. It would do. He needed a disguise in case the cartel recognized him and to get himself and Grace the hell out of Jaco. *Now.*

"How about this one?" Grace said, holding up a flowery Tommy Bahama shirt.

Noah laughed nervously. "I don't do flowers."

"Or this one?" Grace said, holding a shirt with a giant monkey on the front. JUST MONKEYIN' AROUND printed above the cartoon gorilla holding a banana.

Noah snorted. "I prefer to keep my wardrobe pretty simple," he said, standing in front of a mirror with his black shirt. He slipped his shaky arms through the sleeves, staring at himself in the mirror.

What are you going to do? What are you going to do?

The cartel had clearly found a way to find him. Tracker or not, they had eyes.

Noah's mouth grew dry, his breathing uneven as he watched Grace flip through a rack so innocently.

How was he going to get her out without being seen?

"How about this one?" Grace said, holding up a tie-dye shirt.

"Nah," Noah said, making a face. He looked himself over one more time.

"You sure you want to go with that?" Grace said, walking over to him. She had to stand on her toes to be able to look over his shoulder into the mirror.

"What's wrong with this? It's just a plain black shirt."

Grace pressed her lips together. "And it looks great," she said, her eyes sparkling. If Noah didn't know any better, she was stifling a laugh, but he didn't care.

He snapped off the tag and slapped it on the counter for the clerk to ring him up. Then he pulled a pair of sunglasses from the countertop turnstile and pointed at the straw fedora hats behind the register. "I'll take one of those too."

"What's all this for?" Grace said, her nose crinkled.

"You can never be too careful in the sun," Noah said, ignoring the confused look on her face.

He tapped nervously on the counter while the clerk ran his credit card. Slipping on his shades and hat, he signed the credit card slip. "You know what? I think I'd rather take you to a nice dinner," Noah said. "Somewhere out of town."

"You want to take me to dinner... wearing that?" Grace said, pointing to his new outfit.

"We could go to Playa Hermosa or one of the other small beach towns along the coast. A real date."

Grace tilted her head. "I don't need a nice restaurant," she said. "I'm not dressed for something like that." She pulled on her tank top and shorts.

"Okay then… um…"

"Come on, Noah. I'm excited about that ceviche." She dragged him out of the shop.

As they stepped out onto the sidewalk, Noah saw the passenger door of the Sable open. A shiny boot appeared.

Noah tugged Grace in the opposite direction they were headed and darted into an alcove, ducking behind a brick wall.

"Hey!" Grace squirmed. "What are you doing? The ceviche was that way." She shook her arm loose from his grasp.

Noah dipped his head around the corner in time to see the two men from the Mercury Sable in cowboy hats hop onto the sidewalk.

Fuck. Fuck. Fuck. Fuck.

It was them.

They didn't seem on a mission to catch him though, as they lazily strolled into the market. Perhaps they didn't know Noah was there after all.

Noah's pulse pounded in his ears.

"Noah," Grace said, shaking his sleeve. "Noah! You're being weird." He pulled his head back to look at her. Her arms were crossed. "What's going on with you?"

"Um," Noah said, his voice shaking. He had to think of something that was less of a lie but not quite the truth either. His eyes darted from side to side, landing on the giant painted mural behind Grace. He stepped back to take a better look and saw the brightly painted ocean life in a deep turquoise blue. There was a dolphin, a school of fish, and right beside Grace's head was a giant painted sea turtle.

"I wanted you to see this," Noah said. "Look." He gestured

toward the mural. Grace turned around, and her mouth fell open.

"It's so pretty. And there's a sea turtle!" Grace said, looking back at Noah with sheer glee. It broke his heart to lie to her. But she couldn't know the truth. She would never understand or forgive him for getting involved with her while a drug cartel was on his ass. Pure, sweet, innocent Grace, who always played it safe, wouldn't stick around after she knew he had put her in danger.

Noah peeked around the corner again. The men were likely still inside the market. He needed to get her out of there while he still had the chance.

"I just remembered that ceviche can be dangerous to eat if it's not cured right. I'd hate to give you food poisoning. Let's try the taco stand on the other side of town. That way," he urged, beckoning her to take his hand.

"Wait. I want to take a picture," Grace said, pulling out her phone.

Dammit. The mural had backfired. They needed to leave *now*.

Grace snapped a few pictures, admiring them on her phone before looking up at Noah. "Can I get a picture with you?"

Noah let out a whimper. "Sure."

Grace pulled him down next to her, holding out her phone for a selfie. Noah forced himself to smile, but he could see on the screen that he just looked constipated.

"You are such a goof," Grace said. "Can you smile normally?"

"I'm not very photogenic," Noah said.

"I'm sure you are," Grace said. "Let's try again." She held out her hand, about to take the picture when she turned to give him a kiss on the cheek. A genuine smile brightened Noah's face as she snapped the photo.

"There," she said, looking down at her phone.

Her kiss lingered. A heartbreaking reminder of what he'd lose if he didn't get her out of town right that second.

"All right," Noah said, standing up taller. "Let's head out for some tacos."

"Wait," Grace said, walking up to him, threading her hands through his hair. She pulled his mouth down to hers, sucking his lower lip before taking it between her teeth, giving it a soft nibble.

Noah moaned into her mouth, blood rushing between his legs.

Before he could press himself onto her, she was gone in a flash, leaving him stunned and panting. He blinked his eyes open to find that she had already taken off.

"Grace," he rasped. "The taco place is the other way."

"I decided I want to live a little dangerously," Grace said, a mischievous look in her eye. "Take me to the ceviche."

"I really don't think it's a good idea."

"I'm done playing things safe," Grace said. "*Pura vida!*" She turned on her heel, walking directly toward the damn Mercury Sable parked in front of the market.

"Stop!" Noah said, his brain spinning. The drug dealers would be coming out of the market any minute.

He rushed toward her, putting his hat and sunglasses back on. Noah got a glimpse through the paned glass window. The two men in cowboy hats were checking out at the register.

Grace paused in front of the market, peering inside. "Do you think they'd have any snow globes in there?"

"No!" Noah said, barreling toward her. He needed to get her out of their line of sight. He hoisted her up and over his shoulder, taking off in a dead sprint.

"Noah Greene, put me down!"

Noah cringed at his name echoing off the storefront walls. He didn't dare look back to see if they had heard.

A few yards ahead, he spotted a tour bus parked along the street with flashing letters that read DINNER CRUISE. This was his chance to get the hell out of town.

Grace squealed. "Noah! Where are you taking me?" She was laughing at least.

"I've got a better idea," Noah huffed as he ran toward the tour bus.

She pounded on his back with weak fists, laughing and giggling as she bumped along on his shoulder. "Noah!"

By the time he got to the tour bus, he was completely out of breath. He set Grace on the steps and jumped on. Slowly he jutted his head out the door to peek. The two men in cowboy hats stood outside the market, staring directly at him.

CHAPTER SIXTEEN

"What the hell?" Grace said. "Where are we going?"

"Go find us a seat," Noah said, pulling out his wallet. "Please." He turned back to the bus driver, speaking in Spanish. If Grace didn't know any better, she would have thought he was bartering. Noah pointed to his watch and then looked up at Grace, who hadn't moved a muscle.

"Sit down," Noah said softly, pleading with his eyes.

Grace twisted her hair around her finger and bit her lip. It was unnerving to see Noah look so worried, but she did as she was told and turned around. She looked upon the velvet shuttle bus seats. Some were taken by families with small kids. Others were taken by couples. And in the far back of the bus was a group of high school-aged students.

Grace found two seats halfway down the aisle and sat down. A moment later, she heard the bus's engine roar to life. The doors closed. Noah strode down the aisle, his eyes fixed out the back window.

"Noah, I swear to God, if you are kidnapping me—"

"Relax, Blue Eyes," Noah said, sitting down. "My kidnapping days are over."

"What?"

"I'm kidding." Noah chuckled. "Obviously." He looked over his shoulder again.

The bus driver came over the speaker, announcing their departure, and instructed everyone to take their seats. Not a moment later, he pulled forward.

Noah's eyes were still glued to the back of the bus, his forehead wrinkled.

"Is everything okay?" Grace said, tugging on his shirt. She tried following his line of sight but found the high school students sitting angelically in their seats. Through the back window, there was nothing out of the ordinary. People crossed the streets. Cars honked their horns. A homeless white man was digging through the garbage.

"I'm fine," Noah said, turning around to face her. "I just..."

Grace leaned closer, waiting for more. "You just what?"

Noah's eyes searched hers. "I saw something that looked a little shady."

"Shady?" Grace squeaked. "What was shady?"

"Nothing," Noah said, his voice noticeably higher. "I saw some men watching us, and I didn't want to take any chances, that's all."

"Like pickpockets?"

Noah audibly swallowed. "Yeah, something like that. I didn't want them snatching your purse."

"Oh." He was being protective. Grace's chest warmed.

"I was just being paranoid," Noah said, wrapping his arm around her shoulders. "We can relax now and have fun." The weight of his arm was like a shield. She felt safe and warm, and she was touched that he had been looking out for her purse.

"Where are we going?"

Noah's eyes glittered. "It's a surprise."

Grace narrowed her eyes at Noah. "Noah Greene. The last time you surprised me—"

"You jumped off a platform, flew through the air, and had a great time," Noah said, wiggling his eyebrows.

"I don't think I have it in me to do something like that again."

"Nah. This is much tamer."

"Does it include food? Because I'm starving."

"It does, actually." Noah looked behind him again, inadvertently showing off the giant embroidered scorpion on the back of his new shirt. He had been in such a hurry to buy a new one, he hadn't thought to turn around in the store's mirror to see that he looked like a *Mortal Kombat* superfan.

"Hey," Grace said, tapping on his shoulder. "I'm over here."

"I'm sorry." He turned back. "I'm distracted. You deserve better." He took her hand in his, clasping around her fingers.

She cradled his hand in her lap and looked up into his weary eyes. "For a surfer guy, you sure do worry a lot."

Noah snorted. "I'm not usually like this."

"Oh?"

He ran his free hand through his hair, shaking his head. "I'm usually a carefree kind of guy."

"Then why have you been so jumpy?"

Noah stared deep into her eyes. He waited a moment before saying, "Knowing you makes the stakes so much higher."

Grace's lips parted. Her breathing slowed, then she patted him gently across his face. "That is one of your cheesiest lines yet."

He smiled, relief washing over his features, and grabbed her hand and pinned it down to her lap. "Did you just slap me?"

"Don't be so overdramatic. It was a slight pat. And I'd do it again."

"Is that a promise?" His eyes glistened.

Heat crept up her neck. She could feel her own freckles darken from the flush, and she looked away.

Noah leaned down, his lips wisped against her ear, sending a shiver down her spine. "I love it when you blush like that," he whispered.

Grace trembled from the center of her legs to the tips of her ears. She had to remind herself to swallow. She turned, about ready to ravage his mouth when the tour guide's voice came over the speaker. "*Hola*, passengers of the Tortuga Dinner Cruise. We will be at the docks in just a moment. Please have your IDs ready if you plan to drink our complimentary rum punch."

Grace's eyes grew wide. "A dinner cruise?"

"Yeah, is that okay?"

Grace felt as if she could burst. It was the most romantic thing she could have ever dreamed of. An evening under the stars, surrounded by the peaceful ocean, with him. She was living in her very own Hallmark movie.

She tucked away the thought that Hallmark movies eventually came to an end with a happily-ever-after that wasn't possible for them.

This was her night. This was her chance to live her life to the fullest even if it was temporary.

Pura vida, she told herself. "I couldn't think of anything more perfect."

"Good." Noah smiled. "I may not be able to sweep you off your feet with a white horse, so I'm hoping a catamaran will do."

Grace beamed before looking down at his hands, entangled with hers, resting in her lap. Something was missing.

Something he had only moments ago. "Noah, where's your watch?"

"My watch?" Noah said. The same watch he used to barter the bus driver with? The very thing that helped them get on a tour bus without being registered for the tour? The watch his father had given him as a graduation present...

You will do great things had been inscribed on the back.

A piece of his heart had broken off when he exchanged the watch for a quick getaway. But he had no other choice. He had to make sure Grace was safe.

Despite making eye contact with the men, they didn't seem to be following him. Noah had checked multiple times to confirm.

"What watch? I don't have a watch," Noah lied, guilt festering at the back of his throat.

"That's so weird," Grace said. "I could have sworn you were wearing a watch earlier."

"That's weird." His heart sank into his chest a bit more. He hated lying to her. "Hey, look. We're here," he said, grateful for the distraction.

The bus pulled up to a parking lot where a large white catamaran was parked off the dock.

"Wow," Grace rasped. With her eyes glued to the boat, Noah took out his phone and texted Clara.

Noah: The cartel guys are in Jaco. I spotted them on Pastor Diaz and Lapa Verde.

. . .

Clara: What are you doing in Jaco? I thought you were lying low. What do they look like?

Noah: Cowboy hats and boots. Light skin. Dark hair. Jeans. 30-40 years old.

Clara: Head to the police department so you can file a report. They'll need a full description.

"I'm so excited," Grace said, nudging his arm. The tour bus was unloading in front of the docks.

Noah looked through the windows for the Sable, but it was nowhere in sight.

He helped Grace out of her seat and walked down the bus aisle, ignoring the grin from the bus driver, who was currently flaunting Noah's titanium watch on his wrist. Noah stepped out onto the cement lot, leaving a piece of himself behind.

"Do we just follow them?" Grace said, slipping her arm around his.

Noah peered at the giant catamaran. CHARMING TOURS was painted along the side. The afternoon sun reflected off the freshly washed hull of the boat. Caribbean music played from the front deck, and their tour guide was holding a tray of plastic cups with pink punch and tiny umbrellas that he handed out to people with yellow wristbands.

Noah shouldn't be there. He should be taking Clara's orders and finding a cab to the police department. He should tell Grace what was going on and why he had been acting so weird. But this was his last night with her. He couldn't ruin their evening with a giant confession and an evening under interrogation. He'd blow his chance with her forever.

If the cartel guys had known it was him, they would have followed the bus. Plain and simple. Right? It was probably a mere coincidence that they were in the same town.

There was no tracking device, he reminded himself. They were not in town for him. They couldn't be.

Pulling out his phone, he texted Clara one last time.

Noah: I'll go as soon as I can.

Tomorrow, he told himself. He would go tomorrow.

The boat swayed slightly underfoot, and Grace clung to Noah's arm for stability. She peered over the railing toward the giant green rock out in the distance. "Is that where we are going?"

"Yeah," Noah said. "Tortuga Island. I overheard a guy say that people go to the island to snorkel." He gestured to the snorkel equipment piled in a corner. Grace looked around and realized everyone was wearing a swimsuit or a swimsuit cover-up.

"I'm sorry we don't have bathing suits to get the full experience," Noah said.

Grace shrugged. "It's okay. This is enough adventure for me. I've never been on a catamaran before."

The ocean breeze whipped her hair around her face and in her mouth. Grace pulled a hair tie from her wrist and looped it around until she had a loose ponytail. She felt

Noah's eyes watching her while she draped her hair over her shoulder.

A few strands loosened around her face, but she had it under control now.

Noah licked his lower lip, reaching for her hair as if she had something out of place. "May I?" he asked, waiting for the tilt of Grace's chin to proceed with catching a flyaway lock that Grace must have missed. He tucked it behind her ear, grazing her earlobe.

Grace shuddered under his touch, and his eyes flared, as if he knew what his touch was doing to her.

His finger grazed her ear again.

Grace closed her eyes, savoring the slow trail of his finger down her neck. A current rushed through her. She wanted to bottle it up—the shimmering energy that sizzled in her veins.

Noah's finger traipsed to her shoulder blade, lingering there, then trailed down her back to the hem of her tank top before pulling back. The wave of goose bumps he left behind called to him for more.

More.

Grace opened her eyes to find Noah's impish grin, his eyes sparkling with reflections of the sun off the metal bow.

"Flirt," she breathed.

His lips twitched, but he said nothing.

Moments later, the catamaran roared to life. People gathered around the center of the boat, and one of the crew members demonstrated how to put on a life jacket.

Grace listened intently to the safety instructions while Noah couldn't seem to take his eyes off her. His gaze heated her skin.

"Pay attention," Grace whispered, nudging him on the arm. "This is important."

His mouth slid into an easy smile as he turned his head.

She felt his eyes on her from time to time. They nudged

each other with their elbows until she was giggling and receiving looks from others on the boat who were trying to listen to the snorkeling rules and restrictions.

After the crew finished their instructions, they found a spot to stand at the edge of the boat, as the catamaran took off toward the island.

They watched the water splashing against the side as they took up speed. Rogue droplets landed on Grace's hands gripping the railing.

The same thrill she felt earlier had returned—a rush that coursed through her veins. It opened her heart like a window letting in fresh air.

Her whole life she had avoided trouble, avoided parties and drinking and going out on adventures because she assumed it wasn't worth the risk. But Noah made her see what she'd been missing. The thrill and the fun and the happiness that came with giving life a try. Experiencing what life has to offer.

Who would have thought it would take a sexy surfer boy with a megawatt smile to bring her out of hiding? But he was more than a pretty face, if she were being honest. He was sweet and thoughtful and listened better than any other man she had been with before. He cared about what she had to say. His eyes didn't gloss over when she talked about herself.

He was a breath of fresh air, and she couldn't wait to spend the rest of the night with him, whether he knew it or not.

The sky turned gold and pink with big streaks of yellow orange. Grace breathed in the ocean smells, filling her lungs, letting the soft wind caress her face.

She stole a glance at Noah. His face had softened.

"You're glowing," he said, the sun reflecting off the gold flecks in his eyes.

Grace wrapped an arm around his waist and pulled him in for a hug, resting her cheek against his chest. "I'm happy."

He felt so good in her arms, sturdy and strong. It was painful to know that this would end soon.

Grace squeezed before she released him, setting one hand on the cool railing and the other gripping the rum punch that she had barely touched. "Thank you for today."

Noah cupped her chin, tilting it up so he could place his sweet rum punch lips to her mouth. Their kiss started soft, but a feral urge had her gripping the back of his head, pressing harder, wanting more.

Every breath she took was his. Every beat of her heart was for him. She slipped her tongue over his, savoring the taste of him, like a watermelon Jolly Rancher.

Running her hand through his hair, she pressed herself into him, feeling the not-so-subtle hardness between his legs. His tongue retaliated, sweeping the inside of her mouth in a delicious wave that left her boneless and quaking underneath him.

The boat had quieted around them; the chatter had stopped. It wasn't until someone cleared their throat that Grace realized they had an audience. She broke free from Noah's kiss and looked aboard the catamaran to find the entire crew staring at her with their mouths agape.

The cheering and clapping that ensued made her blush so hot it burned her cheeks.

"This is mortifying," she said, looking away, covering her face.

Noah chuckled, pulling her in close as if he were protecting her from the embarrassment.

"I wasn't expecting people to be watching," she said.

"Comes with the territory when you're in public."

Grace managed to avoid eye contact with everyone on board until they arrived on the island.

As the people filed off the catamaran, an older lady appeared to be on her own. She struggled to walk down the ramp with her cane.

"I'm going to go help her," Noah said. "Do you mind?"

"Not at all," Grace said. Her heart almost doubled in size.

Noah bent to greet the white-haired lady in Spanish. He offered to take her cane and stuck his elbow out for her to grab.

The woman looked grateful, smiling up at Noah with a big, wrinkly grin. She threaded her hand around his arm and clutched the railing with the other.

Grace followed them down the wobbly ramp, watching Noah help her off until she was steady on the beach's sand. "*Gracias*," the woman said. She proceeded to talk to Noah in Spanish, pointing to a man who looked like he could be the woman's son. The man took the cane from Noah and thanked him profusely in English. "She's so stubborn, this one. I was in the bathroom for only a minute."

"Bah," the woman scoffed.

"Nice shirt, by the way," the man said. Noah was still completely clueless.

"Thanks," Noah said, drawing his eyebrows together. He turned to exchange a confused look with Grace.

Grace just shrugged her shoulders.

"That was really nice of you," Grace said, slipping her arm through his. There was a lingering smell of lavender around them. "You have a way with older women."

Noah laughed nervously, scratching the back of his head. "It was nothing."

"Come on, let's get something to eat. I'm starving."

They trekked across the sand, coming across a patch of picnic tables with string lights dangling between palm trees. Music played from a portable speaker on a folding table with large buffet-style pans of food. Warm spices mixed with the ocean scent filled her nostrils. Her stomach grumbled in response.

They strolled to the back of the line and picked up paper plates and plastic forks. Noah loaded up his plate so full with different types of meat, beans, rice, plantains, and tamales he needed a second plate to bear the weight.

"You have quite the appetite," Grace said.

"I'm a growing boy," he said, popping a sliced plantain in his mouth. "I also haven't eaten much today."

Grace picked a table on the sand closest to the water. The sun had set, and the sky morphed into an indigo blue with tiny stars sprinkled across the heavens.

"I wonder how the baby sea turtles are doing right now," she said, glancing out at the dark ocean. "I wonder if they're happy."

Noah set his fork down and took a swig of his beer. "I bet they are. I'd be happy too if I lived in the ocean all day."

Grace had to stop herself from frowning.

Of course he would live in the ocean all day if he could. He was made for this place, for a carefree life where he could shuck the responsibilities of his family's business and take a random vacation whenever he wanted.

It shouldn't upset her that this life was suited for him, but it was a nagging reminder that their friendship, or whatever they could call it, would be over tomorrow.

"What happened?"

"What do you mean?"

"Your face," Noah said, pointing at it. "All of a sudden you look sad."

"It's nothing," Grace said, pushing away her inner brooding. She was tired of letting her brain ruin everything. She smiled brightly. "I'm fine."

Noah narrowed his eyes at her, holding them steady while he chewed his food.

Grace's phone buzzed, shaking them out of their stare off. Aunt Judy.

"I have to take this." She straightened her spine and picked up the phone. "Is everything okay?"

"Grace?" Aunt Judy shouted from what sounded like across the room.

"Aunt Judy, can you hear me?"

"I can hear you just fine."

"What's going on?"

"Tamara quit."

"She *what?*"

"Good riddance, if you ask me. Lousy cook."

Grace hunched over, her head in her hands. "Aunt Judy! Tamara was the best one we had!"

"Thanks, Grace," Tamara's voice came on the line, as clear as day. "But I'm not quitting because of your aunt. I got an offer to work at a nursing home."

"You did?" Grace gasped.

There was a shuffling noise before Tamara spoke again. "I'm sorry. It was a hard decision to make, but the home pays better than Sunrise."

"Wait, Tamara, please. There's got to be something we can work out."

"The decision's done. My last day is tomorrow."

Grace played with her ponytail, wrapping the end around her finger. "No one at Sunrise can replace you, Tamara. We're going to miss you so much. Well, *I'm* going to miss you so much."

"I'll miss you too, darling. And somehow God will spite me, and I'll end up missing this cranky ol' thorn in my side too."

"Thorn in *your* side?" Aunt Judy scoffed in the background. "Have you eaten your own cooking? You're the nasty thorn in my withering side."

"Aunt Judy, be nice!" Grace scolded.

"What? She made a mushy casserole without any salt. It was like she dipped rice cakes into water and served it in a bowl."

"I've gotta run," Tamara said, ignoring Aunt Judy's insults as she normally did. "Looks like the night shift just got here."

"Don't let the door hit you on the way out," Aunt Judy shouted.

"Bye, Tamara. Thank you for everything."

Grace groaned. Dealing with other home care workers was such a pain. She could never trust them the way she trusted Tamara.

The phone went silent for a moment.

"Aunt Judy, are you there?"

"I'm sorry, dear, the night-shift worker just stepped in, and he's a handsome-lookin' fella."

"Please promise me you'll be on your best behavior."

"Uh, yes, I believe you're right. Tonight is bath night."

"I didn't say it was—"

"Yep, that kink in my back has been bothering me for a while. I could use a little massage too."

"Aunt Judy…"

"Bye, dear. I'll talk to you tomorrow."

The phone clicked off and Grace stared at it, shaking her head.

"Is everything okay?"

"We just lost our best home care worker. Her last day is tomorrow. And now I'm worried my aunt is going to hit on the new night-shift guy."

"Oh damn."

Grace propped her head in her hands. "I don't know what I'm going to do. Sunrise workers are so unreliable, but it's all I can afford. I keep finding reasons to put her in a nursing home, but I can't do that to her. To us."

Noah bit his lip, watching Grace intently. "What's so wrong with a nursing home?"

"Are you kidding me? She'd be alone. I'm the only family she has."

"Doesn't a nursing home have more than just one person in there? Maybe she could make friends."

"My aunt doesn't make friends. She's crotchety as hell."

"Is she like that because of her MS?"

Grace shrugged. "Possibly. She can hardly get around herself. I can only imagine how frustrating that would be."

"I see," Noah said. "What about you? Don't you need your space from her?"

"Yea, but not that kind of space," Grace said. "She's all I have too. We keep each other company."

Grace took a bite of her rice and beans. She sipped her punch, noticing that Noah was still staring at her.

"What?"

"Nothin'," Noah said, drinking his punch. His eyebrows inched up his forehead.

"Seriously, what is it?"

Noah set his punch down. He opened his mouth but promptly shut it.

"Tell me," Grace urged.

"I just think that you might be using your aunt as a crutch."

"Excuse me?" Grace felt her hackles rise.

Noah shifted on the bench. "You said so yourself. You never leave the house except for work. You don't experience anything because you're scared of what might happen."

"Yeah, so?"

"Well, you're kind of using your aunt as an excuse to not live your life."

"What are you talking about? I'm here, aren't I? I'm literally on an island in the middle of the Pacific Ocean."

"You're here now, but what is your life going to be like when you get home? Are you going to stay in and watch Christmas flicks instead of living your life like a twenty-something-year-old should?"

"Just because I'm not out drinking and bar-hopping and stuff doesn't mean I'm not living. You saw me out there today. I freaking *zip-lined*. I can do stuff. I can have fun."

"And how do you intend to do that when you're having to stay home and babysit your aunt?"

Grace blew hot air out of her nose like a dragon ready to unleash her fire. "I don't know yet, but I'll figure it out."

"Sure." Noah folded his arms, a challenging glint in his eyes.

Grace huffed. "I can have fun. I *am* fun."

"I know you're fun," Noah said with a sly smile. "I'm not talking about that."

"Then what *are* you talking about?"

Noah hesitated, as if he knew what he was about to say would tick Grace off. He traced lazy circles on the table, not meeting her gaze.

"Just say it," Grace said, challenging him.

"I think you're letting your aunt dictate your life choices."

"My aunt isn't dictating my life."

"You told me you wanted to be a preschool teacher, right?" He didn't wait for a response. "Then what's stopping you?"

His eyes burned into hers, cutting into her soul.

Would she rather deal with a room full of crying four-year-olds than people like Jane?

Yes.

Would she rather wipe boogers off tiny little faces and put Band-Aids on scraped knees than spend her time making other people rich?

Absolutely yes.

But the cost was too great.

"You don't know what it's like to be left behind." The ache at the bottom of her throat made it hard to go on. "To be abandoned."

Noah cut in, shaking his head. "But you wouldn't be abandoning her, Grace. You see that, right?"

Grace's jaw tightened, hating the fact that *she* was the one who would feel abandoned, not her aunt.

This whole time she had thought she was doing this self-less thing for her aunt, keeping her at home, when in reality Grace was the one who was being selfish by not letting her go.

Noah leaned back, retreating. It wasn't pity that settled into his eyes but understanding.

"It's okay to be scared of being left behind. You've gone through a lot in your life."

"I'm not ready for her to leave," Grace said tacitly.

"I see that, and I'm sorry. It wasn't my place to push you on it." The moonlight illuminated his profile as he stared out into the distance. "I'm sorry," he said again, just barely a whisper.

"I will let go when I'm ready to let go," Grace said. "And in the meantime, I will find ways to get out more. I don't know how yet, but I'll figure it out. I know something needs to change."

Grace watched two young boys dart across the sand and splash into the water. Their mother chased after them, an exasperated but happy look on her face. She waved at one of the snorkelers who beamed their flashlight in her direction.

The cluster of snorkelers bobbed their heads in and out of the water, and the children played. The water on this part of the island was calm. The waves barely made a fuss, making it safe for children and night snorkelers to roam.

An idea struck. Grace stood up from the table, her eyes brightening.

"Where are you going?" Noah said.

"Proving my earlier point." Grace slipped out of her Keds. She stuffed them under the picnic table bench and dug her feet into the cool sand. She backed away slowly, much to Noah's surprise as he watched her from the bench with his head cocked to the side.

Grace bit her lip, turning toward the water, stepping over fallen leaves and seaweed until the ground beneath her became cold and wet, the gentle waves kissing her heels.

She could do this.

"What are you doing?" Noah called out over the music blaring behind him.

"I'm going in," Grace yelled back, not bothering to look behind her. She stared at her feet, watching the gentle wave roll over her toes. It was cold at first, causing Grace to suck in her breath. But it quickly normalized, giving her the courage to go ankle deep.

"I thought you were afraid of the ocean."

Grace smirked. "This spot seems safe enough, don't you think?" She stepped farther into the cool water, now at her knees. She wasn't sure if she would go any farther, but the idea of immersing herself in the ocean gave her a thrill that she would have never expected.

"You comin'?" she said, looking over her shoulder.

Noah shot up from the table and jogged across the sand, kicking off his sandals and dropping his phone with them.

"You don't have to do this," Noah said.

"Do what?" Grace said innocently.

"Prove to me you're brave. I already know you're brave."

"I'm not proving to you that I'm brave. I'm proving that I will do what I want, when I want to."

Noah's gaze became smoldering, warming her body despite the cold bite of the water hitting her thighs.

Stepping farther into the water, the ocean soaked the hem of her shorts. Not able to punish herself any longer, she sank all the way in, letting it swallow her whole.

It took her breath away.

When she popped her head up, water dripped down her nose. She found Noah standing on the beach still, his mouth open wide.

"I can't believe you just did that."

"Are you coming or what?" Grace said, laughing. The water dripped off her eyelashes, and she swished around underwater, trying to keep her body temperature up.

Noah unbuttoned his shirt and tossed it to the ground. He froze.

Something had caught his eye. He reached to grab his shirt and held it up under the moonlight.

"What the hell?" he said, staring at the embroidered scorpion on his shirt. "Has this been here the whole time?" His face scrunched up, eyes darting from the design to Grace and back again.

Grace couldn't hide her mirth any longer. She burst into a fit of giggles, clutching her stomach.

"No wonder I've been getting so many weird looks."

Grace snorted before dipping her head underwater to hide. When she reappeared, she heard Noah shout, "You knew."

"I kind of liked it," Grace said, still laughing. "It made me feel like you could break out into karate at any moment."

Noah shook his head at her, an admonishing smile across his face. Then he shucked off his shorts.

"Noah! You're not supposed to be in your underwear!"

"Nobody cares," he said, wading into the water, not even bothering to look behind him. He was right. Nobody was looking as far as Grace could tell. The kids were splashing and kicking up sand, and the adults had begun dancing under the string lights.

Noah approached her like a crocodile stalking his prey, his head halfway above water, his piercing eyes fixed on her.

"You set me up. You let me parade around in that ridiculous shirt."

"I thought you knew!"

"Liar." Noah reached for her waist, tickling her sides.

"Noah! Stop!" Grace said, squealing. She got a mouthful of water in the process. The briny tang of the ocean coated her tongue as she spit it out.

Noah stopped, and his face dropped with concern. "Are you okay?"

Grace splashed him in the face. "I'm not the best swimmer."

"Say no more." He grabbed her hips and lifted her up. She was halfway out of the water before he coaxed her to wrap her legs around his waist. "Hang on to me."

She settled against his body, sliding her arms around his neck, connected at the waist. Grace felt the heat of him despite the cool night air. His mouth was a breath away.

His eyes darkened as he held her steady against the push and pull of the swaying ocean. They stared into each other's eyes, the playfulness between them replaced by something deeper. Darker. Carnal.

The soft murmur of voices pulled them out of the moment as they directed their attention to the night snorkelers coming out of the water, a reminder that they were not alone.

"Let's swim over there," he said, motioning toward the end of the beach, away from the muffled music drowning over the ocean waves.

Grace gave him a quick nod and clung to him as he swam

along the beach's edge. The pointed tip of land was covered by fallen trees, but a sandy beach extended just beyond it.

"Do you want to go a little farther?" Noah said. "Beyond that point?"

Grace looked back toward the busy beach where the children played and string lights illuminated the dance party fueled by rum punch and Caribbean drums. Then she looked toward the dark quiet beach, slightly hidden behind the fallen palms.

"Let's do it," Grace said.

Noah's eyes sparkled. "Come and hang on behind me," he said, maneuvering her so she could cling to his neck. They glided around the fallen trees and found themselves in a secluded alcove.

Their own private beach.

The moonlight made everything a silvery hue. It was quiet too. The trees on that little patch of land muffled the music from the other side.

"It's so peaceful," Grace said, wading in the water. She grabbed his shoulders to hold herself steady, unable to touch the bottom.

His breath was ragged from the swim. His face was flushed.

"Do you think anyone can see us?" Grace whispered. She stopped and stared into Noah's eyes. Drops of water clung to his eyelashes.

"I don't think so."

Grace licked her lip, tasting the salty ocean, and her eyes dropped to his perfect mouth.

She had one night. One night to let go of her inhibitions and just be. To live her life the way she wanted.

Grace placed a kiss on the corner of his mouth, then moved to his bottom lip, sucking gently, inviting him to kiss her back.

Noah dove toward her mouth, claiming her lips. He planted a firm grip on her ass; a hand traced a line from her neck down her chest. The wet fabric of her tank top clung to her bra, and her hardened nipples underneath ached to be touched.

Grace moaned into his mouth, arching her back, brushing against his chest.

He peeled himself from her mouth, staring into her eyes. His mouth was swollen and red. Noah seemed to be waiting for her signal to proceed.

Grace grabbed one of his hands, an answer to his silent question, and placed it on her breast, squeezing his hand, encouraging him to go on.

Noah took over, massaging and kneading, pressing himself against her. His tongue parted her lips, and he stormed her mouth.

Tugging and raking his hair, Grace breathed him in. Hot breath and nipping teeth devoured her throat and the arch of her neck. She tilted her hips, seeking the pressure to ease the ache between her legs.

His fingertips found her knees, sliding up her thighs in long strokes, leaving burning trails in their wake. In each stroke, he climbed a little farther up her leg. When he reached the hem of her shorts, Grace sucked in a breath.

"Is this okay?"

Grace bit her lip, nodding her head. There was no room for words, not with the heavy air taking up so much space, her chest aching for that final climb. His fingerprint trailed along the inside of her leg, only a few inches from her panty line. There would be no turning back once he reached the apex of her legs. She was already so close from falling over the edge.

"When you bite your lip like that," Noah husked, his sea-green eyes a pure reflection of the water surrounding them.

"It does things to me." His thumb made the lazy climb to the hem of her underwear, tracing the seam painstakingly slow. Her legs quaked in anticipation.

Grace's chest rose and fell with the waves, and she arched her neck until she saw the stars above them. Noah dragged his tongue down to the crook of her shoulder, his teeth grazing her skin. His fingers lightly caressed the edge of her panties.

Grace released a sound from her throat she didn't even know she could make. Animalistic and wild. She would have been embarrassed if he hadn't whispered in her ear, "That was so hot. And I haven't even touched you yet."

"You're touching me now." Grace panted, wholly focused on the fingers on her legs.

"Not yet," Noah said, his eyes full of mischief. "I haven't even started."

Grace whimpered, unable to imagine how good he'd feel when he finally soothed the aching fire between her legs.

A whistle blowing from the catamaran rang out.

"Shit," Noah said. "We gotta go."

Grace kissed him one last time. "This isn't the end, is it?"

Noah bit her lower lip. He looked up into her eyes. "This is only the beginning."

CHAPTER SEVENTEEN

Noah draped a protective arm over Grace's shoulders, guiding her through the resort lobby. With the cartel in town, he was keeping a careful watch for anything out of the ordinary.

Noah veered away from the pool and down a stone path through the garden. Footsteps echoing somewhere in the distance made Noah jerk his neck toward the sound, but it was another couple on a midnight stroll.

Then a rustling in a palm tree had Noah jump.

"Relax," Grace said, tightening her arm around his waist. "It's not like Jane is going to pop out of a tree. She should be in bed by now."

It wasn't Jane he was worried about, although she *was* a great excuse for his jumpy behavior.

He should have gone to the police and filed a report, but then again, he would have missed out on the perfect date with Grace.

"I am relaxed," he lied.

"You're flinching at the wind," she deadpanned.

"Am not." More lies.

"She texted me an hour ago saying she was heading to bed early so she can go for a run in the morning."

Noah paused, halting Grace along with him. "Jane's in her room?"

"Yeah."

Noah stopped in his tracks. "Do you want to head to my room instead of yours? So we don't risk waking her up?"

Grace looked up at him, her eyes sparkling. "What makes you think we'd be too loud for her to hear?"

"Based on the sound you made in the ocean, I think there's a pretty good chance you might wake up the entire resort."

Under the moonlight, Noah could see the color rush to her cheeks, and he loved how easily riled she could get.

"You must be pretty sure of yourself if you think I'll be making any noise," she said breathlessly.

"Blue Eyes, it's the only thing I'm sure of."

The rise and fall of her chest quickened. She fluttered her eyelashes while she said, "Lead the way."

Noah didn't have to be told twice. He pivoted her around, taking her in the opposite direction. The glowing garden lights illuminated their path to his room.

They were both still damp from their dip in the ocean. The cool night breeze sent a chill down his neck. His teeth chattered as he pulled out his hotel card.

"Are you really that cold?" Grace teased.

Noah shivered. "The temperature dropped twenty degrees, and my underwear is still wet. My balls' teeth are chattering."

Grace snickered.

"How are you not cold?" he added.

She had switched out her wet tank top for his dry scorpion shirt. She wore it all the way home. It seemed like an appropriate punishment for not telling him about it earlier. *Sneaky little minx.* But her shorts were soaked, and her bra had left wet circles at her chest. She had to have been just as cold as he was.

"Spend a winter in northern Michigan, then tell me if you think this weather is cold."

"Brr," Noah said, shuddering. "No, thank you." He opened the door to his room, peeking in to make sure the cartel hadn't ransacked it. "Hold there for just a minute." He stepped in the bathroom and flipped the light on.

No drug lords in the shower.

He moved toward the side table and pulled the lamp's cord, illuminating his room with a warm glow.

No drug lords under the bed or in the closet either.

"All right, you can come in," he said. "Had to make sure my room was picked up." He wasn't lying entirely. "I haven't perfected the art of organized chaos like you."

Noah noticed the playful gleam in Grace's eyes had blown out. She went into the bathroom and hung her wet tank top over the shower rail.

"What's wrong? You were happy just a minute ago." Noah opened his arms to her, bringing her into a hug.

Grace didn't melt into him the way she had before. Her spine was rigid, and her arms hung limp by her sides. Her cold damp shorts pressed against his thigh, but Noah tightened his hold anyway.

"I'm sorry," Grace said into Noah's shirt. "I'm just having a hard time knowing this is all coming to an end soon."

"I didn't realize that was bothering you."

"It doesn't bother you that I'm leaving tomorrow?"

Noah looked into her aquamarine pools. "Are you kidding? Of course it does. I'm trying not to think about it."

Grace's eyes searched his. "Really?"

"I don't think I'll be able to go a day without looking into those beautiful blue eyes."

Grace looked away. "That sounds like one of your lines."

Noah placed his finger under her chin, turning her to face him. "I'm serious. I'm not ready to let you go."

Grace playfully shoved his chest. "You're going to forget about me by the time I touch down for my layover."

"That's not true," Noah said, clenching his jaw. "I could never forget you." He leaned in for a kiss, but she stopped him with her delicate fingertips on his mouth.

"As much as I want my own Hallmark love story, it is just not in the cards for me."

"Don't say that," Noah said, clasping his hand around her fingers still lingering at his lips. He dipped the tip of her pointer in his mouth and sucked.

Grace released a shaky breath, staring at his mouth while he worked his magic, gliding his tongue around the tiny grooves of her fingerprint.

"You're distracting me," she rasped.

"Precisely the point." He moved to her middle finger, wrapping his mouth around the tip.

Grace's lips parted, her chest rising and falling with jagged breaths.

"I can't plan for tomorrow. Or the next day. Or the day after that. I don't have the luxury of being able to think that far ahead right now." He cupped her face. "But I do know this —you're here now, and I really, really like you."

"You do?"

"We don't have to do anything you don't want to do. Okay? This is *your* night. If you want to watch a chick flick, we'll watch a chick flick. If you want to sleep, we'll sleep. As long as I can be the little spoon."

That cracked a smile. *Finally.*

The flicker of light in her eyes was back. She stepped away from him; the corner of her mouth had tucked into a coy smile. Her fingers played with the first button of her shirt until it flayed open.

"What are you doing?" Noah said.

Grace unbuttoned another. "You said this was my night," she whispered. "I'm doing what I want."

Noah's blood warmed under the spell she cast with her eyes. "What is it that you want, exactly?"

"You," she said, biting her lip. Her fingers lingered on the next button by her chest.

Noah swallowed once.

"I'm tired of letting life pass by because I'm scared." She unleashed another button, her pink bra exposed.

"What are you scared of, Blue Eyes?"

She looked to her feet for a moment before flicking her eyes back up to meet his. "I'm not anymore," she said softly. "I just want to enjoy this night with you."

One night with Grace would not be enough. It could never be enough. When she got on that plane tomorrow, it would destroy him.

"Grace, maybe we should slow—"

"Shh." Grace hushed him, placing her finger over her puckered lips. Her eyes were smoldering hot.

Noah's mouth fell open as she released another button, revealing her sweet little navel.

"I...," Noah rasped, unable to finish his thought. His mind had turned to scrambled eggs.

Grace undid the final button, letting the shirt slide down her shoulders, onto the floor.

Noah sucked in a breath at the sight of her tiny waist. Freckles spanned across her chest, dipping behind the satin fabric of her bra.

His fingers twitched, wanting this moment to never end, wanting days and days of this kind of anticipation that scorched through his body.

Grace slid her thumb under her waistband. They should talk before it got too—"Fark"—

She tilted her head. "Did you just say *fark?*"

Noah laughed. "I'm sorry. I have no control over what's coming out of my mouth right now."

Grace smiled, resuming her task. She unhooked the button of her shorts and peeled them from her hips, sliding them down her legs until they flopped on the floor.

The triangle of white cotton underwear taunted him, begged to be yanked and torn into shreds.

She tucked her lower lip between her teeth and stared at him through hooded eyes. Her hands reached behind her back, and the familiar sound of clasps rubbing together had Noah's heart leaping up his throat.

The thin straps of her bra toppled down her arms to the heap of clothes by her feet. A sly smile reached her eyes.

Fuck me. "Where did you learn to do that?" Noah panted.

"What? Get undressed?" Grace said innocently, stalking toward him.

"That wasn't just getting undressed. That was… I'm pretty sure Hallmark didn't show you how to do what you just did."

"Hallmark didn't show me how to do this either," she said, kneeling on the floor between his legs. She reached for the top of his shorts, unfastening the button, relieving the pressure that had been holding down the rocket in his pants.

Holy.

Fucking.

Hell.

He leaned back on the bed and fell to his elbows. All thoughts of tomorrow escaped into the shadows as she tugged his shorts down, springing him free. Her eyes grew wide at the sight of him.

"Grace." A plea. He wasn't sure if he was asking her to stop or begging her to start.

Her fingertips grazed his thighs, making a slow climb to the base of his shaft. She wrapped her hand around him.

Noah shuddered under her touch.

Grace placed a soft kiss at the tip. Her tongue swirled around the bead of moisture until her mouth was fully wrapped around him. And by god, it was the greatest fucking thing he had ever felt.

His jaw slacked and his heart pounded in his ribs as she took him in, deep. The room blurred around her. Nothing in life mattered but that moment with her mouth around him. Warm. Wet. Perfect.

"My god, Blue Eyes."

She squeezed him with her hand, sliding moisture to the base. Her other hand slid across the comforter until her fingers grazed his. She lingered there for a beat, her mouth moving up and down.

He brushed his thumb against the knuckles of her free hand, letting her know how good it felt. That wicked, perfect tongue of hers swirled in response.

Noah moaned, heat building at his root.

She slid her hand up his, intertwining their fingers while she worked him with her mouth.

She was holding his fucking *hand* while she sucked.

He was a goner.

The heat that had been brewing at his base exploded, a fireball so hot and fierce he didn't see it coming. He unleashed into her mouth, every last drop of him, until he collapsed, boneless and cross-eyed.

Grace climbed up his chest and lay in his arms, her hair draped over his shoulder in tickling waves.

Noah shifted to the side, cupping her face in his hands. "You just ruined me."

A soft, satisfied smile reached her lips.

"I hope you're ready for retaliation, Blue Eyes, because it's my turn to ruin you."

Grace lay on the bed under the covers, waiting. Noah had sprung outside to "grab something." It had become so hot in the room; she was glad he'd left the patio door open a crack. The cool night air flowed in, the ceiling fan swirling it around.

The taste of him still lingered on her tongue, and she loved it. Every moment of it. The way he flexed and moaned. The way his jaw slacked when he came. And above all, it was the look in his eyes that had her tingling all over, like an elixir flowing through her veins. Her body shimmered with the light of a thousand stars.

She had been able to push away her fear of what would come next and just live in the moment.

This is life.

This is pura vida.

She was letting her heart be her guide. Tomorrow be damned. Today is what she needed. The here and now. She was finally free.

A soft knock came at the door, and Grace's body stiffened. Could Noah have come around the other side? She got up from the bed to be sure, taking the sheet along with her. The delicate knock came again.

"Noah?" a woman's voice said behind the front door.

Grace's pulse quickened as she tiptoed toward the door and stood up on her toes to see through the peephole. A fish-eye view of Jane appeared in her bathrobe. Her hair fixed up into a messy bun, her lips glossed.

"Noah, are you there?" Jane's voice, a soft hum through the door.

Grace gasped, then took a step back from the door as if Jane could see through the hole.

Please go away. Please go away.

Grace stood on shaky legs, waiting for a sign that Jane had left.

It was dead silent, apart from the murmuring fan behind her.

Grace willed herself to check the peephole once more. As she took a step toward the door, Jane said, "You said I was beautiful."

Grace's mouth dropped. Her stomach hollowed out.

"This is your last chance before I'm gone forever," Jane said.

A hand clamped on Grace's shoulder, and her body jumped. She held in her shriek as she turned to see Noah and a bewildered look on his face.

"What—"

Grace smothered Noah's mouth with her hands, hushing him, letting the bedsheet fall to the floor.

She stood completely naked in front of him.

Noah's eyes flared, about to reach for her, but Grace gestured toward the door to where Jane stood just beyond it.

Noah's face slacked, forming an O with his mouth. He pointed to the door as if he understood now and stepped lightly toward the door to peek out the peephole.

His shoulder immediately relaxed, and he let out a large sigh. "No one's there."

"Oh good. She's gone." Grace gathered the sheet around her again.

"Who was it?"

Grace scrunched her nose. "Who do you think? It was Jane," she whispered.

Noah ran a hand through his hair, and his lazy smile was back. "I thought... Never mind what I thought," he said, pulling her in for a hug.

Grace loved that he hadn't even considered Jane would come to his door. She felt the tension in her shoulders release. When she looked down, she noticed a palm leaf in his hands; its delicate fronds danced in the moonlight seeping in from the patio door.

"What on earth do you plan on doing with *that*?" Grace said.

A slow smile crept over his face. "Retribution."

"You know I hate surprises," she said weakly. Noah ignored her comment, guiding her back toward the bed where she lay down on the soft mattress.

"I'll need you to—" Noah eyed her white knuckles, clutching the sheet wrapped around her like a protective armor. "Is everything okay?"

Grace pressed her lips together, avoiding his gaze while she gathered her thoughts. "Jane said that you told her she was beautiful."

Noah froze. His eyes grew round, darting around the room. "I said it when she was crying yesterday. It was an instinct."

Grace looked down at her hands, biting her lower lip. She could imagine him consoling her, especially if she had been crying. "It's not a big deal."

"Hey," Noah said, pulling out her lip from between her teeth. "You should know by now I think you are more beautiful and perfect than any other woman on this earth."

Warmth crept back to her cheeks. "Really?"

"Yes, really. Can we forget about her now?" Noah said eagerly. "Or do I need to bust out the Kermit voice again to prove that I *only have eyes for you?*" Midway through, he had transformed his voice into Kermit the Frog.

"You really don't have to—"

Noah interrupted her, bursting into song in his ridiculously cute Muppet voice, swaying to the beat with the snap of his fingers.

Grace covered her mouth. "Noah, this is not necess—"

Noah continued, finishing the main chorus of *I Only Have Eyes for You* with one eye open, waiting for her response.

Grace had folded over from laughing.

"You like that?" Noah said, chuckling at himself.

Grace nodded, beaming. "More, please."

"I'll bust Kermit out again later. Right now I have plans."

"Plans?" Grace squeaked, eyeing the palm leaf in Noah's hand.

"Master plans," he said, dipping his mouth to hers. A kiss brushed her lips, sending a ripple of lust through her body.

"Now," Noah said gently, "lose the sheet."

Grace sucked in a breath. The center of her legs dampened under his command, and she let go of the cotton fabric. Noah shifted his weight back, unwrapping her like a birthday present. His hungry eyes raked over her body.

"You are absolutely perfect," he said, placing the palm leaf on the bed near her feet.

He pulled his shirt off, tossing it toward the desk chair. The glow from the bathroom light illuminated his golden skin and created tiny shadows across his delicious muscles.

"Should I be nervous?" Grace said.

Noah stretched over her body, hovering over her mouth for a moment before he kissed her again. "Absolutely not. I want you to just relax." His fingers circled her kneecap and were gone in a flash. "But first I want to cover your eyes."

"Are you serious?"

"I'm dead serious," he said, grabbing the scorpion shirt

from the ground. He whipped it around a few times until it was a tight black rope. "Can you trust me?"

Grace sucked in a breath, squirming under his blazing stare. She nodded, letting him drape the shirt over her eyes. He tied a loose knot at the back of her head.

She let the darkness consume her vision. She could hear the whoosh of the ceiling fan and the rolling ocean waves through the patio door. She could feel his presence, shifting on the bed until he straddled her legs, his weight pinning her down.

Noah's lips brushed hers in a light kiss, but it felt different than before. Electric. His fingers skimmed her arms, down her waist. Every delicate caress became a roaring wave of pleasure.

The air from the ceiling fan rushed over her bare breasts and made her shiver as she waited for him to touch her again.

She waited patiently. Vulnerable. Exposed. Cherished. And then she waited some more. Waited for what, she wasn't sure. But the absence of his touch had become just as sensual as a kiss. She felt her breath grow more ragged with each fleeting thought of what it would be like with him between her thighs.

"Are you there?" Grace said hoarsely.

"I'm here," Noah said. "I'm just enjoying the view before I begin."

She tried to hold still but felt herself tremble in anticipation.

The tip of the palm leaf grazed her foot, then up her shins. The caress was just soft enough that it didn't tickle. It glided slowly to her kneecaps, swirling around in a fluid motion. A river of particles sprang up her legs, radiated her bones, and settled in her pelvis. The trail continued up her thighs and over her right hip bone.

The velvety prongs circled around her navel. Noah continued with featherlight strokes so fine it brought a sea of gooseflesh from the top of her head to the tips of her toes. With painstakingly slow movement, the fronds reached the peaks of her breasts, circling around and around until her nipples were hard and aching.

"Do you like this?" Noah said.

"Yes," Grace panted. Arching her back in response, Noah trailed the blades down her sternum toward her navel. The leaves teased the skin just below her hip bone, gently brushing inside her thigh and over the thin cotton fabric of her underwear.

Grace moaned, waiting, panting, wanting. She tilted her hips toward the palm leaf to ease the growing ache between her legs, but Noah wasn't done teasing.

The fronds glided up her side in a torturous stroke, leaving her center unattended. He circled her breasts again, and she let out a whimper.

Heat was building at the base of her spine, and she tilted her hips again, searching for anything on him that could release the pressure building inside.

The palm leaf was gone, and she was left alone in the darkness, writhing for him, begging him with her squirming hips.

Noah's finger grazed her stomach, tracing a line down to the edge of the cotton, dipping just enough under the hem that she trembled with desire.

"My god," he said, his finger sliding between her folds. "You are so ready."

Grace squirmed under his touch, pressing up into his hand just before it disappeared.

"You're torturing me," she rasped, a ball of twisted tension growing between her legs. She almost had half a mind to touch herself.

Noah went still again for a long agonizing moment.

"Noah. Please."

She felt the weight of him shift on the bed, lying down along her side. His breath softly caressing her right cheek. His fingers were back at the hem of her underwear, drawing circles in teasing rounds just above the spot she needed it most. And just as one finger slid down the apex, his mouth was on her right breast, sucking her hardened nipple.

Grace let out a groan, and his finger slid farther, circling around that center point that had her writhing under his hand.

He removed it again, his mouth gone too, and he shifted off the bed.

"Noah," Grace grunted. "This is cruel and unusual punish—"

She was interrupted by Noah's grip on her underwear. He slid them down her legs and off her feet. A steady stream of cool air blew between her legs, and her body shuddered. It was all too much. She couldn't take it anymore. She tilted her hips and was met with his warm wet mouth locked onto her sex. His tongue flicking the center in sweet, delicate strokes.

The tightened ball of tension uncoiled slowly, releasing a river of fire through her veins. And with one last suck, the room burst into a million fragments. She was sure she let out a groan that could be heard through the walls, but she didn't care.

After Grace's breath normalized, Noah gently untied the blindfold and slid it off. She looked into his eyes and drank up the passion and fire in their depths.

Grace opened her mouth to speak but was unable to make out words. She felt like a shooting star falling into a black hole.

"Was that okay?" Noah said, giving her a light kiss to her mouth. She tasted herself on his lips.

Grace stared into the eyes of a man who wasn't cocky enough to think that her orgasm was anything less than earth-shattering. His question was real. Earnest. A glimmer of worry creased his forehead.

"That was amazing," she said, pulling his mouth to hers again. "But it wasn't enough."

Noah tilted his head to the side.

"I want all of you," Grace said, staring into his eyes.

Noah traced her shoulder with his finger, sending another wave of pleasure down her spine. He cupped her cheek, and a troubled look flashed across his eyes. "Grace. I'd love to have sex with you..."

Grace scrunched her face. "Why do I sense a *but* coming?"

Noah chewed on his lip before placing a kiss to her nose. "I told myself I wasn't going to go all the way because I was afraid of how I'll feel when you leave. It's one thing to feel empty after a one-night stand, but this"—he pointed to her and then to himself—"this is so much more. I don't think I could bear saying goodbye to you if we make love."

Grace felt her eyes moisten as she stared into his. She reached for his cheeks, pulling him down to her. She couldn't handle another second without his mouth on her skin. His tongue stroked hers, and she arched her body against his until they were flush and writhing against each other.

His knee slid between her legs, putting exquisite pressure against her center until she moaned.

"I don't want to say goodbye to you either," she said.

"What if it doesn't have to end?" he said, stroking the hair out of her face. "I don't know how we'll make it work, but we can figure that out later. All I know is that it doesn't have to end tomorrow."

Why should she deny herself the chance to be with a man who made her feel alive and happy? What possible excuse could be strong enough to keep them from each other? She was done with excuses. It was time for her to live her life like a twenty-something-year-old should.

"I don't know how either," Grace said. "But I want to make it work."

"Really?" The hope in his voice made her chest constrict.

"Yes. Really." She pulled him down to her lips again.

He kissed her with more enthusiasm than before, pulling her in tight to his body and grinding himself onto her until his weight was fully on top of her.

"Are you sure you want to do this?" Noah said, stilling his hands on her stomach.

"I've never been more sure about anything in my life."

Noah smiled and leaped off the bed, grabbing his wallet and pulling out a condom. He rolled it on and settled between her legs, nudging his length against her opening. Grace helped guide him until he filled her, every beautiful inch, pressing on a spot that had her gasping his name.

His thrusts were slow at first. His mouth locked on her collarbone and roamed to the nook of her neck. He kissed and licked and grazed his teeth on her skin, pumping in and out of her until her panting blocked out the sound of the ceiling fan.

She felt like she was at the crossroads between reality and paradise. She couldn't believe how quickly she had fallen for Noah. He had become the center of her universe, and she had become his. Gliding down the zip line had nothing on this thrill.

Noah's thumb found its way to the center point of her legs, circling with whisper-light strokes, building a fire in her core until she burst in flames, her orgasm ripping through her.

His eyes flared, watching her as she came down from her high, and he found his own release. His body flexed and jerked inside her with a sweet rhythm, extending the after-shocks of her orgasm.

After Noah disposed of the condom, he nestled in beside her, resting his head on her chest and wrapped his arms around her body, clinging to her as if he would never let her go. His soft snore lulled her into a deep sleep, and she dreamed of a life with Noah by her side, forever and ever.

CHAPTER EIGHTEEN

The morning light seeped through sheer curtains, creating a hazy purple hue. Noah's naked body was sprawled across the bed. Grace had already spent the better half of an hour watching his back rise and fall with sleep. The contour of his shoulders, the dip of his waist, the smattering of freckles across his skin, all burned in her memory.

Noah stirred, rolling over. A slow smile appeared the moment he opened his eyes.

"Good morning," he said, pulling her into his arms. He kissed the top of her forehead and nestled his knee between her legs, wrapping his ankle around hers. She molded her body against him. He was warm and smooth.

They held each other for a long while, gripping tightly to the here and now.

"You tooted in your sleep," Noah said.

Grace gasped. "I did not!"

"You did," Noah said, snickering. "It was cute. There were two of them in a row. Like the little engine that could. Toot-toot."

"Oh my god," Grace said, her cheeks blazing hot.

Noah tickled her sides until she squealed for mercy. "Toot-toot!" he repeated until she smacked him playfully across that menacing grin.

"You are the worst."

"And you are the most adorable thing on the planet," Noah retorted. "Even when you're hot-boxing me in my own hotel room."

That earned another playful slap across the face.

Noah pretended like she wounded him but then quickly snuggled her into his arms. "Last night was amazing."

"It was," Grace said dreamily. "I'll never look at palm leaves the same way again."

Noah laughed, vibrating Grace's chest along with him. "Me neither," he said into her hair. They held each other for a while after that, Noah drawing languid circles over her skin with his finger while Grace listened to his heartbeat through his chest. Like thunderous waves beating the surf, it was the most beautiful sound in the world.

"I'm going to miss this," she said. "Waking up next to you."

Noah's body tensed, and he stopped his caress. "Me too." Then he resumed, pushing her hair off her shoulder and placing a soft kiss at the top. Grace closed her eyes, relishing in the wake of his kiss.

"We can video chat until we figure out how we're going to see each other again," Noah said.

"You'd be okay with that?"

"Sure. It's better than nothing."

Grace pushed her body up to place a kiss against his sealed lips. The contact gave her the soothing confidence she needed. They just might be able to make this work.

"What are your thoughts on phone sex?" Noah said, a twinkle in his eye.

Grace inched closer, even though they were already entangled. "It'd be a first for me."

"Me too, actually," Noah said, running his hand through his mussed-up hair. "I don't know if I'd be any good at it, but I'll take sex with you any way I can."

"You know what they say," Grace said wickedly. "Practice makes perfect."

A low moan escaped Noah's throat. He pressed his growing hardness into her hip as he said, "Just the thought of you touching yourself has me all worked up."

"Good. You'll have something to look forward to then."

Her body shimmered with need, a feeling she was growing to love. She loved being with him. And she'd take him any way she could have him. Forever and—

Forever? Did she really want him forever? The thought made her pause.

Her lust must be clouding her judgment. There was no way she could be in love this soon. Could she?

"Hey," Noah said, nipping her earlobe with his teeth. "Why'd you stop?"

"Oh." Grace didn't realize she had. Unable to process her thoughts, she stared into his eyes, grateful for the time they did have together for now. "I'm sorry. I was just thinking."

"About what?" Noah leaned back, giving her space.

There was no need to worry him. She needed time to process her feelings, not ready to drop the love bomb just yet.

An idea struck. "I was thinking that maybe we could go on another adventure before I catch my flight today. I'd like to take you this time."

Any worry on Noah's face was instantly wiped away as he smiled, coming back to her, pressing his skin against hers where he belonged. "What did you have in mind?"

Grace bit her lip. She hadn't thought that far ahead. Her mind sifted through all the experiences that were put together in their pitch for the Tortuga account. "How about one of those adventure hikes?"

"In the jungle?"

"Yeah. We can *go chasing waterfalls*," she sang.

Noah chuckled. "Would that require going into town first?"

"I think so. We'd have to catch a shuttle from Jaco."

Noah turned to look at the ceiling, resting his head in his hands. He pursed his lips to the side, deep in thought. "What if we just stay in bed all day?" He rolled over, his face softening.

"Stay in bed?" Grace scoffed. "You're the one who's been making me get out of the hotel room. Now you want to stay in all day?"

"Would it be so terrible?" he asked. "For our last day together?" His hand trailed down her arm and settled at the top of her hip.

"I have to check out of my room this morning," Grace said.

"Oh right," Noah said, squeezing her hip. "I can book an extra night. What do you say? Stay with me? Please, please, please."

Grace couldn't help but smile as she said yes. It wouldn't take too much convincing to get her to stay in bed all day, especially since she didn't know when the next time they'd be able to do something like that again.

"I'll call the front desk and ask for an extra night," he said, sliding off the bed. He slipped his boxer briefs on and hovered over the room phone.

As Noah was dialing the front desk, his cell phone buzzed on the opposite nightstand.

"Want me to get that?" Grace said, reaching for his phone.

"Who is it?" Noah said.

"Bruno," Grace said, reading the screen.

"He's probably calling about my van," Noah said, covering the mouthpiece with his hand. "You can answer it."

Grace reached for the phone and answered. A very thickly accented voice came over the line and confirmed Noah's van was ready for pickup. She ended the call, delighted by taking on such a domestic task for Noah.

Her eyes flitted over the screen when she noticed he had two missed text messages from someone named Belinda.

She scrunched her nose, trying to recall the name of the woman who was helping him earlier. When Noah finished with his call, Grace asked, "Who was the woman who helped you with your coffee delivery?"

"Her name's Clara. Why?"

"Oh," Grace said, looking down at the phone. She tossed it on the bed between them. "Your van is ready to be picked up."

Noah grabbed his phone, and his eyebrows immediately pinched together. "Wait. Did you read my texts?"

"No," Grace said, noting the defensive tone in his voice. "But I did see you had two messages from Belinda. Whoever she is."

She looked up into Noah's eyes and saw a flash of pure fear.

"Who's Belinda?" Grace said.

Noah ran a hand through his hair. He stood still, not answering the question. Why was he not answering the question? Grace felt the beating of her heart like a jet engine roaring to life.

"Noah Greene, who is Belinda?"

"She's nobody," Noah said. "Just a past fling. She means nothing to me."

Grace swallowed the lump in the back of her throat. "How long ago did you—?" Grace couldn't get the words *hook up* off her tongue.

Noah looked away, his jaw tense. His fists were at his sides. Why was he being so shifty? She wasn't sure if she wanted to know anymore. She knew he had a life before her, that he had had enough one-night stands to be swearing them off for good.

The thought of it made her sick to her stomach. She almost stopped Noah from answering her question, but she was too late.

"A couple of nights ago," he said, scratching at his jawline. His face had grown pale.

Grace's mouth flew open. "You slept with another woman a *couple* of nights ago? As in *two* nights ago?"

"I told you, that was the old me. And I meant it. I'm ready for something more than that. Something with you."

Grace's skin felt like it would melt right off her bones. She grabbed the top sheet of the bed and covered herself. She couldn't stand the thought of him seeing her naked for another second when he had just been with a woman *forty-eight hours ago*.

"And I'm supposed to believe that you magically changed right before we met?"

Noah winced. "Well, yes. Because it's true. I wouldn't lie to you. About that."

"How am I supposed to believe you? You and your flirting... You could have been feeding me all the right lines just to get laid last night."

Noah shot his hands up in surrender. "Grace. Please don't say that. This is not just a fling to me." He took another step forward, and she realized she was shaking.

"I wouldn't have had sex with you if you weren't willing to give us a real shot. Remember? I meant all that. I can't stand the idea of you leaving me now. Grace. Please. You have to believe me." His eyes were glossy. His throat and nose a shade of pink she didn't recognize. He looked panicked. "This was more than a fling to you too, right?"

He came close enough she could feel his heat. His hands reached for her arms, and Grace let him stroke them until he rested his hands on her shoulders. He looked deep into her eyes, and there was no way she could let a past fling ruin what they had.

Her heart instantly melted. She was either completely blinded by love or she was the ultimate sucker.

Women had been fawning over him since before they met. If it wasn't Jane or the zip line guide or his past hookups desperate for his attention, it would be some other woman.

"Right?" Noah urged, more desperate that time. He knelt down in front of her, looking up with sheer anguish in his eyes.

How could she deny this man on his knees? This beautiful man who had made her feel like the only woman in the world until this stupid text?

A relationship with Noah would not be easy. She'd have to put aside her insecurities and trust him with every fiber of her being. But as she looked into the gold flecks of his eyes, she knew she had to try. The spark she felt with him was unlike anything she had felt before.

"Yes," Grace said. "Yes, this meant more to me than a fling. I want you. But—"

"No buts. Please. No buts."

Grace smiled ruefully and continued despite his pleas. "This is going to be really hard for me when you have women hitting on you all the time. This is only going to work if we trust each other."

"You can trust me," Noah said. "I promise. I'm done with other women. I only want you."

Grace reached down and planted a kiss on his lips, succumbing to the fireworks between them. She couldn't deny him the chance when she was so madly, irreversibly in love.

When Grace came up for air, her eyes landed on the nightstand clock. "Crap. I have to get ready for my presentation." Grace gave him another kiss and threw her clothes on, pulling her tank top over her head.

"Will you text me when you're done?"

"Yeah." Grace slipped on her underwear and her shorts and ran toward the door.

"Wait." Noah stalked toward her.

"I'm going to be late if I don't get in a shower right now."

"You could take a shower here," Noah said, pointing his thumb toward his bathroom. "With me."

"No, really. I need to go." Grace reached for the doorknob before he pulled her back, cupping her face with his hands. His lips crashed onto her mouth in a kiss that had her seeing stars. He finished with a giant "mwah," releasing her as she struggled to stand upright.

"Good luck."

"Thanks," Grace said, stepping out in the hallway. Just before the door closed between them, Noah yelled out, "Toot-toot!"

Grace smirked, not quite able to laugh as easily as she had before. The idea of him sleeping with other women wasn't settling well. Between Noah telling Jane she was beautiful and Belinda thinking she had a chance too, something didn't quite feel right.

She tried shaking off her doubts as she stepped into the hallway toward her room. She hadn't gotten far when she spotted Jane coming back from her jog. She wore high-waisted pink leggings that clung to her shapely legs and a matching sports bra in a cheetah print.

Grace froze the moment Jane spotted her.

"Grace?" Jane said with a huff. Her cheeks had a blotchy

red hue, and a thin sheen of dewy sweat glistened against the sunlight poking through the buildings.

"Jane. Hi."

Jane tilted her head. "What are you doing out here?"

"I was just going for a walk," Grace lied, smoothing down her hair behind her ears. "You know, to blow off steam before the presentation."

"With your purse?" Jane said, looking at the bag she had clutched to her side.

"You can never be too careful," Grace said with a shrug.

Jane narrowed her eyes at her, breathing heavily. She placed her hands on her hips and toe-tapped side to side. "Are you nervous?"

"A little."

"Everything is going to be fine. I've been practicing with the PowerPoint you sent me, and I think I finally have the hang of it."

"Great," Grace said, resuming her walk along the garden path, a nervous hitch in her step.

"Where were you yesterday?" Jane said. "I came by your room, but you weren't there."

"I um… I was out. Exploring the city."

"Oh." Jane bent forward, touching her toes while she caught her breath. "Do anything fun?"

"I—"

"Grace!" Noah's voice echoed off the hotel walls.

Her body stiffened. She closed her eyes, praying she hadn't just heard Noah shout her name from down the hall.

"Grace, you forgot your—"

She turned to find Noah running toward her, holding out the phone she had left in his room.

CHAPTER NINETEEN

Jane's face twisted as she looked between Grace and Noah. Her eyes darkened, settling on Grace's purse. "Exploring the city, huh?" she said flatly.

Noah looked at Jane, then back at Grace, his mouth open in a stupor.

"I… uh…"

"Nice, Grace. Real nice." Jane turned on her heel and stormed down the hallway, picking up her stride until she was back in a jog.

"I am so sorry," Noah said, his arm dropping to his side. "I didn't realize Jane was out here."

"I'm so screwed," Grace said, cupping her mouth. "I'm never going to get that promotion now."

Noah trudged up to Grace. "She can't be that mad, can she?"

"Did you see the look on her face? She'll never forgive me for going behind her back."

Grace fell silent, letting her new reality settle in around her. If Jane didn't make that recommendation for Grace, there would be no home care for Aunt Judy.

She stared at Noah, expecting to be mad at him or herself for letting it get this far. But she couldn't. In fact, she wasn't upset at all. There was a different feeling that she did not expect. A lightness that resembled relief.

If Grace didn't get the promotion, then she didn't need to work at Maritime anymore. She could work anywhere else. She'd be free. Well, almost free. She'd still have to make a plan for Aunt Judy. But she couldn't lie to herself anymore. Her heart wasn't into working for a company run by Jane.

Noah had opened her eyes to a life she now knew she wanted to live. She wanted fun. She wanted adventure. She wanted to spend her time doing something she loved.

But all that came with a price. She'd have to let her aunt go. She'd have to face the world at home alone. But she'd have Noah. And Tessa. But most importantly, she'd have herself. And herself was enough. And Grace was finally ready to face life on her own.

"You know what? It's okay," Grace said. "Whatever happens, happens. I took the risk, and I'll deal with the consequences."

"No." His hands were in his hair. "This is my fault. I messed up."

"I'm telling you that it's okay," Grace said, putting a hand on his arm. His muscle tensed. "I think I'm finally ready to move on from this job."

"Really?"

"Yes. It's time I let go of all my excuses not to live my life the way I should. When I get back home, I'm going to look for teaching jobs."

Noah's face brightened, and his eyes sparkled with pride. "Are you sure? You're not mad at me?"

Grace bit her bottom lip, searching her soul for any inkling of doubt, but none could be found. "I'm sure."

"I still feel bad for getting us caught. You don't need the stress right now."

Grace collected her phone from his trembling hands. "It's going to be okay. I'll see what I can do to smooth things over with Jane so that she doesn't overreact. I need the job until I find a teaching gig."

Noah pulled Grace into a hug. His bare chest felt warm and perfect under her cheek, and his arms gripped her in a way that made her feel safe. That everything was going to be okay.

"I have to go now," Grace said.

Noah looked down at the ground a while before he gave her a weak nod.

"Everything will be fine," she said, attempting to convince herself. There was still a lingering fear that Jane would go ballistic and figure out a way to fire her before she was ready to leave.

But Grace couldn't worry about that now. She turned and marched forward, bracing herself for Jane's wrath.

Jane was sitting in a wicker chair in the lobby, sipping coffee from a to-go cup. Large sunglasses were pulled over her eyes, and she wore a bright red lipstick that popped against a caramel sheath dress.

Grace willed herself to inch closer, but each step felt like moving through quicksand. "Hey Jane," she said softly. "Can we talk?"

"What about? The fact that you lied to me?"

Grace's spine straightened. "I'm really sorry about that. Things just happened. I didn't mean to hurt you."

Jane waved her off. "You know what? It's fine." Her tight-lipped smile hardened like concrete.

"I just think—"

"No, seriously, Grace. I'd rather not talk about it."

"But—"

"It's *fine*. Okay?" Her tone was clipped.

Grace looked down at her hands. "I'm just really sorry. I know you were interested in him first. I should have told you."

Jane tapped her red talons against the table. "I'm actually more worried about you, Grace."

"What?"

Jane let out an exasperated sigh. "I don't expect you to know this, but you're going to learn sooner or later that guys like him don't stick around. They're only after one thing."

Grace narrowed her eyes. "Noah's not like other guys."

Jane clicked her tongue, shaking her head. "That's what they all say."

No. Jane was wrong. She had to be wrong. Noah was not using Grace for sex. He would have been fine watching movies last night. He had said so himself.

"Chin up," Jane said, tilting her head. "A bit of advice though." She brought her voice down to a low whisper. "Use them like they use us, and it becomes an equal playing field." She slid her sunglasses up her forehead, and her hazel eyes twinkled with sin. She winked once, before sliding her shades back on.

Jane's ex must have done a number on her if she was living by such warped rules. But Grace said nothing as she watched Jane sip her coffee.

Grace shook off the uneasy feeling in her stomach.

"Ahem." Diego, the assistant manager, appeared. "Shall we begin?"

Jane plastered on her smile and nodded. "Yes. We're ready." She stood up and followed Diego down the hall, Grace falling into step behind them.

Grace touched Jane's arm just before they entered the conference room. "Are you sure we're okay?"

"Of course," Jane said, "Now let's grab this account by the balls." A flash of excitement glimmered across her eyes before she slipped into the conference room.

Okay then. Grace breathed. Maybe everything would be fine after all.

CHAPTER TWENTY

D*umbass.*

How could he have been so careless?

Only Grace could make a shitty situation a life-altering change for the best. He was proud of her for deciding to pursue a teaching career. She was obviously good at her current job; Noah had gotten a front-row seat to her pitch. But she'd be even better with children because she'd be so much happier.

However, knowing all that didn't stop Noah from beating himself up for being so irresponsible. For leaping out into the hallways without even looking. The cartel could have been lurking in the bushes, for all he knew. He needed to be more careful, or he would lose her forever.

Noah kicked the edge of the bedpost; the vibrations shot up his leg and continued to buzz in his ears.

Oh wait, the buzzing noise was his phone.

Kai's name appeared on his screen, and Noah huffed a few breaths to calm down before he answered it.

"Hey, Noah," Kai said. "I have news."

"What's up?" Noah tried to sound normal, but the words came out strained. Kai would see right through it.

"What's wrong?"

Dammit.

Noah looked at himself in the mirror, staring into his own frantic eyes. The last thing Kai needed to know was that Noah didn't have things under control. "Nothing. I'm just about to pick up the van from the shop."

Kai waited a beat before he said, "Good. Save the receipt. We can expense it."

"What's the news?" He could use the distraction.

"We have a buyer for the business."

"Really?" Noah said. "Can you do that without Raffi?"

"No, but I was able to see him in jail. He's willing to sign the papers."

"How is he?"

"Raffi's fine. He thinks the judge might go easy on him since he's working with the police."

"Do you think he's going to be in for a while?"

"It's shaping up that way, yeah."

Noah meandered to the patio door, looking out over the turtle pool at the young family playing in the shallow end. Raffi would never know what it would be like to have his own family like that. He deserved a long time in jail for what he had done, the burden he had put on Noah and Kai and Ma. But Noah couldn't prevent feeling heartbroken. Twenty-two years of looking up to that shithead, and look what good that did. Noah had turned out just as careless and reckless as the king of dumbasses.

Noah shook off the ache in his chest. "So who's the fool you suckered into buying the company? And do they know about the cartel on our ass?"

"This investor is aware. And they're going to take good care of the employees while they break down the business into parts. Pretty soon it'll just be a coffee roastery with a new name."

Noah heaved a deep breath. His father would have been heartbroken to learn they had to sell the business. But just like everyone else, they had failed him too.

"Either way, I wanted to let you know so you could start finding something to do. You'll officially be out of a job in December."

"I'm already thinking about that."

"Oh yeah? What are you going to do?"

"I'm not sure yet," Noah said.

There was silence for a while before Kai said, "You could stay at my apartment in San José and go to school there."

Noah ran his hand through his hair. "Thanks for the offer." But he couldn't think about school right now. A good education would only be a waste of time for him. "Can we talk about this later? I've got a lot on my mind right now." Noah debated whether to tell Kai about the men he saw in Jaco but decided against it. It would only make him worry.

"Sounds good. And Noah?"

"Yeah?"

"I love you, man."

Noah pursed his lips. His brother had turned into such a sap, although the sentiment still warmed his chest. At least one of his brothers wasn't a complete disappointment.

Noah begrudgingly mumbled, "I love you too" and clicked off the phone.

Clouds hung heavy, threatening rain. The damp air whirled in through the cab window. Noah inhaled deeply, breathing in a mix of salty air and exhaust fumes. The cab driver took him to the auto shop where the OPEN sign was missing an

E. He pulled the front door, and the bells attached to the handle rang in alarm.

American pop music played over the speakers, and two customers in cowboy hats were sitting in chairs, reading automotive magazines. They both looked up at Noah with deep frowns. They were either two very disgruntled mechanics on a break or out-of-towners. No Costa Rican was that grumpy.

He stood in front of the desk, waiting for Bruno, the mechanic he met earlier. Noah tapped his fingers against the desk and got a text message from an unknown number.

4155550809: Hey, it's Kai. I'm texting from Jolie's number. She's trying to convince me to update my phone. Anyway, I've told my landlord to let you into the building in case you decide to stay there while you figure stuff out.

Noah stared at the text for a while. Sure, Kai was babying him like he always did, but what other choice did Noah have? He couldn't go home because of the cartel, and sleeping in his apartment was better than the van. He could drive there tomorrow and wallow in self-pity after Grace had left the country.

Noah: Thanks. I might take you up on that.

After another minute of not being helped, Noah turned to the two men sitting in the lobby chairs. They were looking directly at him. The magazines tossed to the floor.

"Have you guys seen Bruno?" Noah asked in Spanish.

One of the men stood up. He wore black jeans and a white T-shirt stained at the armpits. He had a stubbly face, a cleft chin, and piercing black eyes. "Are you here for the van?" the man said.

Noah caught a whiff of his coffee breath all the way across the room.

"I was told—" Noah froze midsentence as he looked out the glass window and saw a blue Mercury Sable parked outside.

Fuck. "Um," Noah stuttered, swallowing the pool of saliva in his mouth. "Do you work here?" he croaked.

The second man stood up, and Noah noticed the gold bracelets around his wrists and the snakeskin boots on his feet. Not the accessories Noah would expect a mechanic to wear.

"Do I look like I fucking work here?" Coffee Breath said. "I asked you a question. Are you here for the van?"

Noah gulped. "No." *Think, Noah.* "I was here to apply for a job. Bruno told me to come in this morning for an application. But I can see that he's not here, so I'll just come back another time."

Noah tried to pass the man, but Snake Boots blocked his path.

"Don't fucking lie to me, *Noah.*"

"Noah? Who's Noah?" Noah squeaked, his heart thumping wildly. He recalled the name of Grace's crush. "My name's Todd." *Screw you, Todd.*

The man relented for a moment, just long enough for Noah to slip around him.

Relief. Exquisite, pure joy coursed through him as Noah realized these men hadn't known what he actually looked like. They had his name and the location of the van, but they didn't know who he was.

If he could just get the hell out of there and call the police, this whole nightmare would be over. Just as Noah placed his hands on the door to leave, Bruno finally appeared from behind the glass, wiping his greasy fingers on a rag. His face brightened as he walked in, sending Noah back in with the two very distraught, very angry drug dealers.

"Noah Greene," Bruno said with a beaming smile. "Your van is ready to go."

Noah felt his butthole pucker at the sound of his name. Adrenaline spiked. Should he run? He wanted to, but he was frozen in place.

The man in gold bracelets and snakeskin boots walked over to the door, blocking the exit. Even if Noah did want to run, he was trapped.

Bruno walked over to the other side of the desk and pulled up his computer, tilting the screen toward Noah, listing out the details of the repairs. "You're lucky it was just a clogged fuel filter," Bruno said, ringing him up on the cash register.

There was no way out. Noah could feel the heated glares from the men standing behind him. They did not look happy. They looked downright murderous.

Noah wasn't sure how he'd talk his way out of this one. He was already caught in a lie. He pulled out his wallet and his phone and set them on the desk. If he could distract the men and text Clara, he might have a chance at coming out of this alive. But as soon as he pulled out the credit card from his wallet, his cell phone was swiped by the man in snakeskin boots.

"Can I help you?" Bruno said, looking at the men now breathing down Noah's neck. Stale coffee and cigar residue wafted around them.

"We're with him," Snake Boots said, sliding Noah's phone into the pocket of his tight black jeans.

Bruno gave Noah a look, but all Noah could do was stare.

"Tell him," Snake Boots said, elbowing Noah in the ribs with a pointed elbow. Or was it a gun?

"Yep," Noah said, a pitch too high. "They're with me." His hand shook as he signed the credit card slip. The moment he put his card back in his wallet, Snake Boots grabbed it out of his hands.

"Let me take you to the van," Bruno said, maneuvering around the desk. "It could have been a lot worse. I'm glad we were able to get it fixed up for you. I did notice you're low on oil, and you could use some new windshield wipers. Is that something you're interested in?"

"No, that's okay," Noah said casually, following Bruno out the front door. The jingling bells grated his nerves. The two drug dealers kept close behind.

Shit. Shit. Shit.

What was he going to do now? Make a dead sprint? Noah's palms started to sweat. If he ran, these guys would gun him down. And probably take Bruno down with him. There was no way out.

Bruno droned on about the van and all the things he should do to it before "things got really out of hand," but Noah couldn't hear another word.

Blood pumped violently through his veins, pounding in his ears. Then it dawned on Noah that these men probably thought he still had the cocaine. How was he going to explain that he didn't have it anymore? That he gave it to the police?

They would kill him. On the spot.

Double fuck.

Bruno gave him the keys and shook his hand, thanking him for coming in. He eyed the other two men curiously before waddling back to the main office. As soon he was out of earshot, the men closed in.

"Where is it?" Coffee Breath said.

"Funny story," Noah said, looking between the two men. "It's in a safe place."

He needed to call Clara. Clara would know what to do. She could at least summon the police to intercept them somehow.

"My friend is storing it for me. I just need to call her."

"What friend?" Coffee Breath said.

"My *girlfriend*, Clara," he stammered. "I can call her right now."

"Get in the fucking van," Coffee Breath said, pushing Noah forward. The keys to the van fell to the ground, and he had half a mind to consider kicking over Snake Boots as he lunged for the keys.

Opening the back, Coffee Breath pulled Noah behind one of the doors. In one swift movement, he punched Noah in the stomach, knocking the air from his lungs. His body hurled forward, and he was tossed inside like a sack of potatoes.

Through blurred vision, he could see Snake Boots going through his wallet. He pulled out a few receipts. The one from the zip line. The one from the dinner cruise. And then he pulled out the Tortuga Bay Resort room key.

"He's staying at one of the resorts nearby," Snake Boots mumbled to Coffee Breath. "It has to be stashed around there somewhere. Let's go."

"Wait," Noah rasped. His chest burned, fighting for air.

"You're going to show us where you are hiding the cocaine, or you're dead." The barrel of a gun was pointed directly at his head.

Noah froze in terror. He couldn't think. Couldn't speak. All he could do was picture his brain splattered across the van.

The van doors slammed before he could come up with a diversion, shutting out the sunlight that had just begun poking through the thick layer of clouds. The men stepped into the driver and passenger seats.

Snake Boots held the gun pointed at Noah's head as Coffee Breath navigated his way out of the parking lot and onto the streets of Jaco.

CHAPTER TWENTY-ONE

Grace had gone into autopilot mode. She answered questions about Maritime's setup process and showed examples of websites she had worked on. When it came time for Jane to wrap up their presentation, Grace felt numb.

She didn't hear a word of Jane's closing statements. Didn't get excited when Fernando said he was interested in working with Maritime. Didn't feel an ounce of hope when she realized they were close to securing their first-ever international account. All she could think about was figuring out how she would see Noah again after she went back home to Michigan.

Since Jane seemed okay about catching Noah and Grace together, perhaps Grace still had a chance at the promotion. If she could collect a senior sales associate salary for a little while, then she could save enough money to fly back for a vacation with Noah before she began a new teaching career.

She pictured staying at a resort much like Tortuga Bay, only they wouldn't have to duck and hide this time. They could take leisurely strolls on the beach, go swimming in the pool together, spend long mornings in bed. A delicious coil of warmth pooled in her belly at the thought.

Her new plan brought her back to life. Grace felt lighter on her feet, and a genuine smile reached her cheeks as she said her goodbyes to Fernando and Diego and the rest of the Tortuga Bay Resort team.

When the hotel staff left the room, it was just her and Jane. They slipped the boards in Jane's portfolio bag, despite the watermarks from the sprinkler alarm. Grace laughed to herself, thinking if it weren't for those boards, she would have never met Noah. Perhaps she could ask to keep them as a souvenir since she didn't get her snow globe.

"I should be thanking you," Jane said, stuffing the last poster in the case. "For helping me bag this account."

"You're welcome," Grace said, unplugging her computer from the projector. A thank-you from Jane was a pleasant surprise and a good sign that everything was back to normal.

"You know how much I hate the technical stuff."

"It's no problem at all."

Jane paused before walking out the conference room door, turning to look down at Grace. "For the record though, if you think I was going to put in a recommendation after the stunt you pulled behind my back, you have another think coming."

Grace inhaled sharply, staring up into Jane's eyes, expecting her pupils to have turned into slits.

"I didn't want to get your hopes up or anything," Jane said. "So I figured I'd tell you now."

"That's it? I don't get a chance to be considered?"

"Oh, you had your chance, Gracie. And you blew it the moment you wrapped those pretty lips around Noah's... you know."

A strangled gargle escaped Grace's throat.

"Don't think for a second," Jane continued, "that I don't

know what went down with you and him last night. All men are the same, eager to get their *you-know-whats* wet. And I have no doubt he fed you all the right lines to get you to think it was your idea."

Grace gasped. She was utterly speechless.

Noah had fed her lines, sure, but he hadn't been manipulating her. Noah hadn't coerced her into anything. It really had been her idea... right? Last night was for her, he had said. And she believed him.

She attempted to shake off Jane's words, but the poisonous doubt had been planted in her mind. Jane had experience with this type of thing. Unlike Grace, who didn't have a clue what she was doing at all.

"You'll get over it soon enough. I suggest finding another man to help you forget about him. That trick seems to work for me," Jane said, looking down at her phone. "Oh, look at the time. Thanks again for all the technical help, Gracie. I couldn't have done it without you." She turned to leave, then stopped under the doorway. "And one more thing. I have big plans for this company. And honestly, I don't see where you fit in."

Grace's jaw dropped.

"You can keep your job for now, but I'd start looking for other opportunities if I were you."

With the flick of her blond bob, she was gone, leaving Grace alone.

Noah bumped around in the van with the gun pointed directly at his face. He was frozen in fear. He couldn't breathe. His internal organs groaned.

The drug dealers weren't saying anything. Their silence was deafening. Panic settled in. Maybe if he befriended the guys, they would be less likely to kill him. His charm didn't only work on older women. It could work on drug dealers too. Right?

"So, have you been doing this line of work for a long time?"

Snake Boots turned to Coffee Breath. "Shoot him."

"No! You don't want to do that," Noah said, reaching out with his hands as if he could stop the bullet from penetrating his brain. "I'm the one who knows where the cocaine is, remember?"

Well, he sort of knew where it was. He knew it was with the police somewhere.

The gun barrel remained steadily aimed at Noah's head.

"I think you might be mistaking me for someone else. I'm just a coffee delivery boy." Noah's voice was shaky, but he kept going. "I never wanted anything to do with the stuff."

"Shut up!" Coffee Breath said. "We're here."

Noah cowered. His heart clobbered against his aching chest. All he could do was try to steer them away from the main lobby. Away from Grace.

"Over there," Noah said, pointing to a garage at the far end of the parking lot. It was the farthest spot from where Grace would be. She had probably texted him by now or was waiting outside his hotel room.

The van drove over the first speed bump, his stomach clutching his esophagus for dear life. Another speed bump, and Noah almost hurled all over the van bed.

Then they came to a stop, and Snake Boots killed the engine. The men sat silently, looking left to right, scanning the rooftops and the cars around them.

Noah could hear the whistling of Coffee Breath's nose hairs as he breathed in and out, scoping the scene as if he'd done this a thousand times before.

"Is it in the garage?" Coffee Breath said.

Noah panicked. He didn't know what to say or do to stop the train wreck of his life. "If I can just call Clara—"

"Let's go," Snake Boots said, opening the door. Coffee Breath followed, and both men appeared behind the van doors, grabbing Noah and dragging him out of the van.

"If it's not here, you're dead," Coffee Breath whispered in Noah's ear.

Noah was dragged toward the garage. He looked over his shoulders for help, but no one was there.

Coffee Breath growled, landing another punch, only this time it was a solid blow to his kidney. Noah keeled over, dropping to the floor.

A follow-up kick to the stomach had Noah seeing stars. His eyes watered, reeling from the impact. The pain consumed him, wrapping him up like a blanket made of daggers and jagged metal.

Just as Snake Boots lifted his foot for another kick, Noah held his hands up. "I can get you the cocaine," he said hoarsely. He braced himself for the impact, but the blow never came.

Noah took a shaky breath in, relieved and yet still in agony. "I can get it to you. Clara will have it. Please. Please, let me call her."

The two men exchanged glances.

"You have to trust me, okay?" Noah said, struggling to get up on his feet. "She'll be able to tell you where she put it. I promise."

After a lot of angry staring, Snake Boots pulled out Noah's phone. "Call your girlfriend," Snake Boots said, showing him the switch blade that he had pulled out of his pocket.

Noah gulped and limped over to Snake Boots to grab his phone. He was just about to dial Clara when he heard the tapping of running shoes on pavement, coming toward the garage door.

His heart launched into hyperdrive.

Hope.

Someone must have seen him get dragged out of the van and were running to rescue him.

The silhouette of a small woman appeared at the garage's entrance.

Grace appeared, huffing out of breath. "Hey. What are you doing in here?"

Grace had texted Noah with no answer. Panic took over as she knocked on Noah's door.

He was gone. He could have still been at the body shop, but something didn't feel right.

She ran toward the pool to see if he might have gone there and fallen asleep.

Two couples lay sunbathing, lathered up with sunscreen. Caribbean music played over the speakers under the cabana with the bar. But there was no sign of Noah.

Grace plopped down onto one of the lounge chairs and waited.

She was agitated. She needed to see Noah for herself, to prove that Jane was wrong about him. That Jane was wrong about everything.

She waited awhile with no response. Jane's words floated in her head. *Guys like him don't stick around.*

She scoffed. Noah wouldn't have just left. But something was off. Even if he was still at the shop, he would have texted her back. She checked her phone again, but the message she sent hadn't been read.

Grace twitched in her chair; every ticking second felt like

a hammering nail to her nerves. She couldn't wait there at the pool anymore, baking under the sun. If she was going to wait, she would need to sit in the shade.

Grace stood up and meandered toward the resort lobby. The cool air-conditioning chilled her heated flesh. Through the glass windows, she could have sworn she saw the flash of a white van drive across the parking lot. She stepped outside to see if it was Noah's. Her knees buckled at the sight of the Greene Coffee logo.

He came back. Grace felt her shoulders slump with relief.

The van pulled around and parked at the far end of the lot.

Butterflies stirred in her stomach as she marched along the sidewalk toward the van. Too excited and anxious, she picked up the pace, jogging to match the rapid-fire beating of her heart.

As she got closer, she could see Noah wasn't in the van. Voices in the nearby garage caught her attention. Three shadowed figures stood inside. One of them was tall and lean. As she got closer, she confirmed Noah was standing with two other men in cowboy hats. Their faces were stern.

"Hey. What are you doing in here?" she said.

Noah's eyes flared before his face darkened. "Get out," Noah bit out, his mouth in a straight line. His jaw twitched.

"What?" Grace scrunched her face.

"I said, get out of here!" he shouted.

He actually *shouted* at her.

Grace took a step back. Her hand flew to her chest to prevent her heart from spilling out. This wasn't the Noah she knew. He would have never talked to her like that. For a moment she wondered if this was someone else entirely.

"Who's this?" one of the men asked Noah. He had snake-skin boots and a giant gold watch on his meaty wrist.

"Just some chick," Noah said. His eyes were so dark he

was unrecognizable. "I said, get the fuck out of here!" Noah shouted again.

Grace's throat constricted. Something was definitely wrong. Noah would never shout at her like that. He was signaling her to leave, but why? How did he get mixed up with these men? Should she call the police? For what though? She couldn't tell what was going on.

Grace turned to leave when something caught her eye. A metal object in the man's hand. She squinted at the shiny piece.

A *gun*.

A small squeak escaped her throat, and she took off in a dead sprint.

Her feet felt like dumbbell weights attached to tethered ropes. A pair of strong hands gripped her arm, pulling her to a stop. A thunk at the crown of her head shot a painful blast down her neck. Then everything went black.

CHAPTER TWENTY-TWO

Noah woke up in the back of the van with a splitting headache. His wrists were tied behind his back, his ankles bound by wire, cutting into his skin.

He didn't remember blacking out, but Snake Boots and Coffee Breath must have knocked him unconscious and threw him in the back.

The van wasn't moving. In fact, it was very still. He didn't hear the heavy nose hair breathing of Coffee Breath or the grumpy cursing from Snake Boots. What he heard was far worse: the muffled cries of a woman.

Grace.

He contracted his stomach muscles and swung his knees over, hoping he would not see what he feared would be lying next to him. Grace was trembling, her wrists and ankles bound tight, tears falling down her reddened face. She was missing a shoe, and she had a sock in her mouth, taped over with clear packing tape.

Noah attempted to call out, but he also had tape across his mouth, sticking to the tiny hairs on his face. He made a pathetic grunt that got her attention. Grace looked up at him, her eyes wet. She leveled her icy glare, then she continued to sob in pathetic gasps through her nose.

No. No. No.

This couldn't be happening. This couldn't be real.

He had messed up beyond any reasonable amount of messing up, and now Grace was paying the price.

She wouldn't look at him anymore. Turning her body to face the opposite wall, she curled her knees into her chest and whimpered quietly.

This was a nightmare.

The back doors swung open, and Snake Boots reached in, ripping the tape off Noah's face.

Snake Boots held out the phone toward Noah's ear. "Tell her you're all right," he said in Spanish.

It took Noah a moment to realize who he might be talking about. It must have been Clara, but how? "Clara?"

Noah could hear the faint sound of Clara's voice as Snake Boots pulled the phone away and put it to his ear, slamming the van doors behind him. Noah sat up to listen through the door, but the conversation was too muffled through the metal.

He couldn't be sure, but it sounded like Snake Boots was giving her instructions. To what? To their location?

This was good. Clara would send help.

Noah cranked his head toward the windshield. Through the window, he could see they weren't at the resort anymore. They were parked in an empty lot. Palm trees lined the border of the cement ground, and in the far corner of his view he could make out what appeared to be a dock, a sliver of glittering ocean just beyond it.

He couldn't tell where they were or how far they had been taken away from the resort, but by the look of the sunshine beaming down straight overhead, it hadn't been that long.

Grace sniffed, bringing Noah's attention back. Her cheeks were so flushed he couldn't make out her freckles.

He needed to get that tape off before she passed out. He scooched closer.

"Grace," Noah whispered in his most soothing voice. "I am so sorry for this."

Her body stiffened, her eyes shut tight, squeezing giant droplets down her nose.

"I'm going to get that tape off, okay?" He leaned over, falling onto his shoulder. He flinched in agony. The kick he had received earlier had done some major damage to his ribs.

He inched toward her, every movement a stabbing pain in his side, but he continued, leaning over. A sweet orange scent filled his nostrils as he drew near, and Noah's heart broke all over again. He would never be able to smell that scent after this.

His teeth grazed the corner of the tape on her cheek. He had to nudge it a few times, attempting to peel it back, but it was too damn tight. He couldn't get a grip.

"I'm going to try a different way," he said, rolling his body to the other side. The throbbing in his rib was so excruciating it knocked the wind out of him. After a moment to catch his breath, he twisted so that his hands were near her face. His fingers wiggled around wildly until he felt the wetness of her skin and the tape just below the hot air escaping her nose.

His fingertip found a corner, and after several attempts of catching it with his fingernail, he peeled it back. A muffled groan caused Noah to jump. "I know this is going to hurt. But I need you to be quiet, please."

He tugged again and again yanking it with all his body weight until he crashed on his other shoulder. His vision blurred as he held on to his consciousness like a buoy keeping him afloat.

Grace spat out the sock, and it dropped to the floor. She gasped for air, her body trembling.

"What the hell did you do?" she hissed through her teeth.

"Okay, I need to explain," he whispered. "I should have told you this before, but I was trying to protect you. My brother, Raffi, got in the middle of a cartel feud or something, and I got stuck with two hundred kilos of cocaine." He didn't mention that she had sat among the boxes of drugs when they had first met.

"I was working with a detective, Clara. She's been helping me. The police picked up the cocaine the other day. I thought I was in the clear. Well, sort of..." She also didn't need to know he saw the men in Jaco yesterday.

Grace blinked at him, waiting for him to continue. The color of her face had normalized just enough to see her freckles again, but the terror he had seen earlier was replaced by a loathing scowl.

"These guys work for the cartel." He gestured toward the doors. "They think I still have the cocaine. I told them that Clara has it. I'm guessing she figured out I'm in trouble by now. She should be sending help."

"I can't believe this," Grace muttered, squeezing her eyes shut. "I'm in the middle of a *cartel bust*?"

"That about sums it up, yeah."

"You got me in this mess. You did this to me. Why couldn't you have left me alone?"

Noah winced at the sight of her trembling chin. "You have every right to be upset with me. And I'm sorry. I was trying to protect you. I thought I had everything under control." He should have known better. He didn't have control over a damn thing in his life.

Grace turned away from him, whimpering quietly to herself.

Noah's heart shattered in his chest. He couldn't take it

anymore. He couldn't see her suffer. He choked back his own tears. "I messed up. I'm so sorry."

Grace turned back to face him, her eyes glossy. "We're going to die, aren't we?"

Noah's mouth opened, but no words could spill out. He wasn't sure, and he couldn't lie. Not anymore. Not to Grace.

He closed his eyes, ashamed of himself and the world he had pulled Grace into.

"I will never forgive you for this," she rasped, her lips trembling.

Noah felt a burning fire reach his eyes, clogging his nose and throat. He was a grown man, but damn if this situation didn't warrant the tears spilling down his face. Watching her sob with hate and fear in her eyes was ripping him apart.

He fought back the sob that nearly escaped his throat, bearing down. He needed to get his shit together for Grace, to be strong for her.

"Please don't cry," he said, his voice shaking with pathetic hypocrisy. "It kills me to see you cry."

There was a long pause; heavy breathing filled the space between them. Every second in the van felt like borrowed time. He didn't know what to do or what to say to make things right. And for some reason, the fear of death hadn't even settled in his mind. It was the fear of losing Grace that rattled him to his core.

How could she ever forgive him when the only thing she needed was to feel safe? Would they even survive to find out?

The sound of a car on a gravel road approached. Noah held his breath, pressing his ear near the van wall as if that would help him hear better. He heard a car door shut.

Someone had come.

She was going to die.

She was going to *die*. And all because she'd put herself out there again. This was the price she paid for trying to live her life.

It was fitting, really. Just like her parents had gone down in flames, Grace was following close behind. Only instead of a romantic helicopter ride, Grace was in a van in the middle of a drug cartel bust with a guy she had literally just met.

Coffee delivery, my fanny.

He lied to her. He lied to her about everything.

Grace watched Noah fall apart, tears streaming down his face. Her heart ached at the sight, but he had *lied*. She had trusted him. She had believed he was trying to keep her safe. But this… this was the opposite of that now, wasn't it? What other lies had he been feeding her this whole time?

Muted voices grew louder outside the muggy van. She could barely hear over her pulse, pounding in her ears. Sweat dripped down her forehead.

A shout.

Grace stilled.

"Get down," Noah whispered.

Grace straightened in her seated position, ignoring Noah's demand. She needed to hear what was going on too. Pressing her ear against the van wall, she listened as the shouting escalated. Grace couldn't track the number of voices. It sounded like an army in the middle of a battlefield.

"Grace, please. Get down."

She glared at Noah, turning her nose up and away from him as a gunshot blasted, jolting Grace from the side of the van. She crashed to the floor, pressing her cheek against the cool metal.

Two more shots were fired. The sound was so loud it felt like her brain was clanging against her skull.

Grace attempted to curl herself into a ball, but she had

been hogtied like an animal. This was it. This was the end to a life she had barely lived.

Noah lay down next to her, pain and fear in his eyes. She wanted to hate him. To blame him for everything. She wanted to think that he was getting what he deserved, but she couldn't.

In that moment, staring into his eyes, Grace only felt sorrow and heartbreak. Not for herself but for what they could have had. She had found herself hoping they could have worked out a relationship. She would have tried phone sex. She would have tried anything to keep him in her life. But all that was over now.

Kind of hard to keep a relationship when both people are dead.

She had been a damned fool to think she could have had a happily-ever-after with him.

Several rounds of gunshots fired outside. The van shook with every blast.

Tears fell, tickling her nose, dripping onto the floor. "We're going to *die*, Noah."

"The police are out there. They're going to get us out of here."

Grace wanted to believe him, but how could she? "How do you know it's not another drug cartel or something?"

Noah looked away. "I guess I don't know for sure."

Another shot rang out, and they both flinched.

Grace shook her head, the echo of the gunshot still ringing in her ears. "I haven't even lived yet," she muttered to herself. "I was just about to get started."

"When we get out of this—and we will—you can yell and scream at me all you want. You can slap me for real this time. For lying about the cocaine. For getting you in trouble with Jane. All of it. But I need you to know something."

Grace opened one eye as if it would help her hear better.

"I wasn't lying about how I feel about you. I care about you, Grace. I like you so much it hurts." He took a labored breath. Something appeared to be causing a sharp pain in his side. "I think I'm falling—" Noah was interrupted by another shot, and they both ducked for cover.

"Grace, I'm falling in—"

"Stop. No. You can't be seriously confessing your love right now in the middle of a *shoot-out*, Noah!"

"I know it's not one of your Prince Charming movies, but—"

"I cannot hear this right now." Grace cut him off. "Do not ruin this for me." No guy had ever confessed his love to her before, and she refused for her first time to be tainted by an episode of a Lifetime crime show.

The crackling of her heart was interrupted by a blast that broke the passenger side window, shattering glass every-where. Marble-sized chunks scattered across the floor, into their hair.

A huge thump against the van shook the entire vehicle. Grace screamed.

"Grace!" Noah shouted over the commotion outside. Everything was louder now that the window had been broken. "I'm going to cover you." He lunged himself over Grace, rolling his body over hers. The weight of him squeezed the air out of her, and she could no longer scream.

The van was shaking now as it took a series of rapid-fire gunshots. A shower of shrapnel hit the side of the van. Bullets were coming through. One after another, Grace could hear the piercing of metal at one end to the other.

The last shot caused Noah's body to jerk.

"Fuck!" Noah screamed, nearly tumbling off her. He rebalanced himself, groaning with every movement.

"Are you shot?"

Noah grunted through gritted teeth. "They shot my ass. Shit, that hurts."

Grace winced. "You need to get down. Get off me."

"I'm not budging," Noah said, adjusting his head so that it covered Grace. He pressed his cheek to hers, and she could feel his jagged breath. Each exhale was more pained, shakier than the last.

The gunfire stopped, and the van went eerily still. Grace lay under Noah, breathing so hard she was afraid Noah would slide off her.

It was so quiet outside. Somebody had won the shoot-out, but who?

"Are you okay?" Noah whispered.

"I don't know," Grace whimpered. "I'm scared."

"I won't let anything happen to you," Noah said. "I won't."

It was too late for empty promises, but Grace kept her mouth shut. He had taken a bullet for her after all.

They waited for what felt like an eternity. The back door of the van unlatched, creaking open, letting the sunshine into the van.

Grace braced herself for the final shot. The one to end it all.

CHAPTER TWENTY-THREE

Noah craned his neck. His eyes settled on the angel in a blue uniform, her badge reflecting the sunshine from overhead. "Are you okay?" the officer said in Spanish.

"We're alive," Noah said, attempting to roll off Grace, but every inch of his body hurt.

The officer called for a medic in her radio and eased him off Grace. Every muscle fiber and tendon roared in pain, but the absence of Grace's body against his hurt even more.

"Are you Clara?" Noah said in English.

"I'm Valentina," she said, putting pressure on Noah's wound. Searing pain shot through his spine. "You can call me Val."

Noah and Val glanced at Grace, her body trembling.

"I think she's in shock," Noah said.

"Don't worry. It's all over now. I'm going to take good care of you," Val said in English. "Are you hurt?"

Grace shook her head, but her long face said otherwise. Noah knew her pain came from deep inside, fueled by his betrayal of her trust.

Another officer appeared, his eyes darting frantically

around the van. He was a tall Costa Rican man with a goatee and a strong jaw.

"Gunshot wound," Val said in Spanish. "Where is the EMT?"

"Coming soon," he said. He pulled out his pocketknife and cut through the twine around their wrists, then untied the wire around their ankles.

The van bed was covered in blood, soaking Noah's shorts, running down his legs.

Grace gasped, her mouth ajar at the sight.

"Come with me," the male officer said in Spanish, ushering her out of the van.

"She's American," Noah said in English.

The male officer gave Noah a nod in understanding and slipped his arm around her. "I've got you."

"Wait," Noah said, his heart beating so fast. "Where are you taking her?"

"She's coming with me," the male officer said.

"Please. Wait. We need to talk," Noah pleaded.

Grace looked at him with large, sad blue eyes, her lip still trembling. On the brink of tears, she opened her mouth as if to say something but closed it before turning away. She let the male officer help her out of the van without a word.

"Grace," Noah whimpered. *Don't leave.*

She turned at Noah's plea, but her gaze landed on something outside the van. Both hands cupped her mouth.

Grace let out a sob as the officer took her away. Snake Boots and Coffee Breath were likely on the ground, ready for body bags. It was not what someone like Grace should ever see in their lifetime.

"Grace," he muttered again. Noah wasn't ready to say goodbye. There was still so much more to say. She needed to yell and scream and slap him. Anything that would help her get over this rough patch. Okay, so maybe it was more like a gigantic, festering hole. Regardless, he needed the chance to make it up to her before she left Costa Rica for good. Before he lost the chance to be with her forever.

Sirens echoed against the palm trees, and soon a paramedic showed up with a kit and went to work, cutting off Noah's shorts and covering him in gauze. "I think I might have a broken rib too," Noah said, flinching at every jostle of the van.

A stretcher was set up a moment later. They began rolling him toward the ambulance. Noah's eyes darted across the lot. He saw police cars parked with flashing lights. Police officers stood around in small groups, some on the phone, some taking notes.

He eventually found Grace, sitting in a police car with a blanket wrapped around her shoulders. She was staring blankly at the officer who was crouched down on his haunches with a notepad.

"Grace!" Noah yelled as the stretcher was being carried toward the ambulance.

She looked up, her eyes swimming in tears. Sad tears. Goodbye tears.

"Don't worry, Noah. We'll take good care of her," Val said by his side.

"Wait!" Noah yelled as he entered the ambulance. "Stop!" The men holding the ambulance doors open halted the stretcher. "You have to know that my feelings for you are real," Noah shouted. "You and I are *real*! It wasn't all a lie."

Grace wiped her eyes with the back of her hand but held her glare.

"This isn't over," Noah said. "Tell me this isn't over."

Grace stared, tears streaming down her blotchy cheeks. For a moment there was hope, a glimmer of forgiveness in her eyes. But she quickly blinked it away and turned.

"Let's go," one of the men said as they hoisted Noah's

stretcher up into the ambulance. The doors shut, closing him off from the outside.

"Grace!" Noah yelled.

It was too late. The engine kicked on, and the ambulance rumbled forward, away from the crime scene.

CHAPTER TWENTY-FOUR

Noah lay ass-up on the hospital bed while the doctor read his chart. "I don't see any bullet fragments in your scan. You've got a hairline fracture on one of your ribs but nothing to be too concerned about. You'll just need to take it easy for a while."

"What about my butt?" Noah said.

"We'll clean you up and give you a few stitches. You'll be out of here in no time. Gloria and I will take good care of you."

The nurse beside him was preparing a small tray. She was a tall woman with black braids bunched together with a soft fabric hair tie at the nape of her neck. Her skin was a dark ebony, and she had beautiful, full lips.

He would have said something charming if his heart wasn't completely shattered. Noah couldn't get the vision of Grace out of his mind, crying and trembling in fear for her life. And it was all his fault. He knew the cartel had been trailing him. He should have been hiding from everyone, including her.

"You have a visitor," the nurse said, putting on a pair of latex gloves. She gestured toward the curtain.

Noah turned to see if Grace had come to visit. The flutters in his stomach were back. Nervous energy flowed through his veins.

"Hola." A voice that was not Grace's.

Noah sank his head back down into his pillow, his heart so heavy it sagged like an overfilled water balloon.

The woman walking into the room had a head full of spiral curls and rosy cheeks. She was dressed in a suit, with a series of badges around her neck. A walkie-talkie was latched to her belt loop.

"Clara?"

"That's me. I'm sorry, is this a bad time for questioning?" Clara said, her eyes wide, darting between the doctor, the nurse, and Noah's bare ass.

"Fine with me," the doctor said. "I was just about to stitch him up."

Noah felt cold liquid as the doctor proceeded to wash his wound. The pain medication he had taken earlier helped a bit, but every touch felt like a branding iron to his backside.

"I guess it's fine," Noah said, flinching. "Come on in."

Clara took out her notepad and looked into Noah's eyes. "It's nice to meet you in person."

"You too," Noah said.

"This will be just a little prick," the doctor said before Noah felt a sharp pain on his right butt cheek that radiated through every cell in his body.

"Holy fu— Goddamn that really hurts." A scorching fire of torture ripped through him. The needle was worse than the damn bullet. Eventually the pain subsided, and the doctor started on the stitches.

Clara's face contorted in agony before she turned away and focused on her notepad instead of the threaded needle going into Noah's skin. "I'm sorry I wasn't there during the shoot-out."

"Are you kidding? You saved my life."

Clara tucked loose curls behind her ear. "It was a good thing you told those guys to call me. I knew exactly what had happened the moment they opened their dumb mouths."

"They couldn't have been that dumb if they were able to track me all the way here."

"These cartels have connections everywhere. I'm sure they had some people looking for your plates."

Noah cursed under his breath.

Clara clicked her tongue against the roof of her mouth. Her eyes drifted up toward the ceiling. "I should be lecturing you right now, but it doesn't feel right while you're being stitched up for a bullet wound. Are you doing okay?"

Noah felt the tug and pull of string on his backside, but the pain had vanished. "I'm on enough medication to take down an elephant, I think."

"Good. Then you can take what I'm about to throw at you. *What the hell were you thinking, man?*" Clara scolded. "You told me you were going to the police station to identify the men you saw in Jaco."

Noah winced. "I know. I'm sorry."

"You don't need to apologize to me, but you put yourself and that sweet girl in a ton of danger."

Noah stilled, his breathing shallow. "You talked to her? Is she okay?"

"Of course she's not okay, Noah. She's scared out of her mind. You could have prevented that fiasco if you had just done what you were supposed to do."

Noah's chest burned. He gripped the edge of his mattress until he felt the burn in his palms. He couldn't stomach the fact that Grace wasn't okay. That he was responsible for her fear.

"I fucked up."

"I'll say," Clara said, taking a seat. "But I get it. I talked to Grace myself. I can see you were just trying to protect her from everything that was going on."

Noah clenched his jaw. "Did she leave Jaco? Is she gone?"

Clara shook her head. "I can't tell you that. The good news is that you and Grace are safe now. That's all that matters."

But it wasn't all that mattered, not to Noah. He wanted to see her again. To talk things out before she left. He wouldn't accept the fact that they were over before they'd truly begun.

Grace had a flight that night, but it might be possible to catch her at the resort before she left. The thought gave him hope for the future. That is, if he wasn't going to jail.

"Am I in trouble?" Noah said.

Clara looked him over before pulling out a pen from her satchel. "By the looks of things, I'd say you are out of trouble for now. You're lucky it was just a butt wound."

"No, I mean, am I in trouble with the law?"

Clara grunted. "Not unless you stop cooperating with me," she said. Licking her fingertip, she flipped through the pages of notes. "Do you mind if I ask you a few questions now, or do you want me to come back later?"

"Hit me," Noah said.

Answering questions with his buns on display started to feel less awkward over time. Clara asked about that day in Jaco and what he had seen. He described in more detail what had happened in the van and what the men had said.

Clara eventually said, "We figured out who they were. And who they were working for."

"Oh yeah?"

Clara paused to watch the doctor finish up with the last stitch.

"All done," the doctor said, placing a bandage on his

stitches. "We'll be back with a prescription, and then you can be on your way."

"Thank you," Noah said, watching the doctor and nurse toss their gloves into the trash, leaving him and Clara alone in the room.

"So, who are they?" Noah said.

"Juan Alvarez and Pedro Geuvara." She pulled out two photographs out of her notebook and held them out for him to see.

"That's Juan?" Noah said, pointing to the man he had been referring to as Snake Boots.

"Yes. And this is Pedro." She pointed to the man with the square head.

"If Pedro were still alive, I'd suggest he get his teeth checked."

Clara chuckled, then continued to talk to him in a whisper. "They worked for Hidalgo Montezuma, a new drug lord on our radar. We haven't been able to catch him yet, but we did find out that he had targeted the Limón cartel. It was his crew that attempted to hijack the shipment that your brother was involved in."

"Whoa. Wait a minute. Raffi was working with the *Limón* cartel? *The* Limón cartel?" They were infamous in the country. No one messed with them.

"Yes," Clara said. "I'm sorry it took so long for me to figure everything out. I might have been able to stop Juan and Pedro before they got all the way out here."

"Will they be looking for me or my family? Am I even safe to go home?"

"We'll keep your family under surveillance for a little while longer. We haven't seen any suspicious activity yet, but if we come across anything fishy, we'll see about getting you protection."

Noah clenched his fists. "I want to be free from this."

"From my perspective, you already are."

"Then why do I feel like I'm not?"

Clara raised her eyebrows, getting up from her chair. "Because you didn't get the girl. Give it time. She'll come back around."

"How can you be sure?"

Clara shrugged. "Call it a detective's intuition," she said, strolling toward the back of the room. She gave him a salute and then turned to leave, her heavy boots clicking against the tile floor. "Take care of that butt."

Not a moment later, the nurse strolled in. "I've got some scrubs for the way home."

Home. He didn't have one at the moment, but Grace did. And he needed to catch her before she left.

Noah slid his legs off the side of the hospital bed while Gloria helped him get steady on his feet.

"Here, I'll help you," Gloria said. She unfolded the scrubs.

"I can do it on my own, but thanks," Noah said.

"Are you sure? I don't want you to be in pain."

"Nah. I can handle the pain. It's a good distraction."

"Distraction?" Gloria inquired with a tilt of her head.

"It's nothing." *Just the love of my life about to get on a plane and never come back.* Noah reached for the pants and attempted to lift one foot into the pant hole. His vision blurred, and he began to fall forward.

Gloria caught him before he fell, standing him upright and guiding him back toward the bed. "Maybe we should take this a bit slower," she said.

"I really need to get back to my hotel."

"You've just been through a lot. I think you should rest here for a little longer. I can get you a wheelchair—"

"No. Really. I'm fine," Noah said, standing up. The room swirled around him, and he felt the urge to throw up. "Okay, maybe a minute." He lay back on the hospital bed.

"Do you want to talk about why you need a distraction?" Gloria said.

Noah sighed heavily. "Not really. It's been a shitty day."

"It must have been if you have an investigator asking you questions and the cops right outside."

"The police are here?"

"For protection," Gloria said. "You know, my mother always told me that when you're having a bad day, all you need is a hug."

Noah looked up at her. She seemed sincere enough. Not like those desperate women at the bar, looking for an excuse to touch him.

What he really wanted was a hug from Grace though. To feel her in his arms and know that everything was going to be all right between them. But for now he supposed he could settle with a hug from the tall nurse who assisted with putting eight stitches in his ass.

Gloria opened her arms for him, and he obliged, getting up from the bed. She wrapped her arms around him while he rested his head against her giant breasts with nowhere else to go. She smelled like hand sanitizer and vanilla and squeezed him tight. A small part of him did feel better, but the determination to win Grace over only strengthened.

Just as he released his arms around Gloria, he felt her body stiffen, her eyes fixed on something behind him. He turned.

Grace stood across the room, holding up the curtain, her eyes wide with hurt.

CHAPTER TWENTY-FIVE

Grace gawked at Noah's naked butt. One cheek was bandaged and the other barely covered by his gown. His head had been resting on an impressive chest attached to the tallest woman she had ever seen.

"I'm sorry to interrupt," Grace said. She turned to leave.

"Wait," he cried. "Please don't go."

The nurse said something to him in Spanish and left through the curtain on the other side.

"You came," he said.

Grace fought the tears that stung her eyes. "I wanted to see if you were okay."

Noah stood motionless, a pained look on his face. "I'm fine. Are you?"

Grace clenched her jaw, internally assessing if she was. She had been at the police station for a couple of hours of questioning. The terror from the shoot-out had worn off, but her nerves were still frayed. "I'll be all right."

"Come here." Noah reached his arms to her.

She gaped at him, at war with herself. Part of her wanted to be held by him while the other part didn't trust herself. When it came to Noah, she clearly couldn't think straight.

He had lied to her about why he was in town and what he was hiding from. He put her in danger. Not to mention the fact that he let her ride in the back of his van with all that cocaine like a fool.

Grace shook her head. "I'm sorry," she said, quickly wiping away the rogue tear that spilled over.

Noah dropped his arms. Heartbreak was written all over his face.

"Are you mad about me hugging Gloria? She was just trying to help me feel better."

Grace looked away. "I'm not mad about that." *Even if it's just another reminder that women will always be opening their arms for him.* "But how am I supposed to trust you, Noah? You lied about the cocaine. About seeing the drug cartel guys in Jaco when we were there."

Noah's eyes flared.

"Yeah. One of the officers let it slip. You told Clara you saw those men, and you didn't do anything about it. Jesus, Noah, what were you thinking?"

"I didn't want to ruin your last night in town. I was going to go to the police today, but I had to pick up my van first."

"You had a responsibility. And you didn't take it. If you think taking me on a romantic cruise instead of keeping us safe was some gallant Prince Charming maneuver, then you don't know me at all. You weren't thinking."

"You're right. I wasn't thinking. But it's because I was falling for you, Grace. Sometimes you have to live with your heart instead of your head."

Grace pressed her lips together, her blood roiling within her. "I can't live like that." She stewed, shaking her head. "Living your life with your heart has a price, and it's one I'm not willing to pay."

"What are you saying?" Noah said. His hand rushed to his head. He leaned on the hospital bed as if to steady himself. His face turned an ashen gray.

"Are you okay?"

"I've just been a little light-headed, that's all. I'm fine." His eyes darkened. "Please tell me this isn't over."

Her heart wanted to reach for him. To kiss away his pain. But touching him was what got her into this mess in the first place.

"I just don't think this can work out. A long-distance relationship needs to be built on trust, and we don't have that."

"Let me make it up to you. Let me show you that I'm trustworthy. Just give me a chance."

His begging was breaking down her resolve. She needed a new tactic, or this would go on forever.

"You don't even know what you want to do with your life yet, Noah. This isn't the right time for us to be together. We should call this what it is. Just a fling."

"It wasn't just a fling to me."

"I'm sorry," Grace said. "I have responsibilities, Noah. And you do too. You need to focus on taking care of yourself first."

Noah opened his mouth to speak, but nothing came out. His eyes dropped to his knees.

The nurse poked her head through the curtain. "Everything okay in here?"

Grace exchanged a glance with Noah, waiting for him to say something, but nothing came. The silence in the room felt like the slap in the face she needed to get the hell out of there.

"I was just leaving."

"Grace," he whispered. But he did not say stop. He did not beg her to stay. Instead, he hunched over, his sea-green eyes breaking away from her gaze in defeat.

"Goodbye, Noah," Grace said, walking through the curtain that led to the main lobby. She held back her tears for several steps until she recognized the detective she had met at the station, standing by the front doors.

Grace stumbled toward her, tripping over her own feet. She fell into Clara's arms, sobbing into the sleeve of the detective's pantsuit.

CHAPTER TWENTY-SIX

Grace's cab pulled down her quiet street, turning in to the driveway of her two-story brick home. She jumped out into the frigid air and took her carry-on roller bag out of the trunk.

The front porch light had been left on, the soft glow a gentle reminder that this was where she belonged. This was her safe place.

She stepped in through the front door, shutting out the frosty morning. The house was warm and smelled like tuna casserole from the night before.

It was five o'clock in the morning, and her eyes felt droopy. She hadn't slept on the plane due to the frazzled nerves and the broken-heart cocktail she consumed before catching her flight. Her mind raced through all the events of her trip instead.

Too tired to head up the stairs, she hung up her coat and took a seat in the corner of her couch with her laptop. Now that she was home, she needed to face her new life. She wouldn't be working for Maritime forever, and it was time she prepared to put her aunt in a nursing home.

She began searching for homes that didn't look like four-walled asylums. They couldn't afford the nicer homes in the area where a big chunk of the expenses seemed to go to land-scaping. Aunt Judy wouldn't need all that anyway. She preferred being inside. She needed something nice, practical. A place not too far away so Grace could visit her every day.

Grace's eyelids grew heavy in her search. It wasn't until she heard the soft "good morning" from the stranger in her living room that she realized she had dozed off. The man in front of her was middle-aged with a white goatee and a head full of white hair, and Grace expected him to be carrying a bucket of Kentucky Fried Chicken, but the Sunrise Home-care shirt and the small duffel bag at his side indicated he was the night-shift guy.

Grace quickly wiped the drool from her mouth and got up from the couch. "Hi," she said, her voice still groggy from sleep. "You must be Darren."

The man smiled. "And you must be Grace."

"How was she?"

Darren looked down the hall and back. He leaned forward to whisper in her ear, "She's a gosh-darn pain in the ass. But I can tell she has a good heart underneath all that sauce."

Grace smiled ruefully. "Thank you for everything. And for staying the extra night."

"It pays the bills, darlin'. It pays the bills."

Darren gave her a salute before heading out. Shortly after, Aunt Judy appeared down the hall, her hair snarled on one side, big puffy bags underneath her eyes. There must have been too much salt in her dinner last night. Grace made a note to remind Sunrise again that Aunt Judy couldn't eat too much sodium.

"Good morning," Grace said, rushing to her aunt to help her down the hall.

"Did Colonel Sanders leave? I was hoping to get one last look."

Grace giggled. "I'm sorry. He left a minute ago."

"Damn. It was nice having a man around here."

Grace led her to the kitchen table and started preparing her oatmeal.

"How was your trip?"

Grace tilted her head to the side. She didn't want to worry her aunt over what had happened with the cartel and Noah. She would tell her another day when she didn't have a life-altering decision to make. "It was… the trip of a lifetime."

"Oh really? I can't wait to hear about it."

"We need to talk first," Grace said, her eyes landing on the wall clock above her aunt's head. She had less than fifteen minutes until she needed to get ready for work. She had better start talking now, or she'd lose the nerve.

"What is it, dear?"

Grace sprinkled brown sugar in the pot of oats and stirred in the milk. "I realize that I haven't been giving you the option on whether you stay here or go to a nursing home," she said. "And I'm really sorry."

Aunt Judy's eyebrows slid up her forehead. "Oh? You're just realizing that?"

Grace took a deep breath. "The decision was never mine to make," she said softly. "And… although I don't want you to leave, I also don't want to keep you here just because I'm afraid of abandoning you. Or rather, I'm afraid of you abandoning me."

Aunt Judy gawked at her. "Well, I'll be damned. You're ready to have this conversation now?"

Grace fought through the tightening in her throat and the burning in her eyes, but she nodded. "Yes."

"Good. Because Cindy and I found the perfect place."

Grace sucked in a breath. "What? Who's Cindy?"

"Cindy replaced Tamara while you were gone, remember? Anyway, I was going to tell you when you were ready. But Cindy and I have been shopping around. We found a nursing home that specializes in MS patients."

"You did?" Grace's mouth flew open. "You've been looking?"

"When I found myself turned on by Mr. KFC, I knew I'd been cooped up here way too long."

Grace covered her mouth with her hand, stifling her laugh.

"I pinched his butt," Aunt Judy said, looking ashamed.

"Aunt Judy!" Grace shrieked. "You didn't."

"I blamed it on my muscle spasms," Aunt Judy said, sinking into her chair. "I apologized."

Poor Darren. "Shame on you. You're lucky he didn't file a report."

"I know, I know."

Grace sighed as she stirred the oatmeal on the stove, then turned to the coffee maker and added a new filter. She would need an entire pot just to keep herself awake until lunchtime.

"How much is the nursing home?" Grace said, scooping oatmeal into a bowl.

"It's about a quarter of what we're paying for Sunrise."

Grace's shoulders sagged with relief. "That's good." She set the bowl in front of her aunt and sprinkled cinnamon on top.

The cost of living in a home was the only silver lining of the whole situation. Her aunt's social security should be able to cover her living expenses there, which meant Grace might be able to start saving money for once.

"I'm going to miss you, Aunt Judy."

"Meh," Aunt Judy said before attempting to bring a spoonful of oatmeal to her mouth. "You're going to love having the place to yourself. You'll be able to date without my old ass cockblocking you." She waggled her eyebrows.

Grace chortled, shaking her head, ignoring the painful reminder that Noah wouldn't be a part of that plan.

"Speaking of dating, I almost forgot to tell you. When Cindy and I visited the home, we noticed that half their residents are men. *Men*, Grace! I'm going to have a hard time keeping my pinchers to myself."

Grace's head fell into her hands. "You need to come with a warning taped to your forehead."

"Ah, nonsense. I'll behave."

"I didn't know you were so randy," Grace said, shuddering at the word.

"Why do you think I watched all those romance movies with you? I was living vicariously, just like you were doing."

Grace opened her mouth and promptly shut it.

"I'm allowed to dream about my own Prince Charming too, you know. I have MS. I ain't dead."

Grace giggled and got up from her chair to give her aunt a big hug. "Oh, Aunt Judy. Please, just promise to keep it consensual."

"I promise, I promise."

Grace held her aunt for a long time, breathing in what smelled like Vick's vapor rub and lavender essential oil. "What's that smell?"

"Cindy made this concoction for me. Said it would help me sleep. I think she might be a witch because it worked."

Grace gave Aunt Judy her signature disapproving look.

"I'm going to miss seeing that face every day," Aunt Judy said, stroking the side of Grace's cheek with her shaky hand. "We had good times together."

"We did," Grace said, smiling through the growing lump in the back of her throat. "And we still will. I'll come visit you every day."

"About that," Aunt Judy hedged. "This place is in Cadillac, about an hour away."

"Oh," Grace said. "So, not every day."

"You can visit me on the weekends," Aunt Judy said, her eyes wet. She brought Grace in for another squeeze.

They held each other for several breaths.

"So what are you going to do with all this new free time of yours when I'm settled in a new home?"

Grace sighed, smiling to herself. "I'm going to start looking for teaching jobs."

"Really?" Aunt Judy said.

The coffee maker beeped, and Grace leaped toward it. She poured two cups of coffee before sitting back down next to her aunt. "I realized while I was in Costa Rica that sales is not what I want to be doing for a living. I think I want to try giving preschool teaching a real shot."

"It's about damn time." Aunt Judy's eyes were sparkling. "Good for you."

"Thanks." Grace smiled. "After that, I'll probably spend more time with Tessa. I've been thinking about doing something fun. Maybe a girls' trip or something."

Aunt Judy dropped her spoon, and it clanked against her bowl. "Who are you, and what have you done to my little Gracie?"

Grace smiled, looking away. "I met someone in Costa Rica who encouraged me to get out and live my life more."

"And what does this person have that I don't? I've been saying the same damn thing for years now."

Grace pictured Noah's sea-green eyes and the heartbreak written all over his face when she left him in that hospital room.

She sucked back her tears and forced a smile. "*Pura vida.* He had something called *pura vida.*"

Aunt Judy arched a single brow before turning back to her oatmeal.

※

Friday, October 29
   Noah: Did you make it home okay?
   Read.

※

Thursday, November 4
   Noah: I'm so sorry for everything… Can I call you?
   Read.

※

Friday, November 12
   Noah: Grace, can we talk please? I miss you.
   Read.

※

"When you said you wanted to go out, this wasn't really what I had in mind," Tessa said, hopping on her ATV. "I don't even know who you are anymore. ATV riding? Really?"

Grace shrugged. "I told you, I'm done being a homebody. There's so much more to life than cheesy rom-coms."

Tamara had asked to come by and visit with Aunt Judy, so Grace took the opportunity to spend the day with her best friend around Up North trails. She had booked an ATV rental with a tour group so they wouldn't get lost.

"I like this side of you," Tessa said, shimmying her shoulders. Her helmet wobbled around her neck.

"Better tighten that strap," Grace said, placing her own helmet on.

The roaring sound of ATV engines buzzed around her, and she turned on her own engine, tightening her grip around the handlebars. A flutter in her stomach whirred as their group of riders took off.

The train of ATVs crossed the main street before following the trail into the woods, picking up speed. It was a cool morning. The sun was shining, and the leaves left on the trees were still vibrant orange and yellow hues.

As they went faster, Grace couldn't shake the memories of being on the catamaran. She could almost feel the press of Noah's lips with the wind that snuck its way underneath her helmet.

She shivered. The unanswered text from yesterday haunted her thoughts. *Grace, can we please talk? I miss you.*

It had been weeks since she left Costa Rica, and she had hoped by now it would be easier to ignore him. But each day was harder than the last. Still, she couldn't respond, not when she was trying so hard to move on.

The trail wound up and down small hills, making her stomach drop with each dip. She had to navigate carefully. Every turn, every rock was a welcome distraction to the constant torment inside her head.

After an hour of riding around the forest trails, they arrived back at the rental shop. Grace's forearms were sore from all the gripping and steering.

"That was really fun," Tessa said. "Who would have thought Grace would be taking me out on an adventure like that?"

Grace elbowed her friend. They stripped out of their gear and thanked their guide before heading toward the diner across the street for an early lunch.

"Lunch is on me," Tessa said, sliding into a '50s-style red

leather booth. Her brother-in-law had hooked her up with a job at his firm, and apparently the pay was really good. A small jukebox was placed at the end of their table, and Tessa began flipping through the music choices.

"How's the new job going?"

"So good. The men wear suits, and they are oh so scrumptious to look at. Nothing like the tech nerds at Maritime. Hey, maybe you could come and work for the firm! I'm sure I can convince someone there to hire you. You're amazing."

"Oh, thanks. Actually, I've been applying to a bunch of teaching jobs lately."

"Yay!" Tessa's eyes sparkled. "That's great news. Does that mean—?"

"Yes," Grace said solemnly. "Aunt Judy moves into a nursing home after the holidays."

"No way," Tessa said, her jaw dropping. "You're going to be all alone in that house?"

"That's the plan."

"Do you know what this means?" Tessa reached across the table, pulling at Grace's sweater, shaking her aggressively. "This means you can be my wingwoman! You can come out with us when we go to the bars. It'll be so much fun."

Grace shrugged her shoulders. "Yeah, we'll see." Going to bars didn't really interest her so much, but Tessa had been asking her to go ever since she got a fake ID at the age of twenty.

Tessa angled her head in curiosity. "Aren't you ready to date?"

"Yes. Maybe. I don't know."

"What about that hot guy in Costa Rica? Whatever happened with him? You've been very vague in your texts lately. And your emoji game has been subpar."

"Sorry. I've had a lot on my mind lately." And spending an

inordinate amount of time staring at the two pictures she had taken of her and Noah.

The server set down their drinks and let them know their food would be out in a few minutes. Grace and Tessa thanked her before resuming their conversation.

"Tell me everything," Tessa said, sipping the fizzing soda.

"His name is Noah." The sound of his name being said out loud made her squirm in her seat. "Jane saw him first. But he wasn't into her."

"That's shocking. No offense."

"None taken," Grace said. "Anyway, Noah and I got to know each other. He's an amazing listener."

"Amazing kisser too?"

Grace's eyes sparkled in response.

"Stop it," Tessa said, hitting the table. "I need details."

Grace bit back her smile, picturing Noah coming back from surfing, with the sun glistening off his wet wavy tendrils, water dripping down his perfectly chiseled body. "He was incredibly charming." Her cheeks warmed. "And he was sweet too. He took me to see baby sea turtles hatching on the beach. He even got me to go zip-lining."

"No. Flipping. Way. He's the Grace Whisperer." Her hand was at her chest. "You're telling me he got you out of your hotel room?" Tessa's voice had reached a high-pitched trill.

Grace nodded. He also got her to stay *in* his hotel room, but she decided to keep that fact to herself.

"He sounds perfect."

"He *was* perfect," Grace said, slumping her shoulders. "Except for this teensy tiny little thing."

"What?"

Grace cupped her mouth with her hand and whispered, "He was involved in a drug cartel scandal."

"Whoa, whoa, whoa. *What?*"

Grace threw her head in her hands. "He had made up

some story about making a coffee delivery for his family when he was actually delivering *cocaine* to the police and hiding from the *cartel*. It was such a mess. The point is, he lied to me. And that's that."

"Oh. My. God."

Two giant plates of burgers and fries were placed at the table, plus an Oreo shake for Tessa. "Okay. I can't even be excited about this food when you just dropped a bomb on me like that."

Grace laughed, popping a fry in her mouth. "You don't even know the half of it."

"Tell me everything," Tessa said, taking a sip of her shake. Her eyes rolled to the back of her head. "Oh my god." Then she slapped the table once. Then twice. She bobbed her head until her blond hair fell over her eyes. "Damn, that's good."

"I'd give that an eight point five on the foodgasm scale." Grace snickered. "Anyway..." She proceeded to tell her the whole story, despite Tessa's inappropriate display of food affection. Well, almost the whole story.

Tessa was left speechless and stunned, unable to form words. She stuffed french fry after french fry in her mouth instead, staring at Grace in awe.

Grace took that moment of silence to eat her burger.

"So, you haven't texted him back?" Tessa said.

"I can't, right? I mean, it would just open up this gaping wound that I'm trying to heal. If I hear the sound of his voice, it would be the end of me."

"But what if he was actually getting his life together? Wouldn't you want to hear him out? I mean, you said so yourself that you loved his impulsive side. That he was able to get you out of your shell. No other person—not even your own best friend—has been able to do that. He must have something special if he can change my sweet little recluse of a friend into a death-defying daredevil."

Grace smirked. "I'd hardly call going on an ATV ride a death-defying experience."

"No, but you're out of the house, and that's something. You need someone like him in your life to break you out of your hyperfocused sense of duty. I think you should call him."

Grace slumped in her chair, poking at the extra lettuce leaf on her plate with a burned fry. "What good would that do? He lives all the way in Costa Rica. I just don't see how we could ever work."

Tessa took another sip of her shake. "Just because you don't have everything planned out doesn't mean you can't give this guy a real shot. He took a *bullet* for you, Grace. That's like Christian Slater in *True Romance* kind of love."

"That's the thing. Noah isn't Christian Slater in a movie, he's just a guy who wants to live in a yurt on the beach. He wants to surf all day and nothing else. Our lives are just too different."

Tessa leaned back, crossing her arms. "If you say so."

"Don't do that," Grace said, throwing a cold fry across the table. "You obviously think I should text him, but I'm just not ready to get my heart broken again, okay? I need time."

"Okay," Tessa said, pushing her tongue against her cheek.

The ping noise from Grace's phone caught both their attention. Grace opened the text, and her hand flew over her mouth.

Noah: Today the sky was the same shade as your eyes.

Below the text was a photograph of the sky with a thumbs-up in the bottom right corner. Grace held up the phone next to her face for Tessa to see.

"Holy flipping cow. It *is* the exact same color." Tessa gasped.

Grace's chest tightened. He was really making it difficult to move on. She would have to text him to stop or block him from her phone. And she knew in her heart she didn't want to do either.

CHAPTER TWENTY-SEVEN

T he front door swung open.

Noah jolted in the kitchen chair and accidentally knocked all his papers to the floor. "Is it Tuesday already?" Noah turned off his laptop computer.

"It sure is. And you look like shit," Kai said, entering the apartment with a duffel bag in hand. Kai had mentioned that he was going to swing by his apartment to drop off Noah's clothes from home, but Noah had been so wrapped up in his research, he hadn't noticed the time.

"You're early."

"Actually, *we're* late," Kai said.

"You brought Jolie?" Noah got up from the chair and picked up all the brochures from the floor. Then he ran to the coffee table and stacked the three empty cereal bowls and put them in the sink. Clothes were strewn around the room. Empty water cups were on nearly every flat surface of the apartment. It was too late to clean up.

Jolie stepped in the apartment; her eyes went wide, her mouth in the shape of an O.

She had almond-shaped eyes lined with thick eyelashes.

Tanned skin. A slender body. Tattoos up her arms and across her chest, peeking above the hem of her black tank top. She was the polar opposite to Kai, the golden boy in a polo and khaki shorts.

"Oh my," she gasped.

"Sorry," Noah said. "I lost track of time." He looked down at his underwear and smiled sheepishly.

Kai put his hands on his hips and looked around the room. "What's gotten into you, man? You were never this messy back at Ma's."

"It's an organized chaos," Noah said. "I was trying it out. Anyway, you'll be happy to know that I've been applying to schools. Maybe now you can finally get off my ass."

Kai picked up the college pamphlets on the kitchen table and studied them. His eyebrows pinched together. "Online schools?"

"Yeah," Noah said, crossing his arms over his chest. "I want to be flexible so I could take classes while living anywhere I want, especially if the cartel is still on my ass and I need to leave the country."

Kai perked up, his hand gripping the lighter he always had in his hand. "I thought Clara said you were in the clear."

"Calm down. I was just kidding. I should be good. Clara's been tracking them, and it doesn't seem like we have any reason to believe the cartel was after me specifically. They just wanted the cocaine."

"That's good," Kai said, putting his hand over Jolie's eyes. She had been gawking since she walked in.

Noah looked down at his boxer briefs. "Right. I need clothes."

"What you need is a shower. You smell like a hog's ass," Kai said.

"Your face is a hog's ass."

Jolie stifled her giggle behind them.

"Good one," Kai said, pushing him toward the bathroom. "Now take a shower while I clean your shit up."

"I'll pick everything up. Just give me two seconds to shower first. Good to see you again, Jolie," Noah said, stepping into the bathroom.

Under the shower, Noah willed himself to relax. It felt good to wash up. It had been a while since he'd showered and left the apartment. He had been lying low as instructed but also making a plan for his life.

He had been a damn fool to let Grace walk out of the hospital so easily, but she had a point that he couldn't argue. He needed to get his life together first.

He had a plan now. He'd go to school first, then figure out what he was going to do with the rest of his life. It was better than no plan at all, right? Noah just hoped it was enough to get Grace to see he was trustworthy and responsible.

The problem was, she hadn't responded to a single text.

Goddamn, he missed those deep, alluring blue eyes. Her giggles. The way she writhed under the slightest touch. Her taste. The noises she made when she was about to—

"Put down the mascara, and let's go!" Kai called, banging on the door. "Jolie's hungry. And if I don't feed her, she'll turn into a wildcat."

"I'm coming," Noah said, removing the grip on himself. He'd have to finish his thoughts later.

After his shower, he opened the door, and a cloud of steam billowed out around him. With a towel tightly snug around his waist, he grabbed the duffel bag Kai had brought and ducked behind the bedroom door.

"I have news," Kai said from the living room. "We close on the business this week."

Noah stepped out in his shorts and his favorite Hard Rock Cafe shirt from Madrid. "Whoa," Noah said. "How the hell did you pull that off?"

Kai shrugged. "I knew a guy," he said, exchanging a glance with Jolie.

"My father's friend is in acquisitions," Jolie said. "I introduced him to Kai, and they were able to strike a deal."

"Ma wants to split the profit."

"That's Ma's money though. She should keep it."

"It turns out Aunt Ida isn't doing so great, so she'll be in Berlin for a while. I'm selling her house so she can live in a condo when she comes back. It'll be easier to keep up. She'll have plenty of money, and she wants you to take your share."

Noah scratched the back of his neck. "How much is it?"

"Enough to pay for school. Or to build yourself a yurt by a beach somewhere," Kai said. "Just like you always wanted."

He could picture it now, surfing in the mornings. Studying during the day. He could finally have the life he had dreamed of.

Then what was with this sinking feeling in his gut?

He didn't want the yurt on the beach anymore. He didn't want to live alone with no one to share his day with. Or to have to rub crystals hanging from his rearview mirror to convince himself that he was happy.

He wanted Grace.

"Come on. Let's get you something to eat other than Fruity Pebbles," Kai said, wrapping his arm around Noah's head. He pulled him down for a noogie.

"You two are really cute," Jolie said.

"Did you hear that?" Noah said, breaking out of Kai's grasp. "She thinks I'm cute."

"Down, boy. She's taken," Kai said, shoving him out the door and into the apartment hallway.

"Maybe she's ready to upgrade to the new model?" Noah waggled his eyebrows before getting decked in the chin.

Big-screen TVs blared from every corner of the dimly lit bar with brightly colored videos to match the music filling the space.

"Cerveza?" Kai said, ushering the server over. He ordered a pitcher and a plate of nachos.

"Kai told me you took a bullet in the butt," Jolie said. "How did that even happen?"

Noah's eyes fixed on the stone columns of the gazebo in the square, attempting to brush off the pang in his stomach that followed every time he thought about that day. "I was trying to protect a girl," he said flatly.

"What girl?" Kai said. "You didn't tell me there was someone in the van with you."

Noah ran his hand through his hair. "Just some girl," he managed to say. "She showed up at the wrong time and got thrown in the van with me."

"Boy, does that sound familiar," Jolie said, eyeing Kai teasingly. He pulled her into his side, tickling under her arms.

"So what happened to her?"

Noah shrugged. "She's in Michigan," he said, putting his hand up like a mitten and pointing to the top of his forefinger like Jane had shown him before.

The pitcher arrived with three glasses placed in front of them. "Your nachos will be right out," the server said in Spanish. Her hand slightly brushed the top of Noah's shoulder. Bringing his eyes to meet hers, she gave him a wink and rushed off.

"I think she likes you," Jolie said.

"Everywhere we go," Kai grunted, shaking his head. "Without fail."

Noah hadn't even noticed the server until Jolie said something. She had a pretty, makeup-free face and big brown eyes. But she wasn't Grace.

Kai poured each of them a glass and held his beer out. "Here's to making it out alive," Kai said.

"Barely," Noah grumbled, clinking his glass with Kai's.

Kai eyed him over his beer. "Is there more to this girl than what you're letting on?"

"I don't know. Maybe," Noah said, looking away from the beautiful couple sitting in front of him. He was happy that his brother had found love, but it didn't feel great to see what he was missing. "It doesn't matter now. She's gone."

Jolie narrowed her eyes at him, studying him like a textbook. "Have you tried calling her?"

"I texted her a few times, but she's not responding. I fucked it up real bad by getting her in the middle of that cartel bust."

"You knew her before?" Kai asked.

"I met her on my way to Jaco. She's the reason I was staying at that resort."

Kai took a swig of his beer, nodding his head. "I see."

"Like I said, it doesn't matter anymore. She won't hear me out." Noah's eyes landed on the large tray of nachos heading his way. The tray was set between them, and wafts of shredded chicken and cheese filled his nostrils. He'd normally attack a plate like this, but his stomach felt uneasy and a little acidic from all the sugary cereal he had been eating instead of proper food.

"Okay," Jolie said, leaning in close, "tell me everything you know about her, and we'll come up with some ideas to win her over."

Noah was hesitant at first, stuffing nachos in his mouth to buy himself time. But eventually he told Jolie everything he knew about Grace. From her snow globe collection to the name of the home care service she was having trouble with. And everything in between. Together, the three of them came up with a plan that had Noah's heart pounding in his chest.

"You sure this is going to work?" Noah said. Because if it didn't, he'd never get another chance with Grace again.

"If it doesn't, then at least you can say you did everything you could," Kai said.

Kai was right. Kai was always right.

The server showed up a moment later, batting her eyelashes at Noah. "Can I get you anything else, handsome? Tacos? Arepas? A date Saturday night?"

Noah smiled. "I'm sorry, but I'm taken."

CHAPTER TWENTY-EIGHT

A notification popped up on Grace's computer screen, and she groaned. Miranda's staff meeting was in five minutes. It was the one meeting she had every week where she couldn't avoid Jane. Last week they'd had a celebration for landing their first international account. Miranda had bought a gluten-free cake adorned with pink and purple tropical flowers and green palm trees. It read CONGRATULATIONS, JANE across the front. Grace hadn't cared that Jane got all the credit. She was just happy to not have to work with her anymore.

Todd had been next in line. He was assigned to help Jane on her next big account. Grace had to assume he was thrilled about that.

Meanwhile, Grace had returned to the accounts she had been working on and had spent some time putting together her restaurant crawl idea. Grace figured while she was looking for another job, she might as well work on a project she was excited about. She pitched the idea to Miranda a couple of weeks ago, and Miranda loved it so much she asked the tech team to start working on a prototype right away.

She checked her personal email again, a habit she had formed ever since her interview with Pioneer Prep a few days ago. It was the perfect preschool: close to home, with a warm and caring director, and the children were absolutely precious. She'd gotten to take a sneak peek in one of the classes before she left. No email yet.

Grace groaned to herself as she watched the account executive team file into the conference room at the end of the hall. She got out of her chair and forced herself to follow suit.

Leather chairs lined the conference table and along the back wall. As the team settled in, some joking and laughing, others quiet and waiting, Miranda came in and flicked off the fluorescent lights.

Grace couldn't help but notice Jane and Todd were not in the room.

"All right everyone," she said with a clipped tone. "Let's get started." The room fell silent. "We have a special guest this afternoon. Rich Lambert is joining us."

Right on cue, the CEO walked in the room. His heavily creased forehead bore the wrinkles of a man who had worked hard his whole life, but he still looked like a modern-day Paul Newman in his old age with his white hair and the same hazel eyes as Jane. He waved to everyone before taking a seat at the end of the table.

"Don't mind me," he said. "Miranda told me there were a few ideas being pitched today. I wanted to see for myself the amazing work. Just pretend I'm not here."

The collective spines in the room stiffened. Everyone was always on edge in front of the CEO.

"Jane and Todd are currently in Vegas with a potential client, but they will be joining us over our video conference soon," Miranda said. She turned to her administrative assistant and gestured toward the computer. "While Hilary gets us connected,

I can tell you all what's on the agenda for today. We have a couple of presentations and then a special announcement."

The room buzzed in anticipation. Anytime Miranda had an announcement, someone was either fired, hired, or promoted. All eyes fell on Rich.

The air escaped Grace's lungs. Today would be the day of Jane's announcement as the new CEO. She sank in her chair, checking her phone again. She needed that preschool job before Jane decided to kick her out of Maritime. It was a wonder she hadn't already done it.

Still no email from Pioneer.

A moment later, the projector screen was turned on, and Jane's and Todd's faces appeared, sitting in a fancy hotel room. Todd's face was sullen compared to Jane's bright smile.

"Hi, everyone. Hi, Daddy," Jane said, waving through the screen.

"Hi, pumpkin," Rich said.

"You'll be so proud of me," Jane said to the room. "Todd convinced me to use PowerPoint instead of my boards."

Of course Jane would give Todd the kudos for something Grace started in Costa Rica, but it didn't matter. Grace would be long gone from Maritime by the time Jane moved into her new office. Whether it was her decision or not.

The muscles in Todd's jaw flexed, but he said nothing and just stared into the video camera.

"Are you ready to pitch your grand idea?" Miranda said, several decibels too loud. Video conference technology was relatively new to Maritime, and people didn't realize the microphones overhead picked up every sound in the room.

"We're ready," Jane said.

"Let me just share my screen," Todd mumbled. A second later, a PowerPoint slide was up, and Todd and Jane's video minimized to the top right corner of the TV.

Grace had to blink a few times to make sure she was reading the title page correctly.

THE FOODIE TOUR CRAWL

Her jaw dropped. Her pulse quickened as heat rose to her face and ears.

Jane began her pitch, the same idea Grace had shared with her, replacing only a few details. "No lines. No food envy. No hard decisions on where to eat. The menu options would be curated in advance while the guests feel like they are getting the VIP treatment. With just a click of a button on our customer's website, guests will have a day or night planned full of the best food the city has to offer at a competitive price."

Grace whipped her head toward Miranda to see her face had grown pale. Could she be thinking that Grace stole the idea from *Jane*?

Grace's mouth went dry; her tongue felt like sandpaper coated with ash. Her stomach churned with rage as she listened to the stolen idea spew from Jane's mouth through the overhead speakers.

Jane's father nodded in approval with a proud smile as he listened intently.

Jane knew she had the power to steal Grace's idea. She knew she could get away it, that Grace would say nothing for fear of losing her job.

But what Jane didn't know was Grace had had enough. She might not have a job lined up just yet, but she was close enough. Something boiled deep inside her until it escaped her lips. "Stop."

Jane froze, and the whole room's eyes fell on Grace.

"You stole my idea."

"I'm sorry, is there a question?" Jane said.

"This is *my* idea," Grace said, pointing to the screen. "I

pitched this to you in Costa Rica, and you said it was a bad idea."

Jane laughed. "Oh, Grace. Honey. This is not the same idea you had. Not even close."

Grace stood up, not caring that the CEO was watching her accuse his daughter of lying. Not caring if this would cost her job before she was ready to lose it.

"It was my idea, and I've already done all the work. You're just putting your name on it," Grace said calmly, her nose flaring. "I have the presentation and the work ticket to prove it."

"Just because you got a head start doesn't mean the idea came from you," Jane said sternly. "It was my idea first."

Grace looked at Miranda for help, but she just sat there, blinking, saying nothing.

"Are there any further outbursts, or can I proceed?" Jane snapped.

"Proceed," Rich said firmly, glaring at Grace.

"But...," Grace started.

"Sit down," Rich said. "And let her finish."

Grace's tongue felt like a dirty sock in her mouth. She now knew what that was like after all. A lump formed in the back of her throat, and she slinked into her chair.

Jane proceeded with her pitch as if everything was fine, clicking from slide to slide while the room went eerily silent.

No one believed Grace. Or if they did, they were too afraid to say anything. Rich had clearly taken Jane's side for obvious reasons. And now Grace looked like a jealous plebeian, attempting to bring Jane down before her announcement as new CEO.

After their pitch was done, the room clapped awkwardly, some associates not clapping at all. Their eyes fell on Grace as she sat in dumbfounded silence. Miranda's frown spoke volumes, her disappointment written all over her face.

"Good job, sweetie," Rich said. "It's a great idea. I could see why others would want to claim it for themselves."

Grace closed her eyes, ready to run out of the room. But then Miranda called on Ron to share his idea.

The screen flickered as Jane's presentation was pulled off from the video share. Jane and Todd's giant heads flashed up for a brief moment. Todd's eyes fixed on Jane, his jaw clenched.

Maybe Todd had seen how evil Jane could be. Perhaps he was the only one to believe Grace's side of the story. His lips parted as if he were going to say something, but he immediately clamped them shut, then turned off their video.

The screen went black, apart from Todd's printed name.

"Here we go," Hilary said. "Pulling up Ron's presentation now."

Ron proceeded with his extreme water sports idea, flashing images he'd lifted from the internet. Hilary clicked to the next slide with each head nod. By the time he got to his kite surfing slide, a soft murmur came over the speaker.

Ron paused, tilting his head to listen.

The murmuring was clearly Jane and Todd talking in the background. Their video screen had been turned off, but their audio had been left on.

"I'm sorry, can you put yourself on mute, please?" Ron said.

Jane's voice boomed overhead. "I don't care that you think Grace was telling the truth. So what if it was her idea? It doesn't matter. She won't have a job here when I'm CEO anyway."

The room gasped.

"Jane. You're unmuted," her father boomed.

"I don't think it's right that you can get away with stealing her idea." Todd's voice came over the line.

"Listen. If you want to run your own company, you have

to make tough decisions. When an opportunity presents itself, you take it," Jane said.

"Jane, for crying out loud!" Rich yelled. "Mute your microphone."

His loud plea went unanswered, and everyone in the room froze, waiting for the next thing to slip out of Jane's mouth.

"Actually," Todd said, "I couldn't agree more with that."

"Oh really? Are you finally coming around?" Jane crooned.

"I do love a good opportunity," Todd said.

"Jane!" Rich yelled. "For God's sake. Cut her off!"

Hilary's eyes flew to her screen, panicked. She appeared to be searching for a way to mute Jane's video, clicking wildly. Instead of muting Jane, she killed Ron's presentation, and the screen went black again.

"Are you reconsidering what we talked about?" Jane said.

"You'll have to remind me of the terms and conditions," Todd said.

Grace's hand leaped toward her chest as she held her breath.

"One night with me, and I will make you senior sales associate," Jane said.

A series of gasps rippled through the room.

"Goddammit, Hilary!" Rich said, reaching for one of the cords connected to her computer. He yanked it out, but nothing changed. He must have pulled a power cord.

"And what does one night with you entail, exactly?" Todd said.

"You. Me. Naked. Perhaps a little nipple play if you're into it," Jane said.

"So you're telling me if I have sex with you, I will be—"

Rich yanked at another cord, and the black screen shut off. The sound cut out.

Everyone gaped at Rich, whose chest was heaving, his face red.

"Show's over," he gritted through his teeth. "Everyone out."

The following afternoon, Grace was surprised to find Todd at his desk. He looked up, catching her stare. He gestured for her to come over to his cubicle.

Grace gulped, soldiering forward, not knowing what to think after the episode from yesterday.

"You're here," Grace said.

Todd laughed. "Are you surprised?"

Grace shrugged her shoulders, looking around the sea of cubicles. She noticed Jane's desk was empty.

"I wasn't sure what to expect after what happened yesterday. You do know that everyone heard your conversation with Jane, right?"

Todd bit his lip, a twinkle in his eye. "Oh yeah," he said. "I made sure to dial down the volume so she couldn't hear what you all were saying."

"You set her up on purpose?" Grace's fingers covered her open mouth.

"Like I said, I like a good opportunity. When I realized she had stolen your idea, I knew I couldn't be quiet anymore. I had to do something. And she had been harassing me for months."

"What? I thought you had a thing for Jane."

"Hell no," Todd said. "She was toying with me. At first I just kind of let it slide. Then she was finding any reason to touch me, to get me alone. It was creeping me out. When I saw you talking to her at the company picnic, I was going to warn you about her. I was going to tell you to stay away from her."

Grace's fingers slid down to her neck. "I thought you *liked* her then."

Todd stuck his tongue out. "No way."

Grace tried to play back that day in her mind. She had misunderstood the entire situation, assuming he was smitten with Jane.

"I'm so sorry. I should have listened to you. You were trying to get me to stay in that playhouse, and I left you alone with her and—"

"Don't worry about it. You didn't know. I told her to take a hike, although I think that only fueled the fire. The more I rejected her, the harder she tried. And when you came back from Costa Rica, she filed a request to work with me."

Grace's eyes drifted over his face. A face she had once considered the most handsome in the world.

"What happened after yesterday?" Grace said.

"Jane got a call from Rich. She kicked me out of her room when she realized what I had done. I called Miranda and explained everything. I had no intention of sleeping with Jane to become her backfill. Luckily, Miranda believed me."

"What's going to happen with Jane?" Grace said.

Todd shrugged. "I don't know, and I don't care. I'm looking to get the hell out of this job."

"Good. You should."

"What about you?" Todd said. "You must be pretty pissed that nobody believed you yesterday."

Grace sighed, looking down at her boots. "I was, don't get me wrong. But I'm also on my way out too. I've been looking for other jobs myself."

"Good for you. You're too good for this place anyway," he said. "Hey, since we're both going to be leaving, we should grab dinner sometime."

"Dinner?" Grace gulped.

"Yeah." He smiled hopefully. "I've been meaning to ask you out for a while, but... I don't know. I didn't work up the nerve until now. I'm kind of a homebody. I don't get out much."

Grace's head was swirling. Had she just heard him right?

Months ago, she would have killed for a homebody boyfriend. To spend her free time watching movies and eating popcorn. But she wasn't the same person she was months ago. She didn't need someone keeping her home, another crutch, preventing her from living her life.

She wanted to get out more. She wanted fun.

Grace looked up into Todd's honeycomb eyes. There was no spark. No warmth. No fluttering in her stomach as she held his gaze.

He was not Noah, and no man would ever be.

Grace shook her head. "I'm sorry, but I just don't have feelings for you like that anymore. I used to, but not anymore."

He nodded in quiet acceptance. "I'm too late," Todd said, his shoulders slumped.

"I had a major crush on you before. But... I'm in love with someone else."

Grace cupped her hand over her mouth. The truth had escaped before she even realized she said it.

Todd placed his palm over his heart as if he had been wounded. "Ouch. I didn't realize."

"I can't believe I said that."

"It's okay. I get it."

Grace was turning down Todd Freaking Meyers. She shook her head in disbelief. But her heart belonged to someone else. Someone she desperately missed, despite how things ended in Costa Rica.

"Can we be friends?" Grace said.

Todd's face softened. The skin around his eyes crinkled with a smile. "I'd like that."

Grace smiled before turning to leave. She stalked back to her desk, sat in her chair, and pulled up the text messages she still hadn't responded to. The last one in particular resonated in her heart:

Noah: I'll never give up on you as long as you keep reading these messages. Keep reading for me, Grace.

Noah was promising not to give up on her, but she knew deep down he'd eventually move on with his life if she didn't let him in. How long would this window of opportunity last? And what if he did move on by the time she was ready to talk?

She couldn't stomach the thought. She had to text him back.

No. She had to call him. To hear him out. To give him a chance. To give them both a chance.

Grace couldn't stay in the office any longer. It was only four o'clock, but she didn't care. To hell with this place. She was going home early.

She gathered her purse and rushed down the steps, hoping she wasn't already too late.

Grace drove down her neighborhood street, still trying to think of something to text to Noah. A simple "hey" didn't seem appropriate after what they had been through. And a confession of her feelings and how much she had missed him also didn't feel right.

She'd have to slowly work her way into a conversation and hope for the best.

When she arrived at her house, she noticed her lawn had been raked. A trash bag of leaves rested by the garbage can. A neighbor must have helped.

Grace put her car into park and then noticed Christmas lights strung up on the roof. They hadn't been turned on yet, but they were there.

What the heck?

Maybe Cindy, the home care worker, did all this. Cindy was one of the better Sunrise workers, but she wouldn't have raked their leaves and put up Christmas lights. She would have been too busy with Aunt Judy, unless she was able to get her outside.

An icy gust of wind pummeled her window.

No, Aunt Judy wouldn't have lasted more than two seconds out here.

Grace was about to march up to the front door and see if she could get to the bottom of it when her phone buzzed. She scrambled through her purse to retrieve it.

"Hello?"

"Hello, Grace? This is Jennifer from Pioneer Prep."

"Oh!" Grace's heartbeat fluttered in her chest. "Hi."

"Do you have a moment to chat?"

"I do," Grace croaked.

"Wonderful! I'm calling because I'd like to extend an offer for you to work for us at Pioneer Prep."

Grace gasped. "Really? Yes. I'll take it. When do I start?"

Jennifer laughed on the phone. "I haven't even told you your salary yet."

Grace laughed at herself for being so impulsive, but the truth was, the salary didn't matter. She would be doing what she loved, doing what would make her happy.

Jennifer finished giving Grace all the details, and they

seemed fair enough. Grace would have to put in her two weeks' notice with Miranda tomorrow morning. The idea of it thrilled her.

"Thank you so much, Jennifer. I am so excited to work for you."

"We are lucky to have you. See you in a couple of weeks."

Grace gaped at her phone, glowing from within.

Everything was coming together. Well, almost.

She pulled up the last text from Noah and stared at the screen until the inside of her car matched the icy air outside.

She let her thumbs fly free over her phone.

Grace: I'll keep reading if you keep texting. Don't give up on me, Noah. I'm almost there.

She released a shaky breath as she slipped her phone back in her purse and got out of the car. It was time to solve the mystery of the secret do-gooder.

Grace stepped inside her warm house and gasped. Her heart nearly stopped.

Aunt Judy and Cindy were sitting at the dining table, a deck of cards in front of them. At the opposite end of the table was Noah, holding a fan of cards in one hand, his cell phone in the other, and a shimmery look in his eyes.

CHAPTER TWENTY-NINE

"Noah? What in the hell are you doing here?"

Aunt Judy and Cindy looked up at her like squirrels deciding whether to run or cross the street.

Grace tilted her head, noticing the makeup on Aunt Judy's face. The touch of color on her cheeks. She wore her usual attire, a matching soft pink sweat suit, but she looked different. More put together. Her hair clipped back without a strand out of place.

"What in the— Are you playing *cards*?" Grace said, shutting the door behind her.

"Yeah, what's it to ya?" Aunt Judy snapped, doing a terrible job of hiding her smile.

Cindy's face reddened, her eyes shifting between Aunt Judy and Noah.

"Turns out your aunt is a hell of a player." Noah laughed nervously.

Cindy stood up, gathering the cards from the pile and from Noah's and Aunt Judy's hands. "Judy, let's let these two catch up, shall we? Why don't you go down for a nap?"

"And miss this?" Aunt Judy said.

Grace put her hands on her hips and glared at her aunt.

"All right, fine," Aunt Judy grumbled. "As long as you two catch up while making me dinner. It's enchilada night. Grace, you promised."

"Oh, I know." Grace sighed heavily. "You will get your enchiladas after someone explains to me what the heck is going on around here."

Aunt Judy rolled herself away from the table, and that was when Grace realized Aunt Judy had been in her wheelchair.

"Whoa there. Wait a minute. You're in your *wheelchair*? I've been trying to get you in that wheelchair for years. I feel like I've just entered into an alternate universe or something."

Aunt Judy's eyes drifted to Noah and back again, glittering with amusement. "Noah helped me get in it. Turns out I just needed a pair of strong, masculine hands." She winked at Noah.

Grace covered her forehead with her hand. "Please tell me that you didn't inappropriately touch Noah while he's been here for God knows how long."

Aunt Judy's hands flew up in surrender. "I'm innocent."

"I can attest," Cindy said, stepping behind the wheelchair. "I've been with her the whole time, and she's been on her best behavior. I'll get her set up in her room, and then I'm taking off."

"Thanks," Grace muttered, watching them disappear down the hall.

She turned to face Noah, who was looking up through his eyelashes like a naughty child.

"What are you doing here, Noah?" she said softly.

Noah stuffed his hands into his jeans pockets. He was wearing a cable-knit sweater over a collared shirt. He looked like a Ralph Lauren model from the Blue Collection.

"I'm here to make enchiladas, apparently," he said with a smile.

Grace folded her arms. "How did you know where to find me?"

Noah smirked. "I have my ways."

"Were you the one who raked the leaves and put up the Christmas lights?"

Noah shrugged his shoulders. "I fixed your fireplace too," he said, pointing at the hearth. Grace hadn't even noticed it until now.

Across from the fireplace was a giant bouquet of green palms sitting in a glass vase. The delicate fronds splayed out like a giant peacock. Grace felt her cheeks warm from the memory of that night, heat pooling between her legs.

"But... but why?"

"I wanted to show you that I am responsible. That you can trust me. Now where do you keep your enchilada things?"

Grace laughed, still unable to process what she had just come home to. She wanted to jump in his arms and kiss him, but the lingering memory of her near-death experience with the cartel gripped tight.

She didn't know what else to do, so she pointed to the cabinets.

"Thank you for your help," Grace said, opening her pantry. "And for the palms." She pulled out a giant can of enchilada sauce and set it on the counter. "But you didn't have to do all this."

Noah grabbed the can opener hanging from one of the hooks on the side of the fridge and began opening the can. The smell of salty ocean lingered on his skin, and Grace found herself taking a deep breath in.

"I wanted to," Noah said, cranking his wrist until the can top popped open.

Cindy waved goodbye from the front door and shut it behind her with a soft thud.

"So, what's your plan, Noah? You came here to help me around the house? For what?"

Grace pulled out the shredded chicken she had made the day before and began mixing it with sauce and shredded cheese.

"First, please forgive me," Noah said.

Grace stopped mixing in her bowl to look up into his eyes.

"I realize that's completely unfair of me to ask of you because I may never forgive myself for what happened in Costa Rica, but I hope you can forgive me."

Grace swallowed. "And if I do...?"

The corner of Noah's mouth twitched into a grin. "Then we can proceed to phase two of my plan."

"And what's phase two?" Grace said, arching a brow.

Noah looked down at the bowl on the counter. "Filling little corn tortillas." A playful glint flashed through his eyes.

Grace bit back her smile and put a hand on her hip.

"I'm just kidding," he said, nudging her with his elbow. The contact nearly shattered her. Grace's shaky knees were barely holding her upright.

"Phase two involves me going back to school online. I start in the new year."

"You're going back to school?"

Noah nodded. "I'll be going to school to figure out what I want to do with my life. But I know for sure it won't be surfing all day."

"Really?" Her heart beat faster as he stepped in closer.

"Really," he said, reaching his hands toward the sink. His arm lightly grazed hers while he turned on the faucet. Grace's body trembled with desire as he washed his hands.

"And what's phase three?" she rasped.

Noah dried his hands on the kitchen towel before leaning against the counter. "Well, phase three depends entirely on you. You said in your text that you were *almost there*. What do I have to do to get you all the way? To convince you that I'm worth a second chance?"

Grace sucked in a breath, inhaling his ocean scent.

His hands reached for her face, gently cupping both sides of her head, and Grace instinctually tilted her chin up, closing her eyes. She felt the nearness of his mouth, his breath tickling her lips. "Please, Grace. Forgive me."

"I—"

"Good grief, you could cut the sexual tension in here with a knife." Aunt Judy had wheeled herself back into the kitchen. "Is it dinnertime yet?"

Noah jumped away while Grace turned back to her mixing bowl. "Dinner will be ready soon," she said.

Noah grabbed the corn tortillas from the pantry and helped her fill the enchiladas in silence, but the soft brushes of his arm were riling her up, igniting her body on fire.

While the food was in the oven, Aunt Judy instructed Noah where to find the plates and silverware, and before Grace knew it, they were all seated at the dining table. The soft glow of the kitchen light shone down on their faces.

Without even asking, Noah leaned over to cut up Aunt Judy's food into small pieces.

"You're a natural with old farts like me," Aunt Judy said, nodding in appreciation.

Grace was about to roll her eyes when she watched him tuck a napkin into her aunt's shirt and put another one on her lap. Her heart squeezed.

"Well," Aunt Judy said, taking a shaky spoon from her mouth. "I don't know how long you plan on staying, but you have to at least stick around until I move out. I'm going to need all the brawn I can get to move into a new home. And by the look of your rippling biceps—good taste by the way," Aunt Judy said to Grace with a wink, "you seem like you will come in handy."

"Aunt Judy," Grace hissed, her face burning hot. "Keep your roaming eyes to yourself."

"Ladies, ladies. No need to fight," he said in that cocky way of his. Grace wanted to kiss that grin right off his face. "I'd be happy to stay here and help you move. But it's really up to Grace."

Grace's fork froze in the air as she looked at Aunt Judy and back up to Noah. She almost choked on the bite she had just taken. "You mean... you don't have to go back to Costa Rica?"

"I'm a free agent. I can go wherever I want."

"Oh," she said, setting her fork down. "You mean, this wasn't just a quick visit?"

Noah shook his head slowly, his eyes gleaming. "We can talk about that later, but I have some money from selling off our family business. I can rent a place anywhere I want. I could have bought a yurt by the beach, but I figured I'd check out the real estate options in Traverse City first."

Grace's mouth fell open.

"The least we can do is offer you a place to stay tonight," Aunt Judy said, eyeing Grace. "Right, Gracie?"

Noah looked at Grace for approval.

"Of course," Grace croaked out. "You should stay here. For the night."

Noah smiled before taking a bite of his enchilada.

They were quiet the rest of the dinner. Grace's head was spinning with the reality that she and Noah might actually have a real chance.

Aunt Judy claimed that the excitement from the day had tuckered her out, so she asked to be put to bed. Although she wasn't so subtle with the exaggerated wink she gave Noah before wheeling herself down the hall.

Grace helped her get ready while Noah cleaned the kitchen. She held out Aunt Judy's nightgown for her and watched her wash her face and brush her teeth on her own. She would soon have a whole staff of people to care for her in this way. And even though Grace would miss her dearly, she also felt a sense of freedom for both herself and her aunt. They would both be getting fresh starts. New chapters in their own lives.

"He's a good one," Aunt Judy said, sleep in her voice. "Don't let that boy get away, you hear?"

"I won't," Grace said, giving her a kiss on the cheek before pushing herself off the bed.

Grace shut the door and tiptoed down the hall. She turned on the television to add a bit of white noise so her aunt wouldn't hear their conversation.

As she pulled up the news, something caught her eye.

A video of a giant cruise ship sailed across a tropical blue ocean. The headline below in all caps: 200 KILOS OF COCAINE MISSING FROM ABANDONED POLICE VAN.

"Noah," Grace said. "Come look at this."

Noah appeared in Aunt Judy's frilly pink rose apron, wiping his hands on a towel as he stepped into the living room.

The newscaster's face appeared. "An abandoned police vehicle was found on the west coast of Costa Rica. Two hundred kilos of cocaine is believed to be missing from the police van, which had been on its way to a secured location. The two hundred kilos of contraband had been taken into evidence last month."

"Holy shit," Noah muttered under his breath.

"Is that the same—?"

"I think it is."

They both stared at the television in shock.

"Well, I'll be damned," Noah said. "The cocaine is on the loose again."

CHAPTER THIRTY

After Grace and Noah finished putting the dishes away, Noah hung Aunt Judy's apron on the side of the fridge. "Would you like to see your Christmas lights now?" he said with a smile.

With everything going on, she had completely forgotten that he had strung them up outside. "Yes, please!"

"All right. I have to grab something from my bag. I'll meet you outside for the big reveal."

"Big reveal?" Grace said. She was tingling all over with anticipation, just like she did when she was a kid.

"I wanted you to be the first person to see them at night."

Grace cupped her hand over her heart. She could have kissed him, but he whispered, "Be right back" and sprinted across the house toward the laundry room where he must have stored his bag.

Noah was here. In her house. Grace still couldn't believe it as she slipped on her boots and her coat and braced herself for the outdoors.

The sky was a hazy black. The air was frosty, but thankfully the wind had died down. She settled her butt on the hood of her car, looking up at her house. Sizzling smoke escaped through the chimney stack, a sight she hadn't seen since she was a little girl.

Noah's silhouette appeared through the window as he crossed the living room. Her heartbeat quickened at the sight of him on the front stoop with his jacket on, his beanie pulled over his ears.

The faint glow from the house and from the streetlight illuminated the twinkle in his eyes. "You ready for this?" he said, his voice shaking from the cold.

"About as ready as I'll ever be," Grace said, feeling her warm breath turn into a cloud in front of her. "I've been waiting to see Christmas lights up again for a very long time."

"Okay, well. Get ready to have your mind blown," Noah said. "I'm going to count down." He crouched by the panel where the outlet must have been.

"Three. Two. Are you sure you're ready?"

Grace let out a large sigh. "Noah!"

"One."

Grace's eyes grew wide as she took in the brightly colored lights, hanging in disarray. The strings hung in awkward loops and zigzagged in ways that defied reason or any sense of artistic ability.

A laugh escaped her throat before she could stop it. She hadn't wanted to hurt Noah's feelings, but it was just so bad.

She felt the car move under his weight as he sat down beside her, taking in the monstrosity. Like a Pinterest hack gone wrong.

"Ta-da," Noah said, holding his hands out.

Grace cupped her face with her gloved hands. "Wow, Noah. I don't know what to say."

"It's a hot mess," he said, laughing at himself. "I had this whole vision in my head, but it didn't quite turn out the way I wanted to. I'm sorry."

Grace laughed. "That's more than a hot mess, that's—"

"A complete and utter failure?"

"No," Grace said, shaking her head. "No, not a failure."

Noah laughed, sliding his gloved hand onto hers. "It's okay. I've come to terms with the fact that I'm going to make mistakes," he said, not taking his eyes off the colorful mess. "I'm going to fail at a lot of things. But I'm not going to let it stop me from trying anymore."

Grace squeezed his hand. "I'm proud of you."

The silence that followed felt like a warm, healing blanket that had been draped over their laps. Grace looked upon the brightly colored bulbs and scooted in closer, resting her head on his shoulder.

"This might be the world's most underwhelming Christmas lighting ceremony, but you didn't fail. I would call this a success."

"You would?" Noah said. "Do you need to get your eyes checked?"

"No, I mean, it was a success because it made me happy," she said, lifting her head to see his face. She couldn't go another minute without looking into his eyes.

"This made you happy?" he said, his gaze dropping to her mouth.

"Very." She tilted her chin up to catch his lips on hers. His face and mouth were warm, but the tip of his nose was ice cold as it brushed against her cheek. She brought her gloved hands around his neck and pulled him closer. His arms slid round her waist, his tongue tracing the seam of her lips.

She parted her mouth, giving him access. Her back arched in response as she pressed her body into him. His sweet and tender kisses grew ravenous, more desperate with each breath.

Grace's hands were everywhere and nowhere at the same time. There were too many layers. Too much fabric blocking her from his skin. She tugged and pulled, unproductively, gasping into his mouth. "You have too many clothes on," she huffed, her hands moving to his jeans.

"I was just thinking the same thing," Noah said before nipping at her bottom lip. Grace groaned, brushing her hands up his leg until she came across a bulge so hard and large it startled her. She whipped her hand back and stared at the giant protrusion in his pants.

"What the—?"

"Oh!" Noah said, reaching for his pocket. "I almost forgot. I wanted to give this to you."

He reached into his jeans pocket and pulled out a small snow globe. The glow from the Christmas lights illuminated the tiny globe sitting in the palm of his hand. A baby sea turtle swam inside around a swirling snowstorm. On the base of the stand, in bright, colorful letters, read PURA VIDA.

"I went to twenty different tourist shops to find it."

"Oh my god," Grace said breathlessly. Her heart soared at the memory of the little creatures on the beach. "It's so beautiful," she squeaked, feeling the lump in her throat. Her vision blurred from unshed tears. "Thank you. Thank you so much."

"I was wrong." Noah smiled. "Looks like a sea turtle really can live in the snow."

Grace's chest tightened as she looked at the snow globe, giving it a little shake. "I love it so much." Her heart fluttered in her chest. "And I love you."

The words escaped before her brain could catch up.

Noah's breath hitched, launching Grace into a blubbering, mumbling mess of words. "I can't believe I said that out loud."

"Is it true?"

Grace bit her lip, nodding her head vigorously.

"I love you too, Grace Blue Eyes McKinsey. And your orange soda lips, and your Christmas-fetish pj's. I love the way you saw me for me, for calling me out and pushing me to be more, to be better. I may mess things up a thousand times between now and Sunday, but I don't ever want to lose you again. Ever."

Grace leaned into his hand. "I don't want to lose you either."

In one swift movement, he swept Grace off the car and into his arms.

"Where are you taking me?"

"Across the threshold," he said, his eyes twinkling as he walked toward the front door. "It's what Prince Charming does for the princess, right? I've been doing my research."

"Have you now?" Grace drawled.

"I've watched nothing but holiday romance movies since you left."

"Liar."

"I'm serious. I can't say I stayed awake through all of them, but I had them on."

Grace felt her chest tighten. The thought of Noah watching romance movies just to be close to her melted any remaining bit of ice that had coated her heart.

Noah ducked under one of the drooping Christmas lights to get to the front stoop. "I'll take these down and try again tomorrow," he said, his teeth chattering.

"Let's get you inside before you freeze to death, surfer boy," Grace said, squeezing him tight, careful not to drop the snow globe in her hand. "Are you going to miss the life you left?"

Noah nuzzled his cold nose into her neck, tickling her until she squealed, then planted a big kiss on her lips. "Absolutely not. We can have our little slice of paradise, right here. In America's mitten."

Grace was smiling so hard her cheeks hurt.

"If I'm with you, and you're with me, we'll always be living in paradise— *Ow*."

Grace had lightly batted him in the chin with her gloved hand before he could finish. "You and your lines," she said, rolling her eyes—although it secretly warmed her heart.

"One of the many reasons you fell in love with me. Get ready. There's more where that comes from." Noah opened the door, about to walk over the threshold, when the first snowfall hit their noses.

Noah opened his mouth and caught a snowflake on his tongue. His eyes flickered wide as he showed off his catch.

"*Pura vida*," Grace said, claiming his mouth, the snowflake melting against their tongues.

EPILOGUE

Grace waved goodbye to Jennifer and another preschool teacher lingering in Jennifer's office before bursting through the front doors of the school. The sun was shining, and the warmth of summer seeped into her skin.

Noah was leaning against her car, his arms folded with a bright smile on his face.

"Aren't you a sight for sore eyes?" Grace said, picking up her pace. She hadn't seen him all week.

"Are you ready for this?" Noah said, beaming.

"I was born ready," Grace said, dropping her bag and jumping into his arms. She nestled her head against his neck as he twirled her around once. Then he gently pressed a kiss to her lips before setting her down.

Noah popped the trunk and placed her purse next to his duffel bag.

"How'd your finals go today?" Grace said, slipping into the front seat.

"Piece of cake," Noah said, sliding in the passenger side. "You are now looking at an MSU graduate."

Grace smiled, leaning over the center console. "I'm so proud of you," she said, giving him a peck on the cheek.

Noah had worked tirelessly the past three years, finishing up his hospitality degree without any summer breaks. He had a job lined up at the Bayshore Lodge, and they were letting him stay the weekend for free before he began work in a couple of weeks.

Grace rolled down her windows, and a warm breeze flowed in as she drove onto the main road toward the lodge. Noah clasped Grace's hand as the radio murmured in the background and her hair whipped around her face. She was truly happier than she had ever been. Her teaching career was on the right track. Noah would be spending all his time in Traverse City instead of half his time in East Lansing. And the summer had just begun.

They had several adventures planned this summer, and they were kicking off the first one today.

It didn't take long before they entered the Bayshore Lodge parking lot, checked into the hotel room, and changed into their bathing suits. They had arranged to meet up with Tessa and her new boyfriend, Greg. Greg worked at Tessa's firm and had a boat.

Noah and Grace walked up the dock. It glittered as the sun peeked around the fluffy clouds in the sky. Tessa squealed the moment she saw Grace and waved them over to Greg's boat.

"Guys. This is Greg," Tessa said, biting her lip. Her eyes shone with pride as the muscular bald man with a goatee stood up from his seat and shook Noah's and Grace's hands.

"Have either of you done this before?" Greg said, putting his hands on his hips.

"Nope. Can't say I have," Grace said.

"Me neither," Noah said. "But I'm ready."

Greg showed them around the boat, pointing to the life

jackets and harnesses attached to a series of poles and straps. "It'll just be you two in the air," Greg said, pointing to Noah and Grace. "Tess has already informed me she's too chicken to give it a try."

"Really? Tessa! I thought you were all about this," Grace said admonishingly.

Tessa shrugged. "I just like the boat and the hunky man behind the wheel." She elbowed Greg in the ribs. "He taught me how to drive this thing, and now I'm hooked."

Greg bent down and gave her a kiss on her temple. It warmed Grace's heart to see Tessa so happy. Attempting to find a boyfriend at bars had proven fruitless, and none had been as kind and respectful as the man who stood in front of them.

Grace immediately decided that she liked Greg and hugged her friend, thanking them for letting her and Noah come along for the ride.

Greg pulled his boat out of the dock and drove into the open blue water of Lake Michigan. When Tessa took over the wheel, Greg helped Grace and Noah get hooked up in their harnesses. Grace grabbed Noah's hand for strength. The flutter was back in her stomach but in the most delicious way. The bubble of excitement had become something she craved, a link to who she knew she would eventually become one day, an adventure seeker like her parents.

Before Grace could have second thoughts, she and Noah were soaring into the sky with a giant skull-and-crossbones parasail floating in the wind behind them.

Grace's stomach dropped, taking in the sights of the bay and sparkling lake below.

"Woo-hoo!" Noah yelled, his brilliant white teeth on full display. He reached for Grace's hand, and she gripped it tightly in hers. Warmth and light spread through her as she watched the sky turn various shades of pinks and purples as the sun inched toward the horizon.

"This is amazing," Grace said, the wind carrying away her words.

"You are amazing," Noah said, his sea-green eyes twinkling with joy.

❀

Noah and Grace sat in folding chairs on their balcony of the Bayshore Lodge, overlooking the moon's reflection on the lake. A swarm of crickets serenaded them while they played a game of footsie under the coffee table.

"You are no match for me," Grace said, attempting to pin his toes down.

"That is alarmingly accurate," Noah said, fighting back. His left foot joined the battle, causing Grace to rock in her chair. A splash of wine dribbled onto Grace's hand, and she quickly sat up, letting it drip onto the balcony floor and not on the white robe she wore after their Jacuzzi bath.

"Two feet against one is not fair," she huffed, shaking out the last droplet of wine from her hand.

"Oh, there are rules? I would argue those flippers of yours aren't regulation size. If anyone's breaking the rules, it's you."

Grace thwacked Noah's shoulder playfully before sauntering inside to wash up. She set her wineglass next to the sink as she rinsed her hands. The flashing light of Noah's cell phone caught her eye. It was lying beside the bed. She hesitated before reaching for it.

"Noah. Your phone is ringing," she called.

Noah stood up from his chair and strode toward the phone. Grace didn't look at the caller ID before Noah swiped it from the nightstand. He frowned at the screen.

"What's wrong? What is it?" Her heart thumped in her chest.

"It's Ma," Noah said, clicking on the phone. "Hello?"

Noah took the phone to the balcony. Grace's stomach became a nervous pool of energy as she sat on the bed. She watched as Noah's hands ran through his hair, gazing out at the lake. His body seemed tense under the thick, luxurious robe draped over his muscular frame.

After a while, he turned off his phone and stepped back inside. His eyes shimmered with something Grace had never seen before.

"What happened?" Grace said breathlessly.

Noah let out a small laugh before sitting down next to Grace. "That was Kai calling from Ma's phone."

"Is everything okay?" Grace cupped her mouth.

Noah smiled, his eyes dancing. "I'm an uncle."

"Oh my god!" Grace said. Her hands fell to her chest, clutching her robe. "I thought you were going to say something terrible had happened. Jolie wasn't due for a couple of weeks."

Noah shook his head, grinning from ear to ear. "She went into labor early, I guess, but she and the baby are healthy. They named him Isaiah."

"That's wonderful."

Over the past couple of years, she had gotten to know Jolie and Kai through video chat. They had become her extended family, filling the void that had been left after her aunt passed away the year before.

"They want us there for the baptism in a few months. Ma wants to pay for our tickets to fly down."

"Really? That's way too generous of her."

"But you'll come with me?" Noah said, looking through his eyelashes.

"Of course I'll come with you," Grace said, wrapping her arms around his neck. She pulled him down tight.

"Good. Because Jolie and Kai asked if you would be Isaiah's godmother."

"Does that make you—?"

"His godfather? Hell yeah."

Grace pulled him down for a kiss, tasting the wine on his lips. "I can't wait to meet them. All of them."

Both Noah's and Grace's phones pinged at the same time. A photo of a squished little baby face appeared, with red cheeks and eyes shut tight. He had a thick head of hair barely contained by the tiny cap on his head.

"Precious," she cooed at the phone.

"We have lots to celebrate tonight," Noah said, getting up from the bed. He poured the rest of the wine into their glasses and held his out for a toast. "To being the best godparents any little boy has ever had."

Grace held her glass up to his, clinking it lightly. She brought her wine to her lips, letting it tickle her tongue. "It's kind of hard to be the best godparents when we live so far away."

Noah lowered his wine, pressing his lips together thoughtfully. "We'll get to see him at his baptism. And I'm sure we'll be back a few times while he's young."

"Yeah, but you'd rather be there with them, right? With your family," Grace said.

A flash of concern creased Noah's forehead as he sat down beside her. "Grace, we've talked about this before. I love it here." He looked directly into her eyes. "I love being here with you."

Grace pulled away from his gaze and looked down at her wine, letting it slosh around. Her hands trembled slightly. She had been waiting for a while to bring this up and now only felt like the right time.

"Now that my aunt is gone, I have nothing tying me here anymore. I mean, I have Tessa, but… she doesn't need me here. And I can teach anywhere."

"What are you saying?" Noah said, his head tilted to the side.

"I'm saying that if you wanted to move back to Costa Rica, I'd be willing to go with you."

Noah set his wineglass down and moved closer with the grace of a feline cat. He took her wine and set it down before cupping her face in his hands. "Are you serious?"

Grace looked up at him and blinked. "Yes." The truth slipped from her lips as if it were the easiest thing in the world.

Noah crashed down onto her mouth, his tongue swiping hers in an electrifying kiss. His hands brushed over her collarbone, sliding the robe off her shoulders. "I think I'd like that one day," he said, lying her down on the bed. "But not yet."

"Not yet?" Grace said, scrunching her nose.

"I'm not ready to leave Michigan just yet," Noah said, kissing down her neck toward the peaks of her exposed nipples. His warm, wet mouth covered her left breast, sending a shiver of sparks down her spine. "I just got a job. And I like it here," he said, proceeding to her right breast. "But someday, when we're both ready"—his teeth lightly grazed her sensitive pebble, and she trembled underneath him—"we can go back to Costa Rica and start our own family. Would you like that, Blue Eyes?"

He looked up at her with so much hope, filling her with warmth and joy.

"I'd love that," Grace said, tugging him back to her mouth.

"Someday," he repeated on her lips. His mouth traveled down her neck, kissing her sternum, trailing down to her navel. His tongue leaving a trail that cooled under the night breeze.

Her robe fell to her sides as he spread her legs apart. His mouth covered her center, licking with tender, gentle strokes.

Grace's eyes rolled to the back of her head as she arched against his tongue, adding pressure where she needed it most. While his tongue worked her into a panting, writhing version of herself, his finger dipped inside, curling into the spot that had Grace's legs shuddering. The heated coil in the base of her spine was about to unfurl when Grace pressed her hands against Noah's cheeks.

"Wait," she gasped, barely audible through her giant gulp for air. "I want to do this together."

She pulled him to her mouth, kissing him softly before sliding her hands down his stomach, unhooking the tie of his robe. She let the terry cloth fabric fall to the side as she guided him to lie on his back.

A soft whimper left his lips as she straddled his hips with her legs and slid down the length of him, filling her whole. She rocked into him, like she was bobbing in the ocean, rolling with the waves. Noah's eyes flared, his lips parted, drinking her in. "You are so beautiful."

She continued to ride him, filling her with slick warmth and velvety perfection. Exquisite pleasure nibbled at her spine as Noah's hand gripped her hip, the other between her legs, coaxing her to come apart.

"Noah," she gasped.

He bucked in response, sending her over the edge, quaking around him until she fell onto his chest and he lost himself within her, his gaze never breaking hers.

Their bodies stuck together, coated with a film of lust and sweat. They lay in each other's arms, catching their breath, relishing in the afterglow.

The night air flowed in from their balcony door, cooling their heated skin. Noah pulled Grace into his side, pressing her flush against his muscled chest, and he placed a gentle kiss to her forehead.

"We could be in the middle of the Arctic, and that would still be the hottest sex I've ever had."

Grace chuckled, reaching up toward his chin. She pulled him down to her lips once more and kissed him with every ounce of energy she had left.

"Are you sure you'd want to start a family with me someday?" Noah said, stroking her hair.

"You already are my family," Grace said, squeezing him tight. When she opened her eyes, she caught the sparkle of a diamond sitting on top of a golden band nestled between Noah's fingers.

"Then that makes my next question a bit easier on us both," he said, releasing a shaky breath.

ACKNOWLEDGMENTS

I'd first like to thank the hubs, Erik Ebeling, for taking a break from his fine art to design the stunning cover for this novel. A second thanks for listening to me read the story out loud in two days (It was a long two days, I know). And a third thanks for keeping the kids entertained and alive during my writing sprints and my annual writing retreat.

To my daughter, who happened to be listening in during the drug cartel bust scene. Thank you for your relentless teasing about the over-usage of tape. Very helpful feedback, albeit sarcastic. When you are old enough to read this novel (please don't), I sincerely hope you feel that I've struck the proper amount of tape usage for the scene.

To my sister and mother: my tribe, my critique partners, my confidants. Thank you for all the time you've put into reading multiple versions of this story. Our Sunday afternoon chats will be memories I treasure long after the publication of this novel.

Special thanks to Dr. Brett and Dr. Alex for educating me of the realities of working in an emergency room. Your expertise helped make the hospital scene more believable.

"Just a prick" still has me giggling to myself from time-to-time.

To Martha, for sharing what you know about multiple sclerosis, and promptly sending me a very helpful book on the topic.

To my alpha readers: Jenny and Jen. Thank you for taking the time to read an early draft of my manuscript. Your feedback and suggestions were truly invaluable. Without a doubt in my mind, working with you has made me a better writer.

To my beta readers: Uta C, Emma Grocott (mrsljgibbs), Maria, Anna, Juan and Rebecca. Thank you a million times over for your feedback and suggestions with such a quick turnaround. I am so lucky to have this dream team of readers to give me thoughtful advice and the confidence to move forward.

To my ARC team and NetGalley Reviewers: Thank you for giving this book a chance. Your reviews make it possible for readers to find adventure romance novels like mine. Double thanks to those who've shared my book on their blogs or social media pages on behalf of ETTB. Your support means the world to me.

To the beautiful and fabulously talented Sarah Pesce at Lopt & Cropt Editing. Thank you for your partnership, coaching and your thoughtful development edits (and thanks for meeting me a second time so I could get my Covid vaccine). Huge thanks for the amazing line-edits as well. You put in the WORK to help whip this novel into shape, and it shows.

To Anne Victory's proofreading team. Thank you for yet another amazing proofreading job. The little side-bar comments that Annie included throughout the manuscript absolutely made my day.

To you, reader. Thank you for reading Grace & Noah's story, and for giving an indie author like myself a try. I've poured over a year of my life into this novel so that I could give my readers a fun, adventure-filled break from reality, and a story that may hopefully inspire their own adventure, even if it's simply picking up another book.

Happy reading, my friends.

ABOUT THE AUTHOR

Alicia Crofton writes contemporary romance and action-adventure romance novels set in faraway places. When she's not fictionally escaping through the Caribbean, she's self publishing her work, mothering her two rascals, and promoting her husband's artwork on IG @pnw_art.love.

Alicia and her family live in Portland, nestled among Oregon's finest jungle of roses.

Visit www.aliciacrofton.com and sign up for her newsletter for a free e-book!

facebook.com/aliciacroftonauthor
instagram.com/aliciacroftonauthor

ALSO BY ALICIA CROFTON

Coffee, My Love

To My Muse, With Love

Exit through the Jungle (Book 1 in the *Escape in Paradise* Series)

CPSIA information can be obtained
at www.ICGtesting.com
Printed in the USA
BVHW071203030821
613532BV00009B/338

9 781735 235370